LITERATURE OF THE HUNDRED FLOWERS

Literature of the Hundred Flowers is a collection in two volumes of writing that appeared in the period 1956–1957 and that reveals the complex situation of intellectuals in contemporary China. The first volume, *Criticism and Polemics,* includes a general introduction, important writings on the Hundred Flowers movement, criticism of literary problems, and discussions of the major literary issues debated at the time. The second volume, *Poetry and Fiction,* includes articles on poetic issues, poems, stories, fables, and essays, along with articles criticizing them.

LITERATURE OF THE HUNDRED FLOWERS

VOLUME I:
CRITICISM AND POLEMICS

EDITED BY HUALING NIEH

New York   Columbia University Press   1981

Library of Congress Cataloging in Publication Data
Main entry under title:

Literature of the Hundred Flowers.

Modern Asian Literature Series
Includes bibliographical references.
CONTENTS: v. 1. Criticism and polemics.—
v. 2. Poetry and fiction.
1. Chinese literature—20th century—History and
criticism—Addresses, essays, lectures. 2. Communism
and literature—Addresses, essays, lectures. 3. China
—Intellectual Life—Addresses, essays, lectures.
4. Chinese literature—20th century. I. Engle,
Hua-ling Nieh, 1926–
PL2303.L55   895.1′5′09   80-36748
ISBN 0-231-05074-7 (v. 1)
ISBN 0-231-05076-3 (v. 2)
ISBN 0-231-05264-2 (2v. set)

Columbia University Press
New York   Guildford, Surrey

ACKNOWLEDGMENTS

Cyril Birch, who gave me the idea for these books the first time we met. Now we are friends.

John Hsu, for his hard work and for his unique knowledge of China.

Chao Yung-ching, for his generous help in researching these materials.

Malinda Cox, for her close reading of the text.

Ronnie Solomon, for typing and proofreading.

The University of Iowa, devoted to all the arts, including the difficult art of translation. The university has constantly given its support to me personally and to these books.

The International Writing Program, with its intense concern for the writers of the world in their many languages, offered a very congenial atmosphere within which to do this work of many years.

Paul Engle, who kept me steady and confident throughout this complex and often exhausting project. He also kept me steady in my life by his love.

I wish to acknowledge and thank the following two groups of people who worked with me as co-translators:

Y. W. Wong (1972–73)
Dominic Cheung (1973–74)
Dennis Johnson (1972–74)

John Hsu (1974–76)   Daniel Webb (1974–76)
Stewart Yuen (1974–76)   Peter Nazareth (1974–76)

Special thanks are offered to The Northwest Area Foundation, without whose help in supporting translation and its publication this work might never have been complete. The International Writing Program, University of Iowa, was a rich resource for people with a knowledge of Chinese writing and of editing. The University of Iowa Foundation patiently aided this project in many ways.

Hualing Nieh

International Writing Program
University of Iowa

CONTENTS

The Anti-Rightist Campaign

INTRODUCTION

R. DAVID ARKUSH

"In the arts 'let a hundred flowers bloom,' and in scholarship 'let a hundred schools of thought contend,' " exclaimed Mao Tse-tung in April 1956,[1] and what followed was a remarkable year for China. During the Hundred Flowers period from mid-1956 to mid-1957, Chinese intellectuals basked in a new atmosphere of better treatment, greater latitude in which to work, and relaxed pressure for ideological orthodoxy. In the final phase of the period they were encouraged to speak out in criticism of the errors of Party cadres. An unexpected outburst of bitter grievances against the Communists in May 1957, particularly on university campuses, was then followed by a total reversal of the Hundred Flowers policies toward intellectuals.

This extraordinary moment in the history of China since 1949 affords us a unique glimpse into the thoughts and feelings of Chinese intellectuals, and the tensions and issues between them and the holders of political power. One set of issues involved the role of literature in socialist society. In the articles and literature of 1956 and 1957 we can see more clearly than at any other time the disagreement over such questions as whether all literature must support current political objectives or whether apolitical themes should be allowed, and whether or not literature should be used as social criticism to expose the defects in socialist society. The answers to such ques-

---

[1] *Miscellany of Mao Tse-tung Thought 1949–1968* (Joint Publications Research Service #61269, February 20, 1974), I, 33.

tions do not come easily in a society in revolution, when literature seems of crucial importance in the struggle to change people's attitudes and kindle their enthusiasm for building a better world. The issues are still unresolved, and as China begins to grapple with them again twenty-odd years later, the views expressed in the Hundred Flowers period take on fresh interest.

I

Before the Hundred Flowers movement (and for most of the time since), literature had been governed by the strict demand that it serve the interests of the people by increasing popular support for Party policies. Chinese Communist literary doctrine, not greatly different from that of the Soviet Union, was given its classic statement in Mao Tse-tung's 1942 "Talks at the Yenan Forum on Art and Literature," which laid down in no uncertain terms the line that art should serve politics. This was, however, a notion most Chinese writers were probably willing to accept, at least in principle.

China's modern literature, influenced by Western models and solidly wedded to the vernacular, dates from the years around the May Fourth movement of 1919, with its nationalism and enthusiasm for "new culture." The writers who developed this new literature in the 1920s and 1930s were mostly young men and women, born in this century or only slightly before (the greatest of them, Lu Hsün, who lived from 1881 to 1936, was older than most). They were romantic, idealistic, and very patriotic. They read Western literature, sometimes in the original and sometimes in translation, but their thoughts were on China and what could be done to cure the ills of Chinese society. In his article for the *Cambridge History of China,* Leo O. Lee affirms C. T. Hsia's judgment that modern Chinese literature has been marked by an "obsessive concern with China as a nation afflicted with a spiritual disease." For these writers, worried about their society in crisis, the ideal of *l'art pour l'art* had had little appeal; although one group in the 1920s adopted the slogan, their attraction to it was half-hearted and short-lived. In China literature had long been linked to goals of moral betterment, and modern writers have followed tradition in feeling that its mission should be to improve society.

It is not surprising that most of these young, idealistic, patriotic intellectuals became leftists in the 1920s and 1930s, and that not a few joined the Communist Party. By the time of the Japanese seizure of China's northeastern provinces (Manchuria) in 1931, the majority of the better-known modern writers were ready to join Lu Hsün in the League of Left-wing Writers, opposed to the Nationalist government. The most obvious way in which they could use their art to serve the revolution was by exposing the defects of existing society, and this many did, either in fiction or (in Lu Hsün's case) in short, biting essays called *tsa-wen*.

After all-out war with Japan began in 1937, a good many intellectuals fled the Japanese-occupied coastal cities to join the Communists in the rugged northwest around the town of Yenan. Those who chose to go to Yenan, instead of remaining in the occupied territories or following the Nationalists to Chungking and the Southwest, were certainly leftists. Many were Party members. But some, coming from a free, rootless, even bohemian life in cosmopolitan Shanghai, found it difficult to submit to Party discipline and the tough veterans of the Long March. Writers tend to be individualists; moreover, some of these writers had romantic visions of revolutionary heroism which were frustrated in the bitterly hard conditions of Yenan, where just living was a struggle. In 1942 the literary supplement to the Party newspaper carried hints of these dissatisfactions.

The supplement was edited by Ting Ling. An upper-class woman who had rebelled against the traditional culture and its repressive treatment of women, she became well-known in the later 1920s and 1930s for her short stories. Her husband had been killed as a Communist in 1931; she had joined the Party and then spent three years in a Nationalist jail herself. When she arrived in Yenan in 1937 she was greeted in person by Mao Tse-tung, who wrote a poem on the occasion. But all was not perfection there, and she was not one to keep silent. A 1941 story "In the Hospital" presents a depressing picture of conditions in a rural hospital, as seen through the eyes of an educated woman from Shanghai who wanted to be a writer but was ordered by the Party to work there as a nurse.[2] In early 1942 Ting Ling created a stir with an article complaining about

---

[2] For a recent translation of this story, see *Renditions* (1977), 8:123–35.

the unequal treatment of women by Party cadres. And she was not the only dissatisfied writer. The poet Ai Ch'ing wrote that writers deserved more respect from Party cadres. The young Manchurian novelist Hsiao Chün, famous for his *Village in August,* called for more patience and love among comrades, especially for young intellectuals who felt dissatisfied with conditions in Yenan. A colleague of Hsiao's, Lo Feng, wrote that it was still an age for *tsa-wen,* critical essays. The strongest criticism came from Wang Shih-wei, a Moscow-trained Party member, whose essays complained of inequality, of the privileges enjoyed by the leadership, and of Party interference in the work of artists.

Such sentiments were no doubt regarded by Mao as dangerous; in the midst of war, publication of negative views might lead to widespread dissatisfaction and demoralization. The Party had already initiated a rectification *(cheng-feng)* movement to correct erroneous tendencies among its members, many of whom had joined recently, by means of intense ideological study and discussion. A forum on art and literature was convened for most of May 1942, at which some two hundred artists and others aired their views and had heated discussions. Then Mao spoke, and what he said was to become the Chinese Communist doctrine on literary and art questions. It amounted to an insistence on Party control over literature and art.

Mao argued with great force and persuasiveness that art and literature should serve the interests of the masses. This meant first of all that writers and artists should have closer contact with the masses and should popularize their art and make it more widely accessible. Many writers and artists, Mao complained, having come to Yenan "from the garrets of Shanghai," continued to make friends only among intellectuals and to concern themselves with studying and portraying and sometimes defending petit-bourgeois intellectuals. Seldom coming into contact with the masses, they were producing literary and artistic works "which are the self-expression of the petit-bourgeoisie." In Shanghai their audience had been one of "students, office workers, and shop assistants," but now in the Communist-controlled areas they should be aiming at a broader audience of "workers, peasants, soldiers, and revolutionary cadres." They should study folk art forms and the "rich, lively language of the masses," and avoid uncritical imitation of foreign or classical literature. They

should seek deeper understanding of the lives of the common people in order to depict them vividly and convincingly, adopt their
viewpoint, and give expression to their concerns:

China's revolutionary writers and artists . . . must for a long period of time
unreservedly and wholeheartedly go among the masses of workers, peasants, and soldiers, go into the heat of the struggle, go to the only source, the
broadest and richest source, in order to observe, experience, study, and
analyze all the different kinds of people, all the classes, all the masses, all the
vivid patterns of life and struggle, all the raw materials of literature and art.

Second, if art and literature were to serve the interests of the
people, they must be subordinated to political requirements, "because only through politics can the needs of . . . the masses find
expression in concentrated form." Indeed, Mao argued, there could
be no such thing as an apolitical art for art's sake; art always (at least
in class society) served the interests of one class or another. In reply
to those who had called for nonclass humanistic themes in literature,
Mao asserted there was no such thing as a human nature common to
all classes, nor was it possible to love humanity in general without
regard to class.

Mao could not let art be autonomous because he thought it too
important. "To defeat the enemy . . . the army alone is not enough;
we must also have a cultural army, which is absolutely indispensable
for uniting our own ranks and defeating the enemy." "If we had no
literature and art. . . . we could not carry on the revolutionary
movement and win victory." Thus the political effect of a work of art
was of the utmost importance. This did not mean neglecting artistic
excellence, Mao conceded, for works without artistic quality made
weak political instruments; the "poster and slogan style," he said,
lacked force. But the political criterion must come first: art must
serve politics.

Finally, since the way art and literature serve the interests of the
people is by educating and uniting them in their struggle against the
enemy, it must not be divisive. It should not be used to expose the
defects of the people. Satire, social criticism, muckraking were appropriate only as weapons against the enemy. The people had defects, to be sure, but these were best dealt with by criticism and self-
criticism within their own ranks, and not by means of exposure in literature and art. It was wrong to dwell on the dark side when depict-

ing the people: "If you are a proletarian writer or artist, you will eulogize . . . the proletariat and working people."

In the years that followed, writers spent time in villages or factories learning about the lives of common people, wrote for a wider audience, and certainly had much success in reaching a mass public. But many writers felt artistically stifled by the demands of Mao's "Talks," and it is not hard to see why. He called for Party control of literature to ensure that it would fill its function of increasing popular support of current political policies, and this requirement was continued even after the victory of 1949. In the early 1950s we find Chou Yang, the Party official in charge of overseeing art and literature, flatly declaring that "literature and art should, of course, express the policies of the Party." This was to be done in the name of "socialist realism," which Chou explained meant clearly portraying the conflict that exists in real life between what is "progressive and developing" and what is "backward and dying." The practical effect of such a doctrine was, of course, to render suspect any work that departed from a black and white treatment of what the current political line upheld and condemned. How "realistic" such literature would be can be surmised from Chou's instruction that it was better for a writer not to depict character flaws in a hero but rather to "bring out in salient relief the hero's shining qualities and portray him as an ideal personality that all can admire." "Literary works should create positive heroic characters because we want to hold them up as examples to the people."[3]

The stifling tendency of Mao's doctrine was reinforced by the harsh treatment given certain writers who deviated. Ting Ling and others who had voiced discontent in 1941 and 1942 were subjected to public criticism. The one who had been most outspoken, Wang Shih-wei, was branded a Trotskyite and executed in 1947.[4] In the late 1940s Hsiao Chün was sent to labor reform in the coal mines for certain articles critical of Soviet and Chinese Communist actions in his native Manchuria.

After the liberation in 1949 most writers doubtless went

---

[3] Chou Yang, *China's New Literature and Art* (Peking: Foreign Languages Press, 1954).

[4] Mao later expressed regret at this; Stuart Schram, ed., *Chairman Mao Talks to the People* (New York: Pantheon, 1974), pp. 184–85.

through thought reform, that lengthy and intensive study of Marxist and Maoist texts, confession of past errors, and criticism and self-criticism in a small discussion group. In the early 1950s the press from time to time carried campaigns of condemnation of, for example, the movie *Biography of Wu Hsün* or the literary scholar Yü P'ing-po's theories about the eighteenth-century novel *Dream of the Red Chamber*. The harshest such campaign involving the arts was that against Hu Feng in 1955. Hu had been a close colleague of Lu Hsün's in Shanghai in the 1930s, and was now an important literary critic, a member of the executive committee of the Chinese Writers' Union, and on the editorial board of the leading literary magazine, *Jen-min wen-hsüeh* (People's Literature). Then he spoke out to complain about current literary policies, the dogmatic attitude of the literary authorities who enforced them (Chou Yang was an old opponent), and the baneful effect on cultural life. "If we use Marxism as a substitute for realism, then we will block artistic endeavor and will destroy art itself." He opposed thought reform of writers, disagreed with the requirements that literature be concerned only with workers, peasants, and soldiers, called for depicting reality instead of just the bright side, and spoke of establishing a number of literary magazines that would be independent of Party supervision. For these views, a campaign of calumny was mounted against Hu Feng in the press; he was formally charged with being anti-Marxist and a counterrevolutionary, and was arrested and sentenced to imprisonment.

It is strange, then, that only a year after the campaign against Hu Feng, much of what he had been condemned for advocating was suddenly permitted. But the Hundred Flowers policy and its rationale involved more than just literature, and to understand how and why it came about we must for a moment widen our focus to take in the larger political situation.

II

"Let a hundred flowers bloom, a hundred schools of thought contend" was a very Maoist slogan, colorful and vivid, alluding to the exciting classical period of philosophical variety and creativity of Confucius and Lao-tzu some twenty centuries earlier. But the impulse behind the policy was only partly Maoist. The other part,

which was felt first, was to make concessions to intellectuals in order
to win their cooperation in economic development. By the end of
1955 the Communists had been in control of China for six years;
"socialist transformation," that is to say, the collectivization of agriculture and the transfer to state ownership of industry, was basically
completed; and the major task ahead was "socialist construction" or
economic growth. Economic growth requires "intellectuals" (the
term is used broadly in China, sometimes to include those with a
high school education)—scientists, engineers, technicians, econo-
mists, administrators, educators, and so on. They were in short
supply and, moreover, had been rendered somewhat passive and
frightened by the intense thought reform campaigns of the early
years of Communist rule.

In a major speech in January 1956, Premier Chou En-lai announced a new policy toward intellectuals, and it is here, several
months before Mao coined the slogan, that the origins of the
Hundred Flowers policy are to be found. "Science is a decisive factor
in our national defense, economic and cultural enterprises," he said;
but "the state of China's science and technology is still very backward," and "we cannot rely on the Soviet experts indefinitely." He
called for a twelve-year plan to bring Chinese science to world levels.
In order to "stimulate and bring into full play the existing forces of
the intelligentsia so as to carry out the socialist construction of the
country," the premier listed a number of ways in which the treatment of intellectuals should be improved. They should be assigned
work that would make fuller use of their special skills. They should
be given jobs and authority, their views should be respected, and
their research work valued: "we must understand the intellectuals
thoroughly and give them due confidence and support so that they
can work with real initiative." Intellectuals' working conditions
needed to be improved by supplying them with books and equip-
ment and guaranteeing that no more than one-sixth of their working week be taken up with political study and meetings. Finally, he
said, salaries, living quarters, and opportunities for promotion
should be improved: "the tendency toward egalitarianism in remun-
eration systems . . . should be eliminated."[5]

[5] Chou En-lai's speech may be found in *Communist China 1955–1959: Policy Documents with Analysis* (Cambridge, Mass.: Harvard University Press, 1962).

Special privileges for intellectuals, however, was not what Mao was after, not Mao whom the Cultural Revolution of 1966–1969 would show to be so fervently anti-elitist and anti-intellectual. The Maoist impulse behind the Hundred Flowers policy was never spelled out as clearly as the economic rationale was in Chou's speech—Mao's original "Hundred Flowers" talk of May 2, 1956, has never been made public—but in writings from those years (many of them published only recently), it is not difficult to see what his concerns were. His worry was clearly not so much how to get support from intellectuals for economic development as it was political. Mao was becoming concerned with the problem of bureaucratism, and was seeking ways to prevent the regime he had struggled so long to establish from becoming bureaucratic, rigid, unresponsive, and alienated from the people.

Mao had long believed that much of the source of the Party's strength lay in its closeness to the masses, and he had spoken emphatically about the need for cadres to understand local conditions, give expression to the needs and desires of the people, and not act arrogantly toward them. Now, with the tasks of liberation and the transition to socialism essentially complete, he began to turn his attention away from battling the Kuomintang and imperialism to the worrisome possibility of "contradictions" between the government and the governed. Such worries were certainly increased in 1956 by Khrushchev's startling revelations of the dictatorial crimes of Stalin, by the riots in Poland, and by the more serious uprising in Hungary.

In April 1956, Mao write of the danger of "mistakes" due to the high concentration of power needed by the dictatorship of the proletariat, and he asserted the need for "long-term coexistence and mutual supervision" between the Communist Party and the "democratic parties," composed largely of intellectuals. In September, at the Party Congress, he criticized "many of our comrades" for "subjectivism in their way of thinking, bureaucratism in their way of work, and sectarianism in organizational questions." A couple of months later he spoke bluntly to the Central Committee about the dangers of bureaucratism, defining it as "failure to make contact with cadres and the masses, failure to go down and find out about the situation below, and failure to share weal and woe with the masses, plus corruption, waste, and so on."

There are several hundred thousand cadres at the level of the county Party committee and above who hold the destiny of the country in their hands. If they fail to do a good job, alienate themselves from the masses and do not live plainly and work hard, the workers, peasants and students will have good reason to disapprove of them. *We must watch out lest we foster the bureaucratic style of work and grow into an aristocratic stratum divorced from the people.*[6]

It was in response to this danger that Mao developed his theory of two kinds of contradictions, carefully set out in his long February 1957 speech, "On the Correct Handling of Contradictions among the People." The first kind of contradiction, "between ourselves and the enemy," included the past struggle against imperialism, feudalism, and bureaucratic capitalism, and the present conflict with counterrevolutionaries and other enemies of the people. Such contradictions were "antagonistic" and were solved by means of violence. But at present there were comparatively few counterrevolutionaries and most of the contradictions within Chinese society were of a different sort. They were contradictions "among the people," "the people" being defined as all those who support and work for socialism. For contradictions among the people, dictatorial, coercive methods were not to be used. Contradictions among the people, specifically including contradictions between the government and the masses, were to be solved by "democratic methods" of discussion, criticism, persuasion, and education. Mao said he was not calling for Western parliamentary democracy, which was really nothing more than a device for maintaining the dictatorship of the bourgeoisie and could never guarantee freedom to working people. What was needed instead was a measure of true freedom and democracy, combined with discipline and centralized leadership.

Contradictions in society should not be ignored or denied. The Soviet Union had made this mistake, and it had led to political abuses. Contradictions should be brought out into the open and resolved; struggle is what pushes society forward. In art and science it is necessary to be cautious about questions of right and wrong: Darwin and Copernicus were at first thought wrong. It is harmful to art and science to impose one school or style and ban others: "You

[6] Emphasis added. This and most of the succeeding Mao quotations from 1956–1970 may be found in the chronologically arranged *Selected Works of Mao Tsetung*, vol. V (Peking: Foreign Languages Press, 1977).

may ban the expression of wrong ideas, but the ideas will still be there. . . . It is only by employing the method of discussion, criticism and reasoning that we can really foster correct ideas and overcome wrong ones, and that we can really settle issues." The struggle of ideas produces truth and tempers people, vaccinates them, keeps them from being hothouse flowers:

Truth stands in contrast to falsehood and develops in struggle with it. . . . It is a dangerous policy to prohibit people from coming into contact with the false, the ugly and the hostile, with idealism and metaphysics and with the twaddle of Confucius, Lao-tzu and Chiang Kai-shek. It will lead to mental deterioration, one-track minds, and unpreparedness to face the world and meet challenges.

Finally, Mao argued, criticism can be useful in correcting mistakes: "We should allow democratic personages to challenge us with opposing views and give them a free hand to criticize us. Otherwise we would be a little like the Kuomintang. . . . Criticisms that are not wrong can help remedy our shortcomings, while wrong ones must be refuted."

Following Chou En-lai's speech in January 1956, conditions improved somewhat for intellectuals. Ambitious plans were formulated for scientific research, there was an increase in both scholarly and nonscholarly publication, and the Democratic League and other organizations composed largely of intellectuals became active again. In May 1956, Lu Ting-i, director of the Propaganda Department of the Party Central Committee, explained the new policy of blooming and contending for art and science. His speech, which is translated in this volume, proclaimed for literature an end to rigid taboos and formulas as long as it served the people. Socialist realism was not the only method; there should be no restrictions on subject matter as long as the effect was to praise the new society and positive elements and to criticize the old society and backward elements—even writing about gods or talking animals could be acceptable. What followed, rather quickly in fact, was the publication of startlingly new kinds of literature and literary criticism of a sort that could not have been published before, such as Ch'in Chao-yang's long piece, "The Broad Road of Realism," published in September 1956, which argued strongly against the Party's old literary policies, or the remarkable story by Wang Meng (also published in September), "A Young Man

Arrives at the Organization Department," exposing corruption and disillusionment in a Party office in the capital.

Such strong medicine was not easily swallowed by most of those in positions of authority in the Party and government, and there are indications that the Hundred Flowers policy was not popular among the leadership. A careful student of such matters has found that at the Party Congress in September, 62.7 percent of the part of Mao's speech devoted to domestic affairs was on the need to combat subjectivism, bureaucratism, and sectarianism, and on the need for working with non-Party people; but this 62.7 percent got only 11.1 percent of the applause from the Party members listening: "There could have been no clearer indication of the lack of enthusiasm of Party members for united front policies."[7] In November, Mao complained that "among our Party members there are some who are afraid of great democracy, and this is not good." In January 1957, the deputy director of the Army Propaganda Department, Ch'en Ch'i-t'ung, and three others were able to get an article published in the official Party newspaper *Jen-min jih-pao* (People's Daily) declaring that there had been too much "satiric writing voicing discontent" and too little concern with socialist realism and with serving the peasants, workers, and soldiers. Mao in April complained that "Ch'en Ch'i-t'ung represents over 90 percent of the comrades in the Party."

A cold wind was detectable. Wang Meng's story was subjected to harshly negative criticism from authoritative voices in the first few months of 1957. The sociologist Fei Hsiao-t'ung wrote in March that many intellectuals feared the Hundred Flowers policy was like the weather of early spring, "now warm, now cold again." Mao repeatedly had to argue with Party cadres that they should not suppress criticism, most notably in the "Contradictions" speech, and also in a January 1957 talk to Party secretaries:

> Our rural policy is correct and so is our urban policy. That is why a nationwide disturbance such as the Hungarian incident cannot take place here. At most a small number of people may create trouble here and there and clamor for so-called great democracy. On this score I do not see eye to eye with some comrades among you, who seem scared of it. . . . If a handful of

---

[7] Roderick MacFarquhar, *The Origins of the Cultural Revolution, I: Contradictions among the People 1956–1957* (New York: Columbia University Press, 1974), p. 111.

school kids can topple our Party, government, and army by a show of force, we must all be fatheads. Therefore, don't be afraid of great democracy. If there is a disturbance, it will help get the festering sore cured, and that is a good thing.

By March it appeared that Mao was carrying the day. In his words: "The Central Committee of the Party is of the opinion that we must 'open wide,' not 'restrict.' . . . To 'open wide' means to let all people express their opinions freely, so that they dare to speak, dare to criticize and dare to debate." The Central Committee agreed that the Party rectification movement against subjectivism, bureaucratism, and sectarianism would begin that year, and that non-Party people could take part if they wished—that is to say, non-Party people would be invited to criticize the errors of Party cadres.

The rectification movement began on May 1, and what followed was the second phase of the Hundred Flowers period, five weeks of "unchecked criticism."[8] Forums of intellectuals were convened and reported in the press. Many speakers called for little more than greater independence from Party interference in professional work; others voiced pent-up grievances including attacks on the Party's monopoly of power. It was in the universities that things really got out of hand. In wall posters and public meetings students made impassioned and outspoken complaints and demands. They called for freedom of assembly and of speech, freedom to criticize the Party without being persecuted as counterrevolutionaries. They called for justice and legal process, and for righting the injustices committed against people such as Hu Feng, whose case was for them a *cause célèbre* comparable to Dreyfus's. Most of all, the students called for truth, the truth that was not found in the public press: "Long live righteousness, truth, democracy and personal freedom." "We don't want French capitalism, but the French spirit of seeking the truth and fighting for justice." "People who love truth, democracy, freedom, unite!"[9]

That was too much, and in June the Hundred Flowers policy was reversed and an anti-Rightist movement began. It seems clear that Mao had not expected anything like the intensity of anti-Party

[8] Ibid., p. 218.
[9] Dennis J. Doolin, ed., *Communist China: The Politics of Student Opposition* (Stanford: Hoover Institution, 1964), pp. 44, 55, 59.

sentiment that erupted in the wild spring of 1957. In arguing for open criticism, Mao had repeatedly said that erroneous and counter-revolutionary views—what he called poisonous weeds—would inevitably appear, but that they would be few and would be spontaneously rejected by the majority. For China was not like Hungary; Chinese Communist policies had been basically right, millions of experienced cadres had good ties with the masses, and the majority of the people supported the Communists. When it turned out there was more discontent among students and intellectuals than they had thought, the leadership became alarmed about the possibility of this unrest spreading to other groups. As Liu Shao-ch'i put it in late May:

The universities and schools are already on the move. . . . If the worker masses, the teachers from the middle and primary schools, and other mass organizations also start mobilizing, then we won't be able to stand our ground. . . . If we don't control things, then in a jiffy millions of people will be on the move and then we won't be able to do anything. . . .[10]

And so this policy, which had been unpopular with much of the leadership all along, was abandoned. The wrath of Mao and the Party was turned on the intellectuals, many of whom were now perceived to be bourgeois Rightists: selfish, individualistic, unwilling to accept Party leadership or to devote themselves to socialism and the welfare of the people. But now let us go back and take a closer look at what had been said during this period concerning literature.

III

The literary developments of 1956–1957 may be thought of in two categories corresponding with what we have described as the two quite different aspects of the Hundred Flowers policy. In response to the first part of the policy—making concessions to intellectuals in order to win their cooperation in economic development—we can see in the works of literature and criticism translated in this anthology a movement toward more variety and freedom from political restriction for the sake of better art. Permitting less politicized art was a concession on the part of the Party, made largely to the intellec-

[10] Quoted in MacFarquhar, p. 221.

tuals if we assume that the demand for fewer restrictions was coming from writers and the demand for better literature from more sophisticated readers. Corresponding to the second category—permitting outside criticism of those in power in order to counter tendencies to dictatorship—was a movement toward using literature for social criticism.

As to the first, the desire for more variety and fewer restrictions was, we can see, based on the feeling that in recent years excessive political requirements had had a stifling effect on the arts. As Lu Hsün had put it decades earlier, "All literature is propaganda, but not all propaganda is art." Mao in his "Yenan Talks" had called for literature which was artistically moving as well as politically correct, for the simple reason that bad literature was ineffective as propaganda. But many Hundred Flowers writers felt the two aims were not wholly compatible, and in practice in the late 1940s and early 1950s the Party overseers of the arts had been more inclined and more able to enforce ideological orthodoxy than to encourage artistic creativity. One result was simply a paucity of output. Few readers could have been unaware that China's most famous authors, such as Pa Chin or Mao Tun, previously prolific, had since 1949 produced very little. Ting Ling, for instance, was later accused of cynically advising "one-bookism"—relying on the standing won by one famous work, in her case the 1948 novel *The Sun Shines over the Sangkan River,* which had won a Stalin Prize. In 1956, it was reported in Shanghai that some 250 writers had been producing at an average rate of only sixteen pages a year.[11]

Dissatisfaction with the literature that had been produced in the early 1950s was often explicit in Hundred Flowers works. Liu Shao-t'ang made comments on the subject which were with some justice later characterized by an anti-Rightist movement critic (Chou Ho) as "nothing other than a complete repudiation of our literature of the past fifteen years." Writer after writer bemoaned the dull and monotonous quality of current literature. "Why is it that life and characters in so many novels appeared so ordinary, drab, and simple?" wondered a character in Liu Pin-yen's story, "The Inside News of the Newspapers." Ch'in Chao-yang complained that although "ours

[11] Union Research Institute, *Communist China 1956* (Hong Kong, 1957), p. 150.

is a time of rapid changes, a time for unusual personalities and un-usual things," nonetheless "all authors write about events with every-day details like those in a housewife's life." Everyone wrote so much alike, he said, that were the author's name not written on a book's cover, one could never guess whose work it was. Ai Ch'ing was surely satirizing the monotony of recent literature in his fables about a gar-dener who planted only roses and about a cicada who made the same noise morning, noon, and night. There were complaints that poetry had been shallow, stereotyped, lacking emotional impact, and unmemorable—political essays broken into lines, theories without images. Li Pai-fang said the impoverishment of poetic language could be seen in the multitude of poems, all similar, about the sun. Poetry is dull because of the ideological dogmatism of narrow-minded editors, he said, quoting Marx's line that under nineteenth-century German censorship, "it is permitted to produce only one color, the official color."

The problem, said Ch'in Chao-yang, is that "people are afraid of committing errors. . . . Writers have lost the habit of imagining freely, creating freely, searching for artistic style or looking at life deeply." His long article from late 1956 argued for a "broad road" for creative development:

We should consider each author's individual qualities. We should not de-mand the same thing from all authors and all literary forms. We should help develop rather than hinder each author's individual creativity. We should use fewer administrative orders which interfere with literary creation.

There is no question about what Ch'in thought was the cause of the defects in China's literature: "No one should use rigid dogmas to prescribe a fixed, narrow path for others," he wrote later in the same article, and in conclusion cried out, "Let us free ourselves from the bondage of dogmatism." In the spring of 1957 the theme was echoed by the young writer Liu Shao-t'ang in an even more out-spoken article:

We can certainly say that our literary endeavors could and would achieve more were they not so seriously hampered by dogmatism. . . . Dogmatic theories emphasize only the political implications of a literary work, ignoring its various artistic concerns. . . . In a mechanical fashion they dictate stereo-typed protagonists, antagonists, and model heroes.

Ch'in Chao-yang had said he accepted the idea that literature and art should serve politics and the people; he argued merely for interpreting this requirement less rigidly: not asking literature to deal only with "current political propaganda," paying some attention to artistic quality as well as to political content. Liu Shao-t'ang went much further, questioning the appropriateness of demanding that art serve politics once the war of liberation had been won:

> During the years of Japanese aggression when the survival of our country hung in the balance, and during the War of Liberation. . . . literature served as the fastest and most direct weapon in support of the revolution. . . . So writers were required to write according to certain policies and rules. . . .
> But the situation changed following the liberation of our country. . . . The demands made on literature and art ought, therefore, to be different from those of wartime. . . . The old theories cannot deal with the changed situation.

The implication was clear: Liu was boldly suggesting that Mao's "Yenan Talks" were outdated and no longer applied; they were, he said, "based on the historical circumstances of the time, and served as guidelines for literature of that period."

In calling for literature that would be more than just political propaganda, several writers argued for broadly humanistic themes. Current literature was too lacking in "human feelings," said Pa Jen: "Literature should serve class struggle, but its ultimate goal is the emancipation of all mankind, the freeing of human nature," and thus it should appeal to all through the feelings which are inherent in human nature. Ch'ien Ku-jung called for "humanism" in literature, for characters portrayed not as instruments or puppets, but as people "with the same feelings, thoughts, and individuality" as the writer's. The writer should treat characters with sympathy and respect, respect for their individuality; that is why the novels of Balzac and Tolstoy have such force. If the writer's feelings are valid, they will bring us "closer to man and nature, make us love life, our people and our country." Humanism was not in conflict with a class viewpoint, argued Ch'ien, quoting Marx that "the only genuine humanism is communism." That is because the true humanist will always side with the oppressed against their oppressors:

Humanism . . . means to strive for freedom, equality, and democracy and . . . to oppose the oppression and exploitation of man by man and to fight against feudalism and slavery, systems which do not treat people as human beings.

It is clear, then, that writers wanted—and in the Hundred Flowers period were given—more freedom from Party and government control and from rigid restrictions on the content and form of their work. They wanted more time in which to write, and more opportunity to publish. They wanted to, and did, write in different forms: traditional forms, for example, or allegories such as Ai Ch'ing's in which animals speak, or in lyric as opposed to narrative poetry. More varied content was called for and appeared in literature published in this period, some of which had been written earlier but not published. There were works about nature and love and human feelings, not just class struggle. In seeking more freedom from political restrictions, these writers were moving toward art that would be divorced from politics. Yet few, if any, called for complete autonomy; the idea that art should serve politics and the people was, it would appear, too widely accepted to disavow.

These calls for and expressions of greater independence from political control were easy targets for attack in the anti-Rightist movement, after the policy of Hundred Flowers liberalization had been reversed, as individualistic, self-indulgent, and bourgeois. Why, it was asked, were these writers unwilling to sing the praises of the age? Why do they lack enthusiasm for the revolution and socialism? Poems about nature or love were evading reality, life, labor, the realm of politics; such escapism may have been appropriate for intellectuals in the feudal period, but not any longer. The poet Ai Ch'ing, for example, was accused of indulging in petit-bourgeois self-glorification and self-pity. Such individualism and melancholy were called dangerous, for they can sap the will of young people. "The current responsibility of the poet," wrote one critic (Yü Yin), "is to praise the lives and struggles of the workers, peasants, and soldiers who create history."

The secondary tendency to be noted in the literature and criticism of the Hundred Flowers period was not to free art from politics, but to use it for political purposes, by exposing defects in contemporary society. Hundred Flowers writers justified such use of literature by appealing to the principle, inherent in the doctrine of "socialist realism," that literature should indeed be realistic. Socialist realism had been officially defined in the Soviet Union in the 1930s as follows:

> Socialist realism, which is the basic device of Soviet literature and literary criticism, demands of the artist a true, historically concrete portrayal of reality in its revolutionary development, in which truthfulness and historical concreteness must be combined with the task of ideological reform and the education of the working people in the spirit of socialism.

Such a definition, Ch'in Chao-yang argued in 1956 with considerable persuasiveness, was contradictory: to demand of literature that it not only be truthful but educate people in the spirit of socialism will cause it to depart from the truth. Socialist realism, in other words, was not in fact realistic. Liu Shao-t'ang made the same point; the Soviet definition of socialist realism, he said,

> was obviously not formulated in order to encourage writers to base their work on the realities of life, or to deal honestly with these things. . . . If the realities of life are not considered real, and writing itself is supposed to involve the "revolutionary development" of reality, writers are forced to embellish life and ignore its true features. According to the principle of "reality in its revolutionary development," writers should not write of problems in a socialist society or depict the more negative aspects of the society, for these are temporary matters which can be resolved. Then, is there any meaning for "reality" as it pertains to realism?

In this way, writers were able to use the doctrine that literature should be realistic to oppose the literary bureaucrats who wanted literature flattering to the regime. The Hundred Flowers policy, as elucidated by Lu Ting-i in mid-1956, had declared that socialist realism was not the only permissible style. Ch'in Chao-yang called now for a "broad road of realism" which really would be realistic. The key, as Liu Shao-t'ang made clear, was that if writers were to be honest and true to life, they must also depict "the negative aspects of society." Literature as social criticism, thus, was what this discussion of realism was getting at, and in 1956 and 1957 several pieces were published exposing defects in socialist society. This criticism was very mild, to be sure, but in comparison to what had been permitted earlier, it was startlingly daring.

Official privilege and red tape, for instance, were depicted in "A

Visit to His Excellency," about an old peasant from the countryside who comes to the capital to visit his son, a minister of state. The old man first encounters such difficulties with forms and passes that he can hardly get into the building, and then is rather shocked by his son's luxurious standard of living. "The New Election" showed a thoroughly good old worker and union official, one who had been tireless in looking after the well-being of his fellow workers, getting dumped from the list of candidates for union office by a young, ambitious, authoritarian chairman, though in the end democracy triumphs via the write-in vote. A poem called "Song for the Yesman" made fun of those who can only parrot their superiors. Another poem, "Chia Kuei-hsiang," recounted the case of a girl who in 1956 was hounded to death by bureaucrats in her factory.

By far the most important of such pieces were two rather long stories, "The Inside News of the Newspaper" by Liu Pin-yen, and "A Young Man Arrives at the Organization Department," by Wang Meng. The first is about a newspaper that prints only directives and reports and statistics received from above. Reporters who try to respond to the needs and concerns of readers by writing exposés of local problems are frustrated by a chief editor who makes all decisions himself according to what he thinks Party leaders want. Wang Meng's story depicts the similar disappointment of an idealistic young Party member confronting the cynicism of cadres in a Party organization who are content to do nothing about a lazy and incompetent factory director.

Both stories suggest the need for more frankness and honesty in print. "Inside News" explicitly stresses the importance of a newspaper taking the initiative in investigating and exposing social problems in order to remedy them. A newspaper should report the truth and not call every meeting "democratic." Printing some "negative" pieces is not to condemn the Party and the whole society, but to serve the needs of the people, we are told. Wang Meng's young newcomer is disillusioned partly because the literature he has read (he carries a Soviet novel in his pocket) has led him to think all cadres are heroes. More realistic literature, in which social problems are honestly depicted, the author seems to hint, would produce young people better equipped to deal with these problems.

As may well be imagined, such works were not easily accepted by cadres used to being insulated from public criticism. Wang Meng's story was attacked, and defended, in scores of articles published in late 1956 and early 1957. Much of the controversy was couched in terms of whether or not the characters and conditions it presented were "typical," for Engels had once defined realism as "the truthful reproduction of typical characters under typical circumstances." According to Marxist literary theory, the depiction of what was not "typical," even though it really existed, was not realism but "naturalism" and to be condemned. Yet how was one to decide what is typical? In the short run the story was saved by the political decision, reflected in Mao's February 1957 "Contradictions" speech, to go ahead with the policy of blooming and contending. But in the long run, this and the more outspoken criticisms of the spring of 1957 were completely rejected when the Hundred Flowers movement was replaced by the anti-Rightist campaign. As part of this, in July, Mao's speech was published for the first time, with criteria for distinguishing fragrant flowers from poisonous weeds. These criteria, which were surely not in the speech as Mao originally gave it, specified that only expressions not opposed to socialism and the Party's leadership were permitted.

There is no clear line between serving the people by pointing out things that need to be corrected and destroying people's enthusiasm for socialism by depicting the dark side of things. One does not have to posit ill-will or broken trust (not that these must be excluded) to see how those who were trying to lead China to a better life could feel that their efforts would be undermined by critical literature. The "Inside News" story was said to malign older cadres and incite young people to anti-Party activities for personal ambition, cloaked in the guise of "independent thinking" and "daring to oppose conservatives." "Song for the Yesmen" was called

an attack on the Party's leadership and its cadres. . . . A person who honors the leadership by his obedience is a 'yesman' who has no brain and whose 'throat is a loudspeaker,' or a 'parrot' able only to repeat after others. This warping of the cadres' image is apparently aimed at stirring up dissent among them, a familiar method of Rightists.

"The New Election" was not, it was said, an exposé of an individual instance of bureaucratism. Because it did not show the Party rectifying the situation, it was to be considered an attack on the whole structure of unions, suggesting that almost all union officials are bad.

"Writing the truth" was just a camouflage for revealing the darker aspects of society, Mao Tun charged in February 1958. Exposing social defects had been appropriate for literature in the old society, but nowadays "progress and brightness" were the realities, and overly negative writing was a distortion: "The events most worthy of our attention are those that bear on the destiny and happiness of the majority of our society. . . . We believe in our age." Critical literature, it was said again and again, could only have been written for the purpose of turning the masses against the Party.

Political leaders never like criticism, especially those who are used to being protected from it. It is not hard to imagine their anxiety about their prestige and authority in the face of the criticisms of the Hundred Flowers period. They were trying to mobilize a vast nation, short on material resources, to great efforts; they needed literature that would support this effort. We must not forget how important propaganda (the word is not pejorative in China) had been in the revolution. There is no reason to question the sincerity of Mao's fears that "If the paper you publish prints bad news every day, people will have no heart for their work."[12]

IV

The anti-Rightist movement was as sharp and dramatic a turnabout from the liberalism of the Hundred Flowers period as could be imagined. Beginning in June 1957 and continuing well into 1958, thousands and thousands of intellectuals were branded as "Rightists" and denounced in countless meetings and in the press. The enormous number of people who suffered during this time is suggested by an astonishing recent report from Hong Kong sources that 110,000 people who had been arrested during the anti-Rightist movement were being released in 1978, after twenty-one years in prison![13] Writers and artists had their errors condemned in a

[12] *Chairman Mao Talks . . .* , p. 39.
[13] *The New York Times,* June 6, 1978.

lengthy series of meetings. (A sampling of the anti-Rightist articles against them may be found in this anthology.)

Oddly, the younger writers who had been most outspoken in the Hundred Flowers period were not the main targets of the campaign. Apart from Liu Shao-t'ang, who was singled out as the worst of the young Rightists, Ch'in Ch'ao-yang, Liu Pin-yen, and Huang Ch'iu-yün were treated rather gently, at least in print. Wang Meng, perhaps because his story had been given some sort of a Maoist imprimatur in March or so, was not mentioned at all. Most of the attacks in the field of literature were against older writers, long-standing foes of Chou Yang, especially those who had expressed criticism in Yenan in 1942. These writers' old articles were reprinted to show their guilt; and in spite of the fact that most had been rather cautious in 1956–1957, Ai Ch'ing, Hsiao Chün, Feng Hsüeh-feng, and above all Ting Ling were charged with and forced to confess to being individualists, opposing the Party's control of literature, and numerous other matters. Many were removed from their posts and sent to factories and villages.

The two decades following the Hundred Flowers period were not a good time for writers or literature in China. For a while in the late 1950s and early 1960s a great deal was published, but it was not all of high quality. Much was by amateurs, ordinary workers, peasants, and soldiers, as the Party turned away from intellectuals after the Hundred Flowers experience. Encouragement of unrealistic inspirational literature seemed implied by a new artistic ideal of "revolutionary realism combined with revolutionary romanticism." The prohibition of ambiguous "middle characters" meant literary works were to portray only totally good or totally bad people. Then, in the Cultural Revolution and afterward, as Mao's wife Chiang Ch'ing, a onetime film actress, gained control over policy in the arts, even the quantity of published literature dwindled to a few titles. Writers and other intellectuals, including many who had gone unscathed in earlier years, all suffered in various ways. Chou Yang, who after decades of enforcing Party orthodoxy with reluctant writers was himself disgraced and punished in the Cultural Revolution, has recently called the decade from 1966 to 1976 a time when "works were banned, writers and artists persecuted," as the policy of blooming and contending was supplanted by an "extremely reactionary and savage line of feudal fascism."[14]

Now, since Mao's death and the arrest of Chiang Ch'ing and others of the Gang of Four in 1976, once again the situation has changed. Policies concerning intellectuals and literature have been liberalized radically. The "two hundred" slogan, as it is now called, has been revived and indeed enshrined in the 1978 constitution. Much new and old literature is being published, and old writers whose names have not been heard in years—including many whose works are in this anthology—are reemerging into the public light.

The precedent for much of what is going on today is the Hundred Flowers period of 1956–1957, and indeed many of the same issues discussed in the articles in this collection are now, after a hiatus of over two decades, again coming to the surface in the press. We have seen in the earlier Hundred Flowers policy two separable aspects with quite diverse purposes, and it may be useful to keep this distinction in mind in thinking about current trends. It is natural that greater variety is permitted in the arts and better treatment given writers at a time when strengthening science and technology, developing the economy, and modernizing the country are accorded national priority. Educated people are crucial to such tasks, and intellectuals are now assuming more prominent and important roles in society.

But if our understanding of the Hundred Flowers is correct, allowing literature to expose defects is quite a separate matter, and is not necessarily combined with the other policies. Mao, the champion of struggle against bureaucracy and privilege, is gone. As time goes by and less and less can be blamed on the Gang of Four, the new leadership may not find it palatable or easy to accept published criti-

[14] One of the important charges against Chou Yang, Lu Ting-i, et al., was that they had permitted publication in the early 1960s of certain satirical works such as Wu Han's play *Hai Jui Dismissed from Office*, allegedly a veiled attack on Mao and the commune movement disguised as a historical drama about a tyrannical sixteenth-century emperor and officials seizing lands from peasants. Such works must not, however, be thought of as the same sort of literary criticism of official policies found in the Hundred Flowers period, for they came not from outside the Party but from a high official faction; Wu Han was deputy mayor of Peking and had backing from certain Party leaders.

The quoted words are from Foreign Broadcast Information Service, *Daily Report—People's Republic of China*, March 2, 1979, p. E 13.

cism, and there is no institutional necessity that they do so. On the other hand, the Cultural Revolution seems to have produced a younger generation more inclined to speak out, write wall posters, voice grievances, and express political views than before, and perhaps it has left officials less inclined to suppress dissent.[15] It may well be that the Chinese Communists are more genuinely democratic in their ideals than those of the Soviet Union. At any rate, such questions as whether or not literature which "depicts the dark side" in the tradition of Lu Hsün is to be allowed in socialist society are surely worth watching. We need not go as far as Ai Ch'ing, who wrote in 1957 that "The suppression of free speech is the most brutal of all forms of violence," to agree that there are involved here matters of considerable importance in determining what kind of society China is to become.

FOR FURTHER READING

The standard work on this subject, an admirably thorough and scholarly mine of information I have drawn on freely for this introduction, is Merle Goldman, *Literary Dissent in Communist China* (Cambridge, Mass.: Harvard University Press, 1967). Somewhat narrower in focus is D. W. Fokkema, *Literary Doctrine in China and Soviet Influence, 1956–1960* (The Hague: Mouton, 1965). Background on twentieth-century authors may be found in C. T. Hsia, *A History of Modern Chinese Fiction, 1917–1957* (New Haven: Yale University Press, 1961). Chinese literature of the 1950s is discussed in the various articles in Cyril Birch, ed., *Chinese Communist Literature* (New York: Praeger, 1963). An early anthology of Hundred Flowers translations, not primarily about literature, is Roderick MacFarquhar, *The Hundred Flowers Campaign and the Chinese Intellectuals* (New York:

[15] One new development is the beginning of an underground literature of dissent: unpublished novels, stories, and poems circulating in mimeograph or handcopied form. Many of these are by former Red Guards, articulate and politically aware youths. And the example of Lu Hsün, so glorified by Mao, still inspires. The exiled author of the exposé novel *The Coldest Winter in Peking* tells us that after organizing a Lu Hsün study group with some friends, he thought long about the meaning of Lu Hsün's spirit and asked himself "whether I could describe the reality of China as realistically as Lu Hsün had." See Leo Ou-fan Lee, "Dissent Literature from the Cultural Revolution," *Chinese Literature: Essays, Articles, Reviews* (1979), 1:59–79.

Praeger, 1960). One story and the controversy surrounding it are described in R. David Arkush, "One of the Hundred Flowers: Wang Meng's 'Young Newcomer,' " *Papers on China* (1964), 18:155–86. Other relevant works are cited in the notes.

THE SECOND HUNDRED FLOWERS—AFTER TWENTY YEARS

HUALING NIEH

Seventy-five-year-old Ting Ling appeared at the People's Great Hall in Peking on the eve of the 1979 Chinese New Year. Party and state leaders were celebrating the occasion together with 30,000 soldiers, workers, scientists, writers, and artists. The night's entertainment included song and dance, operas, films, puppet shows, acrobatics, martial arts, and chess games. Ting Ling, enjoying the festivities with her family and grandchildren, remarked that she felt like "a country woman who ventured into the city only to be overwhelmed by too many interesting things." Ting Ling had disappeared from public life in 1958. She was accused of being a "Rightist" and was sent to a farm in Hei-lung-chiang Province in remote northeast China, worked there twelve years raising chickens, was in prison five years (1970–1975), and began to live in a village in Shansi in 1975. She appeared in public for the first time in 1979. When asked about her life in the past twenty years, she laughed and said that people should look ahead. She had been writing the continuation of *The Sun Shines over the Sangkan River*.

The Hundred Flowers blooming was made constitutional at the

Fifth National Assembly. Intellectuals are no longer considered
"people to be reeducated and remolded as they were in the earlier
days of liberation; rather, they are members of the working class
engaged in mental labor and are a strong force on which the Party
can rely."[1] The "Rightist caps" were removed from those criticized
during the anti-Rightist campaign in 1957. Writers called out for democracy and demanded the legal protection of their writings as well
as their persons.

Chiang Feng wrote, in his article "Wen-i hsü-yao min-chu" (Literature and Art Need Democracy), published in *Jeh-min jih-pao* (People's Daily), February 20, 1979:

> After 1957, the loss of democracy took place gradually in the literary
> and artistic circles. It became the popular practice to "impose a criminal
> frame on you, grab your queue, dig out your roots, put a cap on you and
> beat you with a club *(T'ao k'uang-tzu, chua pian-tzu, wa kên-tzu, tai mao-tzu, ta
> kun-tzu)*." As a result, members of the literary and artistic circles did not dare
> think, speak, or act out their feelings. There was no academic discussion;
> creative endeavor in art and literature stopped. . . .
>
> Since literature reflects the conditions of a given society, the dark side
> of a society should not be excluded from its literature and art. In simple but
> truthful words, Chairman Mao stated that "The dust will not be gone by it-
> self if the broom doesn't come." Light will not enter until darkness has gone;
> henceforth, we must expose darkness in order to eliminate it and let light
> shine through.
>
> Literature and art without real democracy will wither away like flowers
> without sun.

At a meeting organized by *Wen-i pao* (Literary Gazette) and
Tian-ying i-shu (Cinematography) on January 12, 1979 in Peking, Ai
Ch'ing and other writers concluded that no literary democracy is
possible without a sound political democracy and legal system. Ai
Ch'ing was exiled to Sinkiang in 1959, stayed sixteen years, began to
publish his work again in 1978 after twenty years of silence. He is
living in Peking. One of the many poems he has published since the
spring of 1978 may be symbolic of his life in the past twenty years:

[1] "Wan-cheng de chuen-ch'uëh de li-chieh tang de chih-shih-fen-tzu cheng-ts'ê"
(Comprehensively and Accurately Understand the Party's Policy toward Intellectuals)
Jeh-min jih-pao (People's Daily), January 4, 1979.

Cactus[2]

you like lilac
I like cactus

growing in the tropics
its home is the desert

always blooming
even in drought

kept on the windowsill
dreaming of ocean

Wang Meng, who wrote the controversial story "A Young Man Arrives at the Organization Department" during the Hundred Flowers blooming, was one of the twenty-five winners of the short-story contest sponsored in 1979 by *Jen-min wen-hsüeh* (People's Literature) for his story "Tsui pao-kuei de" (The Most Precious). At the awards assembly, attended by over two hundred distinguished writers and critics, Chou Yang, the vice-chairman of the Chinese Writers' Association, urged the writers to "use independent thinking and write about what they have personally seen, felt, and believed."

Liu Pin-yen, who wrote the sensational story "The Inside News of the Newspaper" in 1957, published in the March 1979 issue of *Shang-hai Wen-hsüeh* (Shanghai Literature) an article entitled "Kuan-yü hsieh yin-an-mien he kan-yü sheng-huo" (On Writing about the Dark Side and Intervening with Life). In it, he described the problems of writing:

Twenty-three years ago, we were in the same situation we are now. . . . In literature, art, and science, a hundred flowers began to bloom, and a hundred schools of thought began to contend. In one year, writing appeared, such as "On the Bridge Construction Site," "The Young Man Who Arrives at the Organization Department," and "The Inside News of the Newspaper," that reflected the inner conflicts of people. These works aroused immediate attention and were welcomed by a great number of readers because they reflected realistic problems, exposed the dark side of society, and defied taboos that had obstructed our progress. Actually, problems raised by these works did not breach the most serious taboos; the stories' criticism of society was not very strong. Nonetheless, the authors

[2] "Hsien-jen-chang" (Cactus), *Hsi-hu* (West Lake), October 1978.

were attacked by some comrades for "writing about the dark side" and "intervening with life."

After the struggle, the writers and those sympathetic to their cause were criticized and defeated. Bureaucratism and other dirt and bacteria in our lives that had harmed the Party and the socialist ideal remained protected; they grew and flourished. This was a great contradiction in modern Chinese history which caused endless disasters. . . .

For a long time one way of thinking was dominant: the leadership had stipulated what was the most important work, or what was needed to propagandize a certain movement. The writer placed events in fixed formulas in order to deliver certain theories and policies. Such writings were regarded as literature. . . . Is this right? No! Literature cannot be an effective instrument for propaganda unless it is truthful in reflecting actual life.

In the past twenty years, twice have we confronted the fact that our newspapers were telling lies. After the Gang of Four, we decided to stop telling lies about our life. Did our literature also tell lies?

Our literature and life diverge in two directions: what is written in books is one thing, what actually happens is another. . . . It seems that our literature is for the sole purpose of promoting the prestige of socialism, and in this, avoids the negative aspects of real life. In fact, these negative aspects have harmed our socialist work and life, and thus, have harmed the prestige of socialism in the eyes of the people. . . .

Since liberation, we have learned a lesson from our literary history: that is, there has been a great gap between what the writer can do for his society and what he has actually done; and attacking the writer for "intervening in life" twenty-one years ago has undoubtedly widened the gap.

The Fourth National Congress of Chinese Writers and Artists was held from October 30 to November 16, 1979. It had been nineteen years since the Third National Congress. Attending the meeting were 3,200 writers, critics, artists, musicians, dancers, actors, and actresses from all parts of China. Certain major problems were argued: should literature and art serve politics? Should literature and art be used as instruments of class struggle? Should literature and art be *only* for workers, peasants, and soldiers? The strongest voice at the Congress was for democracy, against suppression, against bureaucracy, against privileges for Party cadres.

Teng Hsiao-p'ing, vice-chairman of the Communist Party and vice-premier of China, mentioned that many literary and artistic works had been banned and that many writers and artists had been falsely charged and persecuted during the ten years of the Gang of

Four; he extended "warm and sincere greetings" to those who had stood up and fought, adding:

We will still continue to insist on the line in literature and art that Comrade Mao Tse-tung made: literature and art serve the people, above all, the workers, peasants, and soldiers; insist on the hundred flowers blooming, weeding through the old to bring forth the new, making the past serve the present and the foreign serve China. We must encourage free development of various forms and styles in creative work, free discussions of various views and thoughts in literary theory.[3]

He said that the Party should not demand that literature and art obey temporary, specific, and immediate policies. The Party should help writers and artists achieve a favorable life so that they could devote themselves to making Chinese literature and art flourish, to promoting literary and artistic standards and producing good artistic works. He also called for "the liberation of thought," for the authorities to stop giving orders in literary and artistic creation and criticism.

Creating art is complicated mental labor. It requires the artist to make the best of his creative originality. What to write, how to write—these are to be tried and solved by the artist in practicing his art. Don't give orders.[4]

Chou Yang, who had been the spokesman for the Party on literary and intellectual matters and had had an iron hand in organizing the anti-Rightist campaign in 1957, made a report to the Fourth National Congress called "Chi-wang k'ai-lai, fan-jung she-hui chu-i hsin shih-ch'i ti wen-i" (Be Both Successors and Pioneers, Create A Flourishing Literature and Art in the New Period of Socialism). He admitted what was wrong with the 1957 campaign:

Many comrades suffered blows they did not deserve; some views on literature and art as well as some works of literature and art were wrongly criticized, and a large number of men of letters and artists were made to suffer, including some talented, enterprising ones who dared to break fresh ground in this field. This brought setbacks to the lively situation which came about

[3] "Tsai Chung-kuo wen-hsüeh i-shu kung-tso-che ti-ssu-tz'u tai-piao ta-hui shang ti chu-ts'u" (Congratulations on the Fourth National Congress of Chinese Writers and Artists) *Jeh-min jih-pao* (People's Daily), October 31, 1979.
[4] Ibid.

following promotion of the policy of "letting a hundred flowers blossom, letting a hundred schools of thought contend."[5]

Ting Ling gave a talk at the Congress, "Chiang i-tien hsin-li hua" (A Few Words from My Heart). She was grateful to regain the right to talk and to write, for which she had given up hope in the past twenty years. She said that she had felt like someone who had had the mark "Rightist" or "Traitor" tatooed on her face, that she had had to make a way out of a state of almost total darkness, about which she had never even told her daughter.

Now, just as Comrade Ai Ch'ing said, it is over with; no use talking about it. There is no personal grudge against anybody. What happened to us was a social problem. It was not any individual who knocked me down. It was good for me to stay down and see many things and people that I would not be able to see if I had stayed up. I am full of things to write about, but time is running out for me. I wish I could have another fifteen years. . . .

. . . I started to write in 1927; it was fifty-two years ago. Of course, I stopped writing for twenty years after 1958. In the thirties, my books were banned by the Kuomintang; after 1958, my books were banned by our own people. Now, those who are around thirty have not read my books. Several months ago, I received a letter from a reader. He wrote, "Although your name appeared in the newspapers and you were appointed a member of the Consultative Conference, I did not know who you were. In my mind, you were a Rightist. Now, the Party is carrying out a policy of being realistic; even war criminals were given amnesty; so people like you became members of the Consultative Conference. Your image in my eyes did not change until I read your writings. Could a Rightist write works like that?" I was very much touched by that letter. It is clear to everybody that those who were knocked down during the Cultural Revolution were good people, that those who were knocked down by the Gang of Four were also good people. They are favored by the masses. How about those who were knocked down in 1957? They were beaten and turned into shit. Should they all be treated that way? I hesitated whether I should tell you what is in my heart. I am over seventy. I was put in prison by the Kuomintang, and again by the Gang of Four. How could I be indifferent and silent over what has happened and lead a muddled life, as some of my friends, out of concern, told me to do? I just can't. . . .

I have asked some people, what was the root of the troubles we writers and artists suffered? I have been looking for the answer. Some comrades said that it was feudalism. Yes, it was feudalism. But how was it carried out? I started to fight feudalism in 1919 when I was only fifteen; after sixty years, I am still fighting it. It was sectarianism, another form of feudalism, in liter-

[5]*Beijing Review*, December 14, 1979.

ary and artistic circles. It is impossible to look forward, to achieve the unification of the country, to achieve the hundred flowers blooming and the
hundred schools of thought contending if sectarianism is not wiped out. For
people like me it will be over, but we have the young who have a future and
should not suffer the way we did. Our literature should have some influence
in the world. So we must dig out the roots of problems, bring them into the
light of day. We had sectarianism in the twenties, made by a small group of
people who had common interests. It was not bad. When did it begin to
become a terrible thing? It was when people began to have power. I hope
from my heart that it will never happen again.[6]

Hsia Yen, the prominent writer of plays and film scripts, was
beaten by Red Guards; his legs were broken. He was totally isolated
from theater and film and other people for eight years. He was
called a revisionist. Now, at the Fourth National Congress of Chinese Writers and Artists, he was elected chairman of the Chinese Film
Artists' Association. He gave a talk at the final meeting. Pointing out
that there still were people who were suspicious and afraid of, even
opposed to, liberating thought in literary and artistic circles, he emphasized that the liberation of thought had just begun. Real liberation of thought and democracy in literature and art were still some
distance away. He pointed out that although the capitalist system
had had cyclical economic depressions, some imperialist countries
had enjoyed ever improving and changing science and technology
which had greatly accelerated their industrial productivity.

This new situation in the imperialist countries suggests a new subject for the
Marxists and Leninists to study. The world is changing. Society is changing.
Our thought should adjust to changes in the objective reality, and change,
too.

Thus there should be no "forbidden zone" in artistic creation and
criticism. He also emphasized the importance of artistry in creative
work. He encouraged writers to go deeply into life, and at the same
time, work hard at cultivating artistic sophistication. He concluded:
"Our country has entered a period of stability and unification;
writers and artists don't need to worry, to fear such a political campaign as that of 1957."[7]

[6]Chiang i-tien hsin-li hua" (A Few Words from My Heart), *Hung chi'i* (Red
Flag), December 1979.

[7] "Chung-kuo wen-hsüeh i-shu kung-tso-che ti-ssu-tz'u tai-piao ta-hui pi-mu-ts'u"
(Closing Address to the Fourth National Congress of Chinese Writers and Artists) *Jeh-
min jih-pao* (People's Daily), November 17, 1979.

A NOTE ON TRANSLATION

PROBLEMS

The Chinese language is a product of the culture and life of an ancient country. Given the range, implications, subtlety, and the cultural and linguistic complexities of Chinese characters, there is often no English equivalent that can convey the whole meaning of an expression. Certain unique qualities, which the Chinese people treasure in their language, are simply untranslatable. If translated literally, they sound exotic, which is a polite word for "odd." Consider the title of my novel, *Sang-ch'ing yü t'ao-hung,* or *Mulberry Green and Peach Pink.* The full implications of the title are untranslatable: it is composed of two names for one woman, and the implications, associations, and tonal effect of the two names are uniquely Chinese. The following song, from a puppet show in the novel, can also demonstrate certain special qualities of the Chinese language which are untranslatable:

OLD MAN:	*The way to great learning*
FEMALE CLOWN:	is to knock down Teacher.
OLD MAN:	*To understand enlightened virtues*
FEMALE CLOWN:	is to pick up Teacher.
OLD MAN:	*To be close to the people*
FEMALE CLOWN:	is to carry Teacher out the door.
OLD MAN:	*To achieve great virtue*
FEMALE CLOWN:	is to bury Teacher in a muddy hole.

The italicized lines are from the Confucian classics, and this is a satirical song about the Confucian tradition. The old man and the female clown are two types of characters in Chinese opera; the cos-

tumes they wear and the stage voices in which they sing are unique
to the parts. The female clown sings a parody of the old man, who
represents Confucian attitudes. The lines of the song are in rhymed
couplets. Each character of the Chinese language has a fixed tone;
some have more than one, depending on the meaning or the tone of
the character that follows. There are four tones, which make it possible for the Chinese to create a large number of musical and rhythmical variations. The tonal effect and nuances of meaning in the
song, enriched by cultural, historical, and dramatic associations that
are clear to the Chinese, are simply untranslatable.

In addition, the profound differences between the Chinese language and the laws of English syntax make the rendering of some
idioms and expressions awkward or impossible.

Aphorisms, figures of speech, colloquial slang, and proverbs
often seem alien to characteristic English expression, as with a
phrase from the article "On Lyric Poetry" in this anthology: *K'ai-hui
shang li-ch'ang; san-hui hsia li-ch'ang.* These ten characters are translated as "There are those who step up to their position at meetings
and step down from it afterward." This is to say that they can "step
up" to the proletarian class and criticize others from a Marxist-
Leninist point of view, only to "step down" to an individual standpoint after the meetings. The original sentence is divided into two
parts of five characters each, and the parts of speech in each segment are parallel. Such parallelism often appears in Chinese. But it
is impossible to translate the sentence into English with the same
brevity and parallel structure as in the Chinese, so these characteristics are lost.

Puns are often untranslatable. Chinese is full of puns because
the language abounds with characters having the same pronuncia-
tion and tone, but different meaning. When Edgar Snow saw Mao
Tse-tung in China in 1970, Mao told him: "I am a monk under an
umbrella." Mao punned on the characters *fa* (hair) and *fa* (law), but
these characters do not even appear in his expression. It is an understood pun that plays with associations: a monk's head is shaven—no
hair. "No hair" sounds like "no law." Under the umbrella, the monk
cannot see Heaven, which represents the highest authority to the
Chinese. By association, a monk under the umbrella means no law,

no authority. Mao meant that he wanted no law, no authority, above himself. He wanted revolution.

Apart from these difficulties, which any translator will experience in working from Chinese, we have had other special problems in translating this anthology of Chinese Communist literature:

1. Many ideological terms have become part of everyday language in China. The Chinese have coined phrases for certain concepts, ideologies, or movements which, because they are simple, concise, and rhythmical, are easily adopted by the people and readily become idioms in their speech and thought. This helps instruct the people. For instance, consider a phrase in the story "Kai hsien" (The New Election) by Li Kuo-wen. *Liang-hua i-pan* is literally translated as "two -izations and one exemplar." This phrase means that the report on union work is to be presented in a systematic manner (systematization), while the accomplishments are to be listed as statistics (statisticization). The report should also mention certain exemplary people and deeds (exemplars) in order to demonstrate the union's achievements.

Another instance from the same story is the term "economism." This describes the concept of putting the welfare of the workers ahead of their political education. There are many words of the "ism" form in contemporary Chinese. All these ideological terms are extremely difficult to render into characteristic English usage.

2. Hyperbole is a standard ingredient of the political sloganizing common to Chinese writing and speech today: "Rightist literary figures launched a frenzied attack on the Party," "the degenerate soul of the architect of souls." It is difficult to fit such phrases into the quieter tone of the writing as a whole.

3. Marx, Engels, Feuerbach, Hegel, Lenin, and Stalin are often quoted without citing the source. There was some confusion when only the Chinese translation was available, without any mention of the title of the source. In some cases, we had to translate such quotations from the Chinese version alone.

4. In this anthology, we deal with different literary forms: poetry, fiction, and criticism. In addition to the problems all literary forms share, there are also problems unique to each. Contemporary Chinese poetry is written in *pai-hua,* the vernacular language. Poems

in this anthology are mainly concerned with the life of the Chinese in socialist China; the imagery and expressions may be unfamiliar to the average Western reader. For instance, "The Political Studies Class" is the title of a poem. The original, "Hsüeh-hsi-hui" (Studies Class), doesn't explicitly express the word "political." "Studies class" is a regular class in which people study political thoughts or great events and movements. The translation "Political Studies Class" cannot express all the connotations and at the same time sound as idiomatic as the Chinese title. This obvious adjective, "political," deprives the poem of its lyric quality. Certain of the poems may deal with important events, such as the construction of the dam at the site of the Ming Tombs. The image of the dam as New China, replacing the Ming emperors' tombs, or old China, is alien to the Western reader. The imagery and tone of contemporary poetry in socialist China are unique in their brevity and complexity. The expressions for the New Man of New China have no equivalents in English.

In translating the stories, dialogue presented the most difficulty. The characters in the stories are individuals in a collective system. The society, or the Party, comes first; the individual, second. Apart from aphorisms, proverbs, puns, and colloquial slang, the Chinese use many ideological terms in everyday language—for example, "Would you like to be accused of departmentalism?" (from the story "The Inside News of the Newspaper"). "Departmentalism" in Chinese (*fen-san chu-i*) is an derogatory term for those who care only about their own work or their own fields, those who lack a sense of the overall situation. This negative connotation is not expressed by the literal translation of the original, and so requires a footnote; at the same time, this sentence in the dialogue sounds "exotic" in English. Another example is "I'd like to go to the country for awhile," from the same story. The literal translation is "I'd like to go down." *Hsia-ch'ü* (go down) is a term which came out of the policy that people should go to the country to live or work with the peasants. Thus, the English expression "go to the country" does not have the political connotation it has in Chinese.

Translating the criticism was even more difficult. Chinese literature was written in the classical literary language until 1917, when writers began to use the vernacular. It has been the concern of literary people to write in a direct, simple, but artistic language ever since. Poets and fiction writers in socialist China have achieved such a language; most Chinese writers outside China have not. But the language of the criticism included in this anthology is not direct and clear, and may be difficult even for the Chinese reader. Criticism was made in a roundabout way so that it would not be vulnerable to countercriticism. All the articles criticizing Party views were written in a subdued, subtle, and complex style. Their meaning is not in the language, but behind the language. It is like playing chess, attacking and defending at the same time. These unsaid meanings in the critical essays made them the most difficult texts in this anthology to translate. The subtlety and complexity of criticism are lost in translation, which usually sounds long-winded, repetitious, and unclear.

METHOD

Literature of the Hundred Flowers is a product of co-translation. Our hope was to make joint translations of the original, with a Chinese person controlling the sense and an American the English, in an effort to have the Chinese poem or story *sound* like a poem or story in English. This requires a Chinese who not only knows the original language, but also Communist ideology, expressions, and vocabulary, and an American who strives always for a clear and direct American English, avoiding the easy rhetoric that disfigures so many translations. We also believe that when translating imaginative writing, an imagination is necessary. In our case, co-imagination is crucial. Those who have worked on this anthology are poets or fiction writers, either in Chinese or English. We put our languages, our heads, and our sensibilities together in an act of literary cooperation. The co-translation of this anthology was done over a period of four years, with three or four people, both Chinese and American, working together at the same time. Co-translation of this sort has been built into the activities of the International Writing Program at the University of Iowa. If a writer in Hungarian, Polish, Japanese, Korean, or Swedish wants to put into English work of his own or of other writers in his language, a young American writer will be assigned to work with him. After much discussion, often endless consultation, after trying many different shades of meaning for one phrase or one line, a final text is jointly created. *Literature of the Hundred Flowers* is one of the many works of co-translation produced and published by the International Writing Program.

In fact, most translators have engaged in co-translation by consulting others. Ezra Pound based his translation of Chinese poems on the notes of Fenellosa, notes produced with the help of two Japanese professors. It was co-translation. But the co-translating we have done in this anthology, and in many other projects of the International Writing Program, involves a much closer working relationship, a face-to-face relationship, between an English-speaking translator and a translator from the native language. The tiny *co-* must be emphasized: the two translators are equally important. The meaning and spirit of the original are as important as the language into which the text is translated. Co-translation involves a constant dialogue and a close exchange of criticism between two translators of different languages and different cultural backgrounds. All translation is a compromise; co-translators make compromises after thorough discussion and close scrutiny. Because of all the problems mentioned earlier, we believe that co-translation is an efficient way to produce an anthology of such varied and complicated texts.

In translating this anthology, three people worked together at one time. A Chinese and an American made the first draft. The Chinese explained the cultural, political, historical, and literary background of the original text, and gave the literal translation of each sentence. The American rephrased the initial translation of each sentence in English. Then he worked on the entire first draft, reading each sentence, revising and polishing, trying to produce a second draft in clear and idiomatic English. At times the American had to sacrifice elements of the literal translation for clearer expression. For instance, he might change the literal translation "selling dog meat under the sign of a sheep's head" to the simple, direct word "fraud."

After the second draft was completed, I read it and checked it with the original Chinese. Every line was questioned and read again and again, in a state of mixed delight and despair. As writers, all of us love our own languages and take the use of words very seriously. I tried to arrive at a compromise between the Chinese who insists on keeping the "exotic" line, because it is close to the original, and the American who may be too free in his use of English and is careless with the original. The second draft of the translation is attacked, prodded, pinched, forced to accept meanings the American had not appreciated or understood, or to give up meanings the Chinese had cherished too much but no Westerner could understand. I brought up problems for discussion with the Chinese and the American. For instance, "selling dog meat under the sign of a sheep's head," translated as "fraud," was discussed. Finally, the literal translation "selling dog meat under the sign of a sheep's head" replaced "fraud." Sometimes, the three of us fought a cultural war, or a literary war, or an ideological war, or a nationalistic war. There were arguments, accusations of cultural or political chauvinism, indifference to national traditions, contempt for pidgin English or flowery English, or ignorance of a beautiful language (English? or Chinese?). It was an intense and lively confrontation of languages, cultures, imaginations, and egos. Always the confrontation. Always the compromise. In desperation, we agreed to make a third version and let it stand with half the life of the original in English. None of us, Chinese or American, was entirely happy. No translator can be happy. But co-translation may become co-living, on which the survival of the human race depends.

CRITICISM
AND
POLEMICS

PREFACE

Contemporary Chinese literature and art have been guided by the principles Mao Tse-tung set forth in his talks at the Yenan Forum in 1942. Mao's principles of art and literature are these: political criteria should come before the artistic; art and literature are subordinate to politics; writers should submit themselves to ideological remolding by living among the masses; there is no universal human nature, only class nature, such as bourgeois class nature and proletarian class nature. These principles were challenged and debated during the period of the Hundred Flowers. This volume includes the work of some of the most outspoken critics: Ch'in Chao-yang, Liu Shao-t'ang, Huang Ch'iu-yün, Yao Hsüeh-yin, and Huang Yao-mien.

The critics spoke about problems in writing and literary criticism that arose from the dogmatic interpretation and implementation of these principles. Some questioned them indirectly and subtly, others openly but skillfully. Liu Shao-t'ang, the youngest among the outspoken critics, criticized Mao's principles in his article, "Wo tui tang-ch'ien wen-i wen-t'i ti i-hsieh ch'ien-chien" (Some Thoughts on Literary Problems Today). He argued that the principle that literature should serve politics is not the correct attitude toward writing; literature constructed of abstract ideologies has no artistic appeal. Writers should not be forced by administrative orders and rules to write only about workers, peasants, and soldiers; political ideology can only be conveyed through artistic imagery. The value of any work, he said, should not be judged by whether it is valuable as an instrument for ideological education or whether it deals with important events, but by what it conveys and how it moves the reader artistically; further, imposing a unified way of writing on writers strangles their creativity.

Yao Hsüeh-yin agreed with Liu that Mao's literary principles, which had been useful when China was fighting the Japanese for survival, were no longer of value to socialist China when the situation of the country and the life of the people had changed. He said: "Chairman Mao's talks on art and literature were produced under specific historical conditions. . . . These conditions have constantly been changing; many things which were true before should have changed, too." He also said: "History has gone far ahead of us. We are just marking time, reading by heart the outdated lunar calendar. The views which were correct and produced positive results under specific conditions have become stubborn, backward dogmas and taboos, which will be obstacles to the appearance and development of new things." He even criticized Mao's principle that the political criterion should come before the artistic criterion as "not only simplistic, but also rigid."

Critics complained about the lack of originality and imagination in modern writing, the Party's leadership in the literary field, and the fact that writers could praise only the bright side of life. They also complained that literary critics were burdened by too many taboos, that literary works did not satisfy the demands of the people, that writers did not want to whitewash life but could not tell the truth, and that they did not want to close their eyes to the suffering of the people but had to keep silent about things which disturbed their consciences. The most painful obstacle for a writer was not being able to express whatever he had in mind without reservation, having to compromise between what he wanted to say and what he was supposed to say.

Forums were held all over the country during the Hundred Flowers period to discuss various problems in the literary field. Non-Party writers, critics, and editors were invited to attend, and some of their opinions are included in this volume. Forums were also held, to discuss problems of publication, that cannot be included in this anthology but deserve mention. The Administrative Bureau of Publishing Enterprises called publishers together a number of times to discuss their problems. The publishers were unanimous in their opinion that publishing did indeed suffer from dogmatism; they pointed out that books based on authorized views had often been published, yet works with new, unapproved ideas were seldom published. Many Soviet books were translated and published, but few books from other countries. Editors were held responsible for the content and style of writing. As a result, some editors had no respect for the views of the authors and took the liberty of revising their manuscripts. There were so many rigid rules that certain works were deprived of the chance to be published.

The publishers wanted a greater variety of books; they felt that, in addition to works of socialist realism, literature presenting other schools of thought should be published. These should include books translated from foreign languages, as well as classical and modern Chinese works of academic and artistic achievement that did not contradict official policy. A wide variety of forms and styles should be encouraged in literature.

The polemics in this volume concentrate on the literary issues raised during the Hundred Flowers period. China has had a long literary tradition of realism; modern Chinese writers have been greatly influenced by this tradition and by nineteenth-century Western realism. The literary issues debated during the Hundred Flowers movement were mainly concerned with realism and human nature in connection with socialist society. One of the most important was socialist realism as opposed to realism in the socialist era. Socialist realism, as advocated in Soviet Russia, had been the dominant way of writing in China since 1949. Chou Yang, the official spokesman for literary affairs in China during the first years after 1949, defined the literature of socialist realism in an article entitled "Socialist Realism—The Road of Progress for Chinese Literature," published in the Soviet magazine *Znamya* in December 1952:

In judging whether a particular literary work is written in the spirit of socialist realism, the main consideration is not whether it describes real life in its revolutionary development from a socialist standpoint. . . . Socialist realism demands, in the first place, that the writer depict reality truthfully in its revolutionary development. In real life, there are constant contradictions and struggles between what is progressive and new, and what is backward and dying. A writer should give a penetrating picture of these contradictions in life, clearly understand the main tendency in historical development, vigorously support the new and oppose the old. Therefore, in judging the ideological value of a literary work, we must first decide whether this work exposes the class contradictions in society. These contradictions exist in every detail of life. We must also decide whether the exposure of class contradictions goes deeply enough. Any attempt to cover up, whitewash or gloss over the contradictions of life means a distortion of reality; it reduces the strength of literature in ideological struggle and weakens its positive effectiveness.[1]

Some writers and critics criticized these principles of socialist realism. The most outspoken was Ch'in Chao-yang (Ho Chih), editor of *Jen-min wen-hsüeh* (People's Literature). He started the debate on socialist realism by publishing his article "Hsien-shih chu-i: Kuang-k'uo ti tao-lu" (The Broad Road of Realism: A Reassessment of Realism). He coined the phrase "realism in the socialist era" to replace the term "socialist realism." He argued that realism is always the same: truth to art and life. Realism in the socialist era is the depiction of socialist reality from a socialist standpoint in a socialist era. According to this point of view, literature should not be a mouthpiece for any political ideology. Ch'in opposed the principle that the political criterion comes before the artistic criterion in judging a literary work. Only when literature is artistic and true to life can it be effective as a political weapon. Is the world view of Marxism-Leninism the only source for creative writing? No. The writer's experiences in life, his creative methods and his talent, are equally important sources.

Ch'in's views immediately stirred up controversy. During the debates, other terms for realism came up: "writing the truth" and "intervening in life." Writing the truth does not mean objective depiction of life. Rather, it demands that the writer "intervene in life" to unify his subjective experiences with the objective realities and to reflect this unified reality beautifully in an artistic form. To intervene in life means to study, think over, and analyze life and to take action. If a writer lives and works in this way, he will have individual views about life, will not portray characters from an abstract ideological standpoint, and his writing will be true both to art and to life. Liu Shao-t'ang, Huang Ch'iu-yün, and certain other writers strongly and actively supported these views. This group of critics believed that there is a dark side to socialist reality as well as a bright side;

---

[1] Chou Yang, *China's New Literature and Art* (Peking: Foreign Languages Press, 1954). I have revised the translation slightly—Ed.

that literature's main task is to reveal the dark side; and that only by exposing it can a writer intervene in life.

Such views not only aroused controversy, but also greatly influenced many young writers. One group of young writers published a literary magazine called *T'an-ch'iu che* (The Searcher), stating as one of its goals support for the literary views of Ch'in Chao-yang. These views also influenced certain writers whose work became popular with many readers, especially the young. Liu Pai-yü described the situation: "The editor of *Chung-kuo ch'ing-nien pao* (China Youth Daily), who is well informed about the situation of young writers, told me that literary views which are actually in opposition to realism but call themselves authentic realism are very popular among literary young people with petit-bourgeois backgrounds. He was not surprised to find that this was so. Those views revitalized their old habits of thought. Many of them have been stubbornly opposed to being tempered and reformed in revolutionary struggles."[2]

The critics who questioned socialist realism provoked countercriticism in defense of it. Yao Wen-yüan, the most tyrannical of those who offered countercriticism, became an important spokesman for China in regard to literary affairs. In 1965, his criticism of Wu Han's play, *Hai Jui pa-kuan* (Hai Jui Dismissed from Office), triggered the Cultural Revolution. In defending socialist realism, Yao emphasized the importance of the Marxist world view. He argued that socialist realism became *inevitable* in the historical development of literature when the proletarian revolution became inevitable in the development of human society, that the literature of socialist realism was produced during the course of class struggle, and that writers cannot depict the images of the newly conscious proletarian class and its struggles unless they embrace the Marxist world outlook. Yao stated that socialist realism is designed to serve the struggle of the proletarian class for its liberation; that socialist realist art is to be used as an instrument in educating the people and encouraging them to struggle with the ideologies of revisionism; and that socialist realism reflects life from the Marxist standpoint.

Another important literary issue of the Hundred Flowers period was whether there is a human nature common to all human

[2] Liu Pai-yü, "Lun wen-hsüeh shang ti yu-p'ai han-liu" (On the Rightist Cold Current in Literature), *Wen-i pao* (Literary Gazette), August 4, 1957.

beings, or various human natures that represent class natures. Critics like Ch'ien Ku-jung and Pa Jen argued that literature is the study of people, that people are the most important subject of literature, and that human nature is unchanging. They opposed the idea that there is a particular human nature belonging to a particular class. They also argued that if the main concern of literature is socialist reality rather than human beings, literature will become abstract and conceptualized, that it is human nature which leads humanity toward a better life, a life free of oppression and exploitation.

These views also provoked arguments from the opposite side. Yao Wen-yüan commented later in 1958: "Mr. Ch'ien Ku-jung's article 'Lun wen-hsüeh shih jen-hsüeh' [Literature Is the Study of Man], the articles by Ho Chih [Ch'in Chao-yang], and others, represent two separate systems of thought in the same petit-bourgeois literary trend. Ho Chih opposed the concept of class nature in socialist literature and the Marxist world outlook with the so-called theory of 'writing the truth'; Mr. Ch'ien Ku-jung did the same thing, but with the theory of 'humanism.' "[3] The debates on this issue, begun in 1957, continued in writings and at meetings through 1960. Yao Wen-yüan called those later debates "the continuation of the past ideological struggles."

Among those who criticized the literary views of human nature stated by Ch'ien Ku-jhung, Pa Jen, and others, Li Hsi-fan was most active in the debates. In 1952, he and another young man criticized Yü P'ing-po's study of *The Dream of the Red Chamber*. They accused him of failing to recognize the novel as a study of the inevitable collapse of feudal society, and of failing to regard the hero Chia Pao-yü as representing "the spirit of the newly emerging man." As previously mentioned, Mao praised these young men highly, saying that "the whole thing has been set in motion by two 'nobodies.' " By "the whole thing" Mao meant the campaign against the mistaken ideas of bourgeois idealism in literature. Li Hsi-fan became one of the most authoritative literary critics in China.

[3] Yao Wen-yüan, "P'ing Ch'ien Ku-jung hsien-sheng ti 'jen-tao chu-i' lun" (A Comment on Mr. Ch'ien Ku-jung's Theory of "Humanism"), 1958; in *Wen-i ssu-hsiang lun-cheng chi* (Polemics on Literature) (Shanghai: The Writers' Press, 1965).

The criticism by Li Hsi-fan, Yao Wen-yüan, and others of the theory that literature is the study of human beings can be summed up as follows: people have an instinctive nature and a social nature; the instinctive nature, as in love and hunger, is shared by animals; human nature is determined by human beings' social life; a different society at a different point in history will form a different human nature. Human beings cannot be isolated from reality, which always changes in its development. Socialist literature must create images of a proletarian class which have never been created, or have been distorted, in bourgeois literature. The theory that literature is the study of human beings negates the principle that literature serves politics, and the principle that the political criterion comes before the artistic criterion in judging a literary work.

Among the outspoken critics, Liu Shao-t'ang was singled out as an example of how the young can degenerate into Rightists if they do not go through thought remolding. Liu was a very highly regarded young writer from a village in Hopeh who created stories about peasants in a fresh and lyrical language. His talent drew the attention of the Party. In the afterword to his first collection of stories, *Ch'ing-chih lü-yeh* (Lush Branches and Green Leaves), he wrote, "I, a young man who has been raised and supported by the Party, owe all of my accomplishment, if any, to the Party: every bit has been made with the heart and blood of the Party." In 1952, he joined the Party at the age of seventeen. He believed that intellectuals should promote a wider cultural life for the peasants, while the cadres should do the work of promoting production in the villages. By promoting the peasants' cultural life, Liu meant to keep the old customs of weddings, funerals, and festivals, to assimilate the lively activities enjoyed by the country people of Soviet Russia, Eastern and Western Europe, and to make the peasant villages colorful places. He remarked: "The reform I would like to make is a decrease in the intense centralization in the Party system." "In the past, the workers and peasants reformed the intellectuals; now it is the intellectuals who will reform the workers and peasants." Liu Shao-t'ang's criticism and literary views were more often attacked than those of the other critics. In October 1957, several meetings were held in Peking by the Young Writers' Committee of the Writers' Union to criticize him. More than a thousand literary people, including Mao Tun and Lao She, attended the meetings. Criticism of Liu Shao-t'ang was regarded as useful in educating the young.

Another critic deserving attention was Ch'in Chao-yang. He not only spoke out against certain important literary problems and initiated new ideas, but also encouraged and published various controversial writings in *People's Literature,* a magazine he edited. Two stories critical of the system, "Pen-pao nei-pu hsiao-hsi" (The Inside News of the Newspaper) by Liu Pin-yen, and "Tsu-chih-pu hsin-lai ti nien-ch'ing jen" (A Young Man Arrives at the Organization Department) by Wang Meng, published in *People's Literature,* made a nationwide sensation. Ch'in also published Huang Ch'iu-yün's critical article "Pu-yao tsai jen-min ti chi-k'u mien-ch'ien pi-shang yen-ching" (Do Not Close Your Eyes to the Suffering of the People) and other controversial writings. All these works were severely criticized: Ch'in Chao-yang was the Monkey who made trouble in Heaven (The Monkey was Mao's favorite image of a rebel).

The Chinese way of literary criticism may be difficult for American readers who are observers of their society, or artists apart from their society. The Chinese writer is a fighter, a social worker, trying to help bring about a drastic transition from the old feudal system to a socialist system. Thus, Chinese critics deal with an entirely different sort of criticism; they must relate literature to society in the process of change. The opposite sides may have different opinions on the particulars of style and content, but they always have a few things in common: social awareness, a desire to serve their society, and a belief in socialism.

Another characteristic of Chinese literary critics which the Western reader may find difficult is their manner of writing. Many critics, fearing their criticism will in turn be criticized, present ideas in an indirect way; their writing employs a subdued, subtle, and complex style. The meaning is not in the language, but behind the language. It is like playing chess: attacking and defending at the same time.

The great bulk of material concerning Mao Tse-tung in this anthology is found in *Mao Tse-tung ssu-hsiang wan-sui* (Long Live Mao Tse-tung's Thought), an unofficially published volume that includes talks and remarks he made from 1949 to 1968.

THE HUNDRED FLOWERS MOVEMENT

1

ON "LET A HUNDRED FLOWERS BLOOM, LET A HUNDRED SCHOOLS OF THOUGHT CONTEND"

MAO TSE-TUNG

"Let a hundred flowers bloom, let a hundred schools of thought contend" and "long-term coexistence and mutual supervision"—how did
these slogans come to be put forward? They were put forward in the
light of China's specific conditions, on the basis of the recognition
that various kinds of contradictions still exist in socialist society, and
in response to the country's urgent need to speed up its economic
and cultural development. Letting a hundred flowers bloom and a
hundred schools of thought contend is the policy for promoting the
progress of the arts and the sciences and a flourishing socialist culture in our land.

Different forms and styles in art should develop freely and different schools in science should contend freely. We think it is harmful to the growth of art and science if administrative measures are
used to impose one particular style of art or school of thought and to

Mao Tse-tung, "On the Correct Handling of Contradictions Among the People," in
Mao Tse-tung on Literature and Art (Peking: Foreign Languages Press, 1967). The
speech was given at the Supreme State Conference held on February 27, 1957, but
was not published until June 18, 1957, after the anti-Rightist campaign had begun.

ban another. Questions of right and wrong in the arts and sciences should be settled through free discussion in artistic and scientific circles and through practical work in these fields. They should not be settled in summary fashion. A period of trial is often needed to determine whether something is right or wrong. Throughout history, new and correct things have often failed at the outset to win recognition from the majority of people and have had to develop by twists and turns in struggle. Often correct and good things have first been regarded not as fragrant flowers but as poisonous weeds. Copernicus' theory of the solar system and Darwin's theory of evolution were once dismissed as erroneous and had to prevail against bitter opposition. Chinese history offers many similar examples. In a socialist society, conditions for the growth of the new are radically different from and far superior to those in the old society. Nevertheless, it still often happens that new, rising forces are held back and rational proposals constricted. Moreover, the growth of new things may be hindered in the absence of deliberate suppression simply through lack of discernment. It is therefore necessary to be careful about questions of right and wrong in the arts and sciences, to encourage free discussion and avoid hasty conclusions. We believe that such an attitude can help to ensure a relatively smooth development of the arts and sciences.

Marxism, too, has developed through struggle. At the beginning, Marxism was subjected to all kinds of attack and regarded as a poisonous weed. It is still being attacked and is still regarded as a poisonous weed in many parts of the world. In the socialist countries, it enjoys a different position. But non-Marxist and, moreover, anti-Marxist ideologies exist even in these countries. In China, although in the main, socialist transformation has been completed with respect to the system of ownership, and although the large-scale and turbulent class struggles of the masses characteristic of the previous revolutionary periods have in the main come to an end, there are still remnants of the overthrown landlord and comprador classes, there is still a bourgeoisie, and the remolding of the petit-bourgeoisie has only just started. The class struggle is by no means over.

The class struggle between the proletariat and the bourgeoisie, the class struggle between the different political forces, and the class struggle in the ideological field between the proletariat and the bourgeoisie will continue to be long and tortuous and at times will even become very acute. The proletariat seeks to transform the world according to its own world outlook, and so does the bourgeoisie. In this respect, the question of which will win out, socialism or capitalism, is still not really settled. Marxists are still a minority among the entire population as well as among the intellectuals. Therefore, Marxism must still develop through struggle.

Marxism can develop only through struggle, and not only is this true of the past and the present, it is necessarily true of the future as well. What is correct invariably develops in the course of struggle with what is wrong. The true, the good, and the beautiful always exist by contrast with the false, the evil, and the ugly, and grow in struggle with the latter. As soon as a wrong thing is rejected and a particular truth accepted by mankind, new truths begin their struggle with new errors. Such struggles will never end. This is the law of development of truth and, naturally, of Marxism as well.

It will take a fairly long period of time to decide the issue in the ideological struggle between socialism and capitalism in our country. The reason is that the influence of the bourgeoisie and of the intellectuals who come from the old society will remain in our country for a long time to come, and so will their class ideology. If this is not sufficiently understood, or is not understood at all, the gravest mistakes will be made and the necessity of waging the struggle in the ideological field will be ignored. Ideological struggle is not like other forms of struggle. The only method to be used in this struggle is that of painstaking reasoning and not crude coercion.

Today, socialism is in an advantageous position in the ideological struggle. The main power of the state is in the hands of the working people led by the proletariat. The Communist Party is strong and its prestige stands high. Although there are defects and mistakes in our work, every fair-minded person can see that we are loyal to the people, that we are both determined and able to build up our motherland together with them, and that we have already achieved great successes and will achieve still greater ones. The vast majority of the bourgeoisie and intellectuals who come from the old society are patriotic and are willing to serve their flourishing socialist motherland; they know they will be helpless and have no bright future to look forward to if they turn away from the socialist cause and from the working people led by the Communist Party.

People may ask, since Marxism is accepted as the guiding ideology by the majority of the people in our country, can it be criticized? Certainly it can. Marxism is scientific truth and fears no criticism. If it did, and if it could be overthrown by criticism, it would be worthless. In fact, aren't the idealists criticizing Marxism every day and in every way? Aren't those who harbor bourgeois and petit-bourgeois ideas and do not wish to change—aren't they also criticizing Marxism in every way? Marxists should not be afraid of criticism from any quarter. Quite the contrary, they need to temper and develop themselves and win new positions in the teeth of criticism and in the storm and stress of struggle. Fighting against wrong ideas is like being vaccinated—a person develops greater immunity from disease as a result of vaccination. Plants raised in hothouses are unlikely to be sturdy. Carrying out the policy of letting a hundred flowers bloom and a hundred schools of thought contend will not weaken but strengthen the leading position of Marxism in the ideological field.

What should our policy be toward non-Marxist ideas? As far as unmistakable counterrevolutionaries and saboteurs of the socialist cause are concerned, the matter is easy: we simply deprive them of their freedom of speech. But incorrect ideas among the people are quite a different matter. Will it do to ban such ideas and deny them any opportunity for expression? Certainly not. It is not only futile but very harmful to use summary methods in dealing with ideological questions among the people, with questions concerned with our mental world. You may ban the expression of wrong ideas, but the ideas will still be there. On the other hand, if correct ideas are pampered in hothouses without being exposed to the elements or immunized from disease, they will not win out against erroneous ones. Therefore, it is only by employing the method of discussion, criticism, and reasoning that we can really foster correct ideas and overcome wrong ones, and that we can really settle issues.

Inevitably, the bourgeoisie and petit bourgeoisie will give expression to their own ideologies. Inevitably, they will stubbornly express themselves on political and ideological questions by every possible means. You cannot expect them to do otherwise. We should not use the method of suppression and prevent them from expressing themselves, but should allow them to do so and at the same time argue with them and direct appropriate criticism at them. We must undoubtedly criticize wrong ideas of every description. It certainly would not be right to refrain from criticism, to look on while wrong ideas spread unchecked and allow them to monopolize the field. Mistakes must be criticized and poisonous weeds fought wherever they crop up. However, such criticism should not be dogmatic, and the metaphysical method should not be used; efforts should be made to apply the dialectical method. What is needed is scientific analysis and convincing argument. Dogmatic criticism settles nothing. We are against poisonous weeds of any kind, but we must carefully distinguish between what is really a poisonous weed and what is really a fragrant flower. Together with the masses of the people, we must learn to differentiate carefully between the two and to use correct methods to fight the poisonous weeds.

At the same time as we criticize dogmatism, we must direct our attention to criticizing revisionism. Revisionism, or Rightist opportunism, is a bourgeois trend of thought that is even more dangerous than dogmatism. The revisionists, the Right opportunists, pay lip service to Marxism; they too attack "dogmatism." But what they are really attacking is the quintessence of Marxism. They oppose or distort materialism and dialectics, oppose or try to weaken the people's democratic dictatorship and the leading role of the Communist Party, and oppose or try to weaken socialist transformation and socialist construction. After the basic victory of the socialist revolution in our country, there are still a number of people who vainly hope to restore the capitalist system and fight the working class on every front, including the ideological one. And their right-hand men in this struggle are the revisionists.

At first glance, the two slogans—let a hundred flowers bloom and let a hundred schools of thought contend—have no class character; the proletariat can turn them to account, as can the bourgeoisie and other people. But different classes, strata, and social groups each have their own views on what are fragrant flowers and what are poisonous weeds. What then, from the point of view of the broad masses of the people, should be the criteria today for distinguishing fragrant flowers from poisonous weeds? In the political life of our people, how should right be distinguished from wrong in one's words and actions? On the basis of the principles of the Constitution, the will of the overwhelming majority of our people, and the com-

mon political positions which have been proclaimed on various occasions by our political parties and groups, we consider that, broadly
speaking, the criteria should be as follows:

   1. Words and actions should help to unite, and not divide,
the people of our various nationalities.
   2. They should be beneficial, and not harmful, to socialist
transformation and socialist construction.
   3. They should help to consolidate, and not undermine or
weaken, the people's democratic dictatorship.
   4. They should help to consolidate, and not undermine or
weaken, democratic centralism.
   5. They should help to strengthen, and not discard or
weaken, the leadership of the Communist Party.
   6. They should be beneficial, and not harmful, to international socialist unity and the unity of the peace-loving people of
the world.

Of these six criteria, the most important are the socialist path and
the leadership of the Party. These criteria are put forward not to
hinder but to foster the free discussion of questions among the people. Those who disapprove of these criteria can still put forward
their own views and argue their case. However, since the majority of
the people have clear-cut criteria to go by, criticism and self-criticism
can be conducted along proper lines, and the criteria can be applied
to people's words and actions to determine whether they are right or
wrong, whether they are fragrant flowers or poisonous weeds. These
are political criteria. Naturally, in judging the validity of scientific
theories or assessing the aesthetic value of works of art, additional
pertinent criteria are needed. But these six political criteria are applicable to all activities in the arts and the sciences. In a socialist
country like ours, can there possibly be any useful scientific or artistic activity which runs counter to these political criteria?

   The views set out above are based on China's specific historical
conditions. Conditions vary in different socialist countries and with
different Communist parties. Therefore we do not maintain that
other countries and parties should or must follow the Chinese way.

2

LET A HUNDRED FLOWERS BLOOM, LET A HUNDRED SCHOOLS OF THOUGHT CONTEND

LU TING-I

Mr. Kuo Mo-jo, President of the Chinese Academy of Sciences and Chairman of the All-China Federation of Literary and Art Circles, has asked me to speak on the policy of the Chinese Communist Party on the work of artists, writers, and scientists.

To artists and writers, we say, "Let a hundred flowers bloom." To scientists we say, "Let a hundred schools of thought contend." This is the policy of the Chinese Communist Party. It was announced by Chairman Mao Tse-tung at the Supreme State Conference.

In applying this policy we have gained some experience, but it is still far too scanty. Furthermore, what I am saying today is merely

A speech on the policy of the Communist Party of China on art, literature, and science delivered in Huai Jen Tang Hall, Peking, May 26, 1956. This translation originally appeared in a supplement to *Jen-min chung-kuo* (People's China), Peking, August 16, 1956. The Chinese text of this speech was published in *Jen-min jih-pao* (People's Daily), June 13, 1956. At that time Lu Ting-yi was Director of the Propaganda Department of the Central Committee of the Chinese Communist Party. The translator's notes (the numbered ones) also appeared in the original supplement to *Jen-min chung-kuo*.

my own personal understanding of this policy. You here are scientists specializing in the natural and social sciences, doctors, writers, and artists; some of you are members of the Communist Party, some friends from democratic parties, and others non-Party friends. You will readily see how immensely important this policy is in the development of Chinese art, literature, and scientific research—the work you yourselves are engaged in—so if you think I am mistaken on any point, please don't hesitate to correct me. Then we can all do our bit to promote the common cause.

I. WHY THIS POLICY, AND WHY THIS EMPHASIS ON IT NOW?

If we want our country to be prosperous and strong, we must, besides consolidating the people's state power, developing our economy and education and strengthening our national defense, have flourishing art, literature, and science. That is essential.

If we want art, literature and science to flourish, we must apply a policy of letting a hundred flowers bloom, letting a hundred schools of thought contend.

Literature and art can never really flourish if only one flower blooms alone, no matter how beautiful that flower may be. Take the theater, an example which readily comes to mind these days. Some years back there were still people who set their face against Peking opera. Then the Party decided to apply the policy summed up in the words "let a hundred flowers bloom, weed out the old to let the new emerge" to the theater. Everybody can see now how right it was to do so, and the notable results it led to. Thanks to free competition and the fact that the various kinds of drama now all learn from one another, our theater has made rapid progress.

In the field of science, we have historical experience to draw on. During the period of the Spring and Autumn Annals (722–481 B.C.) and of the Warring States (403–221 B.C.), more than two thousand years ago, many schools of thought vied with each other for supremacy. That was a golden age in the intellectual development of China. History shows that unless independent thinking and free discussion are encouraged, academic life stagnates. And conversely, when they are encouraged, academic growth speeds up. But, of course, the state of affairs existing in those ancient times was very different from what it is in present-day China. At that time, society was in turmoil. The various schools of thought did vie with each other, spreading their ideas; but they did so spontaneously, with no sort of conscious, organized leadership. Now the people have won a world of freedom for themselves. The people's democratic dictatorship has been set up and consolidated. There is a popular demand that nothing should be allowed to impede the onward march of science. That is why we consciously map out an all-embracing plan for scientific development and adopt a policy of letting a hundred schools of thought contend to give vigor to academic growth.

One cannot fail to see that in class societies, art, literature, and science are, in the last analysis, weapons in the class struggle.

This is quite clear in the case of art and literature. Here we can see things that are obviously pernicious. The stuff written by Hu Feng is one such example. Pornographic and gutter literature that debauches people and turns them into gangsters is another. Still another example is the so-called literature summed up in phrases like "let's playing mahjong and to hell with state affairs," "the moon in America is rounder than the moon in China," and so on. It is perfectly right and proper for us to look on literature of this pernicious kind as on a par with flies, mosquitoes, rats, and sparrows and rid ourselves of it all.[1] This can only benefit, not harm, our literature. Thus we say there is art and literature, for instance, that serves the workers, peasants, and soldiers, and art and literature that serves the imperialists, landlords, and bourgeoisie. What we need is art and literature that serves the workers, peasants, and soldiers—art and literature that serves the people.

The existence of class struggle is also fairly clear in philosophy and the social sciences. Hu Shih's views on philosophy, history, education, and politics have been held up to public odium.[2] The repudi-

[1] Flies, mosquitoes, rats, and sparrows are considered "four evils" in China as carriers of diseases or pests that destroy crops and food.

[2] In 1917, Hu Shih (b. 1891) joined the movement for a new culture as an advocate of substituting the vernacular for the classical literary language. Later, when the cultural movement associated with the May Fourth movement of 1919 advanced and the ideas of Marxism-Leninism spread among the people, he withdrew to the side of the imperialists and comprador-bourgeoisie as an opponent of socialism and revolutionary action. He was a rabid advocate of pragmatism in its most reactionary, sub-

ation of his views is a reflection of class struggle in the field of the social sciences. We are perfectly justified in denouncing them. We are also justified in denouncing Mr. Liang Sou-ming's ideas.[3] We are also right in criticizing other philosophical schools of bourgeois idealism and bourgeois sociology.

Now let us see how things stand in the field of natural science. All scientists have their own political viewpoint, although natural science itself has no class character. Formerly some who specialized in the natural sciences blindly worshipped the United States, while others tended to be "nonpolitical." It is right and proper to criticize all such things as undesirable—and such criticism is a reflection of class struggle.

We cannot fail to notice too that although art, literature, and scientific research have a close bearing on the class struggle, they are not, after all, the same thing as politics. Political struggle is a direct form of class struggle. Art, literature, and the social sciences give expression to the class struggle sometimes in a direct, and sometimes in a roundabout way. It is a one-sided, rightist way of looking at things to assume that art, literature, and science have nothing to do

jective idealist form. This led him to support the Kuomintang's demagogic theory of piecemeal reform and the whole philosophy of bourgeois individualism.

Politically, he supported the rule of the warlords and opposed the revolutionaries led by Sun Yat-sen. Then after Chiang Kai-shek betrayed the revolution in 1927, he came out as a supporter of Chiang's dictatorial rule at home and capitulation to the imperialists. From then on, he was, and remains today, an enemy of the Communist Party and the people's revolution and a faithful hanger-on of the American imperialists and Chiang Kai-shek. For this reason he is repudiated by the whole nation.

Hu Shih held several important posts in old China's universities and academic institutions, and was thus able to spread his reactionary ideas there. Some of his pernicious influence has persisted in such circles and that is why since liberation, in the course of the general criticism of obscurantism, his ideas have come under heavy fire.

[3] At the time of the May Fourth movement of 1919, Liang Sou-ming opposed the campaign for a new culture. He advocated preservation of the old feudal culture with some slight reforms. Later he promoted a "rural construction movement," the aim of which was, as Liang himself said, to resist the peasant movement led by the Communist Party. He denied that there were any exploiting classes in China and advocated cooperation between peasants and landlords, the formation of armed forces by the landlords themselves to protect the old order, and the setting-up of schools for peasant-farmers to indoctrinate them with feudal ideas. Playing into the hands of the imperialists, he opposed industrialization and wanted China to remain an agricultural country. After liberation he gave his support to the People's Government and became a member of the National Committee of the Chinese People's Political Consultative Conference. Liang's ideas have naturally come in for much criticism.

with politics and that "art for art's sake," or "science for science's sake" is a justified standpoint. To look at things in that way is certainly wrong. On the other hand, it is one-sided and "leftist" to oversimplify things and equate art, literature, and science with politics. This view is equally wrong.

"Letting a hundred flowers bloom, a hundred schools of thought contend" means that we stand for freedom of independent thinking, of debate, of creative work; freedom to criticize and freedom to express, maintain and reserve one's opinion on questions of art, literature, or scientific research.* The freedom we uphold is not

* Several scientists have sent in letters expressing the view that we must guard against people getting off the track in interpreting the policy of letting a hundred schools of thought contend. Here is an extract from a letter from Mr. Yang Chao-lien of the Science Publishing House:

"There is not the slightest doubt," he says, "that to let a hundred schools of thought contend is a thoroughly sound principle. In practice, though, in interpreting it there is the likelihood of aberrations and we should be on our guard against this.

"As the phrase suggests, contestants should be more or less recognized exponents of one or another 'school of thought.' But there are people who happily dabble in knowledge. Such people stumble on something, think they know everything, refuse to carry their investigations further, refuse to embark on a solid course of academic study, fall into a morass and don't know how to get out of it. In fact, they cling to their mistakes and refuse to recognize the truth. Let me give a striking example. Practically everyone accepts that the trisection of an angle simply by the use of compass and ruler and that the construction of a perpetual motion machine have been proved impossible. But there are always some people who choose to waste their time and cudgel their brains in the hope of working a miracle. There are probably quite a few who waste their energy and intelligence in such meaningless and palpably futile attempts. The probability is that among them are some who would welcome the chance of founding a 'school of thought' overnight and creating a sensation by taking part in contention, without all the drudgery of prolonged study. And my experience is that if you suggest they get down to a serious study of things about which well-founded conclusions have been reached, you get some flippant retort like, 'That's a theory concocted by a bunch of bourgeois scholars. It's idealistic!'

"Take another case, somewhat similar. We know from experience that there are people, engineers and technicians in particular, who by the nature of their work have little chance of coming across documents and other material having a bearing on their work. They take enormous pains working things out from scratch without consulting references or seeking advice. Finally they manage to solve their problem correctly. But, alas, they still don't realize that someone else has long since worked out what they have been at such pains to discover—sometimes several decades earlier!

"It takes years of hard work and practice before one can really become a scholar and an exponent of a school of thought and contend eloquently. This is a minimum requirement in understanding the principle, and I think this point needs to be made emphatically. Unless we bear it in mind, the various research and higher educational the same as that based on the type of democracy advocated by the bourgeoisie. The freedom advocated by the bourgeoisie really means freedom for only a minority, with little or no freedom for the working people. The bourgeoisie exercises a dictatorship over the working people. The warmongers in the United States bellow about the "free world"—a free world in which the warmongers and reactionaries have all the freedom and every freedom, while the Rosenbergs are put to death because they stand for peace. We, on the contrary, hold that there must be democratic liberties among the people, but that no freedom should be extended to counterrevolutionaries: for them we have only dictatorship. This is a question of drawing a political demarcation line. A clear political line must be drawn between friend and foe.

"Let a hundred flowers bloom, a hundred schools of thought contend": that means freedom among the people. And we urge that, as the people's political power becomes progressively consolidated, such freedom should be given ever fuller scope.

Among the people there are points of agreement and points of difference. Our country has a constitution and it is a public duty to abide by it—this is an agreement among the people. That is to say, the people agree among themselves that they should love their country and support socialism. But there are other matters on which they do not agree with one another. In ideology there is the difference between materialism and idealism. This difference in outlook exists not only while there are classes; it will go on existing even when there are no classes, when we live in a communist society. While classes exist, the contradiction between materialism and idealism takes the form of contradiction between classes. After the disap-

---

bodies will find themselves having to acknowledge the discoveries and inventions of hosts of 'scholars' or 'founders of schools of thought' who choose to 'contend' with one another. They will have to spend a great deal of precious time going into those things, patiently and carefully explaining why things are impossible, or pointing out that others have discovered them already. All that would, of course, be a sheer waste of energy for all concerned. If, however, one has a correct understanding of the meaning of 'letting a hundred schools of thought contend,' this waste of effort can be reduced and useless effort turned into useful channels."

The opinions of Mr. Yang and several other scientists on how to avoid distortion of the policy of "letting a hundred schools of thought contend" are based on their personal experience and are well reasoned. Such distortion and misinterpretation must be avoided. [Author] pearance of classes, as long as there are contradictions between the subjective and the objective, between the progressive and the backward, between the forces of production and production relations in society, contradiction between materialism and idealism will go on existing, even in socialist and communist societies. The struggle between materialism and idealism will be a protracted one.

Members of the Communist Party are dialectical materialists. We Communists of course stand for materialism and against idealism—nothing can change that. But, precisely because we are dialectical materialists and understand the laws governing the development of society, we hold that a strict distinction must be made between the battle of ideas among the people and the struggle against counterrevolutionaries. Among the people themselves there is freedom not only to spread materialism, but also to propagate idealism. Provided he is not a counterrevolutionary, everyone is free to expound materialism or idealism. There is also freedom of debate between the two. This is a struggle between conflicting ideas among the people, but that is quite different from the struggle against counterrevolutionaries. We must suppress and put an end to the activities of counterrevolutionaries. We also have to wage a struggle against backward, idealist ways of thinking among the people. The latter struggle can be quite sharp, too, but we embark on it with the intention of strengthening unity, ending backwardness, and creating an ever closer unity among the people. When it comes to questions of ideas, administrative measures will get us nowhere. Only through open debate can materialism gradually conquer idealism.*

There will be diverse opinions, too, on matters of a purely artistic, academic, or technological nature. This is, of course, quite all

---

*Some people are of the opinion that there should be no freedom to propagate idealism in China. Others think that since there is freedom to propagate idealism, idealists must have unlimited freedom to do so. Both views are mistaken. Take religion, for example. In our country the various religious bodies have their churches, temples, or mosques, their own publications, their own publishing houses, and their own schools for training preachers. They are free to have these things, which are protected by the state. However, for the sake of unity between believers and nonbelievers and to avoid clashes between them, nonbelievers do not conduct antireligious propaganda in churches, temples, or mosques, and believers do not preach their religious doctrines in public assemblies outside the churches, temples, or mosques. So there is a limit to the freedom of both nonbelievers and believers to spread their views. [Author]

right. In matters of this sort, there is freedom to voice different opinions, to criticize, countercriticize, and debate.

In short, we hold that while it is necessary to draw a clear political line between friend and foe, we must have freedom among the people. To "let a hundred flowers bloom, a hundred schools of thought contend" is the expression of that freedom among the people in art, literature, and science.

Conditions are ripe for this policy. So let us see how things stand now.

First of all, in key parts of the country we have won a decisive victory in every aspect of the work of socialist transformation. In these areas in the next few years the system of exploitation of man by man will be ended. All the former exploiters will be transformed into working people living by their own honest toil. Our country will become a socialist state without exploiting classes.

Second, the political outlook of Chinese intellectuals has undergone a fundamental change, and a still more fundamental change is taking place. Comrade Chou En-lai dwelt on this at some length in his "Report on the Question of Intellectuals." In this connection, let us briefly review the latest struggle we have been engaged in.

This is an ideological struggle against bourgeois idealism; and it must be said that in the course of it most intellectuals have given a very good account of themselves and made remarkable progress.

In this struggle academic circles concentrated their main fire on Hu Shih and Hu Feng, two counterrevolutionaries. These men are not simply idealist in their outlook, they are politically counterrevolutionary. We also criticized the philosophical, sociopolitical views of Mr. Liang Sou-ming and bourgeois individualist ideas in artistic and literary circles. As everybody can see now, it was right to wage this struggle because it was necessary in advancing the cause of socialist transformation.

During this struggle, the Central Committee of the Chinese Communist Party pointed out that we needed to strive resolutely against all ideas that hampered academic criticism and discussion. Such harmful ideas expressed themselves in many different ways. There was idolatry of the "leading lights" of the bourgeoisie, who were held up as "authorities" immune from criticism. There was an overbearing, supercilious attitude characteristic of the bourgeoisie toward young Marxists who were kept in the background. Some Party members, setting themselves up as "authorities," were intolerant of criticism and never went in for self-criticism. Other Party members, afraid of "wrecking the united front," or "doing harm to unity," dared not criticize others. Still others, for reasons of personal friendship or for "face-saving" reasons, failed to criticize others' mistakes, and even covered them up.

The Central Committee of the Party has made it clear that in academic criticism and discussion the principle that should be observed is that no one should have any special privileges. It is wrong to set oneself up as an "authority" and suppress criticism, or turn a blind eye to wrong, bourgeois ideas, to let things drift or even capitulate to such wrong ideas.

The Central Committee also pointed out that academic criticism and discussion ought to be based on persuasion, reasoning, and honest consideration of the facts. That is to say, we should encourage earnest discussion, but discussion on a scientific basis. Criticism and discussion should be the result of careful study; there is no place for crude oversimplification or high-handed proceedings. We should proceed by free discussion, rather than by recourse to administrative measures. Anyone criticized should be allowed to answer back, and such countercriticism should not be muzzled. A minority who hold a different opinion should be allowed to keep it: this is not a case where the principle of the minority obeying the majority applies. Those who make mistakes over questions of scholarship and are still loath, even after criticism and discussion, to publish articles to correct their views, need not be asked to do so. In the academic world, even when a conclusion on any given question has been reached, discussion is still permissible if fresh differences of opinion arise.

The Central Committee also said that while we are criticizing wrong, bourgeois ideas and conducting criticism and discussion on questions of scholarship, we must stick to the policies mapped out by the Party—the policy of maintaining the united front and the policy of uniting and remolding intellectuals. We must make a distinction between people who stick to wrong, bourgeois ideas and those who, while holding such wrong ideas, lean toward materialism, and we should approach them in different ways. A clear distinction must be made between those who are counterrevolutionaries politically and those who merely make mistakes in the academic field. Scholars who hold seriously mistaken, bourgeois ideas in the academic field should still be given suitable jobs as long as they are not engaged in counter-revolutionary activity. It is our job to see that they can go on doing research work for the benefit of society. We should respect any special knowledge they have which is beneficial to society, see to it that it is made full use of and passed on to our young people. We should also encourage them to take an active part in academic criticism and discussion so that they can remold themselves in the process.

All these instructions helped us combat bourgeois idealism and conduct criticism in academic circles without going too far wrong. Now, as we look back on our past activity, we find that we did, in the main, do the right thing in the course of this struggle, and made no bad mistakes either way. But some defects and mistakes there still were—in the way Mr. Yü P'ing-po was criticized, for instance.[4] In the matter of politics, Mr. Yü is blameless. The mistakes he committed were only in the field of literature, and it was necessary for us to criticize him from an academic and ideological point of view. Many articles on Mr. Yü did that and did it very well. But some were not so well written; they were not very persuasive and were couched in too virulent a tone. As to the allegation that Mr. Yü "monopolized the use of rare, ancient Chinese books," that was without foundation. I feel I ought to clear up this point.

So far we have been talking about the past. Now let us see how things are at present.

The situation now is vastly different. It may have been true a year or two ago that bourgeois idealism still enjoyed a wide popularity, that the Hu Fengs did not hesitate to launch furious attacks on

---

[4] Yü P'ing-po is a veteran writer who became well known during the time of the May Fourth movement. He has specialized in Chinese classical literature, and for many years made an intensive study of the famous classical novel *The Dream of the Red Chamber*. He was deeply influenced by Hu Shih's mistaken views on the study of the classics. After the Japanese surrender, Yü joined the Chiu San Society, one of China's many democratic parties. He supported the students' patriotic movement and opposed the corrupt rule of the Kuomintang. He is now a research fellow of the Institute of Literary Studies of the Chinese Academy of Sciences, and a deputy to the National People's Congress.

the ideological front, and that many intellectuals were unable to distinguish idealism from materialism or to understand the harm idealism could do to the cause of socialism. Now, however, tremendous progress has been made in intellectual circles.

In some organizations the campaign against the reactionary ideas of Hu Feng and Hu Shih has not been carried to a proper conclusion, and the work of ferreting out hidden counterrevolutionaries has not been completed. In all such organizations we should carry on, not stopping halfway, because only by carrying through the campaign can we create conditions favorable to the many things that need to be done in the future. It should be emphasized over and over again that well over 90 percent of the people in these organizations are ordinary, decent people (including those who are a bit backward), who should be brought into the common struggle against counterrevolutionaries.

Third, we still have enemies, and the class struggle is still going on inside the country. But our enemies, and our enemies inside the country in particular, have had their teeth drawn.

Who are these enemies? Abroad, we face aggressive imperialist forces with the warmongers of the United States at their head; at home, we face the Chiang Kai-shek clique entrenched on Taiwan and some other stray leftovers of the counterrevolution. These are our enemies. We must keep up a relentless struggle against them; we must not relax our efforts.

Fourth, the political and ideological unity of the people has been greatly strengthened and is growing stronger day by day.

It is because of all this that the Central Committee of the Chinese Communist Party is now emphasizing the policy of letting a hundred flowers bloom, a hundred schools of thought contend. By this policy we shall bring into full play all that is good and useful in society in order to give better service to the people, and pool our efforts to create a flourishing art and literature and put our scientific work on a level with the best in the world.

Under the guidance of the government, many scientists are engaged in drawing up a twelve-year plan of work in the natural sciences. Twelve-year plans for philosophy and the social sciences are also being worked out. The making and realization of such plans is a magnificent task for our scientists. The implementation of the policy of letting a hundred schools of thought contend is an important guarantee of success in this task.

II. STRENGTHEN UNITY

Let a hundred flowers bloom, a hundred schools of thought contend; this is a policy to mobilize all the positive elements. It is also, therefore, a policy that will in the end strengthen unity.

On what basis are we to unite? On the basis of patriotism and socialism.

What do we unite for? To build a new, socialist China and combat our enemies both at home and abroad.

There are two kinds of unity: one is built on mechanical obedience and the other on our own conscious, free will. What we want is the latter.

Are those engaged in art, literature, and science united? Yes, they are. Compare the situation in the days when the Chinese People's Republic was just founded with what we have now and you find we now have a far closer unity among artists, writers, and scientists. This has come about as a result of our work for social reform and changes in our ways of thought. It would be wrong to deny or ignore this. But even so, we cannot say that our unity is all it should be: there is still room for improvement.

In what respect? Well, first and foremost, some Communist Party members have forgotten Comrade Mao Tse-tung's warning about the evils of sectarianism. Success turns some people's heads and they get swelled-headed and sectarian.

In "Cheng-tun tang ti tso-feng" (Rectify the Party's Style of Work)—a speech he made in 1942—Comrade Mao Tse-tung had this to say:

Many of our comrades are much given to swaggering before non-Party people, despising and belittling them, and are unwilling to show them respect or appreciate their good qualities. This is precisely a sectarian tendency. Having read a few Marxist books, these comrades become arrogant rather than modest and habitually dismiss others as no good without knowing that they themselves are really tyros and smatterers. Our comrades must realize the truth that the Party members are always a minority as compared with non-Party people. Suppose there were one Communist in a hundred Chinese, then among China's population of 450,000,000 there would be 4,500,000 Communists. Yet, even if our membership reached such a colossal figure, the Communists would still form only one percent of the whole population, while 99 percent of our countrymen would remain outside the Party. On what grounds, then, can we refuse to co-operate with non-Party people? As to all those who are willing to, or in all probability can, cooperate with us, we have not only the duty to cooperate with them but absolutely no right to exclude them. But, failing to realize this, some of our Party members despise or even exclude those who are willing to cooperate with us. There are no grounds whatsoever for doing so. Have Marx, Engels, Lenin and Stalin given us any grounds for that? No. On the contrary, they have always earnestly urged us to link ourselves closely with the masses and not isolate ourselves from the masses and stand alone. On the contrary, the Central Committee has always told us to link ourselves closely with the masses and not to isolate ourselves from them. Thus any practice that isolates us from the masses has no sanction at all, and it is simply a mischief done by the sectarian ideas of some comrades' own invention. As the error of sectarianism is still very serious in a section of our Party members and hinders the implementation of the Party line, we should start a great educational campaign within the Party to deal with it. First of all, we should make our cadres thoroughly understand how serious the problem is and how utterly impossible it is to overthrow our enemy and attain the goal of revolution unless the Communists are united with the non-Party cadres and people.[5]

As everyone knows, in the past few years we have fought a series of battles in the Party against sectarianism in artistic, literary, and scientific circles. We have waged this struggle in organizations dealing with public health and research in the natural sciences, in literature and art, and in the social sciences. We shall go on waging this struggle and we call on all Party members working in these fields to make an end of this sectarianism.

In the course of these struggles we have gained some experience, and I should like to say something about it.

1. As everyone knows, the natural sciences, including medicine, have no class character. They have their own laws of development. The only way they tie up with social institutions is that under a bad social system they make rather slow progress, and under a better one they progress fairly rapidly. The theoretical side of this question was settled long ago. It is, therefore, wrong to label a particular theory in medicine, biology, or any other branch of natural science "feudal,"

[5] *Selected Works of Mao Tse-tung*, English edition, Vol. IV, pp. 42–43. (London: Lawrence & Wishart, 1956).

"capitalist," "socialist," "proletarian," or "bourgeois." It is wrong, for instance, to say that "traditional Chinese doctors are feudal doctors," that "doctors of the Western school are capitalist doctors," that "Pavlov's theory is socialist" or "Michurin's theory is socialist," or that "Mendel's and Morgan's principles of heredity are capitalist" and so on. We must not believe such stuff. Some people make this sort of mistake because they are sectarian. Others do it unconsciously by trying to emphasize, but not in the proper way, that one ought to learn from the latest scientific achievements in the Soviet Union. These mistakes stem from different causes, so we must not lump them under one head, but deal with them in the light of specific circumstances.

While pointing out such mistakes, we must also point out one of another kind: for instance, denial of the fact that Pavlov's or Michurin's theories are important. The jumping-off point of those who make this mistake is, again, not always the same. Some of them are politically opposed to the Soviet Union, and for that reason inclined to deny even the scientific achievements of the Soviet Union. Others, because they do not belong to the same school of thought, simply won't yield an inch. In the case of the former it is a question of political viewpoint; with the latter it is a question of academic thinking. So these mistakes too must be dealt with in the light of specific circumstances and not lumped together.

2. With regard to works of art and literature, the Party has only one point to make; that is, that they should "serve the workers, peasants, and soldiers," or, in terms of today, the working people as a whole, intellectuals included. Socialist realism, in our view, is the most fruitful creative method, but it is not the only one. Provided he sets out to meet the needs of the workers, peasants, and soldiers, the writer can choose whatever method he thinks will best enable him to write well, and he can vie with others. As to subject matter, the Party has never set limits to this. It is not right to establish such dicta as: write only about workers, peasants, and soldiers; write only about the new society; or write only about new types of people. If literature and art are to serve the workers, peasants, and soldiers, it stands to reason that we must praise the new society and positive people. But at the same time we must also criticize the old society and negative elements; we must praise what is progressive and criti-

cize what is backward. So the choice of subject matter in literature is extremely wide.

Creative writing deals not only with things that really exist, or that once existed, but also with things that never existed—the gods in the heavens, animals and birds who talk, and so on. One can write about positive people and the new society, and also about negative elements and the old. Furthermore, it is difficult to show the new society to advantage if we fail to describe the old; hard to show the positive to advantage if we leave out what is negative. Taboos and commandments about choice of subject matter can only hamstring art and literature, and result in writing to formula and bad taste. They can only do harm. As for questions relating to the specific characteristics of art and literature, the creation of the typical, and so on, they must be the subject of free discussion among writers and artists, letting them freely hammer out differences of opinion till they gradually reach agreement.

In the theater we have already had experience in applying the principle, "let a hundred flowers bloom, weed out the old to let the new emerge." That has been most valuable. What we must do now is to apply the same principle to all other branches of art and literature.

3. In the field of philosophy and the social sciences, our achievements have been great. But for that very reason, there is great danger of sectarianism. If we do not pay prompt attention to this, there is a serious danger of mental stagnation. Since the founding of the People's Republic, the teaching of Marxism-Leninism has spread among the intellectuals. There have been campaigns to remold our thinking, struggles against bourgeois idealism, and a drive to weed out hidden counterrevolutionaries. All this activity is right and necessary, and has borne good fruit. We must, however, consider the seamy side of things as well. Some Party members have a tendency to monopolize academic studies in philosophy and the social sciences. They claim to be always right, fail to see the merits of others, or even forget that others have any merits. They fail to see the progress made by others. They take offense at the critical opinions of others. They always see themselves as the erudite teachers and others as their pupils—mere idealists or bourgeois scholars—now and forever after. This is extemely dangerous. If things go on

like this, they themselves are likely to degenerate, and philosophy and the social sciences in our country will cease to progress and will lose their vitality. These comrades had better stop this self-glorification right away; they had better be modest, listen more often to others' criticism, work harder at their studies, make a point of learning what they can from people outside the Party, and really cooperate with them so as to avoid setbacks to our work in philosophy and the social sciences.

Our People's Republic is nearly seven years old now. Although there are still some people who cling to idealist ways of thinking and bourgeois ideas, many have made great progress. In research and educational work in philosophy and the social sciences, we must consider redeploying our forces, bit by bit, as the situation demands, revising methods and measures which were wrong from the start, or which were right at one time but are now out of date. This is something we must do so that we can mobilize all the positive elements for promoting our work in these spheres. Both philosophy and the social sciences are important branches of knowledge, so we must do good work in these fields.

Here, in passing, I should like to mention the question of modern history. Modern history is an extremely important branch of social science, but we have not achieved much in the past few years in this field. I hear that people are expecting the Central Committee of the Chinese Communist Party to compile a textbook on the history of the Party, after which they propose to write books on modern history based on it. Please don't wait any more. The Central Committee is not going to compile any such textbook. All it is going to do is to publish a chronicle of events of the Party and collections of documents. Our scholars who specialize in modern history should, therefore, get down to independent study of the various problems of modern history. And in research in modern history, too, the policy of letting diverse schools of thought contend must apply; no other will do.

Finish with sectarianism and unite with all who are ready to cooperate, all who possibly can cooperate with us. Put aside the desire to monopolize things. Get rid of unreasonable rules and commandments, and apply the policy of letting a hundred flowers bloom, letting a hundred schools of thought contend. Do not think only of the interests of your own department; try to give more help to others and to other departments. Don't be conceited and cocksure. Be modest and discreet and respect others. That is how to rid ourselves of the shortcomings which have marred our work in building up unity; that is how to strengthen our unity to the utmost.

We hope that writers, artists, and scientists who are not Party members will also pay attention to the question of securing closer unity. And here I would like to repeat part of what Comrade Chou En-lai said in his "Report on the Question of Intellectuals":

We have already pointed out that there is still a certain distance between some intellectuals and our Party. We must take the initiative to remove this. For this distance, both sides usually bear responsibility. On the one hand, our comrades do not approach or try to understand the intellectuals; on the other, certain intellectuals still have reservations regarding socialism or even oppose it. There are such intellectuals in our enterprises, schools, government offices, and society as a whole. Failing to differentiate between friend and foe, between the Communist Party and the Kuomintang, between the Chinese people and imperialism, they are dissatisfied with the policies and measures of the Party and the People's Government and hanker after capitalism or even feudalism. They are hostile to the Soviet Union and unwilling to learn from her. They refuse to study Marxism-Leninism, and sneer at it. Despising labor, the laboring people, and government workers who come from families of working people, they refuse to mix with workers and peasants or government cadres of worker or peasant origin. Unwilling to see the growth of new forces, they consider progressives as opportunists, and often stir up trouble and hostility between intellectuals and the Party as well as among intellectuals themselves. They have enormous conceit, thinking themselves Number One in the world, and refusing to accept anyone's leadership or criticism. Denying the interests of the people or of society as a whole, they view everything only from their personal interests. What is to their personal advantage they accept, what is not to their personal advantage they oppose. Of course, there are very few intellectuals today who have all these faults; but not a small number have one fault or another. Even some of the middle group often hold some of the wrong views mentioned above, let alone the backward intellectuals. And not a few progressives are still guilty of such faults as narrowmindedness, arrogance, and the tendency to view everything from their personal interests. Unless such intellectuals change their stand, however hard we may try to approach them, there will still be a distance between us and them.

That is to say, we must call on Party members and, equally, on people outside the Party to make a great effort to strengthen our unity.

Individualism and parochial prejudice can also be found in artistic, literary, and scientific circles. There is also a lack of mutual understanding between scientific workers of long standing and the newcomers. These things are bad. We ought to—and I am sure we can—get rid of them. If only Party members try to set a good example and work hard with people outside the Party, there should be no difficulty in solving this problem.

III. CRITICISM AND STUDY

In regard to criticism, our policy of letting a hundred flowers bloom, a hundred schools of thought contend means freedom to criticize and freedom to countercriticize.

Some of the criticism we have today is of the thunderbolt variety; some of it is milk and water. How do we tackle this question?

There are two kinds of criticism. One is criticism directed against the enemy—what people call criticism that "kills at a blow," criticism with no holds barred. The other is criticism directed against the honestly mistaken—well-meant, comradely criticism, made in the cause of unity, intended to achieve unity through struggle. In making this kind of criticism, one must always bear the whole situation in mind. The critic should rely on reasoning, and his aim should be to help others. One should never adopt an attitude of "the Revolution is none of your business!" like the "Imitation Foreign Devil" in Lu Hsün's *Ah-Q cheng-chuan* (The True Story of Ah Q).[6]

But in either case, criticism must be the outcome of careful study. One must not dash into print with a criticism the moment one spots something. It should be written only after thorough study and after a good deal of thinking.

The idea that criticism necessarily implies invective is wrong. When we were in Yenan, there was a counterrevolutionary called Wang Shih-wei. Later we had that other counterrevolutionary, Hu

---

[6] Ah Q is the hero of the famous novel *The True Story of Ah Q* by Lu Hsün (1881–1936). Ah Q is a poor odd-job man in a village and lives from hand to mouth. During the revolution of 1911, he is fired with a desire to join the revolution and goes for advice to the son of Chien, the local squire, a pseudorevolutionary called "imitation foreign devil" by Ah Q because he dresses like a foreigner and apes foreign ways, who tells him that the Revolution is none of his business.

Feng. Both of them, in their writings, or in other ways, attacked the Party and the people's regime. It stands to reason that we should give such counterrevolutionaries blow for blow. But it would be wrong to use the same method among ourselves—the people.

Concerning criticism directed against the honestly mistaken, I should like to recommend four articles: (1) "Kai-tsao wo-men ti hsüeh-hsi" (Reform Our Study), by Mao Tse-tung; (2) "Rectify the Party's Style of Work," by Mao Tse-tung; (3) "Fan-tui tang pa-ku" (Oppose Party Jargon), by Mao Tse-tung; and (4) "Kuan-yü wu-ch'an chieh-chi chuan-cheng ti li-shih ching-yen" (On the Historical Experience of the Dictatorship of the Proletariat), from the *People's Daily.* The first three articles are criticisms of two comrades, Wang Ming and Po Ku,[7] who had made serious mistakes; the fourth is a criticism of Comrade Stalin, a comrade known for his outstanding services, who also made very serious mistakes—a comrade whose achievements outweighed his mistakes. When one reads these articles, one realizes that there can be criticism couched neither in excessive nor lukewarm terms—criticism which is a help to many. It can be seen with what great care the authors of these articles studied things before they wrote. And this is precisely the type of criticism we must encourage.

It is a very difficult job to reach the heights in science or art. It is difficult because only those who get to grips with reality make the grade, because there is no room for the smart aleck. We should give every support to our scientists, writers, and artists. In our social system, scientists and artists who do honest work merit support, not blows. When one is engaged in independent thinking, in complicated and creative labor, it is impossible never to make mistakes. In the first place, people make wrong judgments simply because of gaps in their knowledge. In the second place, one can go wrong by exaggerating what is correct and treating it as absolute truth. Lenin said: ". . . it is enough to take one little step further—a step that

[7] Comrades Wang Ming (Ch'en Shao-yü) and Po Ku (Ch'in Pang-hsien) fell into doctrinaire ways and made serious "leftist" mistakes as Communist Party leaders in the years 1931–1935. The interested reader will find the main facts of these events in the "Resolution on Some Questions in the History of Our Party," in Vol. IV of the *Selected Works of Mao Tse-tung* (London: Lawrence & Wishart, 1956). Comrade Po Ku was killed in a plane accident on his way from Chungking to Yenan in February 1946.

might seem to be in the same direction—and truth becomes error."[8] There are people who are genuine advocates of all that is progressive, but who still make mistakes simply because they are a bit over-hasty, and often make mistakes of this kind. And third, some people make mistakes because of their idealist outlook, and there is nothing strange about that, because "human cognition is not (. . . does not go in) a straight line, but a curve, endlessly approaching a series of circles, spirals. Any segment, fragment, or part of this curve can be turned (turned in a one-sided way) into a self-contained, finite straight line which (if you don't see the wood for the trees) will then lead you into a morass, into quasi-religious obscurantism (where it fortifies the class interest of the ruling classes)!"[9] In the process of human cognition, mental sluggishness, the error of seeing things as if they had no connection with anything else (what we call "going into the ox horn") and viewing things one-sidedly are all things that lead to idealistic mistakes.

It is quite common for people to make mistakes in all innocence. There is no such person as a man who never makes mistakes. We must make a sharp distinction between mistakes like this and statements consciously directed against the revolution. Criticism of such mistakes must only be made for the good of others; it must be cool-headed criticism, well reasoned. In making it, we must bear the whole situation in mind and act in a spirit of unity, with the intention of achieving unity. We must do all we can to help those who have made mistakes correct them, and those criticized should have no apprehensions about being criticized.

It is easy to make mistakes. But mistakes should be rectified immediately, the sooner the better. It is sticking to one's mistakes that does the harm. As far as being criticized is concerned, one should stick to what is right, and dissent if others are wrong in their criticism. But if the other party is right, you must rectify your mistakes and humbly accept others' criticism. To admit a mistake frankly, to root out the causes of it, to analyze the situation in which it was made and thoroughly discussed how to correct it is, as far as a politi-

---

[8] " 'Leftwing' Communism, An Infantile Disorder," in Lenin, *Selected Works*, Vol. II, p. 433 (Moscow: Foreign Languages Publishing House, 1952).

[9] Lenin, *Philosophical Notebooks* (Leningrad: State Political Publishing House, 1947), p. 330.

cal party is concerned, the hallmark of a mature party. As far as the individual is concerned, it is the hallmark of a realist. To accept criticism when one has made a mistake is to accept the help of others. Besides helping the person concerned, that also helps the progress of science, art, and literature in our country; and there is certainly nothing wrong with that!

As regards study in general, we must continue to see to it that the study of Marxism-Leninism is organized on a voluntary basis. At the same time, we must acquire a broad range of general knowledge; we must critically study things both past and present, things at home and from abroad, and critically learn from both friends and foes.

Marxism-Leninism is being enthusiastically studied by most of our intellectuals. That is a good thing. The scientific theories of Marx and Lenin are the cream of human knowledge, truth that is everywhere applicable. Once there were people who thought that Marxism-Leninism was not applicable in China, but such ideas have been proved sheer nonsense. Without scientific Marxist-Leninist theory to guide us, it is unthinkable that the revolution could have been victorious in China. It is also unthinkable that we could have achieved the tremendous successes and made the rapid progress that we have in construction and in scientific and cultural work.

There are still, however, many shortcomings and mistakes in our study of Marxism-Leninism, and the main defect is a tendency to doctrinairism.

Fifteen years ago, in May 1941, Comrade Mao Tse-tung wrote the article "Reform Our Study." Later, in February 1942, he wrote "Rectify the Party's Style of Work" and "Oppose Party Jargon." These three articles were the main documents used in the campaign in Yenan to improve Party work. That was an ideological campaign directed against subjectivism, and mainly against doctrinairism. It was the greatest Marxist-Leninist movement in the intellectual life of our country since the May Fourth Movement of 1919. During the period of the bourgeois-democratic revolution in our country, the Chinese revolution nearly foundered on doctrinairism. It was, and is, a bitter enemy of Marxism-Leninism. We must not forget that painful experience. We must also be fully alive to the fact that if academic studies are conducted in a doctrinaire way, and if artistic and literary work and scientific research are led by people who take up a doctrinaire attitude, things are bound to go wrong. That is because such an attitude runs directly counter to the Marxist-Leninist attitude of looking at things as they are.

I should like to avail myself of this opportunity, in speaking to you writers, artists, and scientists, of seriously recommending to you those three articles of Comrade Mao Tse-tung's—"Reform Our Study," "Rectify the Party's Style of Work," and "Oppose Party Jargon"—and the "Kuan-yü jo-kan li-shih wen-t'i ti chüeh-i" (Resolution on Some Questions in the History of Our Party) adopted by the sixth Central Committee of the Chinese Communist Party at its seventh plenary session. I hope that every worker in these fields will read and re-read these documents till he really knows the difference between doctrinairism and Marxism-Leninism, till he discovers why the former is the bitter enemy of the latter and why it is necessary to wage a resolute struggle against doctrinairism.

We must have a broad range of general knowledge.

In medical science, agronomy, philosophy, history, literature, drama, painting and music, and so on, China has a rich heritage. This heritage must be studied seriously and accepted critically. The point is not that we have done so much, but that we have done too little, and have not been serious enough in our approach. There is still the attitude of belittling our national heritage, and in some spheres it is still a really serious problem.

What kind of heritage are we to accept and how?

If we were to accept only what is perfect by present-day standards, there would be nothing left for us to take over. On the other hand, if we were to accept our cultural heritage uncritically, we should simply be taking the attitude summed up in the phrase "everything Chinese is best."

We suggest that in dealing with our cultural heritage the principle should be this: Carefully select, cherish, and foster all that is good in it while criticizing its faults and shortcomings in a serious way. At present our work suffers because we do neither well. There is a tendency to reject offhand even what is good in our cultural heritage. At present that is the main trend. The recent performance of the Kunshan opera *Shih-wu Kuan* (Fifteen Strings of Cash) shows how wrong it was to say that there was nothing good in Kunshan opera. And if there is such a tendency in the theater, what about other branches of art, literature, and scientific research? We must admit that there are similar tendencies in them too, and we must do something about it. At the same time, we can also see a tendency not to criticize, or even to gloss over shortcomings in and blots on our cultural heritage. This attitude is neither honest nor sincere, and that we must alter, too.

Workers in art, literature, and science need to learn from the people. The wisdom of the people is inexhaustible. There are still many treasures among the people that have not yet been discovered or, though discovered, not made good use of. Take medical science, for instance. In the past, acupuncture and special curative breathing exercises were scorned; only now are they being taken notice of. But other "popular" healing methods such as osteopathy, massage, and herbal medicines have even now not received the attention due them.

Then take music and painting. Not enough attention has been paid to our national heritage in these two spheres of creative activity. Wherever there are such tendencies, they must be corrected.

As they come from the people, these things are often not systematically developed or are crude or lack theoretical explanation. Some of them have more than a bit of the "quack" about them, or a taint of the superstitious. There is nothing surprising about that. It is the duty of our scientists, artists, and writers not to despise these things but to make a careful study of them; to select, cherish, and foster the good in them; and, where necessary, to put them on a scientific basis.

We must have our national pride, but we must not become national nihilists. We oppose that misguided attitude known as "wholesale Westernization." But that does not mean we can afford to be arrogant and refuse to learn good things from abroad. Our country is still a very backward one; we can make it prosperous and strong only by doing our best to learn all we can from foreign countries. Under no circumstances is national arrogance justified.

We must learn from the Soviet Union, from the People's Democracies, and from the peoples of all lands.

To learn from the Soviet Union—that is a correct watchword. We have already learned a little, but much remains to be learned. The Soviet Union is the world's first socialist state, the leader of the world camp of peace and democracy. It has the highest rate of industrial development. It has a rich experience in socialist construction. In not a few important branches of science it has caught up with and surpassed the most advanced capitalist countries. It stands to reason that it is worth our while to learn from such a country and such a people. It is utterly wrong not to learn from the Soviet Union.

Nevertheless, in learning from the Soviet Union we must not mechanically copy everything in the Soviet Union in a doctrinaire way. We must make what we have learned fit our actual conditions. That is a point we must pay attention to. Otherwise, we shall run into trouble.

Besides learning from the Soviet Union, we must also learn from the People's Democracies. Every People's Democracy has its own special merits. Some of them have advanced further than China in industry and scientific technique; others are more advanced in other fields. To learn from them all is well worth while. Arrogance in this connection is entirely out of place.

People in countries other than the Soviet Union and the People's Democracies have different social institutions and political systems. Social institutions and political systems may come and go, but the people will live on and continue to progress. It is not without good reason that this is so. We must therefore critically study all their good points—in art and literature, in science, in their customs and habits, in every sphere. Here too a feeling of superiority is quite out of place.

Apart from learning from our friends, we must see what we can learn from our enemies—not to learn what is reactionary in their systems but to study what is good in their methods of management or in their scientific techniques. Our aim in this is to speed the progress of our socialist construction, so as to build up our strength to ward off aggression and safeguard peace in Asia and throughout the world.

I also want to say something about the Party members learning from people outside the Party.

The knowledge possessed by not a few of our Party members is less than it should be. Non-Party people usually lack a fundamental knowledge of Marxism-Leninism, but for many of our non-Party friends who are keen on studying Marxism-Leninism, this is really a thing of the past, or soon will be. Anyhow, plenty of them have bridged, or are bridging this gap, so this question will soon solve itself. The point I want to make is that it is time for Party members to take note of their own inadequacies and remedy them. There is only one way to do so: to seek advice and learn honestly and modestly from those who know. The great majority of those intellectuals who are not Communist Party members study very hard. Members of the Communist Party must not be behind in learning from them. This is an important point as regards our studies.

Now that this policy—"let a hundred flowers bloom, a hundred schools of thought contend"—has been put forward, many problems will crop up one after the other and demand solutions. I hope all of you will do some hard thinking on such questions. Today I have only touched upon some matters of principle, and anything I say is open to correction.

Revised by the author, June 6, 1956.

Postscript: Since I delivered this speech I have had letters from seventy-two people, including Mr. Kuo Mo-jo, some of them written in an individual capacity, others on behalf of groups. Some express opinions on my speech, others say what the writers themselves think of the policy. They have all been a great help to me, and I take this opportunity of expressing my sincere thanks.

3

FREEDOM AND THE WRITER

LAO SHE

I am not a theoretician, either of literature or of revolution. I shall speak frankly, drawing on my own experience—just calling a spade a spade, so to speak.

I was born in 1898, a year marked, as everyone knows, by a coup d'état, part of the political reform movement. During the time from that coup to the 1911 revolution, to the May Fourth movement and right on to the eve of the founding of the People's Republic, I saw with my own eyes how, all through that half-century, Chinese writers stood together with the Chinese people as a whole, fighting for national freedom and freedom of writing. In this protracted struggle a number of writers nobly laid down their lives. I saw all this, and I know what freedom means to writers. That explains why Chinese writers were so overjoyed when liberation came. Freedom, their long-cherished freedom, had come into its own—freedom for them and for the Chinese people as a whole.

CHEERFUL THINGS

It is always a pleasure to tell friends about cheerful things. In the years since liberation Chinese writers have enjoyed more facilities for writing than ever before. For instance, writers can now go on

Lao She, "Tzu-yu yü tso-chia" (Freedom and the Writer), *Jen-min chung-kuo* (People's China), January 1, 1957.

tour or visit any place in the country to gather material, the Union of Chinese Writers paying all or part of their traveling expenses. Writers pay frequent visits to factories or mines and, if they like, live there for a long time and make a profound study of life at first hand. Much of our literary work has been born of such a study of life.

Facilities for these tours and visits are extended not only to Chinese writers but also to foreign writers who visit China. If there is any difference, it is simply that the latter get even warmer hospitality and a still more enthusiastic welcome.

There are a lot more cheerful things I could tell our friends. The fact that forty-six writers were elected to the National People's Congress is one of them. But too much harping on the bright side of things will make people think we are boasting, so let me talk of some of our difficulties and mistakes.

GREAT ENTHUSIASM

There is no denying that, since the liberation, the political enthusiasm of Chinese writers is one of the things that impels them to write. People everywhere in China are living better; writers have better facilities and a place in political life. How can they remain unmoved and silent? Look at me, for instance. I write more now than I did before the liberation. I write every day and don't let up even on holidays. Political enthusiasm prompts me to write about my inner joy, about new people, new things, and the achievements of our new society. I think any writer in China feels the same way. It makes no difference what party he belongs to: the Communist Party, the Democratic League, some other party, or no party at all. You know I'm non-party myself. One thing is common to all of us: we want to write hard and serve the people.

But just because of this very diversity in political affiliation, in experience of life and religious belief, we do not always make a good job of it, no matter how great our political enthusiasm, when we come to write about new people and new things in the revolutionary struggles. I know this well enough. The enthusiasm is there, the impulse to go ahead with giant strides; but the very limitations of my political understanding and experience of life stand in my way when

I try to turn the facts of revolutionary struggle into full-blooded works of art. My writing tends to be empty and thin—for I am writing about things I am not very familiar with. Quite a number of established writers suffer from this. Needless to say, that affects our work adversely.

On the other hand, we have young people who have grown up in the revolution, who have taken part in actual struggles, and who have the courage to write. Their problem is different. Because they have grown up while the revolution was going on, their cultural attainments and literary training are, generally speaking, poor. That handicaps them when they try to turn out sound, well-polished work. If the trouble with veteran writers is that they are good housewives who have to cook a meal without rice, then the young writers are housewives with plenty of rice and no skill to cook it.

A work of literature is assuredly a weapon of political propaganda. But it must be real literature, with power and grip. Literature is subject to its own laws. Nobody will read work which is supposed to be literature but which is full of political jargon.

LITERATURE AND POLITICAL IDEAS

The study of politics is essential to writers who want to improve themselves and turn out work that truly reflects the age they live in. Over the past few years writers, both old and new, have striven to improve themselves ideologically, and willingly and energetically gone in for study. But political ideas cannot be separated from real life. Government policy is decided in the light of what people really want and need. If writers simply lopsidedly stress the political side in their work and fail to see the importance of writing from experience of real life, naturally their work suffers: it is full of stereotyped generalizations and built around cut-and-dried formulas. In the past few years there has been a disease of formulism, of indulging in stereotyped generalizations in the field of literature. It is right and proper for writers to study hard and improve themselves ideologically in order to serve the cause of socialism in a better way. But they are going about it in quite the wrong way if, either by design or accident, they pack their work with didactic ideas, if their plots are nonexistent and their imagery trite.

A writer who is always scared stiff of overstepping set principles or doing damage to the revolution is certain to find himself bound hand and foot and incapable of writing boldly. Boldness and creative work are inseparable. Without creativeness you will always get slavish copying, which is a sure sign of degeneration in literature.

Are we as writers incapable of understanding so self-evident a fact? No, of course not. But all these years it has been our political enthusiasm that has kept us going. We see an honest government, the like of which China has never seen for thousands of years. We see six hundred million people hand in hand pushing ahead toward socialism. We are inspired. We must write. And if we write badly, we have only ourselves to blame: we have let our political understanding of these things lag behind our desire to express them.

The People's Government sets great store by literature and gives it full support. But some government officials, though enthusiastic enough, did things in an incorrect manner, trying to get creative work produced to order. It seems that in a film studio everybody has the right to "correct" a scenario. As often as not, the argument is on some political point. Repeated corrections may make the political ideas a bit clearer, but the artistic worth of the film suffers. Administrative interference, no matter how well-meant, will always stand in the way of creating real art.

LET MANY FLOWERS BLOOM

Now about the question of criticism. In a democratic country, everyone has the right to criticize. Our writing is not only a target for literary critics; every reader wants to have his say about it. Theoretically that is all to the good. Criticism will only encourage better writing. But harsh criticism encourages nobody. On the contrary, it is no better than a good thrashing. Over the past few years we have had much well-intentioned criticism, but also unreasonable thrashings. Thrashings don't encourage good writing; they destroy it.

Here we see why we put forward the policy of letting flowers of many kinds bloom, letting a hundred schools of thought contend. First of all, everyone should write about what he or she is most familiar with. We should not force ourselves to write of things we know very little about. It is good to write about present-day society;

but it is equally good to deal with historical themes. It is true that New China is going ahead by leaps and bounds. No matter how keenly you observe the things around you, you cannot say you understand everything very well, for everyone and everything is changing. The past is fixed, it has definite form, but the living present flows and changes. I understand my elder brother very well, but I do not quite understand my children. Well, let me write about my elder brother, and let the young writers write about my children. Again, we should write about our workers, peasants, and soldiers. But is that any reason why we should not also mirror the lives of intellectuals and capitalists? Every writer should write about what he likes and what he can handle—people, life, and themes. A writer should have perfect freedom to choose what he wants to write about. All writings other than those which poison people's minds are worthwhile and should be published. And by writing them and publishing them we really shall be letting flowers of many kinds bloom.

The same thing goes for ways of writing. It is accepted that socialist realism is a progressive way of writing. But does that mean that all other creative methods are no good? To my mind, no. We should treasure all work that shows itself capable of mirroring people's lives—that is the way to make our literature flourish. Furthermore, we should encourage, not discourage, every writer to have his or her own style—we should give our literary work an infinite variety, not cast it all in the same mold. We should encourage, not discourage, different schools in literature. In this way our writers, irrespective of political affiliation, the "school" they belong to, or the field they specialize in, whether they are veterans versed in classical literature or young writers striking out boldly on new lines, will all blossom brilliantly. Then we shall have a literature brilliant and beautiful, infinitely rich in treatment and subject matter. Only in this way can we do full justice to our policy of letting flowers of many kinds bloom.

NO INTERFERENCE WITH FREEDOM

If a writer wants to sketch an outline of what he proposes to write before he starts, if he wants to invite a number of friends to talk over the theme so that he can benefit by the good ideas of others, the

Union of Writers is duty-bound to help organize the discussion. But if a writer does not want to do so, no one has the right to put such a demand to him. A writer should be allowed to write what he likes and in any way he chooses. He can also send his work to any publishing house for publication. As the writers' organization, the Writers' Union has an obligation to help writers overcome their difficulties; but it has no right to interfere with writers' freedom. The union admittedly has worked on these lines, but not enough effort has been made. Today we want to give effect to the policy of letting flowers of many kinds bloom, so we must do everything we can to guarantee writers their freedom.

Writers should encourage and criticize one another. They should write and criticize freely. That promotes the cause of literature. Neither criticism nor countercriticism should be muzzled. Sober-minded discussion brings out a finer distinction between the right and the wrong. Overbearing criticism damages criticism itself, for truth does not favor impetuosity. From now on we should publish all sound reasoning, no matter what school of thought—materialist or idealist—the writer belongs to. Only frank and open discussion will encourage different schools of thought to contend. Contention aims at bringing out the truth; therefore it should be free discussion, giving everyone who has something to say the chance of saying it, and saying it in full.

PRESERVING THE LITERARY HERITAGE OF EVERY NATIONALITY

China is a country of many nationalities. Our policy of letting flowers of many kinds bloom should apply to the literature of every nationality in the country. Over the past few years we have unearthed and published many epics, folk tales, songs, and dances of the national minorities which have enriched our spiritual heritage and favorably affected the way we write. But in the process of digging them out, when we ran into difficulties in translation or when parts of the original were lost, we deliberately or inadvertently fell prey to dogmatism and to "Great Hanism,"[1] freely changing the

---

[1] The Hans are the largest nationality in China. "Great Hanism" is the kind of chauvinism that disparages and discriminates against the national minorities.

original, adding or subtracting till most or all of the characteristic national style, the flavor of the original was lost. Now this has been put right—as it should be.

I am an assiduous flower-grower. I know new varieties can be produced by grafting. But I cannot be sure if these new varieties will be beautiful or not. A new variety which is ugly, which has no definite character, only excites abhorrence. Culture needs exchange, but there is no reason why we should force others to change something or other to suit our one-sided taste. We must cultivate all flowers with equal assiduousness before they can all bloom brilliantly and vie with one another in beauty. We should, on the one hand, set great store by the literary heritage of our nationalities, not brutally change them. We should also lovingly cultivate the writers of all our nationalities and make every part of our country a garden of literature where flowers blossom in profusion. Writers are now springing up among the Tibetans, Huis, Mongolians, Uighurs, Manchus, and other national minorities. The Writers' Union already has branches in some national minority areas. We must see to it that we make still greater efforts to preserve the literary heritage of every nationality so that new writers appear and new flowers bloom.

LEARN FROM OTHER COUNTRIES

We treasure our literary tradition, and our literary tradition includes that of the national minorities. We also treasure the heritage of world literature and contemporary writing. Dante, Shakespeare, Cervantes, Goethe, Hugo, Pushkin, Tolstoy, Whitman, Ibsen, Tagore, Romain Rolland, Gorky, and others are our teachers. We have already translated many of these great masters and many outstanding contemporary writers, and their books circulate in our country in millions. Today in the theaters of Peking alone we can see Shakespeare's "Romeo and Juliet," Ibsen's "A Doll's House," Chekhov's "Uncle Vanya," Goldoni's "A Servant of Two Masters," and Gorky's "Petty Townsfolk" side by side with our own Peking opera, stage plays, and various kinds of local operas. Fine films from India, Japan, and other countries have had a warm welcome from Chinese audiences. Our film workers have learned much from these films. We have highly acclaimed songs and dances from India, Burma, and

Indonesia and the Japanese Kabuki theater. There is no denying that we have an ancient cultural tradition, but at the same time we should not try to conceal the fact that we are in some ways culturally backward. We must improve our culture, so we need to learn with all modesty from all other countries. We have still done far too little in the way of translating foreign literature. We must do a lot more in the future; and we hope our friends abroad will give us all the help they can.

4

WHY SHOULD WE BOLDLY BLOOM?

HSIAO TEH

The policy "let a hundred flowers bloom and a hundred schools of thought contend" has led to a heated dispute within our literary and scientific circles. Although the policy is broadly supported, the point at issue is whether or not we should boldly air our views.

I

Should we give a free hand to the airing of one's views? If we do so, how should we deal with the poisonous weeds that arise from such contention? Certain of our comrades state that if we allow only the wild flowers to grow, we will have difficulty in dealing with them. Then why should we allow weeds to grow, knowing full well that they are poisonous? What should we do in the event that their poison should spread?

The crux of the matter, then, is whether or not we should allow such poisonous weeds to grow.

That weeds contain poison is a simple fact. Is it advisable to avoid such plants? Yes, but it is also virtually impossible. How can we avoid them when they have existed for thousands of years? Those

Hsiao Teh, "Wei she-mo yao ta-tan ti fang?" (Why Should We Boldly Bloom?), *Chung-kuo ch'ing-nien* (China Youth), No. 9, May 1, 1957.

opposed to the blossoming of such noxious weeds want to prevent their growth by resorting to a mandatory decree. When they discover a trace of poison, whether in the area of art, ideology, or academic matters, they immediately issue an order for its prohibition. This, however, is futile. They mean well in avoiding poisonous plants, but their intentions are ineffectual.

It is not that we have any particular liking for noxious weeds, but we are often unable to distinguish such a plant from a fragrant flower. The plant we destroy as a poisonous weed may often prove to be quite the opposite. Dr. Sun Yat-sen, a fragrant flower, was considered a weed by the rulers of the Manchu dynasty. Communists, too, are fragrant flowers but were regarded as weeds under the Nationalist regime. Even after the liberation certain people were unable to distinguish the two. Wang Meng's newly published story, "Tsu-chih-pu hsin-lai ti ch'ing-nien jen" (A Young Man Arrives at the Organization Department), is a flower but is regarded by some as a weed. A few years ago the theory of birth control was considered to be a Malthusian type of weed, and was only recently accepted as a scented flower. "Ma-lu t'ien-shih" (Angel of the Streets) stands out as one of the finest films to have emerged since the May Fourth movement, yet it continues to be regarded as a weed, and there are those who even propose to ban it. "Yang Nai-wu ho hsiao pai-ts'ai" (Yang Nai-wu and His Little Cabbage) is an excellent opera, but certain people disapprove of its being performed.

New things differ from the old. Conservative individuals who have not accustomed themselves to new developments may often view them as poisonous weeds. We permit such weeds to grow in order to prevent those conventional in their views from rooting out fragrant flowers under the pretext of eliminating the noxious plants. Only through open discussion and the airing of our views can we establish whether a plant is a weed or a scented flower.

Some people assert that we can allow plants, the nature of which we cannot determine, to grow, but we should in no instance allow weeds to grow if we are certain they are poisonous. They believe that if these weeds were allowed to flourish, they would poison the masses. Are the people so frail as to be vulnerable to any pernicious influence? Certain noxious weeds have been in existence for hundreds of thousands of years, and no one has yet died from their poison. Why, then, should such poison be fatal to the masses now? Furthermore, we allow these weeds to grow so that we might have a chance to temper ourselves in combatting them. It is not expected of the young that they acquire Marxist views nurtured in a greenhouse; such views are to be attained through the weathering of storms. Doctrinaire scholars can be nurtured in a greenhouse, while Marxists can only emerge through struggle. If the masses are to raise their ideological awareness, they must personally combat the poisonous weeds and acquire personal experience through the encounter. Only thus can they gradually mold themselves into staunch Marxists capable of sustaining the lashings of wind and rain. Actually, few such people will be affected by the venom, while the overwhelming majority will raise the level of their ideology, their ability, and their perceptiveness through struggle of this sort.

In regard to the problem of scented flowers and poisonous weeds, we may further add that certain flowers and grasses may be neither entirely fragrant nor pernicious. Flowers can mingle with weeds, and vice versa. All this can be ascertained through the open airing of our views.

II

Certain people are leery of allowing poisonous weeds to grow, for they suspect that it would be a violation of the Marxist stance. They assert that our Marxist position can be called into question if we allow weeds which are certainly poisonous to flourish. Is this not the deliberate dissemination of mistaken ideas? Can it be regarded as a responsible attitude toward the masses? To reinforce their argument, these people even assert that many a young person who had read a single pernicious book or viewed one such play succumbed to its influence despite years of Marxist education. People who make such allegations simply do not understand that it is the Marxist position to unite the majority in joint struggle against poisonous weeds. This position should not be interpreted as one which advocates the avoiding of such weeds or the prohibition of their growth. As we have already mentioned, mandatory order alone will not halt the growth of these things. The only way to destroy them is to allow their growth so that we may combat them; this is a genuinely respon-

sible attitude toward the masses. If any young person who has received several years of Marxist education is stripped of his ideology
after viewing a single play or reading a book, then this lends cre-
dence to the view that a youth untrained in struggle, separated from
the weeds and endowed with book knowledge alone, cannot stand
the test.

As the campaign to "let a hundred flowers bloom and a
hundred schools of thought contend" gains momentum, more and
more intellectuals will embrace Marxism of their own accord. At the
same time, this campaign will help those who have embraced certain
elementary Marxist ideas in regard to their world view to further
heighten their political awareness. Only by strengthening our Marxist leadership can we properly implement the Hundred Flowers policy.

III

There are those who object to the open airing of views, fearing that
liberalization may prove troublesome to our leadership. It is their
belief that, even in the absence of poisonous weeds, the campaign is
still troublesome in that it is too complex; it would be better, they
think, if everything were rendered in one color.

Those afraid of difficulties and complexities should examine
our contemporary Chinese society. Although the socialist revolution
has been realized in its essentials, those who retain bourgeois or
petit-bourgeois sensibilities continue to number in the hundreds of
millions. Moreover, they will not remain silent. What should be done
with them? The problem can be approached in two ways.

First, we could suppress the thoughts of the people. Those who
prefer this might think this a way to avoid trouble for themselves. In
reality, however, this would cause them considerably greater trouble.
How can we forbid and suppress an individual's ideas? Ancient
tyrants and modern imperialists have, in turn, attempted to negate
the thinking of the people through violence. All such attempts end
in failure.

Second, we could reason with and persuade the people. This
would entail free discussion and analysis on an equal basis. Such discussion should proceed as gently as a mild breeze and light rain;

there is no coercion or rude attack. This approach may seem inconvenient, but it can solve problems.

This second approach is contingent on the campaign to openly air our views. Those who fear trouble hope to govern by doing nothing; this is wishful thinking.

IV

Certain people are bothered by another consideration. They fear that they themselves may be criticized in the course of "openly airing views." They hold that if we allow people to air their views we must not allow them to engage in debate or criticism; if they want to engage in debate or criticism we should not allow them to air their views. They assert that it is better to let a hundred flowers bloom than to let a hundred schools of thought contend. They further argue that criticism and debate signify the stifling of free expression.

The Hundred Flowers policy involves both the open airing of views and debate. Debate involves reciprocal criticism. Such criticism will not impede the open airing of views. On the contrary, it will allow people a better chance to express themselves. In the absence of criticism there would be "only one flower to bloom, only one school of thought." This is to say that there would be a one-sided airing of views.

In allowing a hundred schools of thought to contend, Marxists can criticize non-Marxists, and vice versa. The truth will become more clearly defined through open discussion. Genuine gold can withstand the test of fire. In an absence of criticism, ideas would become stereotyped and the truth could not be further established.

There is one sort of criticism, however, that would handicap the Hundred Flowers policy: rude and violent doctrinaire criticism. This is the criticism of "death at a single stroke." Such criticism is tantamount to an attack, a suppression of the very policy in question.

Criticism that addresses itself to academic issues should be based on sound reasoning and clearly justified. It should be convincing and well intentioned.

Many people mistake the Hundred Flowers policy as a measure of expediency, soon to be suppressed. They believe that people can air their views only to a certain extent, while the system of control is absolute. In fact, these people are opposed to the.open airing of views because they do not understand that it is a long-term policy. In a Communist society, all flowers should be allowed to bloom rather than being suppressed.

Certain people are of the opinion that only experts are qualified to air their views. This is also a misunderstanding. The spirit of the Hundred Flowers policy is such that it allows people with divergent ideas to have their say, whether they are authorities or not. Moreover, it is quite often the case that an intellectual will seriously apply himself to his studies as a result of his participation in this campaign. In doing so, he himself can become an authority.

5

THE YOUNG ALSO NEED
THE HUNDRED FLOWERS
BLOOMING TO HELP
THEM GROW

FENG HSÜEH-FENG

The policy established by the Party of allowing a hundred flowers to bloom and a hundred schools of thought to contend will enable our literature, art, and academic affairs to flourish. In addition, it will be beneficial to many aspects of our society. It will certainly benefit the cultivation of the young, who have suffered from various unreasonable and unnecessary restrictions. They have even been purposely hampered in their rightful aspirations, interests, and pastimes. Certain young people are penalized for their critical opinions. It seems that there are those who simply won't allow the young to be straightforward, open-minded, and lively. Such people share the moral viewpoint of Ah Q.[1] They regard the young with jaundiced eyes, worried even at the sight of boys and girls conversing. The letters that have poured in to the editor of the magazine *Chung-kuo ch'ing-*

Feng Hsüeh-feng, "Ch'ing-nien men ti fa-chan yeh yao 'pai-hua ch'i-fang'" (The Young Also Need the Hundred Flowers Blooming to Help Them Grow), *Chung-kuo ch'ing-nien* (China Youth), No. 14, July 16, 1956.
    [1] Ah Q is the protagonist of *The True Story of Ah Q* by Lu Hsün. He is noted for his ignorance, cowardice, and feudal ideas.

nien (China Youth) indicate that the younger generation has been hampered in its growth because of these problems. Unless we make great efforts to solve them, the young will not fully realize their initiative and creativity.

In the early years following the liberation we were unable to attend to these problems and remedy the situation. Now, however, we are in a position to deal with them. Most important, we must cultivate among the young a democratic spirit, as well as creativity and an ability for independent thought. It is the purpose of our revolution and the right of every citizen to enjoy a socialist democracy. A democratic spirit and the ideas of socialism are essential to the elimination of the ideas of the old society, and to the construction of socialism. So it is that we should do everything possible to foster the democratic spirit of socialism among the young.

This democratic spirit will enhance our creativity and can be used as a weapon in the elimination of whatever is unreasonable or a remnant of the old society. According to letters received by the editor of *China Youth,* this suppression of the young's initiative takes place not only in the schools, but in villages, factories, and government offices as well. It is not simply a problem of education in the schools; this problem is evidence that the influence of feudalism continues to prevail in our new society. Its influence can be detected in many aspects of our life other than the suppression of the young and the suppression of women. Most of us continue to be affected by remnants of the old society and are given to actions that violate our socialist democracy. Members of the older generation have either become calloused or accustomed to the problems and cannot sense their seriousness. There are even those who, in their sophistication, accept these things despite the fact that they themselves have been oppressed. Such sophistication and resignation to difficulty is particularly objectionable. The young are more sensitive and less cautious; they tend to burst the confines of their oppression. So do certain women, although others continue to be cautious. *Jen-min jih-pao* (People's Daily) and *China Youth,* as well as *Chung-kuo ch'ing-nien pao* (China Youth Daily), have exposed the oppression of women and the young and have tried to remedy the situation. This is a profound revolution in thought.

Not all who unreasonably interfere with and hamper women or

the young are villains. Some of them do so from a biased interpretation of democratic centralism and collectivism. Most are influenced by the ideas of the old system. Others have no respect for the Party system and very little understanding of the Constitution. In *China Youth Daily* of July 5 there appeared the story of a young man, Yang K'ai-hua, who had been strung up, beaten, and forced to confess things of which he was innocent. This was a violation of the law and of our human rights. It did not happen by chance. The solution to problems of this sort lies in the cultivation of the democratic spirit of socialism.

I cannot say precisely what sort of people the young should become. One thing, however, is certain; they will never emerge as certain people have planned, as the fulfillment of their wishful thinking. Plans of this sort have failed in literature. Certain of our comrades devised formats for writers in regard to creative writing. As a result, the work which adhered to this format is not even read by the very people whose format it was. They are forced to admit that such work is "conceptualized," "formularized," and "dull." The cultivation of the young cannot be dictated by the wishful thinking of a few instructors and educators. The young should grow up to be of sound body and mind. This is to say that they should be brave, pure, honest, happy, lively, knowledgeable, and independent in their thinking. They should possess initiative, a responsible attitude, and the courage to get things done. Their individuality, aspirations, and zeal for learning should not be ignored. Young people do need advice and assistance, but they should not be viewed as being incapable or worthless. Their individuality, aspirations, and interests should not be regarded as individualism. The young are more receptive to new developments than adults, and are more eager to make progress. They are highly enthusiastic in regard to the socialist cause, and we should allow them more of a free rein.

Students should be allowed more free time outside of class. Free time should be at their disposal; it would not be wasted. They could read or do whatever they liked. This would enhance creative pursuits, but would not run counter to the spirit of collectivism.

CRITICISM OF LITERARY PROBLEMS

6

SOME THOUGHTS ON LITERARY PROBLEMS TODAY

LIU SHAO-T'ANG

Fifteen years have passed since Chairman Mao's "Talks at the Yenan Forum on Literature and Art." The policy then established of making literature and art serve the workers, peasants, and soldiers has been tremendously successful and has led to great contributions in the cause of the people's revolution. Unprecedented numbers of writers have emerged and many outstanding literary works have been produced.

Since the establishment of the guideline "let a hundred flowers bloom and a hundred schools of thought contend," we face the question of how to interpret Chairman Mao's "Talks" from a new perspective: how to implement his policy in literature and art.

I am a novice as a writer, having produced only several lyrical stories that were sneered at as embellishments of life. I am no doubt unequal to the task of presenting views on this important issue, having only a shallow understanding of life and an entirely insufficient knowledge of theory and history. However, I am encouraged by many comrades as well as by my own internal struggle to speak my mind, although these ideas fall far short of blooming and contending.

Liu Shao-t'ang, "Wo tui tang-ch'ien wen-i wen-t'i ti i-hsieh ch'ien-chien" (Some Thoughts on Literary Problems Today), *Wen-i hsüeh-hsi* (Literary Studies), No. 5, 1957.

I

Chairman Mao's "Talks at the Yenan Forum" have two concerns. One provides tactical guidelines for the literary and artistic movement at that particular time. The other provides theoretical guidelines for the long-term development of our art and literature. It is impossible to identify these two concerns by quotation, for they are implicit in the "Talks."

What was the situation at that time? It was the most difficult period of our war against the Japanese. The reactionary Nationalists, wavering in their struggle against the Japanese, moved toward capitulation and the selling out of the country, while suppressing the people with an iron hand. Literary workers were cut off from the masses and literary creations were removed from the realm of politics.

Everyone is commonly responsible for the destiny of the country. Every Chinese had to do his share, however small. Writers and artists had to assume a more active role, with literature and art the weapons at their disposal. The question was in whose hands the weapons were to be placed and how they were to be used. It was necessary to reform the thinking of the writers and artists and to require that they deeply involve themselves with the struggle of the workers, peasants, and soldiers. It was also necessary to insist that they promptly turn out literary works in support of the anti-Japanese cause. Bricks or stones, however crude, were to be hurled against the enemy. To say that literature should serve politics meant at the time that literature had to serve specific policies. Most plays produced at that time by the cultural troupes in the army and local theatrical groups were for specific propaganda purposes. "Hsiung-mei k'ai-huang" (Brother and Sister Reclaim the Wasteland) is a typical example. It was necessary for writers to produce this kind of work, for critics to theorize on the need for producing it, and for the literary leadership to urge the writers to do so. All this was to be done for the War of Resistance against Japan, for the fight against the enemy.

However, these works reflected the life of a certain period; as they were produced in a hurry, they usually were not artistically excellent and were limited in thought. Few of them have survived as works of art. Still, these works struck powerful blows against the enemy. They succeeded in serving the functions assigned them at the time: the propagation and mobilization of the people. They distinguished our literary efforts. Although not a single great writer nor a single piece of great work appeared during the Anti-Japanese War, the works produced in that period comprise a glorious chapter in the history of our literature. The many anonymous writers involved comprise a great collective Writer, and their works comprise a great collective Work; this is unprecedented in history.

During the War of Liberation and the Anti-Japanese War, the problem of popularization took priority over the problem of raising standards. We had to fight the war. Moreover, people at that time were inadequate in the appreciation of art; they needed the "Hsia-li pa jen" (Song of the Rustic Poor) but could not comprehend "Yang-ch'un pai-hsüeh" (The Spring Snow).[1] It is important for a writer to consider the people's immediate needs and create works they can easily appreciate.

However, since the liberation of the entire country, the people's life has changed tremendously. They are better able to appreciate art and have more opportunities to do so. Works now created to serve policies and lacking a high level of artistic excellence can no longer fulfill the needs of the people. A stable life provides ample time for writers to conceive, plan, and polish their work. To insist on the same old theories and thoughts, and the same old manner of leadership, is a regressive rather than a progressive act.

After the liberation, our theories guiding literature and art remained the same, and have been deeply influenced by dogmatism from the outside. This handicapped the development of literature and art. Thus there were contradictions between the readership and the work itself, contradictions between the people and the writers, and contradictions between the creative work and literary theories. This means there were contradictions between writers and critics, and between writers and those in charge of literary affairs. There was also the ironic situation in which writers had a genuine dissatis-

---

[1] "Song of the Rustic Poor" and "The Spring Snow" were songs of the Kingdom of Ch'u, third century B.C. It is said that when someone sang the more complex "The Spring Snow" in the Ch'u capital, only a few people joined in, but when "Song of the Rustic Poor" was sung, thousands did so.

faction with dogmatism but a poor understanding of Marxism-Leninism. The Hu Feng clique took advantage of all these contradictions to promote counterrevolutionary ideas. The clique confused many writers and the masses, thus making a counterrevolutionary attack against the Party and the people.

Dogmatists interpret and apply Chairman Mao's guiding theory for literature and art of a particular time mechanically, conservatively, exaggeratedly, and in an erratic manner. This gives rise to conceptualized formula writing. This sort of work did play a positive role during a particular period, but it is harmful today. In serving politics, literature does not mechanically serve a specific policy, nor is it governed in its inception by the state constitution, Party regulations, or the law. Of first importance is whether or not the literary piece reveals a class character, whether it encourages the people and educates them—in other words, whether it plays a constructive role in remolding the human soul in accordance with communism. To insist that works of literature and art immediately serve a specific policy is, in fact, a violation of the fundamental principle of materialism. Man's social being determines his consciousness. Literature and art reflect only those things which have already happened. Writers need time to observe, experience, analyze, and study life; it also takes time to conceive and create art. Thus, works of literature and art are inevitably one step behind actual reality. How, then, could literary and artistic works provide stimulus, encouragement, and guidance? The answer, as I mentioned earlier, lies essentially in their constructive role of remolding the human soul in accordance with communism.

To meet certain urgent demands, literary works may have to align themselves with specific policies; outstanding works may be produced because of the artist's rich experience of life and superb artistry. However, this is not the usual creative approach and is no excuse for us to subject literature to specific policies, to formulas and abstract concepts.

Should we emphasize popularization or the raising of standards? Chairman Mao has said that "the raising of standards is based on popularization, while popularization is guided by the raising of standards." The principle is a general one. Today, the primary task we are facing is the raising of standards. This is not wishful thinking but the demand of the people, who are no longer satisfied with the same old "Hsiao fang-niu" (Little Cowherd) and the same old "man, hand, mouth, knife, cow, goat."[2]

Some time ago, there was a dispute about cinema; this fact illustrated the people's demand that artistic standards be raised. The policy of letting a hundred flowers bloom and a hundred schools of thought contend is intended to raise the quality of art and academic studies.

II

Chairman Mao's "Talks at the Yenan Forum" have provided permanent guidelines for literature and art. They contain comprehensive principles that are a profound extension of Marxism-Leninism in literature, relating theory to practice.

Literature and art must serve the workers, peasants, and soldiers; political criteria come first and artistic criteria second in literary criticism; and writers should deeply involve themselves with life and remold their thinking. These are fundamental and permanent guides for literature of the past, the present, and the future. They cannot be revised or rescinded. They do not conflict with the policy of letting a hundred flowers bloom and a hundred schools of thought contend. To reject these principles is to oppose the class viewpoint and world outlook of Marxism-Leninism; to do so would be to embrace capitalism without reservation. No flowers would bloom, no important ideas would be voiced.

We must persist in making literature serve the workers, peasants, and soldiers, for they are the source of literature. Due to the transformation of relations between classes, intellectuals now belong to the working class. So "serving the workers, peasants and soldiers" today means serving workers, peasants, soldiers, and intellectuals. But we must do away with the tendency on the part of authors to write only for intellectuals because they have a common intellectual background. The writer's chief task is to serve the majority of the working people. He should strive to know the life of the workers and peasants and to write about them. Yet you cannot force a writer

[2] Quotations from Mao's "Talks at the Yenan Forum," referring to knowledge and culture at the lower level.

to do this by regulation or administrative order. You must use persuasion and education, bearing in mind the person's personality and situation.

I don't agree with Ch'en Ch'i-t'ung and other comrades that daily affairs and love between men and women are in conflict with the life of the workers, peasants, and soldiers. Are workers, peasants, and soldiers immune to affairs of the household and love between men and women? In portraying the workers, is it necessary to deal only with "blazing furnace, moving wheels, and ringing hammers"? Can peasants only be described in terms of "Heigh-ho! Buck up, work hard, produce more!"? Can soldiers only be described in such expressions as, "Take up your rifles, advance, and fire!"? Can one separate everyday affairs and love from working, producing, and fighting?

There are major literary themes and minor literary themes. Those about workers and peasants should be considered major themes, while those about intellectuals and other classes are considered minor themes. Workers and peasants are the principal creators of life; they are the essential elements of our society. However, we are not justified in concluding that writing on themes of secondary importance will not be worthwhile. The value of a literary work is determined not by whether its themes are of primary importance, but by the way in which the work appeals to its readers, by its artistry and meaning. Literary works of different themes can address themselves to different classes; *And Quiet Flows the Don* can instruct intellectuals, while *The Ordeal* can instruct workers and peasants.

Political criteria first, artistic criteria second; this is how it should be. To reject the importance of political criteria is to deny the class character of art; it is also to reject art as a weapon, to regard it as merely decorative. However, that political criteria come first does not mean that the ideological and instructive role of the work depends on whether the subject matter or the theme is of primary importance. As I said earlier, political thought can be presented in an artistic manner. Chairman Mao has said, "Works of art which lack artistic quality have no force, however progressive they are politically." A political thought which is not presented artistically is as ineffectual as a warrior who cannot subdue a chicken. We should try to realize the goal long ago established by Chairman Mao: "The unity of politics and art; the unity of political content and the most highly artistic form possible."

The foremost problem we face today is to urge writers to explore and pursue the most consummate art. This is the center of all our literary problems.

It is absolutely necessary for the writer to deeply involve himself with life and to remold his thought. By adopting a casual attitude toward life, he will be unable to produce works which truthfully depict things as they are; he will find nothing worth writing about. If he forces himself to write, he will produce only conceptualized formula writing that will eventually be forgotten. As contradiction is absolute and unity only relative, there will always be contradictions between idealism and materialism, the advanced and the backward, even after thousands of years. As long as idealism and backwardness exist, ideological struggle and ideological remolding are necessary. In the absence of a progressive world view—that of communism—a writer will lack the correct stand and viewpoint, and will be misguided in his creative approach. Therefore a good writer of realistic work must immerse himself in life and remold his thought; only in this way can he create works faithful to life and to his era. Only in this way can he produce meaningful works and contribute to the cause of the people's literature. On the other hand, in order to remold his thought, he must genuinely get involved with life.

However, the ways of getting involved with life vary. One can only judge from a writer's works whether he has been deeply involved with life or not. A writer immersed in life is like a fish in water. How does it swim, how does it survive? As long as it is in the water, there is no need for us to define rules for its breeding and swimming. How an animal adapts to its environment depends on objective factors as well as its adaptability. This is also true for the writer. It is a fine thing if he can get deeply involved with life and take a job at a lower rank; but it will also be commendable if he simply lives among the people as a commoner all his life. For remolding thought, persuasion should be used rather than force. This has always been our Party's principle in this regard. Today there is a further development of the principle in the policy of letting a hundred schools of thought contend and of seeking agreement in spite of differences.

Chairman Mao's "Talks at the Yenan Forum" show the proper path for writers to follow in developing their talent and creativity. The policy of letting a hundred flowers bloom and a hundred schools of thought contend is a new development arising from Chairman Mao's "Talks." The basic principle of the "Talks" remains unchanged and will always remain unchanged.

III

It is clear that Chairman Mao's policy for literature has made the realistic spirit of literature develop more widely and deeply than before, and has brought literature and the people closer. Never before has the life of workers, peasants, and soldiers been the primary subject matter of creative works. The policy has unearthed numerous writers from the soil of the people. The tradition of realism has undergone a long process of development from the *Book of Songs,* the most ancient poetry, down to Lu Hsün, the modern Chinese literary master.

However, we must be sufficiently objective and practical to realize that our literature has long been subjected to the same old policy while our historical development has varied, and that the literary construct of our literary works is far inferior to the ideological construct. Having recognized the backwardness of the literary construct, we should waste no time in eliminating it. The policy of letting a hundred flowers bloom and a hundred schools of thought contend is the only way to remove this backwardness and stimulate the growth of literature and art. We must follow Chairman Mao's policy in regard to literature and art and involve ourselves with life in order to remold our thought. We must arrive at a Communist world outlook and master the Marxist approach in order to observe, experience, study, and analyze life. It is also imperative for us to study and absorb the tradition of realism and the artistic skills of the classical masters.

To carry on the tradition of realism, we must get rid of the theory and influence of dogmatism and sectarianism. As long as the writer continues to strengthen the Communist world view, he can choose whatever creative approach he likes. A uniform creative approach based on a fixed definition can only restrict or even destroy the creativity of the writer. Nations can build socialism in different ways according to their different characteristics. Is it impossible for creative approaches to vary among writers, all of whom are working for socialism?

To write in the tradition of realism, the writer should not lose touch with reality. This means being faithful to what is happening, not whitewashing life under the pretext of furthering the revolution. Literature must describe the life of its time and bear the characteristics of the era: the reality of 1957 rather than what might happen in 1967. Literature is not a still life; it is a closeup view of reality seen in a context of motion.

If we were to learn from the art of the classical masters, we would improve our own artistic skills. We would learn how to make language compact and lively, how to make language sound pleasing, how to arrange scenes skillfully and select meaningful details, and how to construct an interesting plot. In a word, to achieve artistic skills, we must work very hard in the spirit of Tu Fu's saying: "I will not die content if my words fail to hold my readers spellbound."

Only in this way can we try to solve the contradictions in our literature. Only then can our literature develop and thrive.

7

DO NOT CLOSE YOUR EYES TO THE SUFFERING OF THE PEOPLE

HUANG CH'IU-YÜN

Some people predict that twelve years from now no one in our country will be unhappy unless, perhaps, his beloved refuses to accept his gifts; no one will shed tears unless they are prompted by a classical tragedy or a fit of laughter.

No one, of course, can be sure that in twelve years our lives will be free of unhappiness. At present, such a paradise is no more than a dream. This is the case even in the Soviet Union, which has achieved socialism. Some artists, however, are so naive as to confuse this dream with reality and to represent it in their work. In the movies, for example, nearly every agricultural cooperative is depicted as having bumper harvests, with sheep and cattle everywhere. In the home of a peasant, various dishes of fish and meat are spread out on the table. Every village girl wears a beautiful new dress. These things, in fact, bear little resemblance to the actual life of peasants in our country today.

Morbid pessimism is harmful to an artist, but cheap optimism is harmful as well. In the current phase of our literature, the latter deserves more attention.

Huang Ch'iu-yün, "Pu yao tsai jen-min chi-k'u mien-ch'ien pi-shan yen-ching" (Do Not Close Your Eyes to the Suffering of the People), *Jen-min wen-hsüeh* (People's Literature), September 1956.

Anyone who has had frequent and profound experiences in life will have witnessed the various miseries of the people. Many shed tears that have not been provoked by hearty laughter, but by the torment of their difficulties and their unfortunate experiences. It cannot be denied that calamities, famine, unemployment, epidemics, and bureaucratism continue to exist within our country. There are also various disagreeable incidents and irrational situations. An honest, conscientious, and sober-minded artist cannot close his eyes and remain silent in the face of the realities of our life and the suffering of the people. If he lacks the courage with which to expose the underlying sickness of our society, to help solve the essential problems in the life of our people, and to denounce all that is abnormal, morbid, and negative in its import, how can he be considered an artist? Is it possible that in writing about the negative aspects of our life we do a disservice to the socialist system we wholeheartedly support? No, this is not so. The morning glow of socialism is radiant and bright. No fair-minded person would mistake a few clouds for an overcast sky. Moreover, we expose these negative aspects in order to rid ourselves of them.

In writing about the darker side of our life, will we destroy our sense of beauty as well as the noble sentiment in our works? Of course not. All that is ugly and unpleasant should be given expression in works of realism, for such things do exist. Realistic art should not besmirch the realities of our life; nor should it shun or embellish these realities. In his *Study of Aesthetics,* Chernishevsky arrived at the following conclusion: beauty in art must be achieved through the reflection of life. Beauty is life. False beauty is like false love: uglier than the ugliest of things, and nauseating.

Fear is unnecessary. It is inexcusable. As revolutionary writers and artists we must identify ourselves with the people; we must share their feelings and never allow ourselves to be separated from them in life or in death. Shallow optimism and indifference should be replaced by a feeling of concern for the destiny of the people. The cowardice of avoiding reality must be overcome by a fighting spirit, by adhering to the truth. Personal interests must be put aside and replaced with a strong sense of political responsibility and artistic integrity. Only in this way can we give expression to the innermost feelings of the people: their love, hate, joy, or anger. Only thus

can we depict their happiness, misfortunes, separations, and re-
unions. Only thus can we do more than simply smile at the people's
happiness while closing our eyes and remaining silent in the face of
their suffering. Only thus can we create works truly worthy and
reflective of our era.

8

WHERE ARE THE THORNS?

HUANG CH'IU-YÜN

I

Two articles by Comrade Liu Shao-t'ang appeared in the April issue of *Pei-ching wen-i* (Peking Literature)[1] and the May issue of *Wen-i hsüeh-hsi* (Literary Studies),[2] respectively. I found them highly thought provoking. Although I cannot agree with certain of his arguments that seem arbitrary and one-sided, I must admit he has raised a significant question in regard to contemporary literature.

We have experienced great achievements in literature since the Liberation. Well-written books have been published and new writers have emerged. It would be unjust to say that we have been without progress, and have slipped backward in this regard. We feel, however, that our literature at present lacks vitality and fails to reflect fully the true nature of our life. There is little work of true artistry that appeals to its readers. What is at the root of the situation? Comrade Liu's articles concern themselves with an analysis of this problem. The effort is worthwhile and necessary.

Addressing himself to the literary situation in the Soviet Union, Simonov once said: "No matter how deep the thorn lies in the body, it must be removed if we are to avoid an abscess. Though its removal

Huang Ch'iu-yün, "Tz'u tsai na-li?" (Where Are the Thorns?), *Wen-i hsüeh-hsi* (Literary Studies), June 1957.
    [1] "The Development of Realism in the Socialist Era."
    [2] "Some Thoughts on Literary Problems Today."

may hurt the pride of a good many people, it must be done in the
interest of our literature, the readership, and socialism." His statement, I think, is so profound in its meaning as to also apply to our
situation. There is a thorn in our side as well. It has lain deeply
buried for so long that certain people have grown accustomed to it;
it no longer pains them. This is the thorn of dogmatism and sectarianism.

It is true that certain contradictions exist in our literature and
art. The most important of these contradictions are not those which
certain of our comrades believe to exist between editors and writers,
young writers and older writers, or writers with Party membership
and those with none. Rather, they are the profound and widespread
contradictions caused by dogmatism and sectarianism. Such contradictions not only exist *between* editors and writers, but also *within* the
editors and writers separately. This is also the case with young
writers, old writers, and so on.

No one would now object to the movement to oppose dogmatism and sectarianism. Of late it seems that dogmatism has suddenly
vanished. Even those who were among the most headstrong of dogmatists in the past have now become stridently opposed to dogmatism. The stronghold of dogmatism has therefore become an empty
camp. However, arguments presented in opposition to dogmatism
usually begin and end in abstraction. In this way they oppose dogmatism with dogmatism. It is no wonder, then, that certain people
believe the situation has yet to be brought out into the open and the
problem remains unsolved. In order for the problem to be solved,
the situation must be made clear. The thorn must be located before
it can be removed.

II

In order to bring the situation out into the open, I must cite a few
facts. Being quite busy, we tend to be forgetful. We need not recall
the events of several years back, or even those of the past two years.
The events that took place within our literary circles since last spring
are themselves sufficient to warrant our profound consideration.

On January 7 of this year *Jen-min jih-pao* (People's Daily) published "Wo-men tui mu-ch'ien wen-i kung-tso ti chi-tien i-chien"

(Opinions on Contemporary Literature and Art) by Comrade Ch'en Ch'i-t'ung and three others. Following this publication, a harsh wave of dogmatism and sectarianism swept over the entire country. *Tsawen* (critical essays) exposing defects and errors in our society have been under ruthless censure. "Tsu-chih-pu hsin-lai ti ch'ing-nien jen" (A Young Man Arrives at the Organization Department) encountered severe criticism from all quarters. In a month's time, a barrage of critical articles condemning "Ts'ao-mu p'ien" (A Family of Plants) appeared in Szechuan. For several days in a row, discussion meetings convened in Kwangtung for the purpose of "reviewing literature." Under this pretext, "Ch'uang-tso ti chieh-fang" (The Emancipation of Creation) by Chou T'ung-ming, "Lao yu-t'iao" (The Old Fox) by Chou Wei, and "Ken chieh-pan jen tsai i-ch'i" (Together with the Successors) by Huang Ku-liu were labeled as "capitulationism," "anarchism," and "bourgeois humanism," respectively. These works do, in fact, leave something to be desired. "A Family of Plants," for example, displays an unhealthy set of sentiments. Trying to do away with such writing in one fell swoop, however, can in no way be justified. We can assume that more such dramatic events could have been staged had Chairman Mao's speech at the Supreme State Conference been published one or two weeks later.

This chilling wave of dogmatism and sectarianism creates a horrible climate for literature. Works criticizing the darker aspects of our society, its abnormality and unhealthiness, and works which describe the hardships and miseries of the people are condemned for "distorting reality, slandering society, and attacking the socialist system." The motive or social effect of the work does not seem to matter. At times, writers are falsely accused of the crime of deliberately maneuvering against the Party and the people. In Peking, while sponsoring the discussion of "A Young Man Arrives at the Organization Department," *Chung-kuo ch'ing-nien pao* (China Youth Daily) mimeographed "Yeh pai-ho-hua" (Wild Lily) by Wang Shih-wei and distributed it among the participants for reference. In Kwangtung, during a discussion of "Together with the Successors," one leading comrade suggested that the participants see the movie "Mo-kuei chi-t'uan" (A Pack of Devils) by way of comparison; the author of the story advocated trust between people as do the counterrevolutionaries in the film. In Szechuan, the criticism of "A Family of

Plants" involved references to the political, historical, and family background of the author. It was even asserted that the author "assumes the reactionary stance of a bygone strata of society, and is hostile toward the people." Under the burden of this, the author nearly committed suicide.

The pressures of this situation are such that quite a few writers are extremely disturbed. They are unwilling to embellish reality against their conscience, yet they are unable to depict life in a realistic manner. They haven't the heart to close their eyes to the hardships and miseries of the people, yet they must keep silent in regard to events which shock their sense of moral values. It is certain that any revolutionary writer will wholeheartedly uphold the socialist system of our country and be filled with confidence in its bright future. Precisely because of this, he is the more intolerant of obstacles in the path of our revolution, of the dust that mires our beautiful life. He is anxious to become involved with life, and to expose the darker aspects of our society. It is his purpose to direct the people's attention to the need for proper remedies, and to educate them in their struggle against shortcomings and mistakes so that the quality of our work will be improved.

It is a pity that such a worthy goal cannot often be realized. One senior Party member asked with emotion, "Will we be permitted to write certain novels for reference among ourselves rather than for publication?" A young fiction writer, in the postscript of his collection, stated ". . . I feel that the most telling weakness in my work is that it is not completely realistic. My hometown lies on the Grand Canal. It has been plagued with disasters and mishaps. My stories, however, often express a spirit of childish complacency in regard to my native land." The confessions of these two writers reveal our predicament in regard to creative work. We all know that the most painful thing for a writer is to be somehow prevented from expressing his ideas clearly and without equivocation. This is the case when he must strike a compromise between what he wants to say and what others expect him to say.

Many of our comrades are concerned over the ideological and artistic decline in our literature, and this is reflected in their discussion of the problem. There can be no denying that our literature is rife with vulgar, pallid works of formularization and conceptualization. Some people believe that the writers are to blame for not becoming deeply involved with life; they are not acquainted with the workers, peasants, and soldiers, and they are not possessed of the proper ideas and feelings. Their artistic technique leaves something to be desired, or they have not acquired an adequate understanding of the characteristics of literature. Others tend to emphasize objective factors. They assert that our society is undergoing drastic changes and that it is difficult for writers to grasp the spirit of the era and of the people. All these arguments are valid. There are many reasons, however, for stagnation in literature, and for the mass production of formulistic and conceptualistic work; no one-sided explanation can address itself to the true situation.

At present, however, it seems to me that literature is suffering from the constriction of dogmatist theory. Such theories impose on writers the idea that literature should praise things of a positive nature rather than exposing the darker side of life. In other words, mention should be made of achievements rather than of difficulties and shortcomings. Work that embellishes life receives undeserved praise while work that depicts things as they are is unfairly attacked and condemned. Our literature shies away from the harsh realities of life, involving itself with meaningless acts of praise. Such work, of course, cannot depict the contradictions and conflicts of our lives and is incapable of reflecting the revolutionary spirit and heroism displayed by our people in their arduous struggle. Inevitably, readers will come to consider such work insipid and unappealing.

The dogmatists are possessed of a strange notion. They believe that so long as our literature incessantly presents the idea that our people lead happy, affluent lives, and that our leading cadres at various levels are infallible, our lives will become rich, happy, and free of contradiction. They dare not expose contradictions and solve them. On the contrary, they conceal and prolong these contradictions. They believe, furthermore, that this is essential to the preservation of the socialist cause. Consequently, in their psychology they develop a conditioned reflex of sorts which causes them to be indignant and fly into a rage whenever they encounter a piece of writing that does not meet their requirements. This, of course, would be work containing truthful disclosures of contradiction among the people.

The dogmatists indiscriminately condemn work of this sort, and even go so far as to suspect the authors of ulterior motives, of being hostile toward and slandering our social system. Some time ago *Nan-fang jih-pao* (Southern Daily) published an essay complaining about the inaccessibility to traffic of a road that was constantly under repair. Certain leading comrades, however, became nervous and claimed that the author was actually making satirical remarks about the Party committee of Kwangtung Province. They felt that an implication was being made that too many automobiles were owned by the committee and that the pavement was consequently being ruined. As a result, the members of the Party committee felt the author's motives should be scrutinized. Imagine! If an essay of this sort could provoke such unwarranted suspicion, how can our writers truthfully depict contradictions among the people and dare to intervene in the affairs of our lives?

To my mind, the most damaging influence dogmatism exercises over literature is the embellishment of the realities of life; it serves to prevent the realistic portrayal of our situation. Of course, the adverse effects on our literature of dogmatist taboos and dictates are by no means confined to this single aspect.

9

OPEN WINDOW, OPEN TALK

YAO HSÜEH-YIN

I

People in the area of science, drama, opera, and cinema have recently pronounced their views in regard to the Hundred Flowers campaign. In the area of literature, however, there seems to be a silence. Is this because writers are entirely free of grievances or complaints that deserve to be aired? I think not. A number of fairly serious problems exist for those involved with literary creation. Some of these problems have been solved, others have not; some have yet to be revealed, while others are known. Fellow writers air a good many grievances in private, speaking pointedly of many exasperating matters. On public occasions, however, they are all quiet. Certain people have said that our literary scene is twofold: the public and the private. This situation continues today, which indicates that problems and contradictions remain.

Why is it that we have so many problems to speak of during private discussions? Why do we seldom discuss problems at public gatherings, if we do so at all? It seems to me that the reasons are varied. Most important, many literary offices and organizations have for a long time failed to follow democratic procedures; such an atmosphere does not lend itself to free expression. In the past, certain

Yao Hsüeh-yin, "Ta-k'ai ch'uang-hu shuo liang hua" (Open Window, Open Talk), *Wen-i pao* (Literary Gazette), No. 7, May 9, 1957.

of our comrades were attacked because they enjoyed the expression of critical opinions and the open airing of views. They became the principal targets during political movements, and were labeled as "consistently opposing the leadership," or, even worse, as "having serious anti-Party sentiments."

These comrades, of course, may have had their shortcomings, great or small. When they were attacked, however, their accusers did not distinguish between right and wrong and expose the true failings. Instead, they tried to contrive as many charges as possible to use as a pretext for accusing these comrades. They even considered the virtue of being fond of airing one's views to be a serious crime. Even if the writers had offered their opinions on nothing other than theories of literature and art, and even if they did actually establish the weakness of the literary ideas and theories of certain leading comrades, when the political movement got underway their previously valid criticism was interpreted as the crime of opposing the leadership. In feudal times, ministers could not discuss their emperor, nor could a son discuss his father. Ours is now a new society, but if one were to dare to contend with the leading comrades, one would be branded as disrespectful of the system, lacking in discipline, and in opposition to the leadership. How can the people speak freely under such circumstances?

Today, the situation has changed greatly. However, the violation of democratic principles that took place within certain literary organizations and society in general continues to exert a negative influence. Certain people fear they may be denounced when the opportunity arises. They believe that the more conspicuous one is, the more likely one is to be crushed. Therefore, they think it better to refrain for the moment from expressing certain things that need to be said. It has been said, "We are now in the thick of the campaign to oppose sectarianism, bureaucratism, and dogmatism. No one will attack you directly if you voice a grievance, but you would incur trouble for yourself at some other time or in regard to some other problem."

This attitude of wisdom for the sake of personal survival should not be tolerated. It is not the viewpoint of the masters of the state. These cautious ones are so concerned with trivial considerations of personal safety that they disregard the interests of the Party and the society in general. Rather than criticizing such overcautious attitudes, however, we should endeavor to correct violations of democratic principle. This would require people to dare to raise questions and offer criticism rather than grumbling in private. On the other hand, leading comrades in our literary departments should emulate the spirit of Emperor Yü,[1] who bowed his thanks for advice. These comrades should courageously accept the opinions of the masses. They should have the courage to examine the shortcomings in their work and in their style of work. In this way, those comrades who dare not openly speak their minds could overcome their reserve.

II

In the administration of literary and artistic affairs, bureaucratism can adopt various forms and is usually accompanied by dogmatism and sectarianism. I would like to cite one or two examples of bureaucratism, leaving the problems of dogmatism and sectarianism for later.

First, bureaucratism can often display itself as a lack of concern for the masses. Let us consider the example of the Wu-han branch of the China Writers' Union, with which I am familiar. It has accomplished certain things over the past years, but has also become seriously infected with bureaucratism. The writers in the Wu-han branch live in very poor surroundings. Not only are they unable to read and write in quiet, they sometimes have trouble getting to sleep. Despite everyone's knowledge of the problem, the situation has dragged on for years. We do not agree that writers should enjoy a better life than the cadres of the state. But we must admit that writers work with their brains. Like scientists, they require suitable surroundings for their work. The quality of the house itself does not matter, but there must be quiet surroundings and sufficient light. The housing problem is severe in a city like Wu-han, but it would not be impossible to arrange ten houses or so for the writers.

This can only be explained by the fact that the leading comrades of the Wu-han branch and the Municipal Party Committee of Wu-han are infected with bureaucratism. They are aware of current

[1] Emperor Yü: the legendary founder of the Hsia dynasty (2005–1766 B.C.). He was purportedly an extremely wise and kind ruler.

problems and hear the writers' opinions daily; they often show their sympathy but never take actual measures to remedy the situation. The writers who live in the writers' dormitory even have difficulty getting three square meals a day, but the leading comrades have ignored the matter. Certain writers have said that because the leading comrades have individual homes with maids to cook for them, they cannot possibly understand the inconveniences experienced by those living in the dormitory. These accusations made in private are justifiable. Our leadership should place itself in the position of the masses in order to think as they do and help them with their problems. In the traditional political thought of China, there is a brilliant maxim: "When others starve, I starve. When others drown, I drown." The Wu-han branch does not have a large membership, but it is a pity that the leading comrades failed to concern themselves with the situation as they might have done.

Let us cite another example. Last year, when there was a general wage increase across the entire country, the allowance for writers in the Wu-han branch was frozen at the level established two years earlier. The wage scale previously established for professional writers in Wu-han was rather low. As a result, those writers who had families to support were without savings and usually spent their earnings in advance. Following the wage increase of last year, the market price of daily necessities went up a bit. This worsened the financial straits of those writers who were unable to produce any work for the moment, or those who were engaged in writing longer pieces. Neither before nor after the freezing of allowances was any explanation offered to the writers. The most curious thing of all was that when there was about to be a wage increase, the leaders quickly reclassified writers' wages as allowances. Accordingly, those comrades who received wages from the state not only were given a wage increase, but also received retroactive payment backdated over several months. Because the writers' wages were referred to as allowances, they were unable to obtain the raise, let alone back payments. This gives one the impression that the leadership searches for ways in which to avoid paying writers, rather than caring for their lives and feelings. Some of these writers are indeed very poor.

I have three preliminary opinions on the matter of frozen allowances. Firstly, this way of administering things does not seem to correspond with the Party's policy regarding intellectuals as it was publicized last spring. Second, even if this mode of administration did agree with Party policy, it does not take into account the actual situation. Third, the mode of administration is too rigid.

In requiring that professional writers support themselves, the Central Committee intended to stimulate and enhance creative activity. When it pronounced the guideline it considered the fact that the majority of the writers had various difficulties. It also understood the peculiar nature of the Chinese intellectual. Therefore, it repeatedly advised the writers not to force themselves to accept this regulation or be bashful about stating their case; if after due consideration they felt they still had difficulties, their allowance could be resumed. This was a truly thoughtful and cautious attitude.

The Wu-han branch, however, did not observe this in practice. Writers there received cursory notice in mid-December of last year that beginning January 1 (although the action was actually enforced on April 1), professional writers should support themselves without exception. Appended to the notice were several regulations. At the end of the notice the writers were asked for their opinions. In all, the notice displayed none of the Central Committee's concern for writers. The writers were to transfer from their jobs or to support themselves fully, even if the latter meant taking short-term loans. Although most of the writers did not transfer from their jobs, there were among them a number of people who suffered from considerable financial and spiritual pressure.

The leading comrades of the Wu-han branch of the Writers' Union could have handled these two problems better than they did. However, because they were accustomed to a subjective mode of administration rather than following the mass line, the results were poor. There have been quite a few such examples; they needn't all be mentioned. It seems that our leading comrades are afraid only of ignoring the instructions of higher authorities. They keep their eyes on those above them rather than those below them. When people read this they will probably accuse me of having the soul of a Philistine, a greed for money, and strong bourgeois ideas. But please, let us be a bit more realistic. Writers are also ordinary people; they are not supermen. They too have wives and children. They must eat and wear clothes as others do. When I am addressing myself to practical problems, I am speaking of what is on their minds.

Please allow me to make a little joke; I have not yet seen a supposedly proletarian-oriented comrade volunteer for a decrease in wages.

III

A second common expression to bureaucratism is the practice of resorting to mandatory order or oversimplified methods in exercising leadership over literary creation. Creative effort is a form of complex mental labor and involves problems of a many-sided nature. Understanding the creative difficulties of a writer and being helpful in developing his good qualities and enabling him to overcome his failings is quite a difficult undertaking. If you must exercise leadership over a number of writers, the task becomes even more difficult. In order to do a good job, the leading comrades must first be knowledgeable in regard to literary pursuits. Second, they must adhere to the mass line, and hold frequent, earnest discussions with writers. Third, it would be good if they set aside a certain period of time each year in order to involve themselves deeply with life in the countryside and the factories. In so doing they could avoid giving instructions in creative matters according to outmoded doctrines derived from books, or according to their own dated experiences.

It goes without saying that leading comrades in the administration of literary affairs should have a thorough knowledge, or at least an understanding, of literary pursuits. Following the liberation, however, the state moved quickly in its literary undertakings. As a result, not every member of the leadership has had an opportunity to arrive at a thorough grasp of literary affairs. If one does not understand something, one should humbly set out to learn about it. One should not ape the man in the proverb who slapped his cheek until it became swollen in order to resemble a fat man. Do not think that simply by being a leader one becomes the embodiment of the truth and can then speak on behalf of the Party, issuing directives as one pleases in regard to any problem.

In recent years, a number of administrators from the Bureau of Culture and the Federations of Literature and Art, who lacked a true understanding of literature, drama, and art, assumed control of creative activities and the reform of the dramatic arts. Despite a few achievements, they have exerted an extremely harmful influence. If a writer under the leadership of others is conceited, he is the one directly harmed. But if a leading comrade is filled with conceit, his influence is much more widespread. If someone is appointed by the Party administrative head, this does not mean he is an expert in literary affairs with no further need of study. After assuming a position of leadership, certain people feel they are superior to the masses in every respect. This is bureaucratism derived from the old society.

Over the past few years, certain of our leading comrades did not understand the peculiar nature of literary creation, although they themselves had at one time engaged in creative writing. They lacked the time or the humility to learn, and they ignored the mass line. They tended to administer literary affairs in a subjective manner, and with oversimplified methods. This resulted in work fraught with inconsistencies regarding Party policy. They did not fully consider the peculiarities of each writer, nor did they fully understand each writer's artistic concerns. These leaders tended to insist on certain general requirements. In doing so, they failed to achieve satisfactory results. Before 1954, for example, certain leading comrades placed particular emphasis on such folk works as poetry read to the rhythm of clappers. In this they displayed a shallow understanding of the Party's literary undertakings. It was their opinion that every writer should first direct his efforts to the production of folk works. If he did not do so and wanted to produce a serious work, he would be considered to be infected with bourgeois literary ideas. He could even be accused of individualist heroism, and thereby become the butt of satire. Each year, we have several opportunities to examine our thoughts. On these occasions, those comrades who were unable to produce folk works had no choice but to conduct a self-examination. They labeled themselves as bourgeois in their literary ideas. Such statements were made with reluctance and resentment.

We must agree that it has been necessary for writers to produce folk works for the masses, especially during the past few years. The writer, however, should do this of his own accord rather than being compelled to do so. Second, it is a fact that each writer is skilled in a particular genre. We cannot insist that everyone employ the same weapon in their struggle. Third, a desire to produce work of some import does not necessarily derive from bourgeois ideas. If such a desire proves to be in the interests of the people, it can be referred to as revolutionary heroism rather than individualist heroism. The subjectivism, the oversimplified methods, and the thinking of the leaders mentioned above have resulted in a number of writers being unable to realize their initiative and potential.

It is absolutely necessary that the leadership urge writers to go off and experience life. If these commendable intentions are implemented in a bureaucratic manner, however, the results will not necessarily be good. For example, certain of our comrades consider sending writers to the countryside to be their foremost responsibility. When the last person has left, their job is done. At some later point, the writers may encounter difficulty in their writing or in their lives. They may stand in great need of the leadership's assistance, only to find that the leaders themselves are too busy to respond; whatever new problems the writers may encounter are no longer their concern. Moreover, the question of whether or not a writer should undertake any work of a practical sort after having gone off to the countryside, or what the nature of his work is to be, has not been properly resolved. The matter is not dealt with according to the writer's individual qualities or the situation in the area where he stayed, but according to the arbitrary demands of the leadership.

Although it is generally a good thing for writers to undertake practical work, it is not the only viable approach. The writer's life, after all, must be structured according to his immediate situation, rather than the wishful thinking of the leadership. If those in the offices of the Writer's Union or the Federation of Literature and Art sit and demand that writers adopt a certain life style after moving to the country, the results will often be undesirable. It was the habit of certain emperors to remain in the palace and command their armies in combat a thousand miles away. This was referred to as "commanding at a distance" and is similar to the mode of leadership mentioned above.

All good writers are willing to experience village life. In this way they can participate in the struggle of the masses. They can undergo continual self-reformation and absorb material for new themes or subject matter in their work. This will ensure the continuation of their creative efforts. But if a writer is in the middle of writing a book and is unwilling to stop, he should not be forced to go off to the villages. Indifferent to the writer's task, certain leading comrades are apt to consider it an aversion to hardship if a writer refuses to go to the country. Through direct admonishment or insinuating advice, the leadership will urge that writer to go. Writers find this a spiritual burden. Occasionally the leading comrades will say, "Why doesn't this person hurry through with his writing and go to the villages?" Such pressure can only serve to rush a writer through his work, or injure his health. In view of this, the leadership should directly involve themselves with writers. They should get in touch with them, talk to them, and try to understand the peculiar nature of writers' creative efforts.

In the past, a writer could to some extent plan the course of his own life and work. This could be done partly by himself and partly by the Party. This arrangement was defined as "combining self-motivation with the intentions of the leadership." If the writer's plan did not coincide with that of the leadership, it could be rejected. In one instance, a writer had planned a long piece of work, of which he had already written seventy to eighty thousand words. The leading comrade involved did not so much as glance at the manuscript. He told the writer to relinquish his goal, simply because he did not think him capable of finishing the project. The writer had no choice but to discard the body of work he had already completed. Today, perhaps, people would ask why the writer did not persist in his plan. But I believe that before the Party propounded the Hundred Flowers policy, and in areas where there was no truly democratic atmosphere, writers lacked the courage to air their views with the leadership. If they dared to do so, the situation would become highly tense and unpleasant.

Moreover, editors were often given to butchering incoming manuscripts, partly to implement bureaucratic instructions from above. This was also the case when the manuscripts were those of certain older writers. The editorial board found the situation embarrassing, and did not want to make changes on their own authority.

Therefore, they sent manuscripts on to the leadership. At this point, the leading comrades should have talked directly with the authors, asking for their opinions and allowing them to make personal changes. Due to the influence of bureaucratism, however, these consultations were never held, despite the fact that the leading comrades and writers worked in the same department of government. With great confidence, the leaders simply deleted whatever they felt was unsuitable and sent the manuscripts on for printing. Sometimes they seemed to have the Midas touch; mostly, however, they only succeeded in transmuting gold into iron.

I feel that in recent years certain of our leading comrades have indeed been very busy. Not only did they have no time to read or study, but they also lacked opportunities to involve themselves with the life of the masses, that of the workers, peasants, and soldiers. They have therefore failed to keep abreast of the progress in our society, and have formed the habit of addressing problems from a subjective point of view rather than from a practical understanding of the complexities of our life. This lies at the root of their dogmatism and bureaucratism. Rather than following the mass line, they have maintained an attitude of lofty indifference. Feeling as they do that the masses are backward, they lost sight of the progress of others. This indicates that it is they themselves who have failed to keep pace with the ongoing realities of our situation. For this reason, it would be better if each year the leaders set aside a period of time during which to involve themselves with the struggle of the masses. This would benefit them greatly.

IV

I feel that dogmatism not only exerts a serious influence on certain leading comrades, editors, and critics, but has a hold on the readership as well. In this it resembles a disease like the flu, spreading itself through the atmosphere into all areas of daily life. Even writers are unable to guard against the influence of dogmatism. Due to their continual involvement with the realities of life, it is easier for certain writers to discover that dogmatism is at odds with the complexity of our existence and the laws of development. These writers are always anxious to rid themselves of the restraints of dogmatism. As a result, they tend to write according to the dictates of the very dogmatism they are struggling to oppose.

In recent years, formularism has also become a serious problem in the area of literature. We cannot ascribe this entirely to a failure on the part of writers to immerse themselves in the realities of life. Instead, we can place the blame on rampant dogmatism. Because a number of our leaders, editors, critics, and readers assess and criticize pieces of literature according to simplistic and doctrinaire criteria, they become a great burden to the writers. There are few writers who exercise their own free will, and who also dare to scoff at dogmatism. Few writers combine a true understanding of life and art with an aversion to dogmatism, and there are few such writers who are not rejected offhand by editors and publishers. Other writers lack their courage. Moreover, if one were to reject dogmatism entirely in one's writing, editors and publishers of magazines would not accept one's work. Even if one managed to be published, certain critics would raise the banner of dogmatism and influence their readers to attack one from the rear. Under these circumstances, how can formularized work fail to hold sway?

First, when writers go to tour the countryside, dogmatism continues to inhibit their thinking. The "guidelines for creation" establish a set pattern for what they are to observe and the way they are to interpret things in their work. In 1942, Chairman Mao stipulated certain guidelines for creative work at the Yenan Forum on Literature and Art. These were no more than a few basic principles which could be extremely flexible in their application, according to circumstance. The current guidelines, however, are so specific and rigid that writers are expected to follow a set pattern in their depiction of life. Therefore, the guidelines are dogmatic. When a writer goes to the villages in search of characters or subject matter, everything is decided beforehand. He simply discovers things in a prearranged manner. As a result of this restrictive pattern, the writer loses his sensitivity to real life. Even if he is aware of certain things, he is unsure whether to address them in his work. It is said that Wen Yü-k'o of the Sung dynasty was so skillful at painting bamboo that the plants seemed to have sprung from his mind. He had studied these grasses thoroughly and could draw them at will with genuine artistry. Bamboo also springs from the minds of dogmatists in the form of prearranged plans. Their plans, however, arise from wishful thinking rather than from the realities of life. The bamboo in their minds is simply a lifeless formula.

Dogmatists tend to oversimplify or formularize the richness and color of life. They often ask, in an accusing manner: "Does such a condition exist in reality?" "Why don't you portray the character of the middle peasant as being alternately drawn toward capitalism and socialism?" "A Party member is made of special stuff. How could he be brought to tears?" "You portrayed so and so as though he were a villain. Could such a person exist among the working class?" Such examples are too numerous to list. In our new society various creative modes should be allowed free expression, but the snares of dogmatism are everywhere. Consequently, a writer cannot help but inhibit himself in his creative efforts. Rather than striving for achievement, he merely wishes to avoid error. As in the old saying, these writers "tremble with fear, as though they stood before an abyss, or were traversing thin ice."

A theory referred to as the "concept of essence" bears some relation to the matter of dogmatism. In the past two or three years, a theory has arisen that writers should address themselves to the essential qualities of things. Art must reflect the essence of its subject. When this concept becomes enforced as dogma, however, it does great damage. It becomes an endless source of headaches, like a tourniquet around the head. If, for example, one were to describe a traveler sitting at night in a "hard seat" compartment, one might add a small descriptive passage concerning conditions in the coach. Such description is sometimes artistically necessary. The dogmatists, however, might consider these things nonessential and suggest that they be deleted. If one were to write of a poor peasant who is relatively backward, or of an old worker who is jealous of the achievements of others, the dogmatists would say: "Your work does not reflect the essential character of the peasantry or the working class. This will not do!" If one revised according to their dictates, one would be forced to trim off the leaves and branches of one's artistry and be left with a dessicated stem. To the stem could be attached a note which read, "This is a plant of the shrub family. It is tasteless, but can improve the respiration and serve as a tonic for neurosis. Upon taking it you become immune to stroke and other such ailments." According to the dogmatists, this is precisely the way in which literature should serve politics.

By adhering to their concept of essence, dogmatists are unable to understand the contradictions among the people. In clinging to the lifeless doctrine which asserts that the struggle between ourselves and the enemy will become more complicated and acute as the course of socialist construction proceeds, they tend to reject the very fact that these contradictions exist. I once wrote a novella in which there appeared, as a minor character, a worker who was politically backward. He was prone to feelings of jealousy and factionalism. If he saw a cogwheel being put in a wrong place, he would simply fold his hands and do nothing. As a result, the machine was kept from operating properly. Certain editors at the publishing house thought this was unseemly behavior for a worker, and insisted he be changed into a spy. I did not agree and, as a result, the manuscript did not go to press.

A certain comrade wrote several novels dealing with life in the villages, but did not describe the subversive activities of rich peasants. A leading cadre criticized the author in the following statement: "At present, the essential contradiction in the rural areas is that between the socialist road and the capitalist road. Rich peasants are the representatives of capitalism in these areas. Why did you not write about the subversive activities of such peasants?" This comrade regretfully replied: "In the area where I live, we haven't found the rich peasants to be involved in subversive activities; not in any of the villages. Perhaps the peasants in China are different from those of the Soviet Union after the October Revolution." "No," answered the leader, "there is not one wealthy peasant who will not engage in subversive activities. This is the essential nature of their class. Therefore, it is certain that these peasants are involved in such activities in your area. Only because you are politically unaware have you failed to find them out." The comrade involved was very disturbed. He accordingly wrote a novel involving subversive activities on the part of wealthy peasants. Because the story and characters were contrived, the novel was a failure. Not until the height of the drive for agricultural cooperatives, when rich peasants joined them, did this comrade feel relieved of his burden.

Not only do dogmatists know nothing of contradictions among

the people, they lack a full understanding of the contradictions between the enemy and ourselves. If, for example, certain authors
write of the struggle between peasants and landlords, or between the
workers and the bourgeoisie during the period immediately preced-
ing the liberation or even earlier, they are required to portray the
way in which an underground Communist exercised his leadership.
Only in this way can the authors be regarded as having reflected the
essence of history. There is a joke involving a young editor with no
knowledge of Chinese history. After having read a manuscript involving a peasant uprising toward the end of the Ming dynasty, he
said with displeasure: "This story sings the praises of spontaneous
struggle. Why does it not write about the leadership of the Communist Party?"

Even after the founding of the Communist Party, oppressed
classes engaged in a great number of spontaneous struggles. Wherever there is class oppression, there is the possibility of explosive
struggle. It is not necessarily true that revolution can only be fo-
mented whenever and wherever a Communist Party member assumes a leading role. The so-called leadership of the Party can assume various forms. Underground Party members provided
leadership during certain of our previous struggles. Other of our
movements proceeded under the influence and enlightenment of
Communist ideas, but without the actual participation of underground Party members. Under the pressure of dogmatism in the
past, certain writers would contrive a way in which to involve an underground Party member as a character in their work. The Party
member, with whom the author himself was unfamiliar, would be
leading a struggle. When such works are published they are not in
the least convincing. Other writers, knowing they cannot construct
the characters of Party members exercising underground leadership, have simply stopped writing.

Why does dogmatism, as it has been described above, lead to
such disastrous results? This is explained by the way in which dogmatists invariably play the role of safeguarding Marxist literature,
under the protective guise of Marxism itself. Dogmatism is bolstered
from above by the leadership and from below by the masses. In this
way it becomes a force in our society. Today, the bastions of dogmatism have been destroyed. If we do not keep alert, however, not only
could the old dogmatism stage a comeback, but a new dogmatism

could emerge at any time. I therefore consider the struggle with dogmatism to be a protracted one. We cannot regard it as merely a passing gale.

V

There has been much disclosure and discussion in regard to sectarianism during the past year. I have no intention of dealing further with the subject, but I want to raise two minor questions. One involves the nurturing of young writers; the other involves arbitrary literary criticism.

Great effort should be directed to the nurturing of young writers. This is absolutely correct in principle. That which is correct in principle, however, may also incorporate a certain falseness or certain unprincipled elements. Precisely because it is essentially a position of principle, its minor shortcomings cannot be easily discerned. What I mean by this is that occasionally, and in certain circumstances, a biased emphasis is placed on the nurturing of young writers, and on the reliability of newly emergent forces. Sectarian sentiments are to some extent involved in this practice. The adverse effects of sectarianism have resulted in the vilification of older writers; they have been made objects of attack. As for the nurturing of young writers, they have been produced in massive quantities but there is a dearth of quality. At times, they have undergone a forced and premature development. The machinations of authority have given various young writers their start. Some are arbitrarily touted as writers; others with some small measure of achievement become arrogant and arbitrary in their opinion of older writers. This is an outgrowth of sectarianism as practiced by the leadership of literary affairs; we cannot place the entire blame on young writers.

As for the matter of criticism, we always stand in need of critical works if they are correct in their views. However, we must reject criticism which adheres to the dictates of sectarianism. I can cite two incidents as examples of the latter. In 1953, as I passed through Chengchow, Honan, the local high school invited me to lecture students on modes of language study and the writing of compositions. I told them that, as a general rule, an essay should not be structurally complicated at the beginning, or begin with a lengthy but purposeless description of scene. These are common failings among high school students. If the students want to write about a certain conflict, it should be developed in the middle of the composition. They should try to effect a powerful conclusion, rather than being sloppy or leaving the composition at loose ends. At this point, in order to illustrate the ideal form of an essay, I quoted Wang Yü-yang, a great poet of the Ch'ing dynasty: "With the head of a phoenix, the belly of a pig, and the tail of a leopard." One year later, when I had forgotten about the matter, I chanced upon an article by the young critic Wang Ta-hai in the *Honan Daily*. In an acrid, exaggerated tone, he criticized me to his heart's content. The main thrust of his article was a criticism of the phrase, "With the head of a phoenix, the belly of a pig, and the tail of a leopard," which he considered vulgar, nonsensical, and reflective of bourgeois artistic ideas. I would not be surprised if this young critic had never read Wang Yü-yang's thesis on poetry and therefore mistook the metaphor as an invention of my own. But why should he go to such lengths of exaggeration? Why should he adopt so imperious an air and pretend the truth was his alone? This is no more than a mischievous display of sectarianism.

This spring, I published in *Wen-hui-pao* an article entitled "Ch'uang-tso tsa-t'an" (Random Talk on Creation). Following this, Comrade Yao Wen-yüan published an article criticizing various of my arguments. Although I disagreed with a section of Comrade Yao's article, I found his attitude pleasant, and the article itself was a source of enlightenment to me. However, a comrade by the name of Ch'en Hsia also published a critical article in *Meng Ya* (Sprouts). His attitude was extremely unpleasant. In certain sections of the article he did no more than spread groundless rumors, attacking not my writing but me. What is at the root of such criticism? Sectarianism.

Sectarian critics believe themselves to be safeguarding Marxist literature. In truth, they are undermining the cultural endeavors of the Party. They regard their opinions to be representative of the truth. Actually, they resemble the radish: red outside and white inside.

I hope that I shall see no more critical writings like those of Wang Ta-hai and Ch'en Hsia, so that we may foster an excellent critical tradition.

10

AWAY WITH ALL TABOOS REGARDING LITERARY CRITICISM

HUANG YAO-MIEN

People are currently discussing what constitutes the major contradiction in the area of art and literature. In my view, the essential contradiction lies in the fact that our literature fails to fill the needs of the vast readership. In general, high school students regard the works we have published as readable. University students, however, find them entirely bland and are dissatisfied. Their interest lies in reading foreign novels. We are therefore confronted with the urgent task of resolving this problem. Over the years we have persisted in the bad custom of praising the work of famous writers. When Comrade Chao Shu-li's novel *San-li wan* (Sanliwan Village) was published, it received many favorable reviews. Comrade Kang Ch'ao also reviewed the novel, although it seemed to me that he was not entirely sure of his opinions. A reader would be left with an ambiguous impression after reading the review.

This custom also affects the readership in our country. In general, college students have little liking for the literature of contempo-

Abridged from Huang Yao-mien, "Chieh-ch'u wen-i p'i-p'ing ti pai-p'an chin-chi" (Away with All Taboos Regarding Literary Criticism), *Wen-i pao* (Literary Gazette), No. 9, 1957. The article was originally a speech delivered by the author at a discussion meeting sponsored by *Wen-i pao*.

rary China. When questioned, however, they volunteer a positive response to these works; they affirm their excellence. This does not result from any true feeling on the part of the students, but from the influence of *Wen-i pao* (Literary Gazette) and Comrade Kang Ch'ao. While parroting the opinions of others, students may actually be burying themselves in piles of Chinese classical works or voluminous novels by Soviet authors.

A strained relationship exists between our writers and critics. Occasionally, critics will rush through an analysis of the merits and defects of a piece of literature before they have arrived at a true understanding of its import. At times they even lose their sense of propriety and are too extreme in their remarks. This evokes discontent and contempt on the part of the writer, and is but one aspect of the matter. Another aspect unfolds if the writer should refuse to follow the critical suggestions and, instead, writes an article in response. The magazine then refuses to publish the article on the grounds that it "does not consider itself ready to discuss the problem." Such an instance of a writer being unable to respond to criticism is one of the underlying causes of the strained relationship between writers and critics.

The leadership espouses a simplistic theory regarding the relationship between literature and one's world view. The inferior quality of our creative efforts is not unrelated to this simplistic theory. It cannot be doubted that one's world view serves to guide one's creative efforts. But the influence exercised by one's world view over one's creative work is confined to the area of one's essential attitudes and standpoint in regard to certain issues. It cannot directly exercise control over the writer's actual understanding of the people's state of mind, their sentiments, and so forth. In order to resolve this difficulty, the writer must accumulate a wealth of knowledge and experience in regard to the realities of life. According to the theory embraced by many of our comrades, however, it seems that creative problems can be readily solved once our writers acquire a proletarian world view.

It is correct to stress the necessity of ideological remolding, but the process of thought reform is a long one. Nor can we wait until writers have remolded their thinking before requesting that they write. Moreover, one cannot expect to reform one's ideology simply by reading a few books on revolutionary theory. Over the past several years, our writers have been fairly well read. Why, then, are certain writers unable to produce works of literature? If progressive thinking is conducive to literary creation, why have certain of our writers been unable to produce, despite having made great ideological strides over the past seven or eight years? It seems to me that one's world view does not exert a direct, comprehensive influence on one's creative efforts. Such an influence displays itself indirectly. Nevertheless, we have ignored this fact in the past. And now there are those who state that as long as one writes the truth, one will produce works of socialist realism. They believe one's world view functions as a peripheral influence that bears no organic relation to creative activity. This will inevitably lead to an oversimplified assessment of the relationship between theory and creative work. In turn, it will also affect the progress of our literature.

Writers often complain that entirely too many taboos and restrictions have been imposed on them by critics. However, the policies and restrictions imposed on literary criticism are equally numerous. Over the past few years I have written very few articles; this alone might suggest the difficulty of writing pieces of criticism. One is not allowed to be rude or satirical, or to make caustic remarks. One must make allowances for the academic authorities, famous writers, newly emerging writers, veteran writers, the leadership of the Party, and writers with whom the Party wishes to become united. One must consider the inclinations of editors, and the opinions prevalent in current Soviet magazines, as well as allowing oneself an avenue of retreat in the event of a policy shift. With so many considerations in mind, one arrives at fewer ideas of one's own. As a result, one strives to write in a careful, unobtrusive manner that will provoke little response.

Many lofty principles and much inflated rhetoric that have been endlessly reiterated continue to be done so on the presumption that readers are possessed of a spirit which enables them to read the same thing a hundred times over without getting bored. Invariably, a positive statement will be followed by a "but"; a negative statement will be followed by a rationalization. Such phrases as "under certain conditions" and "within certain limits" are frequently employed in order to render a person's statements invulnerable. Consequently, one has no choice but to comport oneself in the most upright manner, cautious and ill at ease. In keeping with this, one tends to write articles in a perfunctory fashion and hand them to the editor simply to get the business over with. Style and individuality are almost entirely ignored. When I wrote articles in the past, whether they were good or bad, I experienced a feeling of satisfaction. At present, I often write only for the purpose of fulfilling my duty, not to mention the pressures of the deadline. As a result, I myself am dissatisfied with various articles I have written.

We would like to propose the following suggestions in regard to literary criticism; they are the result of pooling opinions from all sides: (1) There should be a professional group of critics engaged in the reviewing of books. (2) Such critics should be provided with assistants and reference materials with which to conduct their research. (3) One or two comprehensive literary magazines edited by writers should be started on a trial basis. In this way, writers would be in a better position to express their opinions freely. Such magazines might be of lower quality and less authoritative than the official magazines; but in that they would not be as influential as the official magazines, contributors would have fewer misgivings in speaking their minds. Moreover, those who are criticized would not feel so completely disgraced by the criticism. (4) There should be freedom in the area of criticism. When a critical essay has been made public, it should not be censured too severely. Ruthless censure will only prompt critics to produce cautious criticism that is entirely safe and offensive to no one; or they will stop writing criticism and seek another line of work. (5) The writers themselves should be encouraged to write criticism. They should also be encouraged to write of their own experiences in literary creation, or to write a response to criticism addressed to themselves. (6) Critics should be encouraged to imbue their writing with greater artistic technique and a wider variety of styles.

11

THOUGHTS FROM THE HUNDRED FLOWERS BLOOMING

HUANG YAO-MIEN

In order to implement the policy "let a hundred flowers bloom," I believe we must first rid ourselves of various ideological stumbling blocks. Certain of these stumbling blocks derive from the ways in which people interpret the phenomenon of literature. I would like to jot down my thoughts on the subject.

We often hear quoted Lenin's statement that literary undertakings should serve as part of the well-planned, regimented Party cause.

Lenin was entirely correct in this, and we will continue to abide by his ideas. This, however, does not excuse our neglecting the following qualification of Lenin's: "It is indisputable that such undertakings are highly incompatible with mechanical equalization and standardization, and with the subjection of the minority to the majority. It is also indisputable that such undertakings should be provided for with considerable freedom allowed in the areas of individual creativeness, personal interest, imagination, and systems of form and content. All this is certain and can only reinforce the idea that

Huang Yao-mien, "Yu pai-hua ch'i-fang so hsiang-tao ti" (Thoughts from the Hundred Flowers Blooming), *Wen-i pao* (Literary Gazette), June 1957.

literature, as an element of the proletarian party cause, cannot be rigidly equated with the rest of the cause."

It is precisely due to their neglect of this statement that certain people insist on an absolute equation of literature with the Party cause as a whole in the resolution of problems. In keeping a close watch on mechanical equalization, they ignore the characteristics of literature. For the same reason, these people tend to employ standardization in the resolution of problems. They demand that the literary sensibilities of the minority be subjected to those of the majority, or those of the majority to those of the minority. This is an offhand rejection of the considerable freedom allowed for the maneuvering of personal interests under the general policy of serving the workers, peasants, and soldiers.

There are those so overly sensitive that they label anyone an individualist who pronounces his own literary preferences. If one mentions the imagination, one is likely to be branded an idealist or a violator of the principles of realism. If one asserts that an emphasis should be placed on artistic form, one will certainly be accused of formalism.

Lenin was quite explicit in his statements, and there should be no justification for so biased an interpretation. People with so incomplete an understanding of Lenin's ideas, rather than ascribing any blame to the Party or to Lenin, must blame themselves for their own poor grasp of Lenin's work.

People are often fond of saying that literature should reflect the essence of reality, the essentials of man's nature as he lives in society. This statement is, of course, correct. It does not, however, present us with any reason for neglecting the other aspect of the matter; it is through a description of the outward forms of life that literature can give expression to reality. It is therefore not feasible to define any such essence in so excessively rigid a way. A man's life may take various forms, and is a fabric of many interrelationships; its richness and color derives from this. At times a man's mood may range from seriousness and tension to lightheartedness. Relations between men may assume the form of comradeship or of family ties. A man may or may not have given expression to his ideas. It is required of literature that it depict in great detail the various aspects of human life and the interrelationships among people. Such a depiction can be rendered in a straightforward manner, in an oblique manner, or by means of implied description with contrasting effects. Moreover, the depiction can be presented in different styles and in various emotional contexts. Therefore, in that literature reflects the essence of reality through the depiction of various phenomena in life, it need not address itself to such essentials alone. This can vary according to context.

Ignoring the fact that it is through the presentation of life itself that literature reflects the essence of reality, certain people demand that literary works be written in accordance with decisions made at meetings. They assess every character, his words and actions, according to whether or not he displays certain essential qualities. As a result, literature loses a certain richness and its characters lose their individuality. Thus, literature cannot function as vivid and appealing propaganda and is no more than oversimplified indoctrination.

I have often heard it said that literature reflects the realities of life. Life has its beauty, and it is the writer's task to assimilate and typify such beauty, raising it to a higher plane than that of actual life and lending it a more representative quality. This is also true, but there exists another aspect to the matter. It is our task not only to know this world, but to reshape it. Therefore, in their ongoing experiences of life people not only come to know the world, but also form diverse attitudes in regard to objective realities.

It is precisely because they ignore this other aspect of the matter that certain people regard the act of literary creation as picking shells on a sandy beach, in that it is the writer's task to gather and lend order to the facts of life. There are even those who try to identify, one by one, the characters and details in a piece of literature. If these characters and details can be discovered in real life, they will regard the novel as realistic. If not, the work will be considered a violation of realism. In one poem there is a line which reads, "Our hopes are as lovely as the morning glow." There are those who consider this line to be mistaken in its meaning; the morning glow will soon disappear. Will this be the case with our hopes?

If we were to follow their view, creative effort would be an impossible thing and literature would be no more than an accumulation of data. The imagination would be stifled and literature would be a record of events.

If we were to follow their view, a writer would not actively experience life through a process of remolding objective reality but would passively assimilate whatever life had to offer. Only when stirred by some objective situation would he examine it.

I believe that if someone could explain these literary problems it would facilitate the implementation of the policy of letting a hundred flowers bloom.

12

CAN A DRAMATIC ENSEMBLE BE ADMINISTERED LIKE AN ARMY UNIT?

A VISIT WITH THE DRAMATIC ENSEMBLE SUBORDINATE TO THE ART TROUPE OF THE POLITICAL DEPARTMENT UNDER THE PEOPLE'S LIBERATION ARMY

SCHOLARS AND SOLDIERS

How is the Dramatic Ensemble of the Political Department structured as an art organization? At present, the ensemble continues to regiment its actors in squads, platoons, and companies. This basic structure is further divided into actors teams and performance groups, the actors teams being subdivided into a first team, a second team, and so on. Several months ago, actors were still required to ask permission of their team leaders if they wanted to go out during their spare time. Even when they went to observe and study life, they were required to go in groups of several persons. Although it is no longer mandatory that they ask for leave, they are still expected to mention it. Even the actors' living quarters must conform to army barracks regulations. A lamp must be placed two meters above the

Chang Pao-hsin, "Neng yung tai-ping ti fang-shih tai chü-t'uan ma?" (Can a Dramatic Ensemble Be Administered Like an Army Unit?), *Wen-i pao* (Literary Gazette), No. 9, 1957.

floor. This makes it difficult for an actor to read, let alone prepare a role.

The organizational structure of squad, platoon, and company is absolutely necessary to army units. It is doubtful, however, that such a structure lends itself to the creative endeavors of a group of artists or actors. The Dramatic Ensemble has a nominal art committee of its own which is without power. Comrade Lan Ma is the art director, but this is a titular position only. What is his specific position within the Dramatic Ensemble? Comrade Lan has said, "I do not even know myself." The Political Department of the Central Military Committee exercises leadership over the Dramatic Ensemble in the same way it administered propaganda groups in the past. At any time, the higher authorities may phone or send a message requesting that "Wan-shui ch'ien-shan" (Thousands of Rivers, Hundreds of Mountains)[1] be performed for the entertainment of a select few. Actor Feng Kuang-hui states: "Comrades in the Dramatic Ensemble do not know in the morning what they are to do in the afternoon; they do not know today what they are to do tomorrow."

Comrade Lan Ma said that the major impediment to progress within the Dramatic Ensemble is a poor understanding of art on the part of certain leading comrades; they are also incapable of leading the Dramatic Ensemble in a manner suited to the characteristics of an art organization. Comrade Lan once talked with General T'an Cheng, director of the Political Department, in order to discuss the question of staffing. After much discussion, Comrade T'an said, "In my opinion, our staff is quite sufficient." In truth, the current staff does not meet full performance requirements, and the ensemble is forced to engage a large number of temporary workers. The wages paid to these workers amount to $20,000 of the entire yearly performance expenditure. Comrades in the ensemble are anxious to reform the military administration so ill-suited to the demands of an art organization. They would prefer that the Dramatic Ensemble be converted into a People's Liberation Army Theater. This opinion was conveyed to leading comrades. These leaders, however, decided that if the Dramatic Ensemble were to be converted into theater, extra buildings would have to be built. The current housing shortage precluded the possibility of such a conversion.

[1] A play by Ch'en Ch'i-t'ung depicting the hardships of the Red Army during the Long March.

The Dramatic Ensemble is now under the leadership of the Art Troupe, as are the Performing Ensemble and the Acrobatic Ensemble. The Dramatic Ensemble has no power of its own, and everything must be approved by the Art Troupe. Even the selection of a play for stage production is the responsibility of the Party committee of the Art Troupe. In truth, members of the Party committee are for the most part acquainted with acrobatics and song and dance performance. When they are faced with a decision regarding the selection of a play, they do not even read the script beforehand.

The Art Troupe has an office staff of approximately twenty persons. The Dramatic Ensemble, however, lacks an official seal and must send people to the office of the Art Troupe for incoming and outgoing documents. At a full meeting at which people were to openly express their opinions, certain people who wanted to simplify the administrative structure suggested that the leadership consider dissolving the headquarters of the Art Troupe. Comrade Ch'en Ch'i-t'ung, Deputy Director of the Propaganda Department, said: "This suggestion was made at a meeting to openly express people's opinions. Had it been presented at some other time, it would have been an indication of problems in your attitude regarding our system. Today you want to dissolve the Art Troupe. Perhaps tomorrow you will want to dissolve the Political Department and, a few days later, the Party itself. What will the world come to?"

Comrade Lan Ma said to me, "If so military a mode of administration is not changed, there will be no good prospect for the Dramatic Ensemble." The ensemble is unsure of the precise scope of its functions and powers. Because the leaders do not understand the practicalities of performance, they believe that by providing less money and a smaller work force they can fulfill the need for economy. With less money, however, fewer plays could be staged in fewer performances; a good number of actors would be idle. Many idle actors would mean a great waste of human resources, but the leadership takes no notice of this. Is this true economy, or merely a sham?

AN OFFICIAL CAN TRAMPLE THOSE BELOW HIM

Even matters of a purely artistic nature concerning the Dramatic Ensemble are decided by authorities according to rank. One must be absolutely obedient to superiors. The power to select a play for stage production does not lie in the hands of the art committee or the art director; the matter is often decided by a certain leading comrade. After long consideration, those comrades who are responsible for the selection of plays, as well as members of the ensemble, decided to stage "K'ung-ch'ueh-tan" (The Peacock's Gall).[2] When the matter came into the hands of Ch'en Yi, Director of the Department of Culture, he did not make a concrete analysis of the situation. He did no more than say casually, "What's the use of staging this play?" The entire project fell through. When Comrade Ch'en Yi attended the drama festival, "Yang-tzu-chiang pien" (By the Side of the Yangtze River) impressed him as being a good play. He decided to stage the play, and a great deal of effort was expended. It closed, however, after only fourteen performances. The actors were critical of the play at the time. When meetings were held within the Party, however, the actors were admonished, "As Party members, you should say nothing critical of this play." Actress Pai Hui-wen said, "Here we are not allowed to discuss or explore artistic matters. All such issues are determined through administrative pressure." Comrade Li Wei-hsin, one of the actors of "By the Side of the Yangtze River," said to me, "I have my own views regarding the role I play. That which the author praises is precisely what I feel must be criticized. I gave the director my opinion." He said, "This play is chosen by headquarters. I have been working in the army for a long time. I like to obey orders."

An extremely strange system of censorship is enforced within the Dramatic Ensemble. When a play is selected for performance, the script is sent to the authority in charge. He arrives at a decision, although no one can know whether or not he has read the manuscript. If it is decided to stage the play, one can assume there is no problem with the script. The leadership, however, is likely to review the play during rehearsal or in performance, and will probably do so time and again. "T'ung-chih chien" (Between the Comrades) was reviewed during twenty-three performances. "Chao-hsiang na-t'ien" (The Day the Photograph Was Taken) was reviewed six times during rehearsal, but was actually performed only twice. Comrade Ch'en

---

[2] A play by Kuo Mo-jo satirizing the Kuomintang government.

Ch'i-t'ung, Deputy Director of the Propaganda Department, used his authority to make changes in his own play while it was actually in production, rather than in the original script. This was the case with "Thousands of Rivers, Hundreds of Mountains," and with "Between the Comrades." The implementation of changes on stage, even the changing of a single scene, results in a great waste of material and human resources.

A FEW THEORETICAL PROBLEMS

A few years ago, Comrade Ch'en Yi, Director of the Department of Culture, propounded the guideline "focus on the performance of song and dance." This guideline caused great harm to various dramatic endeavors within the army. Experienced and accomplished actors were transferred to other posts, one after another. At present, comrades in the Dramatic Ensemble under the Political Department continue to have difficulty resigning themselves to a lifelong career of dramatic performance. This is because ensembles in the army units are constantly subject to drastic revision, and many people face the danger of being ousted at any time. The leadership has not paid sufficient attention to dramatic endeavors. When Comrade Ch'en Yi addressed the ensembles, it was his habit to focus on matters of song and dance; only at the end of his report would he add a few words concerning drama. It is said that he did not learn the significance of drama until the National Dramatic Festival, at which time he remarked, "So drama can also reflect reality!"

The concept of subject matter also caused considerable problems among the leaders. They thought that only by employing soldiers as characters could drama be regarded as serving the soldiers themselves. Comrade Lan Ma stated: "In serving the soldiers we are not necessarily confined to performing as soldiers. The important thing is that they enjoy our play, and that it enables them to better understand the situation in our country; it should also increase their knowledge in various fields. These fighters lead a soldier's life, and when they come to the theater they are confronted with more soldiers. In their view, the soldiers's life as described by the playwright may often be less interesting than the events of real life. It is necessary to praise our soldiers, but it is not necessary that this be a prerequisite in the selection of a play. If a play concerning soldiers were well written, not only would the Dramatic Ensemble perform it, but other theaters would voluntarily stage it as well. I feel that the criterion for selecting a play must be its quality."

Comrade Ch'en Ch'i-t'ung and others published an article in *Jen-min jih-pao* (People's Daily), for which they were criticized. Even so, he insisted at a full meeting of the Dramatic Ensemble: "We will continue to employ socialist realism. No other creative mode is permitted." Actor Li Wei-hsin stated:

Last year, Comrade Fu To wrote a play entitled "Yu chei-yang i-ke-jen" (There Is Such a Man). When it was staged for censorship, a leading comrade remarked, "How can an army staff officer be unalert?" As a result, the playwright was forced to convert the regimental staff officer in the play to a battalion staff officer, and finally to a cadre at the company level. Even this would not do. What was to be done? The portrayal of army cadres who have lost their vigilance might involve a leak of the army's classified secrets. After much consideration, the playwright finally chose the head of a mess hall for the character who is unalert. When Comrade Fu Chung saw this version, he thought it highly instructive.

WALLS AND GAPS

Members of the Dramatic Ensemble under the Political Department fall into three categories: older comrades who had experienced the war against the Japanese and the War of Liberation, veteran actors who had long been involved with the theater in the Nationalist areas, and young students who have recently joined the revolution. Certain of the older comrades consider themselves privileged, and despise those who had been actors in the Nationalist areas, referring to them as "old actors." At one meeting, Comrade Chou T'su stated: "In our ensemble, one is not supposed to be a good actor unless one is a Communist. I therefore think that if I can manage to give a good performance I might become a Party member." Sun Hsien-yüan stated: "Here a Party member ranks higher than a Youth League member, and a Youth League member is above the masses. Therefore, Party membership is the only indication of one's virtue."

Comrade Hsu Li had performed in many plays, and even starred in movies while living in a Nationalist area. In the past few years, however, he has not had a chance to perform. When "Ti-hsia chang-ch'eng" (The Underground Great Wall) was to be rehearsed, a list of actors was published. According to the list, two comrades without Party membership were to play the leading roles. Two Party members saw the list and made a great scene. The leadership was therefore compelled to replace the two non-Party members with the two comrades who had caused the commotion. Comrade Chou Ts'u told other stories: A comrade from a liberated area who was a poor actor was nevertheless to be trained and encouraged to go on. However, another comrade who was not a Party member, and who was unable to read his lines well, was transferred to another job.

THE PLAY IS PRODUCED IN
AN ABUSIVE MANNER

In the Dramatic Ensemble under the Political Department, the relationship between director and actor is not one of artistic cooperation. The director is usually of a higher rank than the actors. As a result, even in rehearsal they behave toward each other as though a battlefield situation existed, with the corresponding relationship between commander and the lower ranks. This is especially the case with Comrade Ch'en Ch'i-t'ung. He is Deputy Director of the Propaganda Department. When he came to the ensemble, he had a higher rank and more authority than anyone else and could do whatever he chose. When the window in the rehearsal room could not be opened, he simply broke it. It is extremely hard on the actors when he chooses to direct plays. Comrade Li Wei-hsin states: "His method is to first break your pride; then you will accept his will. How did he manage to break people's pride? Through abuse, brutal and arrogant abuse."

Whenever Ch'en Ch'i-t'ung conducts a rehearsal, a murderous atmosphere fills the room, and every actor is panic-stricken. During the staging of "Thousands of Rivers, Hundreds of Mountains" he thought one of the actors had failed to depict his role of a Red Army soldier. He punished the man by forcing him to march double-time. Whenever actors fail in their performance, he tells them, "Dammit! I was wounded before you were born!" Or, "You could not even carry the number of bullets that have struck me, you wretches!" At one point, actor Kao K'un had his own ideas about the role he was to play. Ch'en cursed him loudly in front of others, saying, "You are absolutely rotten!" In another such instance, the workers did not know what was wrong; they became so frightened they took to their heels. He roared after them, "Hurry! Someone catch them and bring them back to me!" He is forever cursing during rehearsals: "Fuck off! Idiot! Good-for-nothing!" If an actor is slow in mastering a role, he or she could be denied the part at any time. Once, when Chu Ch'i missed a performance due to excessive tension, Ch'en threatened, "I'll have your background examined!" He often alleges an involvement on your part in some political problem, or even threatens to have you placed in custody.

At one meeting, Comrade Chao Shen-lin, the leader of the Performance Group, said indignantly, "I received my commission as a major from the state. But Ch'en Ch'i-t'ung is forever threatening to have my commission rescinded." The young actress Pai Hui-wen said to me: "As soon as I enter the rehearsal room my heart begins to palpitate, and I am in no mood for creative effort. How can the actors speak of their art under such circumstances?" Comrade Chao Shen-lin stated: "When you news reporters were accused by a minister's aide, you were able to write articles and editorials in protest. We are forever being accused. We have faced more accusations of greater vehemence than you have."

13

OPINIONS OPENLY EXPRESSED DURING THE RECTIFICATION CAMPAIGN AT THE WRITERS' UNION

Several forums were held during late May and early June by the Party Group of the Writers' Union. Non-Party writers, translators, critics, and editors were invited to criticize problems in the literary field. The following are excerpts of criticisms from some distinguished writers and critics:

MAO TUN: The Writers' Union is under the leadership of the Communist Party, and helps the government to carry out its literary policy. Writers hold the same views. The Writers' Union works that way. But it has ignored writers' benefits, and has become institutionalized. This has given most writers a feeling that the Writers' Union is only a bureaucratic office for carrying out the government's literary policy, not a union for their own interests.

TSANG K'E-CHIA: When we were in Chungking [the capital of China during the war against the Japanese, under the control of the Kuomintang government], Party and non-Party writers could talk to each other about anything. We were quite close in Shanghai, too. But things are different in Peking. There have been fewer intimate con-

"Tso hsieh tsai cheng-feng chung kuang-k'ai yen-lu" (Opinions Openly Expressed during the Rectification Campaign at the Writers' Union), *Wen-i pao* (Literary Gazette), No. 11, June 16, 1957.

versations among friends. . . . In Chungking we had very good relationships with Party writers. But there has been a line separating us from them [in Peking]. Party writers are arrogant. People said that writers from the old areas [the areas liberated by the Communists before 1949] were the main force; that the writers from Chiang Kai-shek controlled areas were not worth much. Some Party writers regard themselves as superior. . . . The Writers' Union should pay more attention to non-Party people. As far as I know, there are many non-Party people who have opinions to express and have complained at meetings. Please get people from democratic parties to attend the meetings. It will be unreasonable not to get them.

CHIN JEN: The Writers' Union should speak for the writers, should become the union for writers. It should not only be a transmitter of the government's policy. We can read about the policy in the newspapers. It should listen to the writer's views first. Then there will be less bureaucracy. In the past few years, the literary policy of our country has been wavering, has always followed that of the Soviet Union. We should have our own independent literary policy. It should be made clear on what our literary undertakings should depend: the writers, or the Party leadership?

HUANG CH'IU-YÜN: The rectification in literary circles has not worked well. The lower levels have too many worries and not enough courage. This happens because the upper levels are not liberal. I've always felt they are not. Some time ago, Comrade Chou Yang criticized Liu Shao-t'ang as "having no sense of how high heaven is and how heavy the earth is" [having no sense of how to behave himself]. These remarks are not nice. They will hurt people's positive feelings. Some leadership comrades talked about Wang Meng's story "Tsu-chih-pu hsin-lai ti nien-ch'ing jen" (A Young Man Arrives at the Organization Department) one way, but later entirely the other way. Chou Yang didn't like the story at all. But his talk with the press about the story sounded quite different. One cannot see how the change came about.

LI K'O: Whether a play can be performed depends on yes or no from the comrade in charge in the Propaganda Department. When we were going to put on the play "Mei-kuo sheng-huo fang-shih" (The American Way of Life), Comrade Chou Yang said that the most important thing was the struggle against the enemy and that the play didn't correctly reflect the American way of life. Comrade Chang Kuang-nien said that the emphasis was on the wrong place. So the play was not performed.

TING LI: It was said that Wang Meng's story "A Young Man Arrives at the Organization Department" was discussed at the meeting of the Party Group of the Writers' Union, and was disapproved at the meeting. I thought of writing about it, but didn't because I was afraid of disagreeing with the Party Group. . . . Some literary manuscripts have to be censored by the Party Propaganda Department, such as manuscripts received by *Jen-min wen-hsüeh* (People's Literature). I don't think such censorship is good. The editors should be independent in their thinking.

TANG TA-CH'ENG: *Literary Gazette* made mistakes. To criticize it was all right. But the Writers' Union did it so harshly that it looked as though it would destroy it right away. . . . Such criticism was horrible because there was no free discussion. No disagreement was allowed. The criticism of one article was final. This horrified writers. . . . Sometimes if your views disagree with those of the leadership, you will also receive harsh treatment from the system. This has caused many literary critics endless worries. Nowadays, there are few literary critics.

SHU WU: I don't fear any harsh condemnation. What I fear is what's behind it—the order from the authorities. It's difficult to do any theoretical criticism. It seems that with Chairman Mao's "Talks at the Yenan Literary Forum," all the problems have been solved, and that the "Talks" are the culmination of truth. The chairman's "Talks" gave directions, but cannot solve all the problems. They paved the way for truth. We have to try it out ourselves.

WANG TSENG-CHI: It is a complicated job to write literary history. A few books of literary history have been published, but all of them suffer from dogmatism. Literary works are evaluated on the basis of the authors' political background. The evaluation of Mr. Shen

Ts'ung-wen is not adequate.[1] He wrote several articles sympathetic to the Communists persecuted by the Kuomintang in the thirties. His situation was complicated and should not be dealt with in a black-and-white way. Regarding his case, a further review is needed.

[1] Shen Ts'ung-wen was one of the most important fiction writers in modern China. He was criticized by the leftists in the thirties as empty and thoughtless because he showed no active interest in the leftist cause. However, because of his critical views of the social conditions of his time, some of his works were censored by the Kuomintang, then the ruling government.

THE POLEMICS OF
REALISM

REALISM IN THE
SOCIALIST ERA

14

THE BROAD ROAD OF REALISM—A REASSESSMENT OF REALISM

HO CHIH (CH'IN CHAO-YANG)

In discussing scholarly problems, people with opinions should express them. If one says something wrong, the correct ideas of others will emerge as an antidote. As long as there is some truth in one's opinions, one can learn from others through the exchange of ideas. It is from this position that I write this essay.

Turning now to the problems of realism, I want to talk about the handicaps stemming from dogmatism.

I

Literary realism is not a set of sanctioned laws. It arises out of literary and artistic practice and then becomes a principle to be followed. Its duty is to be absolutely faithful to actual life, to reflect it artistically and eventually to have some effect on it. When involved in literary and artistic creation, writers must look at life and art. This does not lead to the rigid acceptance of any particular world view, al-

Ho Chih (Ch'in Chao-yang), "Hsien-shih chu-i—kuang-k'uo ti tao-lu" (The Broad Road of Realism—A Reassessment of Realism), *Jen-min wen-hsüeh* (People's Literature), September 1956.

though one could be influenced and governed by a world view. During the whole process of literary and artistic creation, one should take broad objective reality as the subject. One must view this reality as the crux of one's writing, and attempt to influence actual life. The portrayal of life is not a matter of mechanical reproduction. Rather, it is the pursuit of the truth of life and art. This is the basic premise of realism. All the other concrete principles of realism should be based on it. If we sacrifice this when considering some concrete problem, the meaning of realism and of creative technique will become narrow and vague.

Thus, the literature of realism encompasses actual life and all literary possibilities. Since life is broad and rich, the perspective, content, and style of the literature of realism can be very broad and rich according to the author's ability to know and portray life artistically. What a broad arena it gives the author! If literary realism limits the author in any way, it is in how far and how expertly he is allowed to go by the limitations of life, art, and the author's own capability.

The literature of realism has its own criteria, but when we seek these criteria, we must not forget the basic premise of realism stated earlier. We must judge this literature by seeing whether it achieves a true portrait of life and a depth of thought when the author has tried to mirror objective reality. The thought and purpose of the literature of realism are only achieved through a true, artistic portrait.

Here we face a very important question: Is it enough for literature to be based on this premise alone?

One may believe that one respects reality, writes realistically, uses life as the source of one's creative writings, and seeks artistic realism. But objective reality is extremely broad and complicated, as is the way of artistic creation. This is why authors are bound to have many problems when they try to portray life. What, then, is real? What is artistic? How can we achieve the real, the artistic and a high level of thought? How do we discern the different qualities of each piece of work and each author? Deciding what is real and what is artistic is an abstract matter and is not easily grasped. Since ancient times, many authors have dedicated their whole lives to seeking concrete methods of realism. Many succeeded in finding their own methods of realism and produced profound and immortal masterpieces. We should be able to extract some concrete rules and principles for realism from their experiences.

Marx and Engels have offered us many interpretations of this particular problem. In a clear and concise statement, Engels said: "In my opinion, realism does not mean just reflecting the reality of details; it means the true portrayal of typical personalities in a typical environment." This is a famous principle because (1) it comes out of the premise that the source and purpose of realism is life, but works of realism are not just copies of life; (2) it establishes the most reasonable artistic processes by which an author represents life in a nutshell. This principle fully interprets and accords with the characteristics of art. In other words, Engels has shown us a definite way of achieving artistry and true realism. His principle has not reduced the scope of the literature of realism for creating artistically and truthfully. On the contrary, it has pointed out a clear path to the author to make full use of his creative talent.

But people of future generations will not be satisfied with these principles and theories. In the literary realm, many more questions need to be answered. For instance, how does one truthfully portray "the typical personalities in the typical environment?" What is typical and what is atypical? When there are unprecedented changes in history and life, shouldn't there be some developments in literary realism itself? Or should we re-prescribe some of the old concrete principles of realism? When people examine the position of literary creations in certain periods and discover problems, they will naturally bring out some new ideas; but what is the right way of introducing these ideas?

All these questions certainly should be discussed. People should keep on searching and should struggle with various incorrect ideas. While doing so, they will surely find more correct and advanced solutions than before. Some of these solutions may be based on realism itself; some on the direction of the whole literary endeavor; some on the relationship between literature and reality; and some on politics. These approaches are different, but they are all significant as answers to the questions raised above.

For instance, it is an absolute truth now to say that an author's ability to penetrate life will be sharpened if he studies Marxism.

Those against the study of Marxism are actually opposed to the idea that a world view guides and controls realism. They are also opposed to the idea that people should more soberly comprehend the principles of realism. Literary undertakings should be free from the capitalist bonds of money and personal reputation as well as the theory that "art is above all," so that the author can create art freely, can fully develop his creative talents in order to make literature fulfill its function of representing and influencing actual life. The working people have become the self-conscious creators of history and the masters of their time; they are undergoing great and heart-rending struggles in order to change their destiny. But our authors suffer from a fatal weakness—their failure to work with politics and with the masses. Thus, the authors' ability to represent historical reality creatively is hindered, and the development of literary undertakings is hampered.

It was in such a situation that Chairman Mao presented his principles in "Talks at the Yenan Forum on Art and Literature." His words had a decisive and progressive effect on our literary undertakings. There is no doubt that the spirit of his statement will deeply affect the literary undertakings of the future. As for literary problems, there are many other significant statements available for answering a series of esthetic questions, for analyzing an author and his work, and for fully developing the dynamic quality of realism.

However, if we look seriously at the past, we can see that for several years, despite many accomplishments, our literature has suffered from unhealthy symptoms. Sometimes the newly proposed principles in realism are not scientific enough and their meanings are confusing. Sometimes there are inadequate elucidations and one-sided interpretations of correct principles, leading truth to lose its flexible relationship with practice and to be straitjacketed. Sometimes an ambiguous slogan emerges and those who interpret it stretch its meaning to the extreme. . . . In short, the discussions of the problems, the interpretations of the questions, and the formulation of the rules should make the guidelines to realism more concrete, clear, and exact. Instead, they have departed from the major premise of realism and created restrictions in and misunderstandings of realism. They have led to many rigid rules and taboos in the literary field and impeded the development of the principles of literary realism and the creativeness of authors.

II

Let us look at the definition of "socialist realism."

The creation of this term has historical significance because it points to the development of a realistic literature in a new historical era—a more aware and self-conscious era. It reminds authors that they should look at the new life from the conscious, socialist viewpoint in order to be better able to grasp and portray reality. However, since socialist realism was defined in the Charter of the All-Union Congress of Soviet Writers, many people have made wrong interpretations of the definition, as Simonov pointed out in his report to the second All-Union Congress of Soviet Writers. For instance, some believe that socialist realism is opposed to the old realism, that it is merely a positive realism and not simultaneously a critical realism. According to Simonov, this kind of argument is the origin of the "no-conflict" theory. Moreover, there are people who think that socialist realism should prescribe literary style itself and that it should permit the existence of only one literary style.

All these wrong and one-sided interpretations of socialist realism originate from the errors made by the interpreters themselves. But we have to say further that these errors have something to do with the lack of a scientific approach in the definition itself. Let me quote Simonov:

The resolution passed in our First Congress concisely and clearly defined the essential quality of the principles of socialist realism, as follows:

"Socialist realism, which is the basic device of Soviet literature and literary criticism, demands of the artist a true, historically concrete portrayal of reality in its revolutionary development."[1]

This definition is absolutely correct; it can stand the test of time and has expressed essentially the most important requirement our society makes of literary works.

But the resolution goes on to read as follows:

[1] From *First All-Union Congress of Soviet Writers, 1937: Stenographic Report* (Moscow, 1934), p. 666. The translation is based on that of Walter N. Vickery, *The Cult of Optimism* (Bloomington: Indiana University Press, 1963), p. 70.

"Whereby truthfulness and historical concreteness (of artistic representation) must be combined with the task of ideological reform and the education of the working people in the spirit of socialism."

I feel that the second half of the resolution is inexact and open to misinterpretation. It can be understood as a qualification: Yes, socialist realism demands of the artist a truthful portrayal of reality; such a portrayal must, however, be combined with the task of ideologically reforming the people in the spirit of socialism. That is, truth and historical concreteness may or may not be combined with the task; truth and a historical interpretation may not always serve this aim. This kind of arbitrary interpretation of the definition appeared most frequently in the works of some authors and critics following the war. They make the excuse that reality should be represented from the standpoint of progress and that therefore they should endeavor to "improve" reality.

I entirely agree with Simonov's words, but I would further point out that there are illogical elements in the resolution defining socialist realism. If we say that truthfulness and historical concreteness in artistic portrayal does not include "the spirit of socialism," that the former cannot perform the task of educating the people and has to be combined with other things, then what is "the spirit of socialism"? We must assume that it does not exist in actual life and art, that it is merely an abstract idea in the mind of the author, and that it should be forced into literary works. In other words, objective reality is not absolutely worthy of respect. The fixed, abstract idea of the "spirit of socialism" as well as the aspirations of authors are so important that when necessary, "objective reality" should be made to serve an abstract, rigid, subjective concept. Consequently, literary works may depart from actual life and may even become the tool of certain political concepts.

Since the so-called spirit of socialism is one of the subjective concepts of an author, it must be part of the author's world view. Can the author's world view and its effect on his creative practice be separated from "truthfulness in artistic portrayal"? Any accomplished author can prove that the answer is no. The world view talked about here, of course, is the Marxist world view. This world view will have organic, natural effects when the author is in the process of realistic, artistic creation and of experiencing life, creating images, and completing literary works. In other words, the author's thought—his world view and his imagery—will have a dynamic effect on his searching, knowing, and portraying of reality. Therefore this kind of effect is organically present in truth and does not need to be added or combined with anything.

We should try to understand the *truthful, historically concrete portrayal of reality in its revolutionary development* and the *truthfulness and historical concreteness of artistic portrayal* in connection with the principle of *the typical personalities in the typical environment.* Engels criticized Askenazy[2] for her inability to portray workers from the standpoint of revolutionary development and claimed that her writings were not realistic enough; it was in this connection that he stated the principle of "the typical personalities in the typical environment." In our present era, it is hard to imagine how one can portray the typical personalities in the typical environment if one neglects the complex influences of revolutionary development on people or if one ignores the true features of actual life in revolutionary development. Similarly, if one abandons the method of the typical, it would be hard to portray the reality of revolutionary development or to achieve quality in artistic portrayal. This method is not just for portraying characters but also for all kinds of literary forms and creative processes.

The resolution defining socialist realism says that "truthful portrayal of reality in its revolutionary development" and "truth of artistic representation" must be "combined with the education of the working people in the spirit of socialism." We wonder how the first two can be separated from ideology, from the education of the working people. The definition implies that socialist realism can be separated from the problem of the typical because the typical and the education of the working people cannot be separated. This conclusion is misleading because realistic literature, by its very nature, fuses the following things: artistic portrayal, truth, the education of the people, the typical, and the method of typification.

We have other reasons for questioning the definition of socialist realism. Since the definition was established, no one has been able to offer a perfect and conclusive interpretation of its meaning. An interpretation considered quite correct yesterday may be denounced today. Realism is not just a realism of criticism. It is very difficult to classify some of the literary works of realism published in today's

---

[2] A phonetic translation of the name from the Chinese.

capitalistic world and some published in China after the May Fourth movement. What kind of realism do these works belong to? It is difficult to set an absolute line dividing the literature of the new realism from that of the old realism according to the characteristics and content of the works.

We could call our present realism "realism in the socialist era" if we accept that the time is now different, that Marxism and revolutionary movements have had a great influence on human life, that realistic literature has developed to an unprecedented stage where authors have become very conscious about objective reality, and that the realistic literature growing out of such a situation has inevitably developed in certain directions. We can and should call upon authors to learn Marxism and reform their thought and ideology in order to enable literature to better reflect and affect life. However, I think when our experience in literary practice is inadequate, it is difficult and unwise for us to use a few simple terms to create rigid rules and interpretations concerning the literature of realism and realism in the socialist era.

III

I want to examine the defects in the definition of socialist realism because some mediocre ideas arising from it have merged with similar mediocre ideas in China to impose various literary dogmas. This is shown in some people's inadequate understanding and interpretation of "Talks at the Yenan Forum on Literature and Art" and in their interpretation of the relationship between art and politics.

The literary undertaking is part of the people's revolutionary endeavors; it *should* be of service to politics and to the working people. Since ancient times, there has never been any literature which is not tendentious, which is "pure" or "realistic" in a way that does not concern the people. It is of great importance for us to inform those who believe that art is above everything, those individualist and humanists who are isolated from politics and the people, of the principle that literature and art should serve politics and the working people, especially when we are living in an epoch of the people's democratic and socialist revolutions and of an extremely sharp class struggle. At such a time, if authors attempt to escape from the great mass struggle and from significant social change, if they restrict themselves to life and to thoughts of the individualist intelligentsia, how can they tread firmly on the road of realism? How can they give a true picture of the people and the time? How can they not show themselves to be petit bourgeois? How can they not distort reality? To be of service to politics and to the working people means that the author should raise questions from the political point of view. This attitude should be part of the author's world view. It helps perfect realistic literature and heightens the author's consciousness of reality and art. Only when an author has this kind of basic idea about working for politics and the people can he be serious and conscientious enough to participate in the people's fervent struggle, to reform himself and search and work according to literary realism. Only in this way can he penetrate and portray reality.

Looking at the issue in this way differs totally from looking at it through the definition of socialist realism. This is not inconsistent with the principle of realism, nor does it force anything onto realism itself. It is not some kind of "spirit" or thought or wish moving away from artistic truth toward purely abstract ideas that affects artistic truth itself. On the contrary, it encourages authors to reform their thoughts, learn Marxism, and be one with the people and with reality so that they will be able to get at the source of life. With a progressive world view merged thoroughly with their artistic thoughts, they can work out a highly creative way of realism.

All nonpolitical trends are bad for literary undertakings. Literary works produced by those who believe that art is above all are essentially opposed to realism. This was proved a long time ago by literary developments after the May Fourth movement.

For several years, we have accomplished so much in carrying out this principle that our literature has really become the literature of the great masses and taken a great step forward. However, I am not going to talk about this in detail. What I want to discuss is the confused ideas emerging as we implement the principle. These ideas are identical with, combined with, and encouraged by unscientific ideas stemming from the definition of socialist realism; they arise from the degree of understanding of the relationship of literature and politics, of how one can serve politics and the people, and of the characteristics of realism, literature, and art.

How can literature and art be of service to politics and the people? In considering this question, we should first realize that it is a fundamental but long-range literary requirement. It is essential for dealing with the current situation, in which literature and art are separated from politics and the masses; for strengthening the awareness and consciousness of the struggle over objective reality; and for reforming an author's thought and world view. We should constantly strengthen an author's contact with life and encourage the exercise of his thought; we should fully develop the characteristics of literature and art and the principle of realism, and fully develop an author's enthusiasm for politics and his sensitivity to life.

All distinguished progressive literary works have a strong concern with ideological thought and politics. It is obvious that, inescapably, literature has greatly served politics. The reason these literary works possess such great persuasive power is that the authors have been faithful to objective reality and have achieved high artistic quality as well. This is linked with the positive aspects of the author's world view. These literary works were not produced merely to fulfill a certain duty; they have a long-range social significance and are artistic works of great realistic achievement.

Is it possible for literature and art to be of service to every current political line? An author who has great political enthusiasm and a great sensitivity toward life can never feel indifferent to current changes. He will certainly participate in current events. Lu Hsün and Gorky are shining models; every author in our new era should follow them and make this life one of struggle. However, when we demand that authors lead such lives, we have to consider some complex situations and problems.

First of all, the requirement for literature and art to be of service to politics and the people is a long-range one. We should not be so short sighted as to deal merely with current political progaganda, nor should we be satisfied with literary works only because they can have some propaganda effect. Second, we should think of how to develop the characteristics of literary art fully instead of simply regarding literature as a tool of certain concepts. We should realize that literature is artistic and true to life before it becomes effective as a weapon. We should never forget the importance of artistic quality, whether in an essay, a passage of a tale told with drums, or a feature story. Besides, we should consider each author's individual qualities. We should not demand the same thing from all authors and all literary forms. We should help develop rather than hinder each author's individual creativity. We should use fewer administrative orders that interfere with literary creation.

Consider Gorky and Lu Hsün: All their articles on politics, their critical writings, and their literary creations arise out of their profound understanding of objective reality and are therefore portraits of the reality. When they wrote political and critical articles, they always grasped the basic nature of the enemy and the nature of backwardness and then used their unique literary styles to reveal and to attack. They didn't *inform* the readers of certain working or production processes; nor did they write to interpret policy regulations. They never worked mechanically to fulfill any political duty. They were attacking enemies and teaching people how to experience life, how to live, and how to struggle.

We say "political criteria first" because there has never been a literature that has not been tendentious; people always want literature for their own purposes. We must not conclude from this that the most important criterion for literary works is whether or not they follow some temporary political duty; nor should we conclude that artistic criteria are not important. Political criteria should be unified with artistic criteria; but how can they be unified? Certainly not by asking art to disappear for the sake of generalized and abstract political concepts; nor by asking politics and art to be stiffly and superficially "combined." And not by saying we want only art or only politics. What we want is a unification of the author's thought and his art. In order to obtain such a unity, the author should do his best to secure an organic combination of his world view, his creative methods, his artistic thinking, and his rational thinking. This kind of unity should begin with the author's attempt to experience and grasp the truth of life and with his creating the truth of art. In other words, the author starts with political enthusiasm, sensibility, awareness, creativeness, and a zeal for struggle.

Saying "political criteria first" does not mean that accomplishments, weaknesses, or tendencies in literary works should be analyzed according to political standards. Literary creation is a complex mental process. Our ideal should be to achieve a high degree of unity between poetry and rationality, but this is not easily done. A man who is highly sophisticated politically may not be sophisticated and talented artistically and therefore may not be able to write good literary works. There is often a distance between an author's expectations and his actual accomplishment. Although an author's creative activities are guided and controlled by his world view, this world view is not the only factor ruling his creative activities. The accumulation of the author's knowledge of life, his artistic refinement, his experiences, and his abilities are important factors as well. The process of creating artistic images involves complex, dynamic factors. Marxism can encompass but not be a substitute for the creative methods of realism.

If we make light of the premise that only when literary works reflect life truthfully can they influence it, if we disregard the artistic characteristics of the literature of realism, if we neglect the specific conditions of each author and try to use art simply to illustrate politics, then we will inevitably produce unrealistic, conceptualized, and formularized writings or propaganda. If so, even writings that are supposed to reflect life will not be very good.

Although propaganda work is necessary and has its unique, important value, it cannot be a substitute for literary and artistic work. So-called literary and artistic works which are similar to propaganda material will disgust people. They will be less effective even if they are intended as propaganda. People like to listen to political reports and read theoretical books, but no one likes to see movies illustrating formulas or concepts.

If we mechanically make literature do political duty, inevitably few works of good quality will be produced. People will not get artistic pleasure from them. The loss will be invisible. Literature will fail in its original purpose, which is to serve politics.

Let me repeat: each author should learn the skill and have the enthusiasm to portray life. The author should learn to use literature as a weapon, not forgetting the duty and functions of this weapon.

Because we have some confused literary concepts, we have developed confused ideas concerning concrete problems. For instance, some people believe one should not write about the past. Some are overly concerned with whether or not a literary work has done its duty, a criterion they use to evaluate the social significance of all literary works. Some treat literature as a report on the process or execution of policy. Some regard the working processes of certain projects as the purpose and content of the writing and forget the importance of characterization. Some claim that authors should not write about intellectuals, should not depict capitalists or rich landowners as main characters, should avoid exciting and familiar "old subjects" and try to write about the dull and unfamiliar. Some think life itself is formularized and authors should move away from images toward themes and thoughts. Some use administrative orders as guidelines for creative writing, hoping that politics will be combined with art. Furthermore, some say: "If I advocate writing about new people, you should not write about backward people. If you write about backward Party members, you are distorting the image of the members of the Communist Party. In creating new characters, you had better work according to certain rules." People tend to be divided into two categories: progressive and backward. There is argument as to whether one should or should not depict the weakness of a character when he is portrayed as progressive. Some mechanically divide the contradictions of life into major criteria for evaluating literary works. Some criticize literary works on the basis of the author's political position. Some literary magazines mechanically serve political duties. One may argue that depicting new heroes is a socialist act, another may argue that reflecting contradictions and conflicts is a socialist act, and a third may argue that writing based on humanitarianism is a socialist act.

All these arguments have some things in common: all try to simplify and categorize the extremely complex live, fluid, flowing creative process. They all believe that only they have grasped the principles of socialist realism. In fact, they have narrowed, distorted, and deviated from the principles of realism. They all think only they are emphasizing the political quality of art, and even the artistic quality of art, but actually they have in differing degrees lowered the political and artistic quality of literary work.

I don't mean that all have suffered from exactly the same ideas. If that were true, dogmatism would have overwhelmed our literary undertakings and our writers would not have accomplished much. But we cannot deny that the ideas mentioned above have affected people to varying degrees. I don't mean that questions need not be

raised on certain occasions. The problem is that most people are
pedantic and quote classics or allusions, but few work hard enough
actually to study life and see how it figures in creative writing. They
either argue ambiguously or blindly believe in authorities. Sometimes questions lead to good results, but often questions are not
asked concisely, completely, thoroughly, or flexibly. When they have
something to do with evaluations and analyses of specific works, people fail to be concise and fair. All in all, these problems and phenomena have blown over our literary field like gusts of wind. They have
caused quite a few authors, critics, art admirers, amateur authors,
and young and old writers to busy themselves watching which way
the wind is blowing and trying to deal with it. Some have behaved as
though they were producing fashionable hats and have imposed
them on the people.

Some people may want to ask me, "Haven't you underestimated
our literary situation?" No. First of all, I am not talking about our accomplishments and good works, but about our defects. I have often
heard complaints in conversation about our literary situation. People
have been shouting for several years against conceptualization and
the formularization of literature. Are they complaining for nothing?
We will know the answer if we look at the performance of plays this
year: most of the forty-nine plays were influenced by the sort of confused ideas mentioned earlier. A few plays that tried to break the restraints did not achieve even a minimum standard. The history of
our people's drama, including the spoken parts in traditional drama,
has developed for thousands of years, and the standard is very high.
Do our present playwrights have no talent? Of course they do.
Haven't we seen what other branches of the arts, such as movies,
have done in similar situations?

For several years there have been authors with independent
ideas writing good literary works well received by the public. For
several years, there has also been a promising group of new writers
producing works of good quality. Taken as a whole, our literature is
working in the direction of progress; we are doing our best to overcome some of the defects. However, if we count only the number of
good works published in recent years worthy of our age, we will find
that the present standard of our literature is not satisfactory. Besides, how much critical writing with really shrewd insights about

our popular works has appeared? People may not have worked hard enough. Could there be other reasons?

This confusion of ideas is caused by dogmatism: People think from their subjective and one-sided point of view and follow dogma so mechanically that they forget the real situation. The dogmas in the literary field have ignored or destroyed realism, the guideline for literary practice together with experience of actual life.

It is not right to say that the tendency to formulism in literary creation has nothing to do with the tendency to dogmatism in literary thought. How can we ignore this problem? Why can't we break these ideological restraints?

IV

In addition to the definition of socialist realism and the problem of art serving politics, other problems have appeared concerning dogmatism in literature.

In his report to the Nineteenth Communist Party Congress, Malenkov said: "The force and importance of realistic art lies in the fact that it can and must reveal and hold up to the light the high spiritual qualities and typical positive features in the character of the common man, it can and must create his vivid artistic portrait as an example for people to imitate."[3] Zhdanov also said something similar. They had their own reasons for making such statements; but as in the case of other Soviet literary theories, the statements have been superficially understood by our writers and critics and have led to serious problems. We often quote Zhdanov's words. When we talk about "creating new characters," it means "writing about the progressive characters among common people." The effects of the remarks by Malenkov and Zhdanov get mixed up with our own dogmatic concepts. For instance, because we emphasize the need to eulogize the bright side of life and do not have a clear idea about the socialist spirit and the task of education of the people, we have produced the "no-conflict" theory. Because we have mechanically interpreted the principle of serving the workers, peasants, and sol-

[3] From *Current Soviet Policies: The Documentary Record of the 19th Communist Party Congress and the Reorganization after Stalin's Death,* ed. Leo Gruliow (New York: Praeger, 1953), p. 115.

diers, we have reduced the importance of the observation of life and the choice of subjects. Because we are used to taking literature mechanically as propaganda for the masses, we tend to pay attention only to certain kinds of common people: those who look identical, those who have expressed certain attitudes about certain policies, the new type, and those with "backward thoughts." People are afraid of committing errors and adapt to what is simply following other people's secrets of success. Writers have lost the habit of imagining freely, creating freely, searching for artistic style or looking at life deeply. They merely pay attention to the ordinary, average subjects everyone can see. This is one reason why our work degenerates into generalized formulism.

There are characters in literature who have the appearance of common people. However, there are also characters who seem not to be common in real life, but who actually reflect the image of the common people. All workers are common people. An author should recognize not only their common aspects, but also, from their existence and daily lives, those deeply meaningful traits that are not easily recognized and thus seem not so common. Presenting readers with things they have taken for granted and have never paid attention to or fully understood is one of the important ways in which the writer shows his creative originality. It is also a skill every realistic writer should aspire to. Even when a literary work deals with ordinary people and ordinary things, if it has depth and is true to life and creative originality, it will inevitably have an unusual quality. For instance, *Virgin Soil Upturned* describes ordinary peasants and the ordinary practice of collectivism, but many of the characters in the book have unique characteristics. Although all the characters in Lu Hsün's "Benediction," "K'ung I-chi," and so on are common and ordinary, the author's unique, profound vision and feeling and his unusual literary style have given something unique and profound to the characters and to the works. In world literature, such examples are too numerous to mention. The point is, the authors look at people as common people, but they look at reality not with a world view but with profound insight.

Can't common people have an unusual destiny? Can't literature describe this unusual destiny? According to popular ideas, the ordinary but unusual character Grigory in *And Quiet Flows the Don* is a "negative protagonist." Why shouldn't we write about the unusual aspects of a "positive protagonist"? The white-haired girl is an ordinary person with an unusual destiny. Because of this, we are deeply moved by her. During the long years of our revolutionary struggle, we have discovered many ordinary yet unusual personalities. We have discovered many people who resemble unusual characters like Chapayev, Kuo Ju-ho, Chu-ko Liang, Chang Fei, and Li K'uei. Ours is a time of rapid change, a time for unusual personalities and unusual things. Ours is a time when we organize scattered groups of people to carry on our revolutionary struggle, a time for many unusual representatives of the people to appear. Ours is a time when the collective will of each class is recognized, a time when many outstanding heroes and extraordinary villains have appeared. Ours is a time of the emancipation of women and of exuberant emotions, a time when people can demonstrate their unusual qualities.

We have lost many opportunities for creating fascinating typical characters. Our critics and public opinion do not even allow writers to try something new. Several years ago, a writer wrote a work called *Liu-pao ti ku-shih* (The Story of Willow Castle)—a moving story of love and class struggle, convincing and realistic. Some critics, however, argued that soldiers in the Eighth Route Army should not be involved in love affairs because it was atypical and would be a bad influence. The story has vanished.

Generally speaking, every man is a common man. Men have the same ideas, feelings, desires, and habits. Isn't Chu-ko Liang a very unusual character?[4] The ordinary man cannot compete with his position, experiences, wisdom, and knowledge. But there is a proverb that "three cobblers are equal to one Chu-ko Liang." People have always admired him and tried to emulate his wisdom. Examples like this can still be found in literature—because all the unusual personalities share certain qualities with us. No matter how unusual a person is, he is also human. None of us is completely lacking in wisdom. Besides, we all hope to become wiser. Thus, Chu-ko Liang's unusual wisdom is not completely alien to us.

If all the unusual qualities and profound characteristics of individuals are discarded, the individuality and creativity of writers will

[4] Chu-ko Liang is a character in the classical Chinese novel *The Romance of the Three Kingdoms*. He is very wise and an advisor to one of the three Chinese kings.

be discarded too. What is left is only "statistical averages." Writers will be able to create only general, mediocre, and superficial works. They will no longer want to pursue art; their works will no longer possess artistic power. Even in describing striking new heroes, writers fail to depict their psychology, their character, and their lives. This is why there is little difference among our literary works. Many are written with the same style and language and have similar characters and plots.

All authors write about events with everyday details like those in a housewife's life. All the books are good because they are "plain" and "natural." No one commits any errors. If the book did not have a name on it, you could never guess who the author was. Critics cannot get at the faults of the author; they can only get hold of formulism. When formulism was originally advocated, it was clear that no one was allowed to violate it. Critics who try to attack other people's faults perhaps had advocated formulism in the beginning. Now writers take great pains to work on details, expecting that through the careful depiction of them they may overcome conceptualism. People get depressed. People—critics, writers, editors, officials, leaders, and the led—all begin to have one opinion or another.

I am not advocating that writers should search out strange, bizarre subjects like those of the naturalistic authors. The difference between writing about strange, bizarre subjects and writing with daring creativity depends on whether the work has an intrinsic realistic quality. We should broaden the scope of creativity to further understand the nature of realism and to urge our writers to be liberated from the thousand bonds of dogmatism!

In the past two years, we have been talking about problems concerning the nature of art, imagery, and thought. But how many people have studied or promoted a certain author's or work's unique artistic qualities? Has the pursuit of creativity in the arts received proper attention? Literary critics use fashionable abstract language to talk about the thought of the work or to attack certain ideas. As for some new sprouts of creative writing, the critics never offer any support. Sometimes they keep quiet; sometimes they attack the new creative works simply because these do not follow the current fashion in writing, exaggerating the weaknesses of the writing without recognizing or affirming the value of creativity.

In addition to "The Story of Willow Castle," Chen Ch'i-tung's "The Long March" is an example. Some people tried to deny its value and judged it with formulas like "primary contradiction versus secondary contradiction." People think "artistic analysis" means approval or disapproval of the structure, language, style, and imagery of a literary work. Few people think a critic should be a thinker and connoisseur of the arts, that he should be not only a thinker about books but also a thinker about life and art. If he abandons the search for typicality of imagery, if he abandons a deep analysis of life and knowledge of the author's originality and creativity, the critic will abandon realism. Then how can he judge accurately the quality of structure, diction, style, and image? Such critics will rigidly judge literary works with dogmas or with personal feelings and impressions. Thus, criticism will be reduced to remarks in the lounge of the theater after the show is over.

At present, not only writers but also critics themselves are afraid of criticism. In the past, critics would say dogmatically that this work was typical while the other was not. Today, critics have become more clever. They use ambiguous words and try not to ask the question of typicality. The situation today is that one person thinks one work has its good points and defects, another thinks another work has its good points and defects, a third thinks a third work has its good points and defects. No critic dares or is able to compare two or three works with similar subjects or similar characters in two or three works to reach meaningful conclusions. . . . And the final stage is that some people begin to oppose the lukewarm criticism. Dogmatism zeroes in to the attack again.

Dogmatism in creative writing and in literary criticism are twin sisters. So are generalizations in creative writing and literary criticism. But the sisters are not very friendly with each other.

V

In the world of literature and art, as in any other world, dogmatism is harmful. Even the remarks of Marx and Engels on literary problems should not be understood or applied one-sidedly or unrealistically. Engels once said: "If we don't use materialism as a guiding principle in studying history but use it as a ready-made formula and destroy or cut historical facts to make them fit that formula, then materialism will have the opposite result." We should take this attitude whenever we deal with literary theories.

Let us think of the question of what is typical, of how to create typical characters, and of how to write about typical characters in typical environments. If we think of masterpieces written since ancient times, we will find that nobody can create a rigid and narrow formula for judging such writings. Anyone who tries to apply dogmatism to these masterpieces will be defeated.

Has anybody seen men like Don Quixote in real life? Don Quixote wishes to save the world singlehandedly, to make great achievements. He imagines everything he sees as his enemy and tries to attack it with knightly force. He fights with a windmill and imagines a flock of sheep to be a camp of demons. Is there such a person in the world? Is he real? Is he typical? This image of Don Quixote is not used merely to satirize foolish knightly manners. Don Quixote's humanitarianism, his fancy, and his wish to conquer the world—all three exist everywhere. The various kinds of subjectivism we oppose are identical with Don Quixote's subjectivism. On the surface, Cervantes seems to have created an absurd story. However, when we are reading the story we can't help but feel that Don Quixote is a real, living personality. The world he is in is lonely and sad, full of cruelty and injustice; yet it is also full of an attractive life force. We realize and feel that this is exactly the world in which Don Quixote lives— that the world certainly has men like Don Quixote, although on the surface there is only one Don Quixote, in the world created by the book.

Has anybody seen men like Ah Q in real life? His people knock his head against the wall. He is forced to admit that he is an insect. But when he turns around, he says, "My son, beat me," and imagines he has won a spiritual victory. He is humiliated and hurt wherever he goes, but he always imagines he has won a spiritual victory. Superficial readers will think he is funny. Honest readers will feel sorry for him. But readers with insight will shed tears, feel furious, even feel ashamed of themselves and finally want to take some action. Has Lu Hsün created an absurd story? Has this story, as some critics have said, merely condemned certain national characteristics or working people's lack of awareness and paralyzed conditions? Yes, but this is not all. This character Ah Q, like many other universal characters, has risen above his time and space, above the limited world the critics and Lu Hsün himself have prescribed for him. The spirit of Ah Q is helpless, sad, and ridiculous. His human nature is detestable and results from a society that condones the private ownership system, from the existence of class oppression, and from antagonistic relationships among people. It is universal. There is really no one in Ah Q's world who does not possess some kind of Ah Q spirit. This is sufficient to prove the universality of the spirit of Ah Q and to explain the relationship of Ah Q to his world.

Literary realism is a highly creative kind of work. It is realistic, but the writer may create absurd characters and stories in order to represent the profound content of reality. Sometimes it can be so real that it gives the impression of being fanciful. What a boundless arena realism offers the imagination! Imagination can concentrate, universalize, and exaggerate reality—and these can be developed to an astonishing level.

VI

Every immortal masterpiece, as well as every successful writer, possesses a unique kind of creativity. And so the following has often happened: After a good book is published, it will not only be slandered by reactionary critics but also misinterpreted by dogmatists. There is a danger that it may even be buried and forgotten. A good book cannot be turned into a failure by slander, whether intentional or not; either critics will rescue it or it will take root in the minds of readers. Some books have been read and studied for many years even though nobody has thoroughly analyzed their achievement and quality. The study of authors and literary works has become a specialized branch of knowledge. Good authors and works have always contributed new, fresh, and unique things to literature through the content of their books, and their artistic skills, techniques, and styles. Some literary works are highly original and cannot be imitated; they appear in this world only once; they are accepted by readers and touch their hearts, but they are unique and cannot be presented as general examples. That is why there is only one *The True Story of Ah Q,* one *Don Quixote,* one *And Quiet Flows the Don,* one *Water Margin,* one *Romance of the Three Kingdoms,* and only one Lu Hsün, one Ts'ao Hsüeh-ch'in, one Gorky, one Tolstoy. . . . We can learn from these works and from these great authors. We can try to catch up with them in other, newer ways. We can never achieve the level of these authors by using their methods. Only mediocre and repetitive works can be imitated numerous times. Only mediocre critics can give reasons for the success of mediocre works.

I am not encouraging people to aim high and ignore the basics. Having the ambition but not the ability is as inexcusable as following a routine and being lazy. Our great forefathers used their life's energy to complete their works. We can learn from them but we cannot imitate them: we must redouble our efforts to create new paths in literature. Not everyone can reach the same level as our forefathers. But we can at least work honestly and with dedication so that we can achieve something.

We should understand that individual authors have their differences in experience, upbringing, temperament, artistic originality, and so on. You may prefer one style, I may prefer another. You may prefer to emphasize certain subjects, I may prefer analyzing certain types of characters and situations. Mr. A may be determined to create images of a group of new heroes, Mr. B may be interested in writing satires, and Mr. C may like to use revolutionary humanitarianism as a main theme in his writing. Some people want to write only short lyrics, others are more versatile. We cannot and should not ask the same thing from each author. Literary realism is a broad road for creative development, and no one should use rigid dogmas to prescribe a fixed, narrow path for others. All correct theories can help writers find a path in realism that will lead to higher achievements, but they can never be a substitute for the writers' own search for realistic methods.

Realism differs from other theories in that it enables the writer to face reality positively, to seek the truth of life, and to seek artistic truth and originality in order to reflect and affect life as much as possible. Thus, the world of realism is much broader than that of other artistic theories. Writers may have different ways of reaching truth, but their direction is the same and they reach the same destination: the truth of life. Though the truth of life and the truth of art are closely related, there is a distance between them great enough to give writers room to develop their creative talents. Not all concrete details and methods of realism are fixed. Nor has realism been completed. There are still many new, important problems for which we have to work hard to find answers. For instance, there are problems of how to create images of new heroes, how to write new satires, how to combine individual destiny and the destiny of a group, how to portray the organized activities of organized people, how to portray great construction projects and military activities, and how to deal correctly with the increasing importance of science and technology in the daily lives of the people. To solve all these problems, we should first try to get experience through creative practices and not busy ourselves making all kinds of dogmatic rules.

We face a great problem today. We are developing faster than at any other time in our history—so fast that one cannot see clearly, one doesn't get time to think, and one is unable to grasp in time the things one wants to grasp. It is therefore difficult to do creative work, and we are inclined to use ready-made formulas and resort to dogmatism. This is a major reason why dogmatism can grab hold of us. We have to devote much more time and energy to finding our own ways of depicting a little of our great life and of making our new literature achieve a high world standard. However, when we talk about this, we can't help remembering that we have only a small group of writers, and most of them are in charge of various projects in literature and the arts. Thus, writers have to take a vacation from creative writing in order to create. Some writers are restlessly trying to get a chance to write, and many are lucky to get this chance. They are busy writing and living, and are worried that time is too short. Not only are there very few people who get the time to write, but there are few people who get the time to learn. Many people have no time to read classics and foreign works, nor the time or enthusiasm to read current works. Who is working to seek artistic perfection? Who has the ambition to write an epic of the revolutionary wars?

I do not advocate the cancellation of organization in literature. It would not be good to have no administrative organization. However, I feel that because there aren't enough people, and because there is so much work to be done, we have to make a choice and decide what is most important. It is creative writing; let writers have the time to write. If we do not pay attention to creative writing, our literary endeavors will deviate from reality. And this has a great deal to do with dogmatism.

I feel that literature and art are governed by dogmatism in other parts of the world as well as in China. This makes it even more difficult to overcome.

Let us free ourselves from the bondage of dogmatism. Let us bravely and dilligently get the hundred flowers to bloom. We live in a country that has a long tradition of realism. We have many great masters of realistic writing in our history. Each succeeded with new originality, new power. Each succeeded by breaking old rules. Let us learn from them.

15

THE DEVELOPMENT
OF REALISM IN THE
SOCIALIST ERA

LIU SHAO-T'ANG

I

The creation of great literature depends on three prerequisites: (1) the material for creative work provided by the writers' era; (2) the existence of gifted writers with aesthetic sensitivity and talent for observing and comprehending life; (3) theories guiding the writers' thought.

No one would agree with the assertion that our life today lacks the richness and grandeur of the nineteenth century, or even earlier periods. Our age has produced many unparalleled heroes. It should also be able to produce great literary and artistic works—those unprecedented works which are rich in thought and display a remarkable artistry.

No one would say that this age has yet to produce gifted writers. If we were to say, however, that our contemporary writers are inferior to those of previous ages in their ability to observe life and present it through their art, it could serve as an incentive to the

Liu Shao-t'ang, "Hsien-shih chu-i tsai she-hui chu-i shih-tai ti fa-chan" (The Development of Realism in the Socialist Era), *Pei-ching wen-i* (Peking Literature), April 15, 1957.

writers themselves. They could be urged to involve themselves more deeply with life. They would feel compelled to share the destiny and aspirations of the people, to study Marxism, to raise their ideological perspective, to discipline themselves in writing, to develop their creative talent, and to produce works worthy of the era.

A writer's talent, however, depends on theories guiding his thought. If the theories themselves are correct, his talent can be developed more efficiently and to a higher level. Incorrect theories, however, will obstruct his talent. Therefore, in solving our literary problems our most important task is the exploration of the theories that have guided our literary endeavors. I believe that dogmatism has been at the root of all our problems. We cannot expect our literature to progress unless we remove this obstacle.

II

To say that nothing has been accomplished in our literature would be the negative view of a rightist opportunist. It would also be unfair to say that very little has been accomplished. However, we can certainly say that our literary endeavors could and would achieve more were they not so seriously hampered by dogmatism.

It is justified to ask why we have yet to produce works of the same stature as *Iron Flood, Chapayev,* and *The Rout*—works produced in the first few years following the Russian revolution. Is it true that we do not have a life of great struggle, that we do not have heroic revolutionary figures to portray in our writing, and that we do not have writers of the same greatness as Serafimovich, Furmanov, and Fadeyev, all of whom were tempered by revolution and hazardous experiences?

No, this is not true. We have all of these. The difference lies in the fact that immediately following the victorious close of the Russian revolution, literary dogmatism was not popular. Therefore, Russia not only produced these works, but soon began producing such momentous epics as *And Quiet Flows the Don* and *Virgin Soil Upturned.* We, however, were affected by dogmatism from the very beginning.

Dogmatic theories emphasize only the political implications of a literary work, ignoring its various artistic concerns. They neglect the complex and colorful realities of life. Dogmatists blindly demand of writers, "Can our life really be like this?" In a mechanical fashion they dictate stereotyped protagonists, antagonists, and model heroes. For didactic reasons they propound various regulations and taboos. Among these is the rule that a writer should never depict the weaknesses of a model hero.

Such dogmatism prevents writers from addressing themselves honestly to the realities of life. Instead, it encourages them to adhere to dogmatic concepts about life and character. It forces writers to ignore the essential nature of their art in order to fulfill a didactic role, as though literature were a branch of the social sciences.

Dogmatic theories have for a long time been regarded as "orthodox" guidelines for literary creation. Numerous pieces of literature have been produced according to those guidelines. The course of Russian history proves that prior to Stalin's blunders, and before subjective dogmatism came to dominate literary creation, writers were able to produce such masterpieces as *And Quiet Flows the Don, Virgin Soil Upturned, Cement,* and *And Then the Harvest.* These works mercilessly reflected the life of the people and the momentous changes in their destiny. Twenty years later, however, when writers were allowed to write only of the superiority of socialism and to serve particular propaganda purposes, when they began to misrepresent the realities of life and ignore conflicts among the people, literature became the adornment of a false prosperity. It was then that the concept of "no-conflict" came to prevail. As a result, the literary works of the second twenty years were greatly inferior to those of the first twenty years after the Russian revolution.

Over the past few years, our literature has also convinced us of the negative influence of dogmatism. It is evident in conceptualized formula writing, which lacks life experience and artistic appeal. It is especially evident in screen and play writing. One might say that it is tragic to have such a state of affairs. These facts indicate that we have deviated from the essential spirit of realism and from the worthy tradition of the classical realists.

III

Literature has a more direct and systematic tradition than the social sciences. In the history of literature, writers of realism have always dealt honestly and extensively with the realities of life. Such writers have always been deeply concerned with the fate of the exploited and the oppressed, and have attempted to educate the people by writing about problems that exist in their lives. These writers were in sympathy with the people: they loved and praised them without concealing their weaknesses or miseries. They offered a profound depiction of the reality of life in all its aspects, so that the people could grasp their situation and realize their strength.

Classical realists objected to systems in which people were exploited. They hated social injustice and corruption, and gave their sympathy and support to the people. The evolution of their progressive ideas was a long process. A younger writer inherited the thought of older writers, started from where they left off, and advanced even further. It was in this way that realism began to embrace elements of socialism and undergo a socialistic development. Lu Hsün and Gorky were realists who carried on past traditions and pointed the way for those who were to follow. Although they were not yet Communists at the time, they had already imbued realism with the spirit of socialism as a natural result of social developments.

But these innovators who first conjoined realism and socialism were puzzled by the many problems they encountered in their study of life, and in the process of their art. They needed a valid scientific and philosophical doctrine with which to interpret life. It was for this reason that they embraced Marxism. It is Marxism that stimulates and directs the development of socialist elements in realism.

The founding of the Communist Party and the success of the socialist revolution have imbued realism with a new life and spirit; socialist elements now predominate in realism. This new spirit is represented in the socialist life of the people, and in the writers' Communist world view. To be more specific, the realities of life that serve as the basis for all literary creation have themselves undergone a change. The thinking of writers who depict these realities in their work has also changed.

Both the life of the people and the thinking of writers have become richer and more profound.

Realism, therefore, has not died during the socialist era. On the contrary, it has grown. This powerful current has not dried up, but has opened out and become even more widespread. Realism has been imbued with a clearly defined Party spirit, and has begun to serve the people under the guidance of the Party's principles.

Nevertheless, literature differs from the social sciences. The social sciences demonstrate the superiority of socialism through conceptual reasoning and analysis, and through the study of social and political systems and their economic functions. The basis of all literature and art, however, should be the realities of contemporary life. Writers, therefore, should not only boldly and realistically depict the positive aspects of life, but also the negative aspects of life in a realistic and appropriate manner. This is the one realistic attitude that seeks to derive truth from the facts. This alone is the spirit of realism for those who wish to remain faithful to the realities of life.

IV

Nevertheless, according to dogmatic theories, literature and art are to be equated with the social sciences. Dogmatists admit to only one difference between the two—literature and art can explicate conceptual reasoning through illustration. As a result, literary work has become entirely divorced from the realities of life, serving the cause of certain concepts.

The charter of the Union of Soviet Writers has defined socialist realism as a term, and has prescribed a standardized creative technique. This manifesto regarding technique "demands of the artist a true, historically concrete portrayal of reality in its revolutionary development; whereby truthfulness and historical concreteness must be combined with the task of ideological reform and the education of the working people in the spirit of socialism."[1]

A creative approach of this sort was obviously not formulated in order to encourage writers to base their work on the realities of life, or to deal honestly with these things. Rather, it encourages writers to depict life in relation to "reality in its revolutionary development." Such a depiction, furthermore, must be combined with a sense of "duty." Writers, therefore, are quite confused in regard to the issue of reality. If the realities of life are not considered real, and writing itself is supposed to involve the "revolutionary development" of reality, writers are forced to embellish life and ignore its true features. According to the principle of "reality in its revolutionary develop-

---

[1] From the *First All-Union Congress of Soviet Writers, 1934 Stenographic Report* (Moscow, 1934), p. 666, as cited in Walter N. Vickery, *The Cult of Optimism* (Bloomington: Indiana University Press, 1963), p. 70.

ment," writers should not write of problems in a socialist society or depict the more negative aspects of the society, for these are temporary matters that can be resolved. Is there then any meaning for "reality" as it pertains to realism?

This great concern with educational value and "duty" in literature has resulted in writers' selecting their subjects carefully and fearfully avoiding any critical delineation of life in detail. But life is rich and splendid; it encompasses a wide variety of situations and colors, and many details of life may have no educational value in themselves. After they are arranged and selected for their educational value, however, these details are robbed of all vitality. Only their "educational value" remains. Works designed to conform to this theory cannot be regarded as artistic creations, for they lack artistic appeal, which can be achieved only when life is depicted through specific images of reality.

Ridiculous as it is, according to the theory of educational value and duty, the great classical works are unacceptable, while conceptualized formula writing, which whitewashes life, is regarded as the best. Such works depict "reality in its revolutionary development," have great "educational value," display a high level of ideological sophistication, and deal with protagonists, antagonists, and model heroes—practically everything you could ask for. What they lack, however, is the least bit of artistic appeal. Such works are no more enduring than a news release.

Let us ask ourselves whether the character Grigory in *And Quiet Flows the Don* is a protagonist of positive aspects, or an antagonist. What concrete educational value does he possess as a character? Grigory is said to represent the tragic figure of an individualistic small landowner. Why then is such a character so deeply moving to readers as a figure of subtlety and valor? Why do readers not despise him? Why do they sympathize with him and weep for him? If we classify Grigory as a counterrevolutionary because he joined the White forces during the Russian revolution, how are we to regard Aksinia, who gave her life and all she had to Grigory? True, we might classify her as a counterrevolutionary as well. But the timeless and exemplary nature of Aksinia's character has exerted a positive influence on people. Many men wish for lovers as beautiful and faithful as Aksinia; many women seek a conscience and love as pure and noble as Aksinia's. If we were to adhere to dogmatic theory, we would have to say that the educational value of these two characters is virtually nonexistent. Would this, however, be a fair way of evaluating the characterizations?

Let us pose another question. In *Virgin Soil Upturned*, is the "left-wing" opportunist Nagulnov of the agricultural collectivization movement a protagonist of positive aspects, or an antagonist? Since he is vehemently opposed to Party policy, he should be considered an antagonist. But his rigorous perseverance as a Bolshevik and the tragedy of his personal life are more appealing than his ideological convictions.

It is simply impossible for us to discover model heroes in Sholokhov's works. Davydov in *Virgin Soil Upturned* does not, of course, merit the status of a model hero. Because he does not display a revolutionary alertness to the antirevolutionary wealthy farmer, Ostronov, and because he had carried on an illicit liaison with the promiscuous Lukeria, he is not even a positive figure in the true sense of the term.

As a matter of fact, the one and only model hero is God. It is a pity that only Christians can believe in him. Even Christians, however, have no conception of God's personality or character. Therefore, they must turn for assistance to glib ministers or extremely ignorant painters.

V

There is a historical background of dogmatism in our literature. During the years of Japanese aggression, when the survival of our country hung in the balance, and during the war of liberation when the people overthrew the semi-feudal, semi-colonial reactionary government, literature served as the fastest and most direct weapon in support of the revolution. We would quickly produce a short opera in order to urge that lenient treatment be accorded war prisoners. We would hastily compose a verse play with clapper accompaniment to launch a drive for effective army training. We would promptly produce a *huo-pao* drama[2] exposing the conspiracy behind the false

[2] A type of play performed in the streets primarily for purposes of propaganda. In order to obtain a more realistic effect, the players are not required to wear cos-

peace proposals of the Kuomintang. So writers were required to write according to certain policies and rules; their work was more effective than if we had issued flat verbal statements. Because it was their duty to fight, writers did not have time to deliberate over their work, to improve its aesthetic quality. Literary guidelines were necessary at the time to ensure that writers would adhere to the policies of the moment. It was also necessary to criticize those writers who did not respond to the demands of the times.

But the situation changed following the liberation of our country. There was a great change in the life of the people, and in their social environment. The people are now better able to appreciate the arts. The demands made on literature and art ought therefore to be different from those of wartime. It is unfortunate that the theories guiding our writers remain similar to those of the past. A certain amount of progress has been made, but the old theories cannot deal with the changed situation. Our writers have felt inhibited and our literary progress has been obstructed.

Under such conditions as existed during the long wars, it is understandable that the hasty production of literature, the requirement that art serve politics, and the fact that literary works had a predominantly political content were all considered acceptable. There was little emphasis on artistic technique. Consequently, a misconception has arisen that political and artistic criteria are separate affairs. In other words, Chairman Mao's statements have been misinterpreted, and this misinterpretation has seriously obstructed writers in their pursuit of artistic excellence. Writers must be satisfied only with "ideological content" and "important subjects." Actually, Chairman Mao explicitly stated that the political nature of a work must be assessed through the artistry of its presentation, and that the ideological quality of a work is not determined by whether its theme or subject matter is political. If we were to say, for example, that physical well-being is our foremost concern, we do not mean that working and studying should be set aside in order to maintain a well-developed body.

Chairman Mao's "Talks at the Yenan Forum on Literature and

tumes. The dramatic form itself lies somewhere between traditional Chinese opera and contemporary drama. It occasionally employs folk songs and traditional acrobatics.

Art" comprise a comprehensive and classic statement on artistic theory. His remarks were based on the historical circumstances of the time, and served as guidelines for literature of that period. Chairman Mao outlined the direction our literature and art would follow in the years to come, and at the same time defined their function in 1942. We must study and try to understand the historical significance of Chairman Mao's statements, so that we will not be oblivious to the importance of his long-term program for literary and artistic development.

It is an urgent and glorious task for our literary historians and critics to make a conscientious study of literature produced after 1942. If we are unable to evaluate and examine the past scientifically, we will be unable to direct the future of our literature. Literature produced after 1942 has made great contributions to the development of realism. The socialist elements of realism have fully matured; the popular nature and Party spirit of realism have become clearer and more firmly established. We should say, however, that these works have made an ideological contribution rather than furthering the artistic development of realism. This was due to a period of war and the influence of dogmatism, as stated above.

If this analysis is correct, can we therefore assert that the major problem in our literary endeavors is the conflict between the tenets of realism and those of antirealist dogmatism, a conflict which has resulted in the artistic impoverishment of realism itself?

VI

Chairman Mao told us that revolutionary literature is produced by the revolutionary writer reflecting the life of the people. Lu Hsün, moreover, instructed us that a revolutionary writer should participate in the revolution, that he should feel the pulse of revolution and become a fighting proletarian. Then, no matter what such a writer's subject or sources may be, his work will be significant, now and in the future.

As realism advances into the socialist era it demands that the writer be revolutionary in his thinking, and that he become a fighting proletarian. In other words, he must have the most advanced of world views, the Communist world view. As a result, his work, which reflects the writer's image of the life of the people, will be of value whatever its subject happens to be, and his work will be realistic.

No one has propounded such clear and simple guidelines, which are at the same time strict and practical, as Chairman Mao and Lu Hsün.

The practice of dogmatism should be ended immediately.

Henceforth, if we seriously study the creative techniques of the masters of realism; if we depict life in the same fashion as Lu Hsün, Gorky, and Sholokhov; if we regard their classic works as standards by which to assess the validity of our theory and the degree of realism in our own works, our literature will be transformed.

SOCIALIST REALISM

16

IS REALISM FOREVER
CHANGELESS?

YAO WEN-YÜAN

Following the publication of Ho Chih's article in *Jen-min wen-hsüeh* (People's Literature) last September, a revisionist trend has gradually entered the area of literary theory. According to the dictates of this trend, the essence of realism is "writing the truth"; realism is believed to be forever changeless; socialist realism is no different in its methods from the realism of the past; and there is no essential difference between socialist literature and capitalist literature. Emphasizing the significance of the realistic mode of expression in art, this trend divorces the writer's thought from his creative skill, asserting that a high degree of artistry will automatically involve the writer's thought. Those who support this trend refer to socialist realism as "realism in the socialist era."

The publication of Liu Shao-t'ang's article in *Wen-i hsüeh-hsi* (Literary Studies) amounted to a complete rejection of the orientation of literature toward the workers, peasants, and soldiers. It was also a negation of the achievements of past literary movements. This revisionist trend received considerable support from young writers of

"Hsien-shih chu-i shih wan-ku pu-pien ti ma?" (Is Realism Forever Changeless?) This article was first written and published in 1957. It was later included in a collection entitled *Polemics on Literature,* which was published by the Shanghai Editorial Branch of the Writer's Press in September 1964. This abridged version was taken from the second edition, which appeared in August 1965.

intellectual background, and exerted a certain influence on their work. In Nanking, several young writers planned a magazine edited by fellow writers, entitled *T'an-so-che* (Explorer). One of its proposed guidelines supported Ho Chih's opposition to socialist realism in favor of pure realism. In analyzing certain works of literature, we can more clearly discern the influence of this revisionist trend.

The methods of literary creation are different from those of mathematics, physics, or handicrafts. Literature serves to reflect society, and is the outgrowth of a writer's viewpoint, his observations and thoughts. Literature reveals the attitude of the writer, and offers comments on various aspects of life. Chairman Mao has stated: "Literature, as the creation of ideas, is a reflection of the life of the people as viewed by the author. Revolutionary literature is a reflection of the life of the people as viewed by a revolutionary writer." This is the essential principle for any study of creative methods in writing.

Obviously, a writer's creative approach and his actual skill are two very different things; also, the writer's world view is not the same thing as his creative approach. Comrade Mao Tse-tung has stated explicitly that "Marxism can encompass, but not serve as a substitute for, realism in literary creation." As in the other arts, literary writing requires skill. For example, one cannot portray the realities of life without having mastered the complexities of language; one must also have absorbed the literary heritage of one's predecessors, and have learned the basics of creative writing. Although literary writing requires skill, certain people condemn the mere mention of the word "skill" as formulaic. I consider this a rash and biased attitude. Lu Hsün urged young writers to develop their skill. Neglecting to do so will impede our task of raising artistic standards. We shall certainly not deny the importance of skill, but will strive to acquire it.

Skill, however, is not the essential factor in literary creation. We have a wealth of experience accumulated by previous writers, but no definite skills can be singled out of their experience to be universally applied to literary writing; one cannot become a great writer simply by understanding the skills of the best writers. We do not mean that there are no principles governing literary creation; it is simply that such principles are not concerned with skill alone; the writer's convictions are another decisive factor. The portrayal of life, and the acquiring of expertise in observing and giving expression to the realities of life, are invariably related to the author's attitude toward life itself. They are also related to his understanding of life and his approach to experience in life. The ideological factor is intrinsically related to the factor of skill and serves to govern the exercising of the latter. Consequently, a shift in one's ideology will often result in a revision of one's creative method. One's world view is not the same as one's creative mode, but the creative mode will invariably reflect one's ideas about life. A different world view and a different way of thinking will bring about a different understanding of reality, and will effect a different portrayal of reality in art. In other words, they will cause one to change one's creative method.

As class struggle proceeds, society is in a state of constant change; a writer's position in society changes as well. As a result, the writer's viewpoint and understanding of life are in a state of flux. The creative method of realism continually evolves and enriches itself in keeping with the development of the entire society. In history, there is no unchanging realism; realism is constantly and definitely evolving into something different.

This thesis is a prerequisite in our study of creative methods. The fundamental difference between our position and that of Ho Chih lies in this issue. He states:

This [literary realism] does not lead to the rigid acceptance of any particular world view, although one could be influenced and governed by a world view. During the whole process of literary and artistic creation, one should take broad objective reality as the subject. One must view this reality as the crux of one's writing, and attempt to influence actual life. The portrayal of life is not simply a matter of mechanical reproduction. Rather, it is the pursuit of the truth of life and art. This is the basic premise of realism.[1]

Ho Chih's essential point here is that the creative method of realism is free of ideology, and is only indirectly influenced by one's world view. Since this influence is an indirect one, the creative method of realism can be studied in a manner entirely independent of one's world view or a specific ideology, as though it were a piece of fruit

[1] Ho Chih (Ch'in Chao-yang), "Hsien-shih chu-i—kuang-k'uo ti tao-lu" (The Broad Road of Realism—A Reassessment of Realism); *Jen-min wen-hsüeh* (People's Literature), September 1956. The article is translated in this anthology.

plucked from a tree. In this way, Ho Chih not only dissociates the realistic creative method from one's world view, but places the two in contradiction with each other.

From the perspective of Chinese history, realism has gone through various stages. At each stage, the characteristics of realism were connected with the world view or life style of a certain class, and with the need of that class to place art at the service of politics. Certain writers who had been influenced by European realism and who were critical of society converted, after the liberation, to revolutionary realism. The crucial factor of their conversion lies in the transformation of their world view and attitude toward literature, as well as in their shift in life style from an isolated existence apart from the masses to a life involved with the workers, peasants, and soldiers. Only when a writer has progressive sensibilities will he be able to want and to realize truthfulness in life and art. Conversely, a writer's mistaken, reactionary ideas always prevent him from arriving at a correct understanding and reflection of the realities of life. Such ideas also tend to hamper the writer in making typical representations of life in his art. There has never been an instance of a reactionary writer producing an immortal character.

The Communist vision has become the greatest reality of our era. In order to portray this reality in an era of proletarian revolution, we must give full expression to the revolutionary aspirations in the minds of millions of working people. To do away with the aspirations of life is to rid it of its truthfulness. Certain current works of literature dismiss idealism in life under the slogan "writing the truth." Consequently, through their disclosure of partial truths, such works offer a depiction of life that is discouragingly gray or even pitch-black. They substitute the bourgeois dissatisfaction with reality and the individualism of the petit bourgeoisie for the vision of Communism. The initiators of this revisionist trend refer to this as "realism in the socialist era," which is intended to be distinguished from social realism and revolutionary realism. Moreover, they try to introduce a variety of other concepts as connected with "realism in the socialist era."

17

AGAINST A NIHILISTIC VIEW OF SOCIALIST LITERATURE: AN EXCHANGE OF VIEWS WITH COMRADE LIU SHAO-T'ANG

CHOU HO

Comrade Liu Shao-t'ang began the two articles "Realism in the Socialist Era" and "Some Thoughts on Literary Problems Today" with the same statement: Our literature has made considerable progress, yet the influence of dogmatism has prevented it from making the greatest possible achievement. The content of both articles, however, seems to contradict this entire statement. One gets the impression that all this talk of "achievement" is nothing other than empty praise, and that he recognizes no such achievement at all. One feels this way because Liu's articles fail to cite the positive aspects of our literature and because the essential argument of his discussion tends to contradict the statement cited above. A closer examination of his views will make this clear.

Abridged from Chou Ho, "Fan-tui tui she-hui chu-i wen-hsüeh ti hsü-wu chu-i t'ai-tu" (Against a Nihilistic View of Socialist Literature: An Exchange of Views with Comrade Liu Shao-t'ang), *Wen-i pao* (Literary Gazette), No. 15, 1957.

A COMPARISON OF LITERARY DEVELOPMENTS IN
POSTREVOLUTIONARY CHINA AND THE SOVIET UNION

According to Comrade Liu Shao-t'ang, three elements determine the creation of great works of literature: (1) the material for creative work provided by the writer's era; (2) the existence of gifted writers with aesthetic sensitivity and talent for observing and comprehending life; and (3) theories guiding the writers' thought.

It is his view that the evils of dogmatism have not only retarded the development of socialist literature in the People's Republic from the very beginning, but also have weakened what has been actually produced. In all, he believes our creative life is now almost entirely stifled. We have produced nothing comparable to the literature of the Soviet Union in the first two decades following the Russian revolution. Comrade Liu asserts that this failure derives from the fact that our theories guiding the writers' thought were affected by dogmatism from the very beginning. He traces this "beginning," moreover, not to the early days of the People's Republic, but way back to 1942 when Chairman Mao delivered his "Talks at the Yenan Forum on Literature and Art."

Liu states that in the past fifteen years we have produced nothing but formula writing, such as *Hsiung-mei k'ai-huang* (Brother and Sister Reclaim the Wasteland). Such work illustrates certain political principles and serves the temporary purposes of propaganda and education, but as literature it "lacks enduring artistic appeal," and is "limited in thought." If this is actually the case, what "achievement" is there to speak of? Yet Comrade Liu affirms our achievement. From his "historical standpoint," he confirms the positive value of "conceptualized formula writing." He even tries to defend the shallow writing produced during the Anti-Japanese War and the War of Liberation: "They succeeded in serving the functions assigned them at the time: the propagandization and mobilization of the people. They distinguished our literary efforts." He continues, "Although not a single great writer or a single piece of great work appeared during the Anti-Japanese War, the works produced in that period comprise a glorious chapter in the history of our literature. The many anonymous writers involved comprise a great collective

Writer, and their works comprise a great collective Work; this is unprecedented in history."

Although I do not understand what he means by a "great collective Work," I do see that Comrade Liu is trying very hard to affirm
our "achievement." And because he is unable to discover a single author or piece of work worthy of his praise, he must give a positive
"historical evaluation" to these shallow, propagandistic writings; he
concedes a distinguished position in our literary history to these
anonymous writers.

Comrade Liu's seemingly affirmative analysis is actually nothing
other than a complete repudiation of the literature of the past fifteen years. If it were true that during these years we produced
nothing but conceptualized formula writing, it would then follow
that we had not only failed to produce a single work or writer of any
stature, but had no true body of literature at all. But is this actually
the case? Is it true that we have produced nothing since 1942 but
works which Comrade Liu Shao-t'ang describes as being written
"from certain propagandistic motives," like the verse play *Brother and
Sister Reclaim the Wasteland*? Are such works as *Pai-mao nü* (The
White-Haired Girl), the novels of Chao Shu-li, *T'ai-yang chao tsai
Sang-kan ho shang* (The Sun Shines over the Sangkan River) by Ting
Ling, *Pao-feng tsou-yü* (The Hurricane) by Chou Li-po, *Wang Kuei yü
Li Hsiang-hsiang* (Wang Kuei and Li Hsiang-hsiang) by Li Chi,
Chang-ho shui (The Waters of the Chang River) by Yüan Chang-chin,
Pien-ch'ü tzu-wei-chün (The Militia on the Border) by Ko Chung-
p'ing, *Kao Kan-ta* by Ou-yang Shan, K'ang Cho's early short stories,
Sun Li's stories, Liu Pai-yü's stories and essays—are all these works
merely conceptualized formula writing, unable to withstand the test
of time? If this is the case, why do people continue to read them,
and what particular policies and directives do they supposedly expound? Moreover, do all the excellent plays, films, essays, fiction,
and poetry that appeared following the liberation lack "enduring artistic appeal," and are they "limited in thought?" I believe that any
reader with realistic sensibilities and a proper historical perspective
would think otherwise. I am not altogether denying the existence of
certain phenomena cited by Comrade Liu; but he presents only part
of the picture. To exaggerate so insignificant an aspect of the situa-

tion and obscure the true achievement of our struggle is like painting a man's face white and calling him a clown.

And when Comrade Liu makes observations on the Soviet literature of the twenty-year period following the Russian revolution, he
does so from an unscientific point of view. To lend force to his
argument, he adopts a stance refuted by Soviet critics themselves:
that the literature of this period is superior to that of the following
two decades. There is no need to deny that Soviet literature was
badly affected by the dogmatic ideology of the cult of Stalin. However, Liu states: ". . . when writers were allowed to write only of the
superiority of socialism, and to serve particular propaganda purposes, when they began to misrepresent the realities of life and ignore conflicts among the people, literature became the adornment
of a false prosperity. It was then that the concept of 'no-conflict'
came to prevail. As a result, the literary endeavors of the second
twenty years were greatly inferior to those of the first twenty years
after the Russian revolution."

Again, this is a distortion of the facts. Actually, Soviet literature,
in spite of various difficulties, showed a strong development during
the second two decades. It is not necessary to list all the great writers
who appeared in the thirties; such people as Alexi Tolstoy, Leonid
Leonov, Ilya Ehrenburg, Konstantin Fedin, Feodor Gladkov, Alexander Tvardovsky, Valentin Katayev, Nikolai Tikhonov, and Alexander Korneychuk all produced works of lasting value. Mikhail Sholokhov, whom Comrade Liu apparently admires very much and
mentions often, completed his epic, *And Quiet Flows the Don,* in 1940.
The second volume of his *Virgin Soil Upturned* is an even more recent
work. Alexander Fadeyev, author of *The Rout,* wrote *The Young
Guard* after World War II. Many of the new writers who appeared
after World War II have produced works comparable both in artistry and thought to those of the twenty years immediately following
the revolution. These comprise but a segment of the entire body of
work, but they are sufficient to display the bias of Comrade Liu's
negative evaluation of Soviet literature of the second twenty-year
period.

The zeal with which Comrade Liu slanders the history of our literature over the past fifteen years, and that of the Soviet Union during its second twenty-year period, derives from his desire to prove

that in our theories guiding the writers' thought the principles of dogmatism have replaced those of realism. This, he feels, has resulted in a tragic backwardness and poverty in our literature. Liu considers the problem of theories guiding the writers' thought to be basically a problem of literary leadership: if the leadership errs, our literature cannot help but fail.

THE ORIGINS OF DOGMATISM

Comrade Liu has labeled himself an antidogmatist. He has tried to attack dogmatism at its very roots. His daring has won him the admiration of many of our comrades. They believe that his views have pinpointed the real problems of our literary situation. Some of them have rallied to his support. Others, although in disagreement with his views, are touched by his "courage." I would not say he is entirely wrong in his opinions, but I do believe his basic attitude in no way deserves our support.

What, then, are the origins of dogmatism? Comrade Liu informs us that from all his probing and research he has discovered that the trouble lies with theories guiding the writers' thought. He states that dogmatism has been at the root of various problems concerning theories guiding the writers' thought, and that our literature will not progress until the obstacle is removed. Liu informs us that the trouble arises from two facts which manifest its nature. First, socialist realism as defined in the charter of the Union of Soviet Writers runs counter to the true spirit of realist literature. Second, Chairman Mao's "Talks at the Yenan Forum on Literature and Art" has two parts: one outlines the tactical guidelines for the literary and artistic movement at that particular time; the other provides guidelines for the long-term development of our art and literature. According to Comrade Liu, "Dogmatists interpret and apply Chairman Mao's guiding theory for literature and art of a particular time mechanically, conservatively, exaggeratedly, and in an erratic manner." The Soviet dogmatic theories have joined our own in such a way as to impede rather than further the development of our literature and art. This is what Comrade Liu has discovered to be the crux of our literary problems. And in the eyes of various of our admiring comrades, this discovery constitutes the thrust of his argument.

Comrade Liu was not the first to say there are problems in the definition and application of socialist realism. He is unique, however, in his mode of reasoning. After citing the official Soviet definition of socialist realism, he comments:

A creative approach of this sort was obviously not formulated in order to encourage writers to base their work on the realities of life, or to deal honestly with these things. Rather, it encourages writers to depict life in relation to "reality in its revolutionary development." Such a depiction, furthermore, must be combined with a sense of "duty." Writers, therefore, are quite confused in regard to the issue of reality. If the realities of life are not considered real, and writing itself is supposed to involve the "revolutionary development" of reality, writers are forced to embellish life and ignore its true features. . . . Is there then any meaning for "reality" as it pertains to realism?

Socialist realism as a creative mode is incompatible with monotonous, mediocre formula writing, and the notion of no-conflict. This creative mode demands that a writer observe life from a Marxist point of view. In so doing, he is able to observe and depict life in the most comprehensive and incisive manner; he is provided with the broadest possible perspective for his creative exploration. This has been proved by the writers of the Soviet Union and other countries where socialist realism is the creative mode. The "truthful, historically concrete portrayal of reality in its revolutionary development" is not an approach that ignores or embellishes the realities of life. On the contrary, it raises the writer's consciousness and allows him to penetrate the structure and rhythm of life in all its dynamic movement.

Actually, socialist realism requires a writer to portray life in a more comprehensive manner, and in no way allows him to "ignore reality." Soviet writers have produced innumerable excellent works dealing with the realities of life. These works have unmasked the truth of actual life in a severe manner. On what does Comrade Liu base his assertion that this creative approach does not "encourage writers to base their work on the realities of life," but, rather, leads a writer "to embellish life and ignore its true features"? If a writer applies the principles of socialist realism, he can never produce work that is "unfaithful to the realities of life" or that "embellishes life." Socialist realism, moreover, is by its very nature in contradiction with such work. Those writers who have produced pessimistic, mediocre work have not done so through the application of the principles of socialist realism; they have violated these principles or applied them in a mistaken manner. After having twisted the original definition of socialist realism, Comrade Liu blames various failures on the creative approach itself.

Liu Shao-t'ang may indeed be the first person to discover two different concerns in Chairman Mao's "Talks at the Yenan Forum on Literature and Art." This "discovery," however, is nothing but a serious distortion of the meaning of Chairman Mao's "Talks." The history of our literature over the past fifteen years testifies to the epoch-making significance of these "Talks" as a landmark of revolutionary literature. Liu, however, claims to see in them only "tactical guidelines for the literary and artistic movement at that particular time." He blatantly asserts that the long-term application of these guidelines has produced dogmatic, conceptualized formula writing. He further states that works produced under these guidelines had a "positive effect" at the time, but that the theories are now entirely inadequate. Although he never explicitly states that the "Talks" are as a whole outmoded, his reinterpretation of their meaning and his refutation of part of them are clever ways of insinuating the same thing. Anyone who has seriously studied the "Talks" will realize that it was not their purpose simply to resolve the immediate, tactical problems regarding propaganda and education in that time and place. Rather, it was their purpose to resolve the problem of our basic attitude toward revolutionary literature and art.

We can certainly say that, were it not for the "Talks," we would not have made so considerable an achievement in revolutionary literature and art; we would not have had many writers employing their talents in the service of workers, peasants, and soldiers. Comrade Liu's attempt to extract "tactical guidelines for the literary and artistic movement at that particular time" from the "Talks" is in contradiction with the original spirit of the "Talks." It is only natural that so comprehensive a set of guidelines should apply both to the present and to the future. Indeed, the "Talks" exerted a profound influence on our art and literature at the time Chairman Mao propounded the guidelines. But Liu's assertion, that to require literature to serve politics is to require literature to serve specific policies, is his own misinterpretation of the "Talks"; that policy is not required in the "Talks." True, there have been many misinterpretations of the "Talks," and our literature has suffered as a consequence. These misinterpretations are a problem in themselves, and Comrade Liu could criticize them in a definite manner. However, to attribute all the blame for our literary difficulties to the "Talks" by reading into them "tactical guidelines for a particular time" is a distortion of the situation and of the "Talks" themselves.

Furthermore, during the Anti-Japanese War, the War of Liberation, and the period following the founding of the People's Republic, our literature was not simply guided by the "tactical guidelines"; our literature was not merely a vehicle of propaganda, advocating various policies and doctrines. Although historical circumstances have at times compelled us to devote much of our energy to propagandistic work, it has been our abiding principle never to lose sight of the essential characteristics and particular qualities of literature. This is clearly stated in Chairman Mao's "Talks," and we have carefully observed this principle throughout the entire course of our revolutionary literature.

Since the liberation, we have continued to stress the importance of the popularization of literature. This is not because we have adhered to the "tactical guidelines for a particular time." We have done so because our literature continues to be divorced from the masses, and there has yet to be any marked improvement in the situation. It has always been considered an important task to popularize literature and art among the masses, whenever possible. That literature and art are becoming increasingly accessible to the masses is a direct result of this policy. Comrade Liu, in his peculiar manner, connects such efforts toward popularization with the explication of specific political policies. He then cites the concept of raising artistic standards by way of opposing popularization, asserting that the historical situation is such that we no longer need popular literature. Today, he believes, only raising artistic standards is needed.

This idea is also wrong. Comrade Liu has entirely failed to grasp the dialectical relationship between the popularization of literature and the raising of artistic standards, which is implicit in the "Talks." Consequently, he believes the former to be a thing of the past; today we require only the latter. In fact, these two concepts are not the opposites Comrade Liu imagines them to be. The raising of artistic standards was necessary in the past as well, and we encouraged this. It is true that we are now in greater need of such an effort, but this must be done with a view toward the popularization of literature and art. Both now and in the future, these two concepts must continue to influence and transform each other; they must not be regarded as separate entities, or as being in contradiction with each other. No one would object to the raising of artistic standards or the level of ideas in our literature. It would be a different matter, however, if one tried casually to dismiss the literary achievements of the past under the pretext of "raising artistic standards." It is an even graver error to make a false accounting of our literary situation, and, in a roundabout manner, to blame various imaginary faults on Chairman Mao's "Talks."

It is dangerous to probe the question of dogmatism in the manner chosen by Comrade Liu Shao-t'ang. The object of his attack was not dogmatism itself, but the correct guiding theories of our literary movement, which he simply discards as dogmatism. As a result, even the correct views that appear in his articles are overshadowed by his nihilistic and liquidationist arguments.

Perhaps Comrade Liu considers dogmatism to be the only obstacle in the path of literary progress today, and thinks that if it were removed we would produce great writers and great works of literature. Such a belief displays both his naïveté and rightist thought. We must realize that bourgeois ideology has always been the greatest enemy of our literary endeavors. Not only do bourgeois ideas find expression in the work of nonproletarian writers, but we ourselves may be influenced by such ideas. If we do not adhere to our point of view, and distinguish between right and wrong, such ideas may begin to influence our thinking; we ourselves may begin to talk like bourgeois writers. It seems to me that the erroneous views apparent in Comrade Liu's two articles actually derive from rightist sentiments. Thought reform continues to be a necessary task for all of us.

18

ON THE SPECIOUS CONCEPT
OF "WRITING THE TRUTH"

MAO TUN

During the last year and a half, a number of literary figures have noisily supported the concept of "writing the truth." Some of these people have revealed themselves as rightists antagonistic to the Party and to socialism in general. Nevertheless, the term "writing the truth" continues to attract and mislead too many young writers and artists. They have yet to learn that the term is for the most part employed by revisionists. The purpose of this essay is to discuss certain of the more obvious problems relating to "writing the truth."

I

Literature should be realistic in nature; that is undeniable. This has been true since ancient times, particularly of those works which we refer to as "great" or "timeless."

But what, exactly, is "writing the truth?"

There are two conflicting answers to this question, each as old as literature itself. According to one point of view, a writer attempts to represent his personal understanding of reality in his work,

Mao Tun, "Kuan-yü so-wei hsieh chen-shih" (On the Specious Concept of "Writing the Truth"), *Jen-min wen-hsüeh* (People's Literature), No. 2, 1958.

disregarding the objective laws of the real world. The other course for a writer is to adhere faithfully to these laws without subjective prejudice.

The first concept, that a writer should offer us his subjective, entirely personal world, is one of absolute idealism. Writing of this sort has little to do with objective reality, and therefore is not realistic in the true sense. The second concept, however, which asserts that the writer reflects objective reality, is in keeping with dialectical materialism. Such writing is truly realistic in nature.

In order to examine the enormous disparity between idealism and dialectical materialism, we might begin by examining the way in which each addresses itself to the crucial issue confronting any author: how to explain social phenomena.

The idealist believes that history is governed by "the hero," that events which are turning points in history are brought about through the will and deeds of great men. According to the idealist, these "heroes" are capable of influencing the course of events by virtue of their innate superhuman qualities.

The Marxist materialist realizes that the working people determine the course of history, and that the most powerful force in social development is the way in which material production is achieved. The actions of the "hero" effect change only when they coincide with the laws of social development, and with the best interests and expectations of the people.

Which of these two explanations of social phenomena is more in keeping with objective truth? History supports the latter.

Nevertheless, the exploiting class will insist that history is fashioned by the hero. It is quite obvious that the truth to which they refer is that of the ruling class, rather than that of the proletariat.

With which version of truth should the writer concern himself? In order to arrive at a decision, he must ask himself: from what standpoint can we discern the truth?

The rightist has a different understanding of reality from that of the people. For eight years, rightists have been telling us that the task of constructing the country is a "mess." The people have denounced this foolish talk. If an author observes social realities from the standpoint of the people, his work will serve to portray objective truth accurately. To adopt any other stance is to guarantee a distortion of things as they are, and ensures that the author's work will assume a quality of unreality.

This is the first and most important thing we must recognize about the truth. We must not become confused in our point of view if we wish to avoid the pitfalls of revisionist thought and to prevent our work from becoming essentially rightist in nature.

II

The rightist slogan "writing the truth" is nothing other than "revealing the darker aspects of life." One need only refer briefly to their works to see that this is the case.

The exposure of unpleasant facts had its place in the literature of the old society. However, it is absurd for this to become the sole function of "writing the truth" in our new society. Even in the old society, bleak as it was, the portrayal of ugliness for the purpose of merely exposing it occupied no more than half of the writer's attention. This was because, in the midst of their oppression, the working class lent a brighter aspect to things simply by engaging in struggle. A writer who ignores this aspect of the old social order does not present the truth in its entirety.

The situation is different in our new society. We have rid ourselves of oppression, and the socialist system is being established. The sustaining force of our new order is generated by the diligent, brave, and contented working class. Therefore, the progress and brightness of our society are the realities of our existence. Life, of course, has its negative aspects as well, but these exist in the midst of progress. They are the remnants of the old society and the object of our struggle. If our works of literature depict an untroubled existence, free of problems or struggle, they are mere decorative frauds from the fantasy world of no-conflict. But if it is the intention of an author to reveal only the negative aspects of our recent history, he will not only denigrate our social system but will also present a distorted image of our society as a whole.

The point, therefore, is not that the negative aspects of our society must never be portrayed, but that the writer must determine the attitude and position he will adopt in offering such a portrayal. One must not play the detached spectator while depicting the sordid obstacles that impede our progress. A writer who adopts such an attitude has divorced himself from the working class. He becomes a mere bystander, and his work will produce negative effects.

It is even more important that one not take pleasure in the calamities that happen to us. To do so would be to view unhappiness with the attitude of a rightist, and consequently that of a capitalist. Writing of this sort is extremely venomous.

The proper attitude is one that stems from the views of the working class, an attitude of love for our social system and an abhorrence for anything which hinders our progress.

We are opposed to theory that ignores the conflicts in our society. However, we are even more strongly opposed to the absurd, ill-founded assertion that "writing the truth is the exposure of the darker aspects of life." This theory has been secretly promoted in our society under the guise of opposing the theory of no-conflict.

III

Those who advocate "writing the truth" in this fashion have yet another idea. They choose to believe that an author is justified in addressing himself to any phenomenon so long as it is a reality of life rather than a product of his imagination. The phenomenon must be treated as "true."

Actually, this is an extremely stale notion. It is a reiteration of the capitalists' fallacious theory of objectivity. Capitalists justify their decadence as a "fact of life," because it is to their advantage to do so. Under the guise of "recording everything," they have created a yellow journalism of the sort that benefits capitalists while corrupting the working class. However, these capitalist journalists never seem to be able to "record everything" regarding the glorious struggles taking place in socialist countries that threaten their system.

We support socialist realism. We believe in our age; the events most worthy of our attention are those that bear on the destiny and happiness of the majority of society. Foremost among these are the great social revolution and the evolution of human thought. A work of literature has little value if it does no more than depict the superficialities of the social revolution. A work must also describe the effect of this revolution on the consciousness of the masses—the changing modes of human thought in the midst of social change. And in my opinion, to describe the inner world of individual people is to achieve this purpose. Pointless witticisms, the meaningless portrayal of the details of daily life—these things have no relationship to the individual's inner world if they do not serve to reflect the subtle changes in a person's thinking in the midst of social change. It is not my intention, of course, to say that one must never make witty remarks or write about matters that seem trivial. Such things can be of use when they are needed to reveal a person's character. But these details must be skillfully and carefully selected if the writer is to avoid the pitfalls of naturalism, which has different principles from those of realism.

Hu Feng and others of his sort frantically declare that "life can be experienced anywhere." Such people employ this equivocal slogan to oppose the Party's call to describe the vigorous class struggle, the struggle for production, and the men and events arising from these struggles. It is imperative that we note the way in which the term "writing the truth" lends itself to Hu Feng's absurd claim that "life can be experienced anywhere." Those who assert that writers must write the truth ridicule the absence of the complicated plots and laborious character development that is characteristic of certain works of literature. Naturally, little pleasure can be derived from a story so simplistic in its plot and characterization that the reader will be able to predict the outcome after glancing at the first few pages. It is our belief, however, that the fault of such works lies in the author's inability to experience life in depth, or to arrive at an understanding of the people; the fault cannot be attributed to the author's failure to provide the reader with nonsensical jokes or meaningless trivia.

We would like to emphasize the following point: the rather immature works dealing with events of great social import, despite their inferior artistry and their imperfections of plot and characterization, are correct in the principle that they are for and about the realities of peasants, workers, and soldiers; they are based on the Party principle that literary works should be written for the proletariat. Works of the sort mentioned above have served to reflect the realities of our society accurately. They are deficient in their artistic quality alone. Our Party Central Committee has often emphasized the importance of getting rid of conceptualized formula writing. The committee has repeatedly urged authors to involve themselves with the struggle of the lower classes. Such involvement will enrich their experience and allow them to eradicate the roots of formula writing and conceptualism.

The rightists, however, in promoting "writing the truth," have used slogans against conceptualized formula writing as excuses to attack works that concern themselves with great social events, the men of the new era, their class struggle, and their struggle for production. The rightists have labeled these works "unrealistic" and are now presenting their own examples of writing the truth. These works deal only with the darker aspects of our society. Certain feeble-minded young people are following this course. As a result, there is considerable confusion about what is of value in literature and art.

This paradoxical slogan is essentially derived from bourgeois literary thought. It must be analyzed and refuted in theory and in practice. This matter of selling dog meat under the sign of a sheep's head must not be allowed to continue.

The paradoxical slogan is misleading, especially for those young people who are incapable of discrimination. This situation now involves a struggle regarding our literary and artistic direction. When we engage in a national debate on this subject, we must engage in repeated discussion and analysis of concrete examples in order to defeat the revisionist influence on the young and to strengthen their Marxist education. We must do so in a thorough, step-by-step manner. We must focus on these problems in depth, and avoid abstract and inflated arguments.

This rather brief essay is by no means a thorough examination of the matter of "writing the truth." I have done no more than bring up certain problems and present arguments of principle. I have not analyzed or criticized any specific rightist works. I find that I am not satisfied with my efforts, and would be grateful for the reader's criticism and advice.

HUMANISM AND
LITERATURE

HUMANISM

19

LITERATURE IS THE
STUDY OF MAN

CH'IEN KU-JUNG

Gorky once suggested that literature be called "the study of man."
We often quote this suggestion to show that literature must place
man at the center of description and create vivid, typical characters.
However, our understanding stops there—we stress the importance
of man and cannot go any further. In fact, the implication of
Gorky's suggestion is extremely profound and wide. We can use it as
a master key to unlock all literary problems. Whoever wants to penetrate into the recesses of art and literature, whether a creative writer
or a theorist, has only to grasp this key. Without it, a critic will not be
able to explain certain artistic and literary phenomena, while a creative writer will not be able to produce genuine artistic works that
appeal to human emotions.

The suggestion is not merely Gorky's invention. Many philosophers and literary masters have expressed similar ideas, and all the
outstanding literary works of the past prove its authenticity. It was
only after Gorky had read far and wide in the masterpieces and absorbed the literary concepts advocated by past philosophers and literary masters that he was able to put the basic characteristics of literature in such clear and concise words.

Abridged from Ch'ien Ku-jung, "Lun wen-hsüeh shih jen hsüeh" (Literature Is the
Study of Man), *Wen-i yüeh-pao* (Literary Monthly), May 1957.

The purpose of this article is to explain some implications of Gorky's suggestion and then to use it to discuss some controversial issues in current artistic and literary circles.

I

The subject and object of literature should be man: Man in action, and man in various complex social relations. This is common sense and needs no further explanation. People, however, tend to regard the portrayal of man as no more than an instrument of literature: as Dimofeiyev says in his *Theory of Literature,* "The portrayal of man is an instrument used by the artist to reflect total reality." In other words, the reflection of total reality is the immediate and foremost function of writing. By this definition, man plays only a subordinate role in literary works; the writer has no interest in "man" himself. Although he portrays man, what the writer thinks and concerns himself with is the depiction of so-called total reality. If this is so, how can this character be vivid, alive, and have his own genuine personality? How empty and abstract a concept this so-called total reality is! If a writer sets himself the task of "reflecting total reality," if he starts to create from such a vague and abstract principle, he can only turn his characters into illustrations of reality as he perceives it; he can only extract the feelings, thoughts, and soul of his characters and turn them into puppets.

It should be admitted that Dimofeiyev still places some emphasis on the characteristics of literature and art; there are many keen perceptions in his *Theory of Literature.* The book has been severely criticized and condemned in the Soviet Union, in my opinion not entirely correctly, but the theory of using man as an instrument is accepted in the Soviet Union and China. Because Dimofeiyev's theory has authority in our literary circles, a lot of literary writings based on it have emerged. Concerning the reflection of reality, these writings are correct and comprehensive. But if man is used as an instrument to reflect reality, he becomes an instrument without feelings and does not arouse the slightest interest in people.

Do I imply that literature cannot or does not have to reflect reality? Of course not. Literature can and must reflect reality. What I am against is taking the reflection of reality to be the primary function of literature and especially taking man to be an instrument for reflecting reality. To do so is to take literature as social science, it is to violate the nature and characteristics of literature. Dealing with the portrayal of man in this way, the writer can never create a character and a genuine man; and his work will become abstract.

How, then, should we understand the function of literature? And how should we portray man?

Outstanding philosophers and writers of the past usually regarded literature as an effective means of influencing and educating the people. They felt that all things must begin with man and all things must serve man. In his early writing, "Mo Lo shih-li shuo" (Theory of the Poetic Power of Mo Lo), Lu Hsün said that the highest achievement of the poet is to be able to "transmit his wonderful tune, communicate his feelings and sensibilities, beautify and perfect our emotions, and ennoble our thoughts." The reason he recommends and admires masterpieces since Homer is that after one has finished reading them, one is able to get closer to life—to "see clearly the good things and the defects of life and therefore to try harder to achieve perfection."

Lu Hsün does not hold this opinion alone. We can say that nearly all the outstanding poets of the past who had a great love for life share this view. Talking about the function of literature, Chernyshevsky says: "A poet guides people to approach a noble concept of life, noble ideas and sentiments; as we read a poet's work, we hate things vulgar and disdainful, we see the charm of the beautiful and the good, we are encouraged to become better and nobler." All the arts, including literature, have as their purpose the improvement of the quality of human life. They provide eager hopes and noble ideas that will move men to achieve the beautiful and the perfect. These are the ideals that drive all great poets to write. In order to improve the life of man, we have to improve man himself, to clear away his weakness and evil, and to cultivate and elevate his tenacity as well as his courageous, fighting spirit. In "The Readers," Gorky talks about the goal and duty of literature:

The goal of literature is to help man understand himself; to elevate his confidence; to develop his desire for the truth; to resist vulgarity; to discover good qualities; to arouse in him the sense of shame, of anger, of courage; to make him strong and noble; and to arouse man with a beautiful and noble spirit.

All literary masterpieces regard as their primary function the singing of the praises of good people and good deeds, and the condemnation and the reproaching of evil people and evil deeds. The fight between good and evil, right and wrong, has become the primary theme in literature in which good conquers evil, right wins over wrong. Even when evil gets the upper hand, the people's sympathy is always on the side of the good and the right. As Corneille says about the function of drama: "Although good men may have misfortunes, everyone still loves and sympathizes with them; a bad man may succeed, yet everyone hates or dislikes him." The reason for this lies with the writer who, in describing his characters, does not use them as instruments for his own purpose. Instead, he looks at them as men like himself. He cannot but love those who are kind and conscientious, hate those he thinks wicked and evil. In his writings, he laughs and weeps with the good people; he is happy over their happiness, worried over their worries. In regard to the bad people, he always bears the greatest hatred and contempt for them, revealing their hypocrisies and depicting their ugliness. He gives his characters life through his strong feelings of love and hate. It is the characters with life who move the audience; the audience then, like the author, loves the good people and hates the bad.

The author can further stimulate his audience actively to help the good and to fight to exterminate the evil in real life. This is also the reason why, when we are told of the literary masters who have created distinguished works, we feel great respect and gratitude. If an author has his eye only on the so-called total reality or "the essence of life," "the law governing the development of life," as some people call it, man will be used merely as an instrument of reflection, and the author will never produce works that will move people, or that will make a great impact.

Does this mean, then, that the link between literature and reality will be severed and the function of literature to reflect life abolished? Such concern is unnecessary. Unless the writer is incapable of portraying a real character, he will surely be able to depict the time a man lives in, the society, and the current, complex class relationships. Because man cannot exist outside the context of a specific time, society, and class relationship, if there are none of these, there can be no "man" and no "character." From each concrete man, we can see the marks of time, society, and class. And nobody can remove these marks. Did Ts'ao Hsüeh-ch'in write *The Dream of the Red Chamber* in order to reflect the collapse of feudalist society and to reflect the decline of the bureaucratic gentry class? Of course not. He was driven to write by his deep, complex, and sustained feelings toward characters like Chia Pao-yü and Lin Tai-yü. Nevertheless, what we see in this novel is not just the personal life of Chia and the others, but the whole society of that time. We can also say the same thing about works like *Hamlet, Don Quixote, Oblomov,* and *The Story of Ah Q.*

Man and man's life cannot be separated. However, there is the question of which is essential and which is subordinate. Man is the master of life and the master of social reality. To grasp the nature of man is to grasp the nature of life and social reality. On the other hand, if you take the reflection of social reality and the revelation of the essence of life as your objective in creation, not only will you not be able to create a genuine man, but the reality you reflect will be fragmentary and incomplete. Consequently, the essence of life will not be revealed. *That is why, in order for literature to achieve its goal of educating and improving mankind, it must deal with man as its focus of attention. Even while reflecting life and revealing the nature of reality, literature begins with and dwells on man himself. When we say that it is the function of literature to reveal the nature of life and the laws which govern its development, we are denying literature and its true essence; we are eliminating the distinction between literature and the social sciences. In doing so, we are depriving literature of its force.*

The theory that we should represent social, historical phenomena through types is wrong. It is equally wrong to regard as the primary function of literature the revelation of the essence of life and the reflection of the way life develops, while the portrayal of man is merely an instrument to perform such a function. But people have still not noticed it is wrong. In fact, these two wrong theories are correlated and their nature is similar. If the function of literature is to reveal the essence of life and to reflect the way life develops, it would appear that we must create typical characters. The simplest way is to present certain social and historical phenomena through stereotypes. There is nothing ridiculous about these two theories. In fact, they are quite practical. However, if taken as a prerequisite, they become harmful. They ask us to pay attention to unnecessary things which, as a result, lead us to neglect things deserving our attention. If, for instance, we say that food is passed through the esophagus instead of the bronchus into the stomach, we are perfectly right. However, if we say to a child, "Take care, you must let food pass through the esophagus into the stomach instead of through the bronchus!", what would be the result? The child would choke himself and feel that eating was an ordeal. This is the result of unnecessary emphasis. This is the kind of result the two theories would have.

Gorky used to think that literature should not have any negative function. If the function of literature is limited to the reflecting of life, we do not need literature. If we demand that literature reflect reality only in a generalized way, reveal only the essence of reality, then science would be more precise and dependable. Consequently, literature would lose its meaning as a special realm for the mental activities of man. However, people do not give up literature because they have science. Thus, we can see that literature has a special kind of function which cannot be replaced by science. (Such a function, according to Gorky, is to influence, educate, and encourage people to transform reality and the world so that man may have a better life.) Furthermore, if we take the reflection of reality as the primary function of literature, we would have difficulty explaining why all the outstanding lyrics and great works of romanticism that originated from individual and subjective sentiments and ideals are so cherished and respected by the people. This is why Gorky wants to call literature "the study of man," a term that not only explains the object of literature but also unifies the object of literature with its nature, features, responsibility, and function.

There is a special need today to emphasize Gorky's suggestion of calling literature "the study of man."

II

As we have said above, the portrayal of man in literature is not only an instrument; it is also the very purpose and function of literature.

The history of world literature proves this. The world treasury is actually a gallery of characters. If we take away their portraits, the treasury will be emptied. All great writers, past and present, have poured their efforts into characters through whom they served their country and their people. We judge whether the works of a writer are good or bad and the writer's quality noble or low according to how he portrays and deals with man in his works. Why do we reject decadent and naturalistic writers? The main reason is that in their works they have twisted and disparaged man. We respect and are deeply grateful to humanist writers because they have praised and embellished man in their works and made the image of man larger. By calling literature "the study of man," Gorky implies that *we should not only take man as a focus of literary portrayal, but also appraise a writer and his work according to how he portrays and deals with man.*

How to portray and how to deal with man are questions related to the writer's thoughts and to his world view. However, a man's "world view" is actually the sum of his various views. They are both unified and contradictory. In dealing with a specific problem, not all views function to the same degree. Some have greater weight than others. *In the field of literature, since everything depends on how one portrays and deals with man, a writer's attitude toward man and his aesthetic ideal and humanist spirit are decisive elements in his world view.*

Balzac and Tolstoy are the best examples. If you look at their class status and political ideals, these two men are reactionary. But their works are essentially good for people and are progressive. How should we explain this? According to Engels' criticism of Balzac, the advanced creative techniques of these writers broke through their backward world view. This is attributed to the triumph of realism. Such an explanation is not convincing, however, because it would mean that creative techniques and world view can be separated. In other words, a writer can view reality in one way and write about reality in another and the result can be good works influencing and educating man. Even common sense tells us this cannot be accepted.

The Hu Feng clique seized Engels' statement and used it to advocate their reactionary theory of negating the decisive role world view plays over creative techniques. Other people have tried to explain this through the contradiction between the writer's subjective ideas and the work's objective ideology; again, this is not convincing. Even if there is such a difference between the subjective ideas of the writer and the objective ideology of his work, the difference is actually one of degree and the two are not entirely contradictory.

Some people have tried to explain it by finding contradictions in the world views of Balzac and Tolstoy, using a great deal of material to prove that there are reactionary and progressive elements in the world views of these writers. These people decide it is the progressive side which plays the dominant role in their works, and conclude that their creative method and their world view coincide. However, such conclusions still lack substantial analysis. Which are the progressive or reactionary elements in their world views? On what grounds could we decide that their world views are mainly progressive? A person's world view in the narrow sense is his philosophical point of view; we could hardly call the philosophical point of view of Balzac and Tolstoy progressive.

In issue No. 4 of *Wen-hsüeh yen-chiu* (Literary Research), published recently, there are two articles concerning the relationship between world view and creative method by Comrade Wang Chih-liang and Comrade Wen Mei-hui. These two articles base their analysis on the three major works of Tolstoy; Wang Chih-liang deals with *Anna Karenina* and *Resurrection;* Wen Mei-hui deals with *War and Peace.* They determine the basic relationship between Tolstoy's world view and his creative methods and come to a unanimous conclusion: there is a basic congruence between Tolstoy's world view and his creative methods. There are also contradictions, but the negative, reactionary elements in his works are less than those in his thoughts. The cause of the contradictions is the loyalty of the writer to real life and his strict observance of artistic law; in other words, his method of realism has triumphed.

This conclusion was not reached for the first time in the two articles; in fact, we have already mentioned the same idea earlier in this article. But the two articles are valuable not only because they have brought to light definite evidence to prove the prevalent views and make them more scientific, but also because the approach of the two comrades is so serious, their evidence so reliable, and their method of analysis so correct that they have called our attention to the key point of the problem and provided us with many useful clues for its solution. Regrettably, they failed through their correct analysis to reach the correct solution. They are bound by preconceptions, and when they come to a crucial point, they rush to a ready-made statement and stop further exploration. Based on solid materials, they convincingly analyze the contradictions in Tolstoy's world view, pointing out which are reactionary and which are progressive and further proving that his reactionary thoughts occupy a smaller portion in his works than the progressive thoughts do in his thinking.

This might have naturally led to the correct conclusion about the relationship between a writer's world view and his creative method; it might have clearly pointed out which elements in one's world view play the immediate and dominant role in the creation of literature and which elements can play only an indirect or secondary role. But at this point, their eyes slide over the conclusion that is really already evident. They suddenly see the destination they first set out to reach and they rush toward it. Finally, they stop at the conclusion they had hoped to find: the triumph of realistic creative methods.

Is it really true that because Tolstoy is loyal to life and art, his reactionary ideas do not occupy as big a position in his works as in his ideology? Is this really the triumph of the creative methods of realism? I don't think so. Such a conclusion is inadequate. If we attribute it to Tolstoy's loyalty to life, to the force of reality, then *we cannot explain why Tolstoy was so faithful to reality in his creative works and often came to correct conclusions but in his philosophical and literary articles often distorted reality and drew the wrong conclusions. Does this mean that Tolstoy was faithful to life only while he was creating?* As the two comrades have pointed out, the progressive thoughts of Tolstoy exist not only in his writings, but also in his thoughts. Thus we can see that the problem is not why Tolstoy possessed such progressive thoughts, but rather why in his creative work these progressive thoughts can play a dominant role and why it is the reverse in his articles. We cannot explain the problem merely with the idea that Tolstoy was loyal to life. These two comrades also quote Gorky, who says: "Tolstoy in his *Resurrection* cannot but admit and also prove the correctness of waging active struggles." This is similar to what Engels once said—namely, that "Balzac cannot but revolt against his class sympathy and political prejudice." We see the power real life exercises over the writer, but since the explanation given is "Tolstoy cannot but," "Balzac cannot but," we have to find other explanations in the consciousness of these two writers.

Comrade Wang and Comrade Wen said "it is not enough to explain that the objective meaning of the works outweighs the writers' subjective prejudice merely because of their experience of life." They know there are many kinds of writers who may be rich in experience, but whose works could never break through the limitations of their own world views. Consequently, in addition to rich experience and loyalty to life, the two comrades suggest strict observance of artistry in realism. Comrade Wang has put it very nicely:

When the writer is in the process of creating, the work develops its thesis and plot and the artistic image begins to take a realistic shape and become more definite. Then the character and his surroundings begin to organically unify. A real relationship grows between one character and another. As a result, the character that has been given life and individuality by the pen of the writer will become forceful, so forceful that it will require the writer to continue writing on the basis of the reality and unity which have already been achieved. It will also require the writer not only to take care of his own thinking, but also to take care of the character, which has already become a complete personality. This is where the artistic strength of realism lies. If the writer is a really great artist and knows and respects the workings of art, and if also he is excited and encouraged by the characters who come to life under his pen, he will go on to write according to the logic of how the character should develop, and then he will unconsciously let things in his own thinking which are incompatible with this logic be relegated to a secondary position. This is the triumph of realism we have been talking about.

We all know this happens in literary creation. The most familiar example is *Anna Karenina*. Tolstoy first tried to reproach Anna as a guilty wife, but later "could not but" give her his deep sympathy, even to the point of praising her. Comrade Wang explains this in a vague way. He says: "The character will be so forceful that it will require the writer to continue writing on the basis of the reality and unity which have already been achieved." What kind of force is this? Can it exist separately from the consciousness of the writer? Can it remain uninfluenced by the writer's thoughts and attitudes? Of course not. If Comrade Wang had used plainer and clearer language, there would be nothing vague. However, if he had done so, his conclusion would have been quite different.

We have already mentioned that in literature, everything depends on the portrayal of man. A real artist will not use his character as an instrument or a puppet, but will regard him as a man who has the same feelings, thoughts, and individuality as himself. He must fully respect the individuality of this character, and he can portray him through his own sense of right and wrong, love and hate. Through his portrayal, he can express his approval or condemnation, affirming or negating him. As in real life, he can express his opinions of a man by evaluating him. However, he could never impose his own will upon his characters and demand that they submit to it. This is true in life, true in writing.

The force Comrade Wang talked about must come from the character's personality, and there is nothing vague about it. To know and respect the workings of art is to know and respect the character's personality. So the important thing is the writer's attitude toward his characters and his evaluation of them. Is he able to respect the individuality of his character? Is his evaluation impartial and correct? If a writer does not respect the character he creates, if he has made wrong evaluations of his characters, there would be no such a thing as the "artistic power of realism." The writer's attitude toward his characters and his evaluation of his characters are not problems of whether there is realism or not, but of what the writer's aesthetic and humanistic views are. The fact that Tolstoy's reproach of Anna finally becomes sympathy and praise of her was the triumph not of realism but of humanism. How could a real humanist reproach a suffering women like Anna instead of sympathizing deeply with her? Anyone can see that in *Anna Karenina*, it is triumph of Tolstoy's humanistic sympathy toward the unfortunate Anna over his reactionary thoughts about women and family problems.

The situation in *Resurrection* is the same. Tolstoy used to have contradictory attitudes toward the people's revolutionary struggles. Although he expressed some sympathy for the revolution of 1905, this sympathy was slight in the framework of his total viewpoint. However, in *Resurrection* he has described the revolutionaries essentially as a group of brave, honest people who would sacrifice their privileges and lives for the people. He even goes against his principle of "nonviolence" to praise and sympathize with the violent struggles of the revolutionaries. He presents this not as a crime, but as a glorious deed. This is because Tolstoy no longer faces his own thoughts, abstract principles, dogmas, problems of political platforms, or social ideals: he faces concrete man and concrete behavior. He saw that the revolutionaries took violent action after they were in danger of losing freedom, life, and the things that every man values. It is after they were treated ruthlessly by other people that they naturally adopted the policy of "an eye for an eye." How could a real humanist oppose such revolutionary action? Here again, Tolstoy is shown as a friend to the persecuted and an enemy to cruelty and slavery, his great humanist spirit conquering his reactionary thoughts against revolution.

This is not only the situation of Tolstoy, but also that of Balzac. Although Balzac comes from a common background, he admires aristocrats and adds a "de" before his name. In politics, he is a royalist and his sympathy is on the side of the aristocrats. In his works, however, Balzac uses stinging satire and malicious ridicule to deal with the class with which he most sympathizes. And he describes his political foes with clear appreciation. Why? It is because Balzac, as a great humanist, could not adopt any other attitude toward his characters. Aristocracy, as a class, is what he sympathized with and had hopes for. Republicanism, as a political platform, is what he hated and repudiated. Nevertheless, what he portrays and criticizes in his works is neither aristocracy as a class nor republicanism as a political platform, but concrete men performing concrete actions. Balzac evaluates them in accordance with their actions. He ridicules those who should be ridiculed, praises those who should be praised. This is why we all like his works and respect him as a great writer.

The examples of Balzac and Tolstoy fully demonstrate that in literary creation, characters appear in concrete and sensitive forms and are dealt with as human beings. There is no place for abstract and empty concepts and generalized principles. This is why in *The Human Comedy,* the royalist Balzac and the Catholic Balzac have to give way to the humanist Balzac. It is the same with *War and Peace, Anna Karenina,* and *Resurrection:* what appears distinctively before our eyes is a Tolstoy who sympathizes with the persecuted and the exploited. The Christian anarchist Tolstoy is but a dim shadow.

III

Am I recommending humanism too strongly and overestimating its spiritual function? Speaking of literature, I am afraid that the spiritual function is even greater than I have said.

There are many reasons for our fondness for and appreciation of the valuable literary works of the past. The basic reason is that these works are full of deep humanism, and the characters are portrayed with respect and sympathy. Mass awareness, patriotism, and realism may not be good criteria for judging every literary work, but almost every literary work can be judged by whether it is humanistic.

Every classical literary work, no matter in what time or country it was written, has a humanist spirit. We have many works that were not written with the creative methods of realism, that may not have mass awareness, and that may not be patriotic. For instance, the poetry of Li Yü (937–978), about which there has been debate in literary circles, belongs to this kind of literature. It would be difficult for us to find any mass awareness or patriotism in his works unless we infinitely expand the meaning of these two concepts. Then how do we explain the fact that so many people like the works of Li Yü? It is because of the humanism that affects literary work and our evaluation of them.

The works of Li Yü are concerned mainly with his personal sorrow and happiness. He had very little concern for his country and almost none for his people. After he lost his kingdom, he was filled with sadness, with sentimental and nostalgic feelings toward his past. Literary works are intended to express mainly the human sentiments of happiness, sorrow, separation, and reunion; to express people's aspirations and yearnings for a happy life and to express sadness over misfortune. It is through the artistic expression of those thoughts and sentiments that literature performs its function as a weapon of class struggle. Even if what the author wants to express is the life and work of the broad masses, it must be reflected through the writer's personal sensibility. *Otherwise, it cannot be a literary piece.*

Since everyone has his own particular experiences and thoughts and sentiments, he should be able to sing out his own joys and sorrows. If his songs are sincere and touching, why can't they arouse our affections and sympathies? If a writer is not a detestable rogue, and if the feelings he carries are deep and true, no matter whether they are about man or nature, the individual, the masses, or the state, he will have our approval. He brings us closer to man and to nature, he makes us love life, our people, and our country. Li Yü had such feelings, and Wang Kuo-wei praised him for his pure heart. Not only Wang Kuo-wei, but all who love Li Yü's poetry most appreciate his pure feelings. Look at the following poem:

> Again, the lakka flowers
> Bloom on their old stems.
> A desolate evening
> Of mist over the pavilion.
> Against the railing, alone
> whom do I expect to see?
> I let my tears fall.
>
> Confined by these many walls
> I am denied the beauty
> Of your presence.
> Through the pleasures
> Of the festival, a sadness
> Clings to me, unbearable.
> And what is the use
> Of that old misty moon?
> Here by the hyacinth pool
> I weep for you, for your beauty.

This poem was written in remembrance of his beloved wife, the queen. Here are two other poems:

> Mountains beyond mountains
> Off in the distance.
> The sky is deep, the river cold.
> My love for you: the deep red
> Of maple leaves.
>
> Chrysanthemums bloom and wither
> Wild geese fly high above.
> Still, you have not returned.
> Beyond my curtain,
> The indifferent wind and moon.

>   "Ch'ang hsiang-ssu"
>   (Long Remembrance)

Half the spring has passed
Since last we parted,
And what I see before me
Leaves me broken with sorrow.
The plum petals swirl down
In disorder like snow
On the steps. I brush
Them from my robe
But again I am covered.

The wild geese arrive,
The mail does not.
The road is long and old dreams
Are difficult to grasp.
Like spring grass,
The sorrow of parting
Is with you and grows
Wherever you wander.

"Ch'ing-p'ing le"

These poems are said to have been written in remembrance of his younger brother, Ts'ung Shan, who was detained in Sung and did not return. In these poems, feelings are deep and true; diction is fresh and natural. How could they not arouse our appreciation and sympathy? The poems he wrote lamenting his life after he had lost his kingdom are also popular and even more moving.

If the criteria for our evaluation of every work is confined to whether it has mass awareness, to whether it is patriotic, and to whether it is realistic, the poems of Li Yü, Wang Wei, Meng Hao-jan, and many others would be excluded from our classics. If we did this, not only would our literary treasures be considerably depleted, but we would find that such action is against the liking and desire of the people.

Before we make any negative comments on naturalistic and decadent writings, should we first see if there is mass awareness and patriotism? If the works have such an antihumanist level and if they are against human nature, then every normal and good person would immediately find them revolting and reject them. The people may not know what "mass awareness" or "realism" are, but they do possess a certain literary appreciation and judgment. Their only

standard (always the most dependable one) is to look at how the
writer portrays and deals with characters: Does he have respect and
sympathy for man? Does he have a positive attitude toward man? In
a word, though the people may not understand what "humanism" is,
they want to know if the literary work is based on it.

Here, it is inevitable that I be reproached: Are you trying to
employ the principle of humanism to negate and overthrow the
principles of mass awareness and realism? According to what you
have said, is this a literary view that transcends a class view of literature or that comes close to the literary theory of human nature? Are
you trying to deny literature as a weapon for class struggle?

In order to reply to all these probable reproaches, I have to
make the following explanation: First, as I have said, I am definitely
not opposing the vital significance of the principles of mass awareness and realism. What I am denying is that these two principles be
used as *the most basic and universal principles* in evaluating literature. I
do not think that the principle of humanism is the only reliable, efficient standard against which to evaluate literature. I only look at it
as the most *basic and essential standard.* As to the relationship between
humanism and mass awareness or humanism and realism, I think
they are closely related rather than opposed. We could put it in this
way: *Humanism is the essential element in mass awareness and realism.
Without humanism, there is no mass awareness or realism.* Second, *a real
humanist would sympathize with the oppressed and the exploited and hate the
oppressor and the exploiter.* He would definitely align himself with the
former against the latter. This is why humanism does not conflict
with a class viewpoint; it is incompatible with the abstract theory of
human nature. Third, since literature is the reflection of people's
ideas and feelings, it is inevitable in a class society that it should subordinate itself to class and politics, serving the class struggle and the
political struggle. Some people have tried to deny this fact, but it is
true just the same. At the same time, we should note that most classical writers, as well as petit bourgeois writers today who still believe
that literature can transcend class, have not consciously used literature as a weapon in the class struggle. We are different from them;
therefore we cannot substitute our literary point of view for theirs.
As to our own writers, we should, of course, demand that they use
literature *consciously* and effectively as a weapon for class struggle.

Although the term "humanism" has been debased by the capitalists and frequently used as a tool to oppose proletarian revolution and proletarian dictatorship, we cannot simply discard it, just as we cannot simply discard terms like "freedom" and "democracy" because they are also debased by the capitalists. On the contrary, we should spare no effort to expose the antihumanist activities of the capitalists in order to defend real humanism.

Although humanism arose in the sixteenth and seventeenth centuries in Europe in opposition to medieval feudalism, its spirit and ideals have survived in the mind of the people from ancient times. It still can be seen in the conversations and writings of the people. We can still find this idea in the works and writings of Asian philosophers like Confucius and Mo Tzu and in Western philosophers like Socrates and Plato. Although the content of humanism has continually changed because of the changes of the era and of social conditions, we are still able to recognize some enduring elements. The most enduring element is to *treat men as human beings*. This means that man must defend his own rights as an individual as well as recognize and respect other men.

So humanism, in a positive sense, means to strive for freedom, equality, and democracy, and in a negative sense, to oppose the oppression and exploitation of man by man and to fight against the system of feudalism and slavery, a system that does not treat people as human beings. For thousands of years, the people have been struggling to achieve this genuine humanism; as Marx has said, "The only genuine humanism is communism." All great literary masterpieces of the world, past or present, in China or abroad, are good reflections of the struggle of the people toward this ideal.

Albert Maltz, a progressive American writer, has pointed out in his article, "Writer: The People's Conscience," that writers who occupy a major position in the history of literature are all "well-known for loving and sympathizing with peple." He says:

How could it be otherwise? Since a writer is a man, he is moved by the miseries of others. If a writer does not choose the life of the people as his theme, what else can he choose? If his heart is full of sympathy, his intelligence good in exploration, his eyesight piercing, how could he avoid portraying an imperfect world or avoid not desperately dreaming of a better world? Since writers have come into existence, humankind has been living a life in flux; the world has always been on the move or in convulsion. There has never been a day of peace. Every day there are people who suffer. Every day there are people who hope and dream of change.[1]

Maltz thought that most world literature is created from such fundamental situations. The outstanding works of world literature can be divided into two kinds: one kind exposes and scourges "the imperfect world," while the other dreams and yearns for the "better world." Most realistic writings are of the former class; all progressive romantic writings are of the latter. The starting point for both is sympathy and love for the people, a desire to improve their lives, to help them emancipate themselves spiritually. Every great man in world literary history is entitled to the same honor given by the Russian workers to Tolstoy—"An enemy of brutality and slavery, a friend of the persecuted." If a writer could not become such a humanist, he would never be able to create works that touch the people, regardless of whether he is a realist or a romantic.

The realists Balzac and Dickens are great humanists. The same applies to the great romantics Byron and Hugo. We do not like and respect Balzac and Dickens simply because they are realists. Similarly, we do not like and respect Byron and Hugo simply because they are romantics. We praise them because in their works there is severe criticism of the exploiting class and deep sympathy for the oppressed, as well as a humanist spirit that respects and cares for man. Lenin said: "Art belongs to the people. It should derive its deepest source from the basic level of the working masses, it should be understood and loved by the people, and it should unite all the feelings, thoughts, and wills of the masses and heighten them." To treat man as man is to recognize his rights and to respect him. Such a humanist ideal has very deep roots in the people.

Literature is the study of man. The historical position and social significance of literary work is decided by how it portrays and deals with man. The progressive art of every era is against decadent art mainly because it is different in its attitude toward man and in its idea of man. If we accept this, we will not doubt that humanism occupies a supreme position in literature.

[1] Translated from the Chinese.

20

ON HUMAN FEELINGS

PA JEN

I have encountered a number of veteran revolutionary fighters who prefer classical drama, whether Peking, Szechuan, or Shaohsing opera, to the new drama in the form of opera or plays. They state that the content of the new drama is familiar to them already, that it is overly politicized and lacks human feeling. I have also encountered various professionals engaged in revolutionary work who frequently read works of the new literature. They consider these writings to be lacking in common sense, and believe that the first concern of such work is the preaching of "dogma." When senior members of our literary circles discuss current literature, they also complain of an absence of human feeling.

The opinions of people from these three categories are almost identical. It seems that the attraction of literature lies essentially in its "human feeling" and "common sense." As the old Chinese saying goes, "If you understand human affairs, that is knowledge; if you understand human feelings, you can write."

I know little of the ways of the world, and am not very sensitive to human feelings. I usually do not appreciate pieces of writing about trivial but human details. I have done very little writing in recent years and have paid little attention to the ongoing discussion of the role of human feeling in literature. At times, however, I seem

Pa Jen, "Lun jen-ch'ing" (On Human Feelings), *Hsin kang* (New Harbor), January 1957. Reprinted in *Wen-i pao* (Literary Gazette), No. 2, 1960.

to have certain thoughts about this matter. I greatly dislike reading collections of my own work; at times I feel like throwing them into the toilet. Nevertheless, publishers urge me to revise them for publication. There is no more difficult task. Why do I feel this way? Perhaps it is because my writing deals with dogma and lacks human feeling that I myself cannot enjoy it. This is a matter requiring much consideration.

We often encounter this very problem in our daily lives. I have some young friends of bourgeois or landlord backgrounds. Following the liberation, they became revolutionary cadres, as League or Party members. During the period of land reform and the Three Antis and Five Antis campaign,[1] they attempted to draw an ideological line between themselves and their landowning fathers and brothers. They all adopted the same tactic: the breaking off of family relations. In order to demonstrate the firmness of their position, they ignored the complaints of their fathers and brothers. They continued to do so even after the end of the campaign, when their families had been reformed. They would not send a penny to their families when they had financial difficulties. At heart, however, they were not so steadfast. Recalling their father's or brother's love, they wept in private. They thought of writing letters to their families, but were afraid that the Party might suspect them of losing their class stand.

A young comrade once told me of such feelings. He believed that the process of drawing an ideological line between himself and his family involved the severing of all family ties. I told him that the Communist Party had drawn a clear line between itself and the bourgeoisie. However, the Party keeps in touch with the bourgeoisie in order to encourage an acceptance of socialist reform on their part. Why can you not, I told him, employ your affection for your father and brothers to persuade them to surrender to the people, to

[1] The Three Antis and Five Antis campaign was launched in 1951–1952. The Three Antis were (1) antibureaucracy, (2) antiwaste, (3) anticorruption in government offices. The Five Antis were directed against (1) bribery, (2) tax evasion, (3) stealing from the government, (4) cheating on contracts, (5) stealing state secrets, perpetuated by businessmen.

confess their sins and errors, to forsake oppression and exploitation, and to become new men?

Only when one is sensitive to human feeling will one's reasoning become convincing. Feeling belongs to humanity; reasoning belongs to the proletariat. To draw an ideological distinction is to realize one's class stand through sympathy with human feelings.

This example drawn from the realities of life bears some relation to the realities of literature. In designing their work to serve class struggle and illustrate the ideology of the proletariat, certain authors refuse to address themselves to the feelings of the common people. They believe that a piece of literature will lose its class position if it dwells on the nature of human feeling. This is sheer affection. All earthly accomplishments are human accomplishments. With no understanding of human feelings, one cannot realize one's class stand or one's ideal; on the contrary, one is likely to sacrifice both.

What, then, are human feelings? They are what people have in common with one another. Food and sex are common desires; the fragrance of flowers and the singing of birds are common delights. It is everybody's first desire to survive, then to have adequate food and clothing, and finally to develop himself. If anyone impedes the satisfaction of these desires and delights, rebellion and struggle will surely follow. These desires are instinctive in human nature. However, human nature is suppressed in a class society, hence the class struggle. This is always the case.

Actually, the proletariat advocates class struggle in order to emancipate all humankind. Class struggle is therefore a struggle to emancipate human nature. The greatest works of literature are those that embody the highest degree of humanism. Such works encourage people to free themselves from class bonds. They arouse resentment toward the inhuman life led by the majority of the people. Such works oppose social injustice and the bonds restraining the development of individual talent and wisdom. They express the hope that people will lead a life that fosters human nature. When these works make their appearance in a class society, they become weapons to upset the social order. Such works display the deepest human feeling.

If we say that current works of literature lack human feeling, we mean that they do not address themselves to those things which appeal to all of us, that they lack a humanism based on an understanding of man's innate nature.

Some might say that this explanation reflects "individualist humanism" in literature. I do not think that this is true. Literature should serve class struggle, but its ultimate goal is the emancipation of all humankind, the freeing of human nature. It would be wrong of us to forget this. To write about class struggle is to bring people to a realization of the detestable nature of a class structure. We should not only urge the proletariat on in their struggle, but also bring our class enemies to a dispirited state in which they tremble with fear and shame, on the verge of collapse. To achieve this purpose, literature must be structured in such a way as to appeal to all of us. The element of common appeal is human feeling, a humanism based on our innate nature.

"Class nature" is but an alienated form of man's innate nature. We want literature to serve the class struggle. This is because we want man to "come back to himself" when classes cease to exist. In other words, we want man to return to his innate nature, to develop and enrich himself.

Can this be regarded as "individualist humanism?" Let us quote from Marx and Engels. At this point, I must "dogmatize" a bit. In his "Conspectus of *The Holy Family* by Marx and Engels," Lenin offers the following "conspectus":

The propertied class and the class of the proletariat present the same human self-alienation. But the former class feels happy and confirmed in this self-alienation; it recognizes alienation as its own power, and has in it the semblance of human existence. The class of the proletariat feels annihilated in its self-alienation; it sees it in its own powerlessness and the reality of an inhuman existence. To use an expression of Hegel's, the class of the proletariat is in abasement and feels indignation at this abasement, an indignation to which it is necessarily driven by the contradiction between its human nature and its conditions of life, which are the outright, decisive, and comprehensive negation of that nature.[2]

[2] *The Collected Works of Lenin*, Institute of Marxism-Leninism, Central Committee of the CPS (Moscow: Foreign Language Publishing House, 1960), fourth enlarged Soviet edition, Vol. 20, p. 17.

This is to say that the proletariat seeks its own liberation in order to return to human nature, and to develop and enrich that human nature. It seems, however, that our literary theoreticians of class theory have failed to grasp this important concept.

The proletariat can and must achieve its freedom because "it has happened that the proletariat has lost every vestige of common humanity. They have even lost their human appearance, because all that is inhuman has reached its climax in the conditions of proletarian life. The proletariat have also lost themselves. They are aware of this loss in theory. Furthermore, because of inevitable, obvious, crushing poverty, and because of the pressure of such poverty, they must strike out in anger against the inhumanity of their lives."[3]

The proletariat must struggle to eradicate "all that is inhuman" in modern society, which has "reached its climax in the conditions of proletarian life." They must "strike out in anger against the inhumanity of their lives," in order to regain their status as genuine human beings and recover their human nature.

If our literature is to serve class struggle, it must be suffused with human feeling; class heroes must be exemplary in their display of human nature. What arguments could we present against this idea?

If we say that our current literature is lacking in human feeling, if it lacks a humanism based on human nature, then I am afraid this is because we have a mechanical understanding of class theory in our writing.

Men have a class nature, but they also have an innate human nature. "Give back to us the soul of literature: our human feeling."

[3] This is the translator's English version of the passage, as quoted by the author of the article. The official translation can be found in *The Collected Works of Lenin*, p. 28.

21

A MEMO IN LIEU OF
AN ESSAY—

A REPLY TO CRITICISM OF
"ON HUMAN FEELINGS"

PA JEN

April 21, 1957

Comrade Editor,

You asked me whether I wanted to write something about the article in *Hsin kang* (New Harbor) that criticizes my article "On Human Feelings." This is certainly a good way to solicit contributions; men tend to be interested in their own business, and literary men always feel their own writing is the best. But I do not enjoy reading polemical articles, particularly those that pounce on the small flaws of others to soundly beat them.

However, I would still like to talk about how I wrote "On Human Feelings" and about some related matters.

"On Human Feelings" was written last December. After studying documents of the Eighth Party's National Congress, I thought we should reassess everything in the light of what had really happened, including a reassessment of art and literature. The policy

Pa Jen, "I-chien tai-wen" (A Memo in Lieu of an Essay), *Pei-ching wen-i* (Peking Literature), May 1957.

"Let a hundred flowers bloom and a hundred schools of thought contend" means "strive for differences and seek unity so as to flourish." When I recalled my work in the foreign service, the ambassadors I met would say, talking about Chinese movies, art, and so on, "the political atmosphere is too strong while human feelings are missing." Hence I decided to write on this subject.

I wrote the article as the pen dictated without an overview. I didn't wish to get it published as a research paper, for I merely put down my thoughts at random. Afterward, I heard that literary circles in Tientsin were quite "shocked" by the article and had some discussions about it. This is good: it means I have raised a genuine problem. Then I received the proofs of the article criticizing "On Human Feelings" from *New Harbor*. I just glanced through them and mailed an immediate reply, for I did not have the time or capability to discuss the problem. During disputes, those who raise questions may justifiably stand aside and watch the battle.

In my reply, I explained the main idea of my article—namely, "When you understand feelings, you will be good at reasoning. Feelings are human, reasoning is proletarian." But I know that the latter half of my article involves abstract theories which might lead to trouble. I said that writings should have something common to all people as a foundation. I also said that "the so-called class nature is but a deviation from human nature." "We want literature to serve class struggle because we want man to 'return to himself' when classes perish—in other words, to return to human nature, to develop and enrich it." I made those remarks because I wanted to show that right now we should do more work to seek unity. But some people would consider my article one-sided.

Before the third issue had come out, I received a letter from a young man via *New Harbor*. Clearly, he wrote it after reading my article. This is the letter, without any change except for the omission of the writer's name, as I haven't asked for his permission:

February 17, 1957

Dear Comrade Pa Jen,

How are you?

I am a young revolutionary cadre from a landlord family and like to read modern fiction. Maybe because I haven't read enough and my understanding is not deep enough, or maybe because it is my background, I have an ideological problem which I hope you'll help me solve. In all the stories I have

read, the firmest, the most outstanding model revolutionary characters are all
from a proletariat background, while there has not been one who comes from a
nonproletarian background and, through his understanding of revolutionary
truth and ideological reform, has fostered love for the cause of revolutionary
struggle and become loyal to the cause of Communist construction. I think
from now on authors should pay more attention to this aspect. This will help
bring out all the positive resources that can be mobilized to make our country a
great socialist state. It also has a realistic significance in encouraging the old
intellectuals, old functionaries, and other non-proletarian progressive people
to lay down the burdens of their old selves and deal with their historical and
political problems and to study Marxism-Leninism and Mao Tse-tung
Thought in order to strengthen ideological reform and endeavor to do a good
job in revolutionary work. Whether my understanding is right or wrong,
please criticize and instruct me. I look forward to hearing from you.
   Salutations.

                                                    Yours respectfully,

   The handwriting shows that the writer of the letter does not
have a high cultural level. I am very pleased that he has understood
the basic meaning of my article and also developed it further by asking a new question about literary creation. He makes me think that
the "class theory" in literature is by no means the same as "judging a
person only by class origin." The gist of my reply is this: In fact,
Marx, Engels, Lenin, and many revolutionary leaders in our country
are not from a proletarian background. In order to mobilize all po-
tentially positive resources, a writer can create characters from his
opponent class or from alien classes who, through revolutionary
tempering and reform, become model revolutionary characters. Furthermore, there indeed are people like this in actual life. We don't
have to bother about what literary theorists say: a writer cannot close
his eyes to these historical and realistic facts.

   I am reassured by the fact that my article was not misunderstood by a reader who has not reached a high cultural level. Thus it
may not be as bad as poisonous weeds.

   Last week, an author friend whom I met in Southeast Asia came
to my home and talked about my article, which is such a problem
now. He agreed with my views and mentioned many works as examples in support. One of them was *A Man's Fate* by Sholokhov,
which appeared in the April issue of *I Wen* (Literary Translations).[1]

[1] *I Wen* (Literary Translations) is a monthly journal of translations from foreign
literature, published in Peking.

He thought what I required of writers in "On Human Feelings" was illustrated precisely in *A Man's Fate*. He also thought that because the novel was published in *Pravda*, it showed how important it is.

The discussion was sparked by the following words of mine: "To portray a revolutionary fighter," I said, "You should describe not only his bravery in killing the enemy on the battlefield, but also his shedding of tears over the death or suffering of other people; then the image of the fighter would become more complete and be truer to life." The description may seem contradictory, but in fact it has a dialectical unity. It's just like our policy regarding a prisoner of war; when on the battlefield, we have no alternative but to kill him; but once he is captured, we treat him leniently as a human being. Humanism has a different content at different historical periods, and the proletarian policy is the supreme expression of humanism. It was after this that my friend talked to me about *A Man's Fate*.

I felt ashamed that I had not had the time to read the novel. I started reading it that night, after my friend left. I was excited to read about the hero demonstrating a very complex but essentially unyielding ˙pirit when fighting against the German Fascists and after he was taken prisoner. I shed tears when I read the episode in which, after the war, he lost his wife and his son and adopted an orphan. In his pursuit of paternal love, he has shown his great love for mankind. At the time, I was also in bereavement over my son. I recalled him, a seventeen-year-old boy who, lacking in discipline and education from his parents, pretended to be twenty years old and courageously joined the artillery school in Chiamusu.

After three months of shock training, he participated in the battle to defend Harbin. He dug trenches along the Sung-hua River and for several months faithfully guarded the ack-ack position as a lookout. The long time in the trenches left his body covered with fungus and boils; he became weak and his health declined. Then he fought in the battle at Chinchou, the battle at Shenyang, and the battle at Tientsin. At the age of seventeen, though tall, he was not developed, healthy, or robust. We met again when the troops bivouacked at the airport in the Western suburb of Peking. He wrote to me one day, saying he had emitted blood during a military drill. I didn't pay much attention to this except to comfort him a little as a father. Less than two months later, his unit informed me of his death. He had accompanied his commanding officer to Nanwan to

take a batch of cadets to the Naval Academy when he suddenly
vomited blood and developed acute pneumonia. He died after two
weeks' illness. I felt deeply that I had not only lacked fatherly love
toward him, but also had not had the least human feeling. I could
not help being ashamed and tearful over the spirit of the hero in *A
Man's Fate*. . . . Well, where have I digressed to! Let me stop here. I
think it is not necessary for me to reply to anything further. Here is
the article you asked me to write.

Salutations,
Pa Jen

22

NOTES ON THE
ISSUE OF HUMAN NATURE

WANG SHU-MING

A Comment by the Editor of Wen-hsüeh p'ing-lun (Literary Criticism)

Our previous issue presented commentaries by Comrades Chang Kuo-min and Huang Pin-liang on Comrade Wang Shu-ming's article, "Lun jen-ch'ing yü jen-hsing" (On Human Feelings and Human Nature). That article originally appeared in the July 1957 issue of *Hsin kang* (New Harbor), and was reprinted in our last issue together with the commentaries. Comrade Wang now indicates that he may have erred in publishing the article in support of Pa Jen's theories, considering the criticism elicited by Pa Jen's "Lun jen-ch'ing" (On Human Feelings). Comrade Wang asserts that there is an essential difference between his theory and that of Pa Jen; Comrade Wang thinks his theory does not support humanism. He has provided us with these notes concerning human nature, inviting us to publish them in defense of his arguments.

We believe these notes were written three to six months after the publication of his article, "On Human Feelings and Human Nature." Some of his comments differ from those in the article. For example, he has revised his assessment of "the love between man and woman" and the "love between parents and children" as elements of "human nature." He states in these notes that he does not regard love, fear of death, the desire for survival and for adequate food and clothing to be elements of "eternal human nature." In "On Human Feelings and Human Nature," Wang asserts that if literature has a "universal appeal" and a "timeless image," it is because of an innate

Wang Shu-ming, "Kuan-yü jen-hsing wen-t'i ti pi-chi" (Notes on the Issue of Human Nature), *Wen-hsüeh p'ing-lun* (Literary Criticism), No. 3, 1960.

human nature common to us all. In his notes he goes no further than admitting that literature does "have universal values, but within definite limitations." Nevertheless, these notes are informed by the same dominant theory of his previous article, that of humanism.

Comrade Wang insists on the existence of an unchanging, abstract human nature which he refers to as "the innate nature of man." He repeatedly states that this essential human nature "strives upward, leading men to a better life, a life free of oppression and exploitation." "For centuries," he states, "working people have undergone an endless struggle for the normal development of this human nature." He believes that in addition to man's social character he has an innate human nature, but that "this human nature is greatly impeded in its normal development." He does not consider the oppression and exploitation of others by landowners and the bourgeoisie to be representative of the true nature of these people. We regard such a theory as essentially humanist.

We must thoroughly debate these questions. Which is valid, class theory or humanist theory? Does man have an "innate human nature," a nature that is abstract and unchanging? We are presenting Comrade Wang's notes in order that the theory of humanism can be debated further.

There has been much discussion recently on the issue of human nature. This has involved a discussion of both bourgeois and proletarian human nature. It is believed that human nature bears a class character. The cruelty and exploitative nature of the bourgeoisie are believed to represent their human nature as well, because these are the characteristics of their class.

I do not agree. The term "human nature" refers to the innate nature of humankind, as opposed to whatever inhuman qualities man may display. It is the innate nature of men to strive upward, to lead good lives, lives of the sort demanded and struggled for by working people over countless generations. The bourgeois characteristics of cruelty and exploitation are contrary to human nature. Marx states in *The Holy Family* that working people are reduced to a state of inhumanity under the oppression of capitalists. In *Economic and Philosophic Manuscripts of 1844,* he defines communism as "the complete return of man to himself as a social (that is, human) being—a return become conscious, and accomplished within the entire wealth of previous human development."[1] This is to say that

[1] Karl Marx, *Economic and Philosophic Manuscripts of 1844,* translated by Martin Milligan (New York: International Publishers, 1964), p. 135.

human nature can only become unified and avail itself of the wealth of previous human development when men live in a Communist society. Obviously, the cruelty and exploitative nature of the bourgeoisie serve to impede the complete return to human nature, and are therefore contrary to human nature. How, then, can it be said that such cruelty is an aspect of human nature?

Chairman Mao said: "We believe in human nature as it pertains to the proletariat and the masses." Therefore, when we speak of human nature today, we do not do so in a general way or without a definite point of view; we do so from the position of the proletariat.

October 18, 1957

What is human nature? Human nature strives upward, leading men to a better life, a life free of oppression and exploitation. But the oppression and exploitation of others by the bourgeoisie, as well as the ideas and emotions that accompany such acts, are contrary to human nature. They are inhuman. We are not speaking of human nature in a generalized manner; we are addressing it from the proletarian stance. Therefore, we cannot agree that the oppressive and exploitative behavior of the bourgeoisie are innate elements of human nature, although the bourgeoisie may itself believe that this is true.

Marx never offered a concrete definition of human nature in his works. When he spoke of man's natural character and man's social character, his intention was merely to differentiate between man's social and animal natures. In the absence of such a differentiation, there would be no distinction between men and animals.

When we use the term "human nature," its connotations are more definite and concrete. We do not agree that there exists an eternal human nature which is unchanging. We would not say, for instance, that love, fear of death, and the desire for survival and adequate food and clothing are universal human qualities. This is to say that we do not consider them to be permanent. Otherwise we would be forced to regard human nature as an abstract concept. There can be no generalized references to human nature; it must be represented in concrete terms.

Animals also have sexual desire and the desire for survival. In

this respect they are no different from men. These tendencies, however, are essentially animal in nature. In human society, the sex
drive is transmuted into feelings of love, and the desire for survival
is expressed in the relationships between men who are engaged in
production. These desires, then, take on a social character and become specific qualities. We must not confuse animal nature with
human nature; the two must be differentiated.

However, man's social character differs from the specific qualities of his human nature. It would be a mistake to think that talking
about man's social character is the same thing as talking about his
human nature. Man's social character establishes a clear distinction
between man and animals. Both his human nature and his social
character are the forces that define him as a man. The qualities of
human nature, meanwhile, are something about which we can be
more specific. Among these are the ideas, feelings, habits, and psy-
chological traits manifested by men in their daily lives. In a class society, these qualities of human nature are stamped with a class character. In such a society, where men oppress and exploit other men,
man's true nature cannot develop normally. Men are compelled to
struggle with inhuman behavior and situations. For many centuries,
working people have undergone an endless struggle to secure for
themselves a life in which human nature can develop in a normal
way.

December 2, 1957

In his *Ludwig Feuerbach and the Outcome of Classical German Philosophy*,
Engels offers the following statement: "The possibility of purely
human sentiments in the intercourse with other human beings has
nowadays been sufficiently curtailed by the society in which we live,
which is based on class antagonism and class rule."[2]

"The society in which we live" refers to a capitalist society.
Under this system, capitalist exploitation of workers had reached a
state of inhumanity. Marx's assessment of the situation is identical to

[2] Frederick Engels, *Ludwig Feuerbach and the Outcome of Classical German Philosophy*,
Vol. XV of *Works of Marxism-Leninism*, Marxist Library (New York: International Publishers, 1941).

Engels' contention that "the possibility of purely human sentiments in the intercourse with other human beings has nowadays been sufficiently curtailed." It was Marx's belief that "the complete return of man to himself as a social (that is, human) being—a return become conscious, and accomplished within the entire wealth of previous development" could only be realized in a Communist society. Not until such a society is established can there be the possibility of a unified human nature capable of full development.

January 8, 1958

In his *Economic and Philosophic Manuscripts,* Marx repeatedly states that capital's exploitation of labor leads to the inhuman treatment of workers. The following quote is from the *Manuscripts:* "Certainly, eating, drinking, procreating, etc., are also genuinely human functions. But taken abstractly, separated from the sphere of all other human activity and turned into sole and ultimate ends, they are animal functions."[3]

This is the notion that people now hold: "It is the common man's desire first to survive, and second to acquire adequate food and clothing."[4] This is also the humanistic concept of Feuerbach, the old materialist who returned man to his natural being by freeing him from Hegel's absolutist theory. But Feuerbach regards man as merely a natural man, a part of nature; he does not address man as a social being or as a totality of social relations. It is Marx who, beginning with man's natural character, discovers man's true essence, his social nature.

Man's social nature distinguishes him from animals. A recognition of this concept distinguishes the historical materialist from the humanist.

Eighteenth-century philosophy, limited by the state of the natural sciences at the time, could only regard man as an element of nature. He was regarded as a static element of general biology, the essential nature of which was revealed in his animal functions. In truth, the difference between men and animals lies in man's ability

---

[3] Marx, *Economic and Philosophic Manuscripts,* p. 111.
[4] See Pa Jen, "On Human Feelings."

to shape his own history, and in the fact that his instinctive functions come to acquire social qualities during the course of evolving in a human society. Marx states that in a capitalist society, the oppression of labor by capital results in the following:

. . . man [the worker] only feels himself active in his animal functions: eating, drinking, procreating, or at most in his dwelling and dressing-up, etc. And in his human functions he no longer feels himself to be anything but an animal. What is animal becomes human, and what is human becomes animal.[5]

The point he is making is that such oppression results in the loss of human nature. Man's natural qualities can never display themselves freely in a capitalist society. This was Engels' meaning in stating: "The possibility of expressing purely human sentiments in relationships with other human beings has . . . been greatly curtailed."

January 9, 1958

Hegel stated that great works of art can transcend space and time and achieve the status of masterpieces because of their timeless influence from one person to the next, and from one era to the next. This, he stated, is because authors are able to depict the universal qualities of human nature. In *Lectures on Aesthetics*, he states:

Human nature and artistic excellence are universal qualities that transcend national differences and the changes of many centuries. Therefore, men of different races and eras are able to comprehend and appreciate the same object. By virtue of this universal duality, Greek poetry remains thrilling to people of different races, and has always been a source of imitation. In its content and artistic form, it is emblematic of purely human qualities in a grand and beautiful sense.[6]

In his article "Hegel's Aesthetics and Universal Human Nature," Bernard Bosanquet offers the following interpretation of this passage:

People may say that there is no universal nature whatever, that human nature is defined by history; for there is no common man, but only man as he is governed by historical conditions. Certainly, there is no man free of such

[5] Marx, *Economic and Philosophic Manuscripts*, p. 111.
[6] This is the translator's English version of the passage, as quoted by the author.

influence. But man has universal values. Furthermore, man has certain universal responsibilities. (But this does not concern us—AUTHOR.) If no such universal character exists, there can be no mutual understanding between one people and another. There can be neither an understanding of separate eras, nor a comparison of them. In particular, there could be no work of art that could be introduced to people of different eras and races. But it is a simple truth that such works of art do exist. This is the starting point for our discussion. Those who affirm this truth will accept the concept of a universal human nature.[7]

Like Hegel, Bosanquet explains that the immortality of great works of art is due to their expression of universal human qualities. In the absence of such a common nature, the people of one culture or era would be unable to understand those of another.

Is this true?

I do not agree that the timelessness of art stems from its appeal to a universal human nature. Great works of art are always realistic, reflecting their era and the people's need for progress. This spirit of progress and the need for it Bosanquet refers to as "universal values" possessed by men, but "within definite limitations." This is true although the specific nature of these values varies from era to era, as men progress from one historical phase to another.

Therefore, we should not arrive at the forced conclusion that the timelessness of art stems from a universal human nature. There has never been a human nature in the abstract. There is no universal man; there is only social man. The fabric of human nature will vary according to class in a class society.

January 12, 1958

Marx borrowed a number of terms from Hegel and Feuerbach: "alienation," "objectification," and others. Among these was Feuerbach's term "human essence," which was frequently employed in Marx's earlier works, and less frequently in his later writings. Marx eventually arrived at a clear definition of man as "a totality of social relationships."

In a letter to Engels, Marx chuckled at Feuerbach's use of the term "human essence" to explain the "significance of man." The fol-

---

[7] This passage was translated from the Chinese, as quoted by the author.

lowing is an excerpt from page 31, volume one, of *Marx-Engels Correspondence:*

As for Feuerbach's "The Essence of Christianity," I skimmed a few pages from *Heir of the World.* Except for certain clear and concise commentaries, the topical content of the work is stale. At first, as he strictly confines himself to the subject of natural religion, he displays a reliance on empirical thought. After this, however, his reasoning becomes confused. Terms like "natural essence" and "man" are endlessly repeated. The entire work—about sixty pages—begins with the following definition of nature, which is different from human essence: "There exists something which is different and independent from human essence and God (!!)—that is, from the content of 'Christian essence'. It is (1) a mode of existence independent of human essence, (2) a type of human characteristic, (3) a type of human character, (4) nothing other than nature." This is truly a masterpiece of thundering repetition.[8]

Marx obviously came to be contemptuous of Feuerbach's repeated use of the term "human essence."

January 15, 1958

I am well aware that when Marx employed such terms as "human essence" and "man's innate nature," he intended them to represent the opposite of man's natural or animal qualities. Meanwhile, he clearly stated that although man is a natural creature possessed of an animal nature, his most distinctive feature lies in his nature as a social animal: "The true nature of man is a totality of social relationships."[9]

Marx made such statements when he criticized the views of the older materialists such as Feuerbach. Although Feuerbach established man in the province of reality rather than that of theology, and although this was progress of a sort, he regarded man solely as a natural creature, ignoring his social character. Herein lie Feuerbach's limitations.

Marx often employed the term "human nature" in describing the relationship between capital and labor. It was his belief that capi-

[8] This passage was translated from the Chinese, as quoted by the author.
[9] From *Theses on Feuerbach,* as cited (in English) in Karl Marx, *Selected Writings in Sociology and Social Philosophy,* trans. T. B. Bottomore (New York: McGraw-Hill, 1964), p. 68.

talist exploitation and oppression of workers prevented men from leading the life that was rightfully theirs. I have already quoted such a passage from *Economic and Philosophic Manuscripts*. Now, in *The Holy Family*, I have discovered a passage of similar import:

. . . the class of the proletariat is in abasement. It is filled with indignation at this abasement, an indignation to which it is necessarily driven by the contradiction between its human nature and its condition of life, which is the decisive and comprehensive negation of that nature. . . .[10]

It is apparent that when Marx speaks of "human nature," he means that men's essential qualities and desires are such that they require a good life for themselves. Whether men struggle with nature or with society, it is their object to lead fulfilling lives. To prevent their attainment of this goal is inhuman and destructive of human nature.

January 16, 1958

[10] Karl Marx, *The Holy Family* (1845; reprinted 1956, London: Lawrence and Wishart), p. 51.

CRITICISM OF HUMANISM

23

MAN AND REALITY: A REFUTATION OF "LITERATURE IS THE STUDY OF MAN"

LI HSI-FAN

All revisionists tend to pose as discoverers of the truth. They tend to represent their views as having developed from Marxist thought. If, however, we arrive at the essential nature of their ideas and strip them of the Marxist phraseology they have coopted in order to confuse right and wrong, they will lose their attraction and we will be able to discover the true features of their various insinuations.

Ch'ien Ku-jung's "Literature Is the Study of Man" is one such article. It was published in the May issue of *Wen-i yüeh-pao* (Literary Monthly). In order to embellish his literary views, Ch'ien stole from Gorky, the master of socialist realism, the profoundly philosophical statement, "Literature is the study of man." Actually, it was his intention to revive the literary views of the bourgeoisie under this beautiful disguise. Nevertheless, an attractive appearance cannot disguise the true nature of Ch'ien's insinuations. *Wen-hui pao* praised this article as "original in its ideas, sound in its reasoning." Let us examine this article and decide what original ideas it actually presents.

Ch'ien Ku-jung presents the thesis of his article at the very

Abridged from Li Hsi-fan, "Lun jen ho hsien-shih" (Man and Reality), *Wen-i yüeh-pao* (Literary Monthly), October 1957.

beginning: "Literature must place man at the center. . . . This can be used as a master key to unlock all literary problems." And again, ". . . all things must begin with man and all things must serve man." He claims that many philosophers and major literary figures have expressed similar ideas, the summation of which is Gorky's profound statement, "Literature is the study of man." If we apply Ch'ien's thesis in an exploration of essential literary problems, we will certainly lead literature into the blind alley he has constructed. If, however, we consider the problem carefully, we will come to see that the way in which Ch'ien raises the issue is an old idealist trick: the substitution of half-truths for the truth itself in regard to literary theory.

The portrayal of man has always been the crux of Marxist literary theory. The proletarian teachers, Marx and Engels, regarded typification of characters in works of realism as the key to success or failure in literature. It was Engels who propounded the famous thesis, "a typical character in a typical environment." This is the formula for typification in the literature of realism. On the basis of their wide creative experience, the great proletarian writers Gorky and Lu Hsün advised young people on several occasions that the portrayal of man was of primary importance in their creative efforts. This is understandable. It is the purpose of literature to portray the realities of life in a given society, and man is the agent of all social activity. Marx refers to man as "a totality of social relationships." A writer portrays life and reflects reality through a presentation of man's complex activities and involvements. Men are the cells of society. In the absence of man's diverse activities, there would be no social life.

Literature differs from the sciences in that it does not appeal to its readers with its knowledge of truth derived from rational conclusions. Rather, it does so with truth depicted and embodied in artistic images, and educates its readers by virtue of aesthetic appeal. Since this sort of writing is intended to reflect the realities of life, it cannot divorce itself from the affairs of man. This principle has been accepted by writers of realist literature. Even reactionary writers cannot reject it. However, can this generally acknowledged principle be employed as a solution to every literary problem? The point at issue, regardless of the literary school, is not whether man should be at the center of writing, but the manner in which he is to be portrayed. Is man to be portrayed as he is in reality, or as he is in the wishful thinking of the writer? The literature of realism, including the literature of revolutionary romanticism, concerns itself with the depiction of man as he is in real life; the literature of counterrealism portrays man according to the writer's subjective fancy.

Ch'ien defines the concept of literature as the study of man in the following manner: "Man is the master of social reality. To grasp the nature of man is to grasp the nature of life and social reality." This is a mistaken concept, and he intends to employ this paradoxical view of literature to place out of proportion the idea of man as the focus of literary writing. His purpose is to insinuate bourgeois ideas of literature that transcend reality and distort realistic literature.

Man created by the artist in his work is a self-contained entity. He is a living man with feelings, thoughts, and actions. But man does not exist in isolation from society. It is the truthfulness of the events in his life that justifies his presence and makes the characterization convincing and appealing to the readers. The development of his character and the complex reality of his existence must be realized in connection with the events in his life. Man cannot be separated from the realities of life. These realities determine his ideas, behavior, and character. This is the plain truth; it is especially true of literature as "the study of man." Chia Pao-yü, Lin Tai-yü, Ah Q, Hamlet, Don Quixote, and Oblomov all fall into the category of "a typical character in a typical environment" as defined by Engels. They cannot be dissociated from the realities of their lives. They are unique because each particular character is made by a particular reality.

Ts'ao Hsüeh-ch'in did not write *The Dream of the Red Chamber* entirely for the purpose of depicting "the decline of the aristocratic class." If, however, Ts'ao had not been familiar with the life of this class, and had not entertained such complex feelings of disapproval and sadness about the realities of the aristocratic class, he would have been unable to write the novel. Ch'ien states that Ts'ao "was driven to write by his deep, complex, and sustained feelings toward characters like Chia Pao-yü and Lin Tai-yü." Even so, these two characters would have lost their authenticity and impact had Ts'ao lacked a clear understanding of their environment, and had he been unable to present a vivid picture of the complex life of the aristocracy. He would have been unable to produce characters as well-defined as Chia and Lin had he focused on their characterization alone. Characters cannot exist in isolation; their existence is significant only when seen against the complex realities of their lives. This is the case with Chia Pao-yü and Lin Tai-yü; it is particularly true of Ah Q.

Ch'ien Ku-jung denies that "the reflection of total reality is the immediate and foremost function of literature." He states: "All of the arts, including literature, have as their purpose the improvement of the quality of human life. They provide eager hopes and noble ideas that will move men to achieve the beautiful and the perfect. These are the ideals that drive all great poets to write." It would be difficult for us to find fault with these remarks. All scientific and literary activities are intended to improve the quality of human life. Marx states in *On Feuerbach* that "philosophers have interpreted the world in many ways; however, they all hope to change it." The question is how to interpret the world correctly, where to begin and what conclusions to draw. Ch'ien's reply to this is: "In order for literature to achieve its goal of educating and improving mankind, it must deal with man as its focus of attention. Even while reflecting life and revealing the nature of reality, literature must begin with and dwell on man himself. When we say that it is the function of literature to reveal the nature of life and the laws which govern its development, we are denying literature its true essence; we are eliminating the distinction between literature and the social sciences. In doing so, we are depriving literature of its force."

Such ideas concerning the relationship between man and reality and that of literature and reality were not created by Ch'ien Ku-jung. European bourgeois scholars have grumbled over these hackneyed ideas for a hundred years. Liang Shih-ch'iu and others who followed the third road also raised a furor over them twenty years ago. However, these attitudes were long ago rendered meaningless under the counterattack of Lu Hsün and the left-wing writers. In the midst of the surging wave of socialist revolution, Ch'ien struck up the old tune to lend force to the bourgeois rightists' attack on the principles of socialism. It was his purpose to revive subjective, bourgeois idealism in literature.

Ch'ien considers the idea that literature should reflect reality to be "an empty, abstract concept." He considers man to be an individual independent of reality. He says that if a writer allows his creative work to be governed by this abstract principle, his characters will become no more than sketches of reality as the writer sees it. For this reason, Ch'ien insists, "all things must begin with man and all things must serve man." However, is it true that a writer always begins with situations out of real life which give his characters a living force?

The lofty, fervent ideas that present themselves to great writers, ideas concerning the improvement of life, do not arrive from nowhere. They arise from the stimulus of complex, objective reality. In explaining why he began writing fiction, Lu Hsün said: "It was for the sake of life and to improve life." His subject matter, he said, was "for the most part derived from the unfortunate people of a diseased society." "It is my intention," he stated, "to expose the diseases so that people can direct their attention to their cure." Lu Hsün did not inherit these views at birth. His mother's family lived in the countryside, and through his contact with a number of peasants he came to understand the oppression and misery of their lives. When Lu Hsün acquired a command of writing, he saw the actual life of the peasants even more clearly. He began to employ literature as a means with which to struggle for the working masses. This is an instance of creating literature for the service of man, but the motives involved came from the writer's experience of reality.

The idea that literature comes out of an understanding of man arises from the writer's understanding of reality. If a writer confines his attention to man alone, without addressing himself to the complex realities of life that comprise the background of man's existence, he will inevitably arrive at a false understanding of man. As a result, man depicted in the writer's work will be lifeless and distorted.

The nature of realistic art is not that of a photograph of the realities of life. Realistic art involves a complex process of artistic synthesis. The crucial factor here is the complexity of life. Chairman Mao states: "Life as reflected in works of literature and art can and ought to be on a higher plane, more intense, more concentrated, more typical, nearer the ideal, and therefore more universal than actual, everyday life." But this state of affairs cannot be brought about through wishful thinking divorced from reality. It must be achieved by a profound involvement with the realities of life, "in order to observe, experience, study, and analyze all the different kinds of people, all the classes, all the masses, all the raw materials of literature and art."

The process of creating realistic literature involves a close relationship between the writer and the realities of life. This cannot be explained by the abstract concept that "All things begin with man, and all things must serve man." Man in literature is also man in life. His relationship to the realities of life should be one of unity, rather than one of opposition. Therefore, the portrayal of man and the depiction of the realities of life are inseparable in the literature of realism. Ch'ien Ku-jung's discussion of man as detached from the realities of life is simply intended to disguise his opposition to realism.

The creation of typical characters is a specific artistic process. The way in which man is created in works of literature further demonstrates the relation between literature and the realities of life. Ch'ien introduced his own views when we debated Ah Q as a typical character. He criticized various opinions that arose during the debate over the typicality of this character. He maintains that those opinions were influenced by the theory that "typification is no more than a summing up of the historical situation in a specific society." Since Ch'ien protests the injustice done to Ah Q, let us reply with a quote from Lu Hsün, the author of *The True Story of Ah Q*. The following is a statement presented twenty-seven years ago:

Without addressing itself to man, literature cannot express man's nature. When man is presented in a class society, his character cannot help but be influenced by the nature of the class to which he belongs. We cannot impose a class character on man; it is his natural attribute. Certainly, happiness, anger, sorrow, and joy are human feelings. Poor people, however, can never experience the disappointment of those who suffer losses at the stock exchange. The petroleum magnate can never know the miseries of a woman who earns her living by gathering coal cinders in Peking. Those who suffer hunger in areas of famine will probably never raise orchards like venerable gentlemen or rich people. Chiao Ta, the old servant in the house of Chia in

The Dream of the Red Chamber, will not fall in love with the frail Lin Tai-yü. The simple mention of factory sirens or the name of Lenin does not necessarily imply the literature of the proletariat. Nor does the inclusion of the phrases "all things," "all the people," or "things are going well and men are happy" indicate that such literature serves to express human nature. If literature that gives expression to common human nature is literature of the highest quality, then what of literature that expresses the even more universal nature of animals: their nourishment, respiration, movement and procreation? Or what of literature that expresses the nature of a living organism, a nature of even a more universal sort? Would not such literature be of even "higher quality?" If we must confine our literature to the expression of human nature on the grounds that we are men, then the proletariat must address its efforts to proletarian literature on the grounds that they are the proletariat.

It is our belief that a typical character must be rooted in the realities of life. Therefore, a character cannot but express its class nature. Perhaps, as Ch'ien believes, there are characters of a type representing the "kind benevolence" or "purity and honesty" common to landlords, merchants, peasants, and workers. We, however, have never seen such types, at least in the literature of realism. It must be the task of people like Ch'ien to provide examples of such characters in order to educate readers. Even so, this would indicate that he is in sympathy with Liang Shih-ch'iu, rather than being a Marxist.

Nobody denies that if a great writer creates works that benefit mankind, it is because the writer is capable of giving his work his own great humanist spirit. He can reveal his well-defined feelings of love for those who are ruled and hatred for those who rule. Such a spirit of humanism naturally affects the creative process. Literature, however, must adopt the rich and colorful realities of life as its concern. It must give expression to love and hate through artistic imagery in an honest depiction of these realities. The writer's attitudes can help describe reality, but they cannot describe the nature of reality. Any piece of literature with a subjective orientation that entirely disregards the realities of life and indulges itself in an arbitrary exaggeration of the concept of humanism is certain to be lifeless.

Ch'ien Ku-jung stresses the writer's subjective attitude of humanism; that is, respect for man. He asserts that the writer cannot impose his will on his characters and force them to go his way. He attempts to use this attitude to explain the complexity of the creative process. His explanation, however, is unconvincing to the reader. In whatever way one chooses to explain it, humanism is no more than a writer's attitude toward man. One cannot create an authentic character through a reliance on humanism. A writer, no matter how lofty his humanist spirit, will be unable to produce vivid artistic images if, in Gorky's words, he does not have a wealth of experience and impressions of life.

Ch'ien attempts to dissociate man from the realities of life and deny him his true character, his class character. He stresses the so-called human nature common to all men, and maintains that creative work depends on the writer's humanism and his aesthetic ideas. Such concepts are common in Ch'ien's literary thought. It is his purpose, in fact, to suggest that all literary problems will be resolved through the writer's subjective motivation and attitude, both of which are viewed as transcending class structure and the realities of life. He denies the concept that the essential character of realistic literature is the reflection of the realities of life. He discounts the role of a writer's world view, closely associated as it is with actual life. He denies the importance of class identity, but stresses the influence of abstract humanism and aesthetic ideas regarding literary creation. He believes that one can produce good writing only if one regards man as a human being, and can move the heart of the reader regardless of class position and class feeling. This is idealism in the extreme.

Clearly, all this is not "original in its ideas, and sound in its reasoning." These ideas are gathered at random from bourgeois literary doctrine. They are the theories of subjective idealism. They are thoroughly exploited by the bourgeois rightists in their opposition to the Party's literary ideas.

24

HUMAN NATURE AND LITERATURE: A CRITIQUE OF PA JEN'S AND WANG SHU-MING'S HUMANISM

YÜ HAI-YANG AND OTHERS

Pa Jen's article *Lun jen-ch'ing* (On Human Feelings), and Comrade Wang Shu-ming's *Lun jen-ch'ing jü jen-hsing* (On Human Feelings and Human Nature) have been refuted by many comrades. In advocating an abstract human nature, these two articles support the ideology of the landlords and the bourgeoisie.

Pa Jen asserts that, in a class society, men have a common human nature and common human feelings. He states: "Men have a class nature as well as an innate human nature." It is evident that Pa Jen regards the innate human nature as the essential basis of human beings. And he regards class character as alienated from innate human nature.

And what are human feelings? Pa Jen states:

They are what people have in common with one another. Food and sex are common desires; the fragrance of flowers and the singing of birds are common delights. It is everybody's first desire to survive, then to have adequate food and clothing, and finally to develop himself.

Abridged from Yü Hai-yang and others, "Jen-hsing yü wen-hsüeh" (Human Nature and Literature), *Wen-hsüeh p'ing-lun* (Literary Criticism), No. 3, 1960.

Comrade Wang Shu-ming calls what people have in common the "normal nature of human beings." He regards the love between man and woman and the love between parents and children as elements of the "normal nature of human beings."

In applying this theory to literature, Pa Jen believes that literature should give expression to human feelings which are common to all men. He thinks that the greatest works of literature are those which embody the highest degree of humanism. Comrade Wang also believes that literature should give expression to the "normal nature of human beings" and that the "universal appeal" and "timeless image" of good literature stem from its expressions of this "normal nature."

It is a fact that in a class society there can only exist a specific class nature, rather than a general human nature which transcends the structures of class. Of which class, then, are the "human feelings" or the "normal nature of human beings" advocated and praised by Pa Jen and Comrade Wang Shu-ming?

Pa Jen makes an issue of man's desire for survival, food, clothing, and self-development at a time when our country is proceeding with its socialist revolution and construction. It is common knowledge that the proletariat is at the vanguard of revolution in our country. The proletariat has excellent prospects. It is moving forward with a boundless vitality unrivaled by any other class. Clearly, it need not concern itself with problems of survival, food, clothing, and self-development. Therefore, it is not for the benefit of the proletariat that Pa Jen promotes his theory. The peasant class, moreover, is the strong, reliable ally of the proletariat, and as such it naturally does not need to worry about these matters. The peasant class is not anxious about its future. Rather, it is elated at the brilliant prospects that await it. Naturally enough, Pa Jen's theory does not represent the desires of the peasant class. On whose behalf, then, does Pa Jen propound his ideas? In New China, workers, peasants, and the urban petit bourgeoisie need not concern themselves with the matters listed above. Only the declining bourgeoisie need feel threatened in this regard. Under the present historical conditions in our country, Pa Jen's statement is no more than an expression of the desires of the declining bourgeoisie. It must be pointed out that Pa Jen's article, "On Human Feelings," was published in January 1957.

At that time the bourgeois rightists were launching a frenzied attack on the proletariat. The historical situation at the time the article was published helps us to understand his theory.

Wang Shu-ming's idea that the love between man and woman and the love between parents and children stem from the "normal nature of human beings" is also the idea of a specific class. The human nature Comrade Wang advocates is that of the feudal class, not that of the proletariat.

As Chairman Mao pointed out when he criticized the theory of human nature:

Is there such a thing as human nature? Of course there is. But there is only human nature in the concrete, no human nature in the abstract. In class society there is only human nature of a class character; there is no human nature above classes. We uphold the human nature of the proletariat and of the masses of the people, while the landlord and bourgeois classes uphold the human nature of their own classes, only they do not say so but make it out to be the only human nature in existence.[1]

Pa Jen and Comrade Wang Shu-ming are the kind of people, as Chairman Mao pointed out, who regard the nature of the landlord class and the bourgeoisie as the "innate human nature" or the "normal nature of human beings." They consider it to be a universal and unchanging human nature possessed by the whole of mankind. They then apply this concept of human nature to the creation of art and literature.

Pa Jen employs the humanism of the bourgeoisie as a criterion not only for the literature of the bourgeois era, but for all works of literature. He obviously desires that we assess literature from the standpoint of bourgeois humanism so that our literary works will serve as expressions of that humanism. Pa Jen disapproves of proletarian humanism. He shows no interest in our literary works, which display the noble qualities of love for the people, a spirit of self-sacrifice, a concern for the happiness of the people and the proletarian class, and a disdain for one's personal misfortunes. The human feelings he appreciates are those of personal sorrow—the feelings of bourgeois youths who shed tears in private after having informed on their fathers. There is no place in our literature for personal feelings

[1] *Mao Tse-tung on Literature and Art* (Peking: Foreign Languages Press, 1967).

of this narrow sort; we have no use for the melancholia of the bourgeoisie as they face their doom. And because our literature does not express such feelings, it is condemned by Pa Jen for an absence of human feeling. He complains that our works of literature "do not address themselves to those things which appeal to all of us; they lack a humanism based on an understanding of man's innate nature." He even goes so far as to cry, "Give back to us the soul of literature: our human feeling."

The origin and growth of proletarian literature and art in China have been closely associated with our struggle against bourgeois literary concepts. From the time of the May Fourth movement in 1919, such revolutionary writers as Lu Hsün have often bitterly opposed the concept of human nature. Chairman Mao, in particular, made a profound and thorough criticism of this concept. As a result, it long ago lost its theoretical validity in China. Nevertheless, it continues to make an appearance from time to time. A review of our recent history will indicate that the reappearance of the concept of human nature has been closely associated with the situation of class struggle in our country. Such bourgeois spokesmen as Liang Shih-ch'iu and Wang Shih-wei resorted to the concept of human nature in their vicious attack against the proletarian revolution. In 1957, when bourgeois rightists launched a frenzied onslaught on the proletariat, they employed this concept as an ideological weapon.

Pa Jen, of course, cannot be identified with bourgeois rightists in an absolute sense. Comrade Wang Shu-ming has even less in common with them. However, the concept of human nature embraced by Pa Jen and Comrade Wang Shu-ming is similar to that of the bourgeois rightists. Furthermore, the concept of human nature that currently prevails in our country not only reflects the political sentiments of China's bourgeoisie, but is also an echo of the international revisionist trend. All those who advocate the concept of human nature, both at home and abroad, follow the same pattern. They praise the bourgeois concept of human nature, promote bourgeois sentiments, seek compromise in class conflict, and weaken the fighting will of the proletariat in an attempt to oppose socialism and restore the capitalist system. From this it can be seen that although the concept of human nature has long been a meaningless theory, we cannot relax our vigilance under current conditions. In order to defend Marxism and to further the development of the proletarian revolution, it remains extremely important that we expose and criticize this concept thoroughly in our literary endeavors.

THE ANTI-RIGHTIST
CAMPAIGN

25

IMPORTANT SPEECHES PRESENTED BY LU TING-I AND CHOU YANG

AT THE 27TH EXPANDED MEETING CONVENED BY THE PARTY GROUP OF THE CHINA WRITERS' UNION

Addressing the meeting, Comrade Lu Ting-i stated that the struggle within our artistic and literary circles against the Rightists and anti-Party elements is progressing well and has led to great victories. He then analyzed the formidable task of carrying on with the socialist revolution and examined certain fundamental problems revealed by the anti-Rightist campaign.

"Lu Ting-i, Chou Yang tsai tso-hsieh tang-tsu k'uo-ta hui-i shang tso chung-yao chiang-hua" (Important Speeches Presented by Lu Ting-i and Chou Yang at the 27th Expanded Meeting Covened by the Party Group of the China Writers Union), *Wen-i pao* (Literary Gazette), No. 29, 1957.

The Party Group of the China Writers' Union held twenty-seven expanded meetings from June 6 to September 17, 1957, to critize the Rightists and anti-Party elements. Lu Ting-i, Director of the Propaganda Department of the Chinese Communist Party, and Chou Yang, Deputy Director of the Propaganda Department, gave the concluding speeches.

LU TING-I'S SPEECH

SOCIALIST REVOLUTION AND THE PROBLEM
OF BOURGEOIS INTELLECTUALS

Comrade Lu Ting-i stated that the socialist revolution is the most profound revolution. Everyone who experienced the democratic revolution knew it had not been easy. The revolution, dated from the Opium War, began a hundred years ago. If we were to date it from the founding of the Chinese Communist Party, the revolution could be said to have begun thirty-eight years ago. It was won after much bloodshed. Socialist revolution, more profound and more extensive than the democratic revolution, has as its purpose the destruction of the exploitative system of capitalism. It would end thousands of years of the exploitation of man by man, and would prevent the revival of any further system of exploitation. This revolution has been an ongoing process in our country for a brief period of time: eight years from 1949, and four years since the general line for socialist transformation was inaugurated in 1953. In this short time we essentially completed the socialist transformation of agriculture, handicrafts, and capitalist commerce and industry. All this comprised a socialist revolution on the economic front that changed the ownership of the means of production. Having resolved the issues of political power and ownership of the means of production, the socialist revolution was in the main concluded. The bourgeoisie ceased to exist as an exploiting class, and the era of mass class struggle ended.

But this does not mean that everything is over. The struggle currently being waged against the bourgeois rightists is a socialist revolution on the political and ideological fronts. This struggle is not peculiar to our country; many other socialist countries have experienced such struggle. In the Soviet Union there was a struggle against the Trotskyites. Hungary experienced a counterrevolutionary incident last October. Trotsky was a bourgeois intellectual, as were the leading figures of the Petöfe Club in Hungary.

Although the issue of state power has been resolved and the socialist revolution on the economic front completed, the capitalists continue to desire a resurgence of influence. Leading them are the bourgeois intellectuals. The capitalist rebellion in the Soviet Union met with defeat, but the rebels in Hungary briefly overthrew the state power of the proletariat. Here in China we face the same problem. With the Chang-Lo alliance [1] as their base of power, the bourgeois rightists have savagely attacked socialism. Whether in the Soviet Union, Hungary, or China, it is the goal of the bourgeoisie to overthrow the socialist revolution through rebellion, and to revive the reactionary rule of the counterrevolutionaries.

Comrade Lu pointed out that the revolution on the political and ideological fronts cannot be accomplished at a single stroke. It is possible that ten to fifteen more years will be required for its completion; it is a severe class struggle and will remain so as long as imperalism and capitalism exist.

Proletarian intellectuals can be nurtured in large numbers under a socialist system, but it is also possible for bourgeois intellectuals to emerge. These bourgeois intellectuals are capable of being reformed; however, some of them will resist ideological reform to the bitter end. The latter are bourgeois rightists; they remain hostile to socialism, the Communist Party, and the people. Certain of these bourgeois intellectuals, like Feng Hsüeh-feng and Ting Ling, formally joined the Party; but even many years' education by the Party could not remold their thinking. We must also be aware that bourgeois intellectuals can emerge from a socialist society: such people as Tseng Yen-hsiu, Chung Tien-fei, Ch'en Yung, Liu Shao-t'ang, Liu Pin-yen, and Kuo Wei. Some of these persons joined the revolution while quite young, and were raised in the liberated areas; others were raised after the liberation of the entire country. They were educated in a socialist society, and yet became bourgeois rightists.

How can a socialist society produce bourgeois intellectuals? Comrade Lu offered the following explanation. First, he stated, man's awareness tends to lag behind his social character. If intellectuals full of democratic ideas fail to undergo ideological remolding, they will be unable to adapt their thinking to the realities of socialism. Second, bourgeois ideas continue to exert a measure of influence on our society, and will continue to do so for a long period of time. Third, bourgeois rights still hold sway in regard to the dis-

[1] The Chang-Lo alliance: Chang Po-chün and Lo Lung-chi were prominent figures in the China Democratic League, and were branded as ultrarightists during the anti-Rightist campaign in 1957.

tribution of daily necessities. Such distribution is not conducted in accordance with personal needs; rather, it is conducted in accordance with the person's labor, and is based on the principle of equal value in the exchange of commodities.

Comrade Lu stated that in a capitalist society, equality means that the millionaires and the poor stand equal before the law. But this is a false equality. Controlling the means of production, the millionaires are in a position to oppress and exploit the penniless poor. How could there be equality between them? Things are entirely different in a socialist society. With state and collective ownership of the means of production, no one can employ private ownership for the exploitation of the masses.

A socialist society still retains a measure of inequality when compared with a communist society, however. This inequality lies in the distribution of daily necessities. The principle of socialism is embodied in the phrase, "From each according to his ability, to each according to his labor." Since one's reward corresponds with one's work, there is bound to be some measure of inequality. Certain people are physically stronger and are capable of greater effort; such people will earn higher income. Others are weaker and will earn less. A family with many mouths to feed and fewer hands for work will have a smaller income than a family with fewer mouths to feed in proportion to its production. In *A Critique of the Gotha Program*, Marx stated that, in a socialist society, "equal rights are restricted by bourgeois confines in one respect." He was referring to the distribution of daily necessities. Although in a socialist society various sorts of assistance and relief funds are provided for people with low incomes, certain inequities continue to exist. Only when the productive force of our society greatly expands and the society advances into the phase of communism can we implement the principle of "from each according to his ability, to each according to his needs." This would serve to eliminate such inequities.

Our country has already entered its socialist phase, but capitalists nevertheless continue to exist. This is explained by the fact that they continue to receive fixed interest—a form of exploitation. The state must pay one hundred and ten million dollars annually, and this will continue to be the case until 1962. Our socialist society has accomplished the socialization of capital goods, but at the same time certain inequities continue to exist regarding the distribution of daily necessities. These inequities constitute the material base of bourgeois ideas. Therefore, in a socialist society, the proletarian ideology of selflessness and wholehearted service to the people is accompanied by the bourgeois ideology of selfishness and profit at the expense of others. The two ideologies are locked in a protracted struggle.

Bourgeois intellectuals are the representatives of bourgeois ideology, Comrade Lu stated. They have propounded many slogans: "one-bookism," "be proud," "a gentleman should be willing to die for his dearest friends," "be loyal to one's friends," "personal feelings have priority," "become an expert before becoming a revolutionary," "with a knowledge of natural science and engineering, one can go anywhere in the world," "struggle for money," "one can achieve both fame and wealth as a writer," and so on. These arrogant, smug bourgeois intellectuals contend for fame and reputation, scorn manual labor, and are unable to endure a hard life. They shirk discipline and care nothing for collective interests. Contemptuous of other people, they gossip, insinuate, and conspire. Some even go so far as to become absolutely corrupt and turn against their country.

In sum, the country that produces many proletarian intellectuals also produces bourgeois intellectuals. Our socialist society, conceived in the womb of the old society, has inevitably retained ethical, economic, and ideological remnants of the old. For this reason, the construction of a socialist society requires a resolute struggle of proletarian ideology against that of the bourgeoisie. Socialist society will perish if such a struggle fails. Furthermore, we must fight offenders and their crimes through the courts and prisons, in conjunction with the police.

Of the intellectuals nurtured by a socialist society, some will inevitably degenerate into bourgeois rightists. If we do our work well, however, we can bring this number to a minimum by learning from past experience.

THE TWO-LINE STRUGGLE IN LITERATURE AND ART

Comrade Lu offered a concise explanation and analysis of the long-standing two-line struggle in literature and art, a struggle that has been going on since the Yenan Forum on Literature and Art in

1942. The divergence between the two lines essentially has to do with the relationship between politics and literature, literature and the Party, and the respective roles of literature, the writer, and the artist.

It has always been a principle of our Party that politics should lead literature. This requires that literature submit itself to the Party's leadership and dedicate itself to the service of the people. In evaluating a work of literature, its political implications should be of primary importance; artistic merit is secondary. Writers and artists must study Marxism and align themselves with the workers, peasants, and soldiers, sharing their thoughts and feelings. It is Party policy to strive for unity in order to serve the revolution. For this purpose, we must organize an extensive united front within our literary circles, educating and promoting unity among all writers and artists. Under the principle of serving the workers, peasants, and soldiers, we wish to make "a hundred flowers bloom and a hundred schools of thought contend." Revolutionary literature and art advance themselves through open competition, and workers in literature and art can be educated through open competition.

What is the proper role of literature and art? Comrade Lu maintained that revolutionary literature and art are a vital element of revolution. However, people such as Wang Shih-wei, Hu Feng, Feng Hsüeh-feng, Ting Ling, and Chiang Feng conceive a literature and art in an entirely different way from that of the Party. They assert that literature and art should take precedence over politics, and that artists should be given free reign in the realms of art and literature. They reject Marxism, refuse to serve the workers, peasants, and soldiers, and scorn the concept of political and artistic criteria. They reject the concept of a national form, and repudiate the principle that the elevation of standards must be based on popularization. Asserting that "life can be experienced anywhere," they refuse to ally themselves with the working people. Renouncing the united front, they would discard everything for the absolute authority of the individual writer and artist. This is an anti-Party, antipeople, and antisocialist line regarding art and literature. The struggle between these two lines has been a long one, and will continue in the days to come. It is of great importance, and will exercise a crucial influence on art and literature. A victory in this struggle will greatly bolster the Party's leadership in this area.

TWO SPECIFIC POLICIES
REGARDING WRITERS AND ARTISTS

Writers reflect social life and participate in class struggle through the medium of literature, stated Comrade Lu. And what is the nature of literature? Comrade Mao states: "Works of literature and art, as ideological forms, are products of the reflection in the human mind of the life of a given society. Revolutionary literature and art are the products of the reflection of the life of the people in the minds of revolutionary writers and artists."

A writer cannot wrench his creative work from thin air, but must reflect the life of the society. A revolutionary writer reflects life in a society from a revolutionary point of view, while a counter-revolutionary does so from a counterrevolutionary position. Willingly or unwillingly, directly or indirectly, a writer's work serves a political end, revolutionary or counter revolutionary. Works of literature that reflect the society will have considerable impact on the political situation.

Comrade Lu pointed out that every class has its spiritual architects. There are spiritual architects for the slaveowners, the feudal landlords, and the capitalists, as well as for the working class. Regarding the latter, "spiritual architect" is a title to spur writers to further efforts, not to make them arrogant. Writers and artists are not the only spiritual architects. The Party, educators, lecturers on Marxism, and Youth League workers play the same role. This is also the case with parents, instructors of the Young Pioneers, and nurses in the day-care centers. In fact, anyone whose purpose it is to educate others can be considered a spiritual architect. However, all educators must be educated themselves; writers and artists are no exception. All builders of the spirit must reform their own spiritual nature before helping others to do so. If writers and artists do not strive to remold themselves in their spiritual nature and become proletarian writers, they will come to resemble worms that feed on the souls of others.

There are two ways of dealing with writers and artists. One

approach would be to sing their praises, offer them encouragement in the form of material benefits, and tolerate their mistakes at the expense of neglecting their political and ideological education. In so doing, we would appear to be playing the role of patron to writers and artists. Actually, we would be impeding their future development, corrupting them and bringing about their political and ideological destruction. We must avoid this. Another approach would be to delegate art and literature to their proper roles, and to warn writers and artists to maintain constant vigilance against feelings of conceit. They must be urged to integrate themselves with the workers, peasants, and soldiers, and to study Marxism-Leninism. They must live in the midst of the masses, and writers with Party membership must be placed under the leadership of the Party's basic unit. If they make mistakes, they must be criticized just as other Party members are criticized; a genuine effort must be made to correct their errors. This sounds like restricting their "freedom." That is right: they are not very free. However, in relinquishing their freedom to develop as bourgeois intellectuals, they gain the freedom to progress toward the status of proletarian intellectuals.

Comrade Lu cautioned us that our revolutionary writers and artists should take great care in political and ideological matters; they must be ever on their guard against individualism and liberalism. The more success and prestige a writer achieves, the greater care he should take in conducting himself modestly and prudently; he should be all the more respectful of the working people and the Party. The highest consideration should be given to the masses, the interests of the revolution as a whole, and to the Communist Party, the leader of the revolution. If the "self" were given precedence, it would collapse in the face of the masses. Only those who efface themselves to the point of altruism can win the esteem of the masses.

Comrade Lu stressed the necessity for writers and artists to submit to the leadership of the Party, and to earnestly serve the cause of socialism. With prudence and modesty, they must allow themselves to be instructed by the masses, and to serve as the nuts and bolts of the machinery of revolution. They must place themselves in the humblest position, serving the people with all their heart and soul. We must tirelessly promote this attitude among writers and artists.

SETTLE AMONG THE MASSES FOR A LONG TIME, WHOLEHEARTEDLY AND WITHOUT RESERVATION

Comrade Lu emphatically stated that writers and artists must "settle among the masses for a long time, wholeheartedly and without reservation." The slogan "experience life" has its merits, but it also has had certain ill effects. It was beneficial to writers who had little opportunity to involve themselves with the workers, peasants, and soldiers under the reactionary rule of the past, for it served to bring them closer to the masses. But on young writers, and on those from liberated areas, it has exerted a harmful influence. Such writers have already lived for a time among the masses, or would have, had not the slogan "experience life" prevented them from doing so. Comrade Lu told the story of the play, *Marriage of a Fairy,* as an example. The seventh daughter of the Jade Emperor in heaven comes down to earth in order to marry Tung Yung, a peasant. She intends to live with Tung Yung forever, but the Jade Emperor will not tolerate it. She is therefore able to "experience life" for no more than one hundred days.

The call to "experience life" has done even greater harm to the younger generation. Various young people who wish to be writers are placed in a "creative workshop" and prematurely become "professional writers." Certain young people who lived in the midst of the workers, peasants, and soldiers for several years have composed a number of literary works of great merit, only to live in big cities divorced from the realities of life thereafter. Only occasionally do they tour the countryside in order to "experience life." As a result, they gradually lose contact with the source of their inspiration and fail to produce new work of any merit. Certain of them are heading for a fall. In particular, the case of Liu Shao-t'ang should be a warning to us.

Comrade Lu stressed the necessity for young writers not only to "experience life" on occasion, but also to "settle among the masses for a long time, wholeheartedly and without reservation," as Chairman Mao said. It will be good for them, first, to participate in manual labor, and second, to work at the grassroots level. They should work together with the workers, peasants, and soldiers, share their lives and hardships. As for writers who are advanced in age or poor in health, we must make other appropriate arrangements for them. But this should not alter our basic principle. To serve as an example to younger writers, veteran writers should do what Chairman Mao suggested at the Chinese Communist Party's National Conference on Propaganda Work: 70 percent of all veteran writers should go, group by group, to villages or factories within eleven years. They would have the choice of either looking around briefly ("looking from horseback at the flowers"), staying for a closer look ("dismounting from the horse to look at the flowers"), or "settling down" for several years. Writers in large cities should find access to the masses whenever possible.

ON SOCIALIST REALISM

Comrade Lu has stated his opinion on the issue of socialist realism. Quoting Chairman Mao, he said: "China's revolutionary writers and artists of promise must go among the masses; they must do so wholeheartedly, without reservation, and for a long time. They must go among the masses of workers, peasants, and soldiers, the only source, the broadest and richest source. They must do so in order to observe, experience, study, and analyze every manner of people, every class, the whole of the masses, all the vivid patterns of life and struggle, all the raw materials of life and art. Only then can they proceed to their creative work." According to Comrade Lu, this statement forms the basis of the creative approach of socialist realism.

We uphold the principle, "Let a hundred flowers bloom and a hundred schools of thought contend," because we desire free competition among works with different creative approaches, different themes, and different styles. We do not regard socialist realism as the only creative method; however, it is the best. If one divorces oneself from the workers, peasants, and soldiers, one will not produce works of socialist realism, no matter how eloquently one voices one's support of the mode. Anyone who intends to produce works of socialist realism must "go among the masses of workers peasants and soldiers for a long time, wholeheartedly and without reservation."

Certain literary works tend to be formulaic and conceptualized. This is not because, as Hu Feng alleged, writers have involved themselves with the workers, peasants, and soldiers. Conversely, it is because writers have failed to achieve a comprehensive understanding of the life of the common people.

Comrade Lu talked about the issue of exposing the dark side of our society and criticizing our shortcomings. He stated that the question of what comprises the dark side also has a class character. We have, for example, done away with such places of debauchery as brothels and nightclubs. To the proletariat, this was an entirely positive achievement. Certain bourgeois individuals, however, may have regarded this as something negative. The point at issue is the question of class viewpoint. It is entirely permissible to criticize our shortcomings and mistakes; we are certain to encounter all kinds of difficulty and make various mistakes, wherever we work—factory, farm, school, or shop. The outcome of all this, however, will be difficulties overcome, mistakes corrected, and the achievement of success. If we are creating works of socialist realism, we will inevitably write about difficulties and mistakes, but we will also write about the manner in which they are overcome. The primary subject of our writing will be achievement, while our difficulties and mistakes will become secondary. Furthermore, our successes often exceed our expectations. There are failures as well, from which we can learn lessons even as we describe them. Liu Shao-t'ang, for example, was an instance of a failure on our part in cultivating young writers. Why could we not write about him?

Comrade Lu pointed out that the dark side of our society can and must be exposed. The Ting-Ch'en anti-Party clique is the dark aspect of our literary circles. Our effort to expose them is an important lesson to us all.

Comrade Lu pointed out two things to be expected from writers and artists. First, writers should conduct a long-term, comprehensive study of the development of our factories, agricultural cooperatives, schools, and stores. Studying one unit in each of the four categories will give the writer a basic understanding of the features of our society; this will help him to make correct judgments about many issues. The Writers' Union should collaborate with the Party committees to facilitate an involvement on the part of writers with the realities of life. Second, writers with Party membership should be integrated with Party organizations at the basic level of production or administration in the neighborhood. It is not a good thing for writers to form a separate organization that estranges them from the masses. There are those who believe that committees at the municipal level, committees at the provincial level, or the Central Committee should exercise leadership over writers, rather than committees at the basic level. In criticizing this mistaken idea, Comrade Lu stated that writers with Party membership must not consider themselves privileged Party members. They must obey the Party constitution and observe Party discipline. This holds true for young members, and even more so for veteran members.

THE THREE HARDS

In the last section of his speech, Comrade Lu propounded the requirement of the three "hards": strike hard against the Rightists, strive hard to improve one's work, and struggle hard to remold one's thought.

Bourgeois rightists, he declared, are antisocialist reactionaries; they are counterrevolutionary, and are our enemies. The conflict between them and the people is one of life and death; there can be no compromise. Therefore we must strike hard against them. We must adopt stern measures in dealing with Rightists and anti-Party elements; we must, however, avoid extremes in order to allow for the possibility of repentance on their part. Those who do not repent will serve as a negative example in educating the people. If, however, they commit crimes, they will be subject to legal action.

Comrade Lu went on to say that we have many shortcomings and have made various mistakes in our work; we lack mature, systematic experience in the administration of literary affairs. Our experience in this regard is not equal to the task of implementing Chairman Mao's guidelines on literary work, and the task of organizing and nurturing a literary contingent of the working class. Our shortcomings and mistakes are the result of various factors; among them are the influence of Rightists, lack of experience, bureaucratism, sectarianism, and subjectivism. It is necessary for us to conduct a thorough review of our work, and to encourage people to offer criticism.

Comrade Lu stated that it is imperative for non-Party members to remold their thought, even more so for Party members. Apart from studying relevant documents and articles, thought reform involves experiencing the life of the workers, peasants, and soldiers, and going to work in the country, factory, or army. It will help writers remold their thought and create good socialist literature; it will also help reform the old habits of our society. In particular, young comrades and comrades from liberated areas should go to live among the peasants, workers, and soldiers for a long time, unconditionally and wholeheartedly. Of course, writers who are old or in poor health should not be forced to go off to the countryside or the factories. As was mentioned earlier, we must make special arrangements for these writers.

In concluding his speech, Comrade Lu stated that we are fully confident that under the Party's leadership, united and striving, the literary contingent of the Chinese working class will develop and grow strong; our literature and art will enter a new era.

CHOU YANG'S SPEECH

In explaining the significance of the struggle against the Ting-Ch'en anti-Party clique, Comrade Chou Yang criticized its anti-Party ideas and analyzed its historical origin. He also pointed out what work we should do in the future. The struggle, he said, must continue; the successes achieved so far must be consolidated and carried forward. We must continue our debate on the issue of art and literature, and learn from it.

Comrade Chou first spoke of lessons to be learned from the present struggle. Why is it that older left-wing writers and artists such as Ting Ling, Feng Hsüeh-feng, and Chiang Feng went the anti-Party route? How did it happen that such people as Chung Tien-fei, who joined the revolution while in his teens and was brought up in the revolution, set out on the anti-Party road? Why did Liu Shao-t'ang do the same? He was even younger and had received his education and training as a writer after the liberation of the entire country. We should reflect on this question.

THE CONFLICT BETWEEN TWO WORLD VIEWS

As early as 1930, when the League of Left-wing Writers was formed, Lu Hsün warned that if left-wing writers divorced themselves from reality, placed themselves in a superior position, and considered their writing the most important thing, they were likely to become right-wing. Comrade Chou stated that this prediction has come true. Most left-wing writers have come from a feudal-landlord or some other exploitative class. In terms of their upbringing and world view, they are bourgeois intellectuals. After the May Fourth movement in 1919, we began to get in touch with Western science, and democratic and socialist ideas; we also read a great many Western literary works of realism which are full of democratic ideas. We were influenced by many of the pernicious elements of Western literature. Finally, we accepted Marxism, an ideological weapon for the emancipation of all mankind. But at that time, communism was no more than an abstract belief to us. There had been no change in our individualistic world view, or in our egocentric ideas and sentiments. To a large extent, many associated themselves with the revolution for personal motives. However, we were committed not only to a democratic revolution, but also to a socialist revolution; our egocentric nature became incompatible with collectivism.

People may be divided into two categories. First, there are those who, educated by the Party and tempered by the struggle of revolution, have gradually discarded their burden of individualism. They have slowly freed themselves of their burden, step by step, at last becoming unfettered and free. They have identified themselves with the collective, become of one mind with the Party, and finally have become fighters for collectivism. People of the second category will never discard their individualism; they cling to it. They will never discard their individual interests or free themselves of their personal motives. They cling to their individualism when challenged, nourishing it and cherishing it within themselves. They become increasingly antagonistic toward the Party and hostile toward the collective. The stronger the Party becomes, the more constrained they feel. They credit themselves for any small achievement. They have no respect for the Party, or for anybody. Such people are unable to withstand the test of certain crucial moments, and easily set off on the anti-Party road. We are now facing the difficult job of socialism. We must become determined soldiers of communism and oppose any individualistic careerist.

People seriously infected with individualistic ideas, observed Comrade Chou, are unable to remain true to the Party and the people. He cited a wealth of evidence to demonstrate that Ting Ling, Feng Hsüeh-feng, and others became dissatisfied with the Party over a long period of time and that they were no longer of the same mind as the Party. When they consecutively held the position of chief editor of *Wen-i pao* (Literary Gazette), they regarded the journal as independent of the Party. Desiring only praise, they rejected criticism. They accepted those ideas of the Party that corresponded with their own, and rejected all others. Our journals are the organs of the people and the working class; how can they act independently of the Party? These people continually felt constrained by the Party. But they failed to understand that, within the Party, discipline is joined with freedom. Party members can air their opinions at meetings, but are not allowed to act in a clandestine manner against the Party's interests. Those who are faithful to the Party will not despair. In 1955, the Central Committee reviewed the case of the *Literary Gazette*. On the surface, Ting, Feng, and others accepted the investigation, though not without reluctance. At heart, however, they became increasingly discontented with the Party. The Hungarian incident was a source of encouragement to them. When Rightists launched an assault against the Party this year, their own anti-Party activities reached a climax. That Ting Ling and her like should oppose the Party is the inevitable consequence of their profound egotism. It is also a reflection of the problems within the Party when great transitions are taking place in our society.

Comrade Chou was emphatic in his criticism of "one-bookism."[2] He stated that the conflict between the Communist and bourgeois world views bears on the question of the way in which we are to educate the next generation of writers. Are we to educate and cultivate the younger generation according to the Communist world view or the bourgeois world view of individualism advocated by Ting Ling? It is our hope that every writer will write good books—and not only one book. What does it mean to be a writer, if not to create? However, we are resolutely opposed to one-bookism. In the eyes of certain people, the bloodshed from the struggle of millions is less im-

[2] During the anti-Rightist campaign in 1957, critics coined the term "one-bookism" to criticize Ting Ling for her idea that a writer should care about his art more than anything else and that it was better to write one good book than to write many bad books.

portant than the book about the bloodshed. Such people view their writing as more important than the struggle of the working people, and use their books as chips with which to bargain with the Party. They immediately change their relationship to the Party after writing a book; they believe they can advance themselves without assistance.

Writing is a matter of individual effort; it requires diligence and talented labor. The Party considers this an important activity. One-bookism, however, can only lead writers to their own destruction. There have been numerous men of letters in the past who wrote in the spirit of one-bookism. However, only those books by great authors who wrote for the people have survived. We have to struggle against one-bookism and emphasize the importance of the Communist world view. No matter how much writing an author produces, he should always be aware that he is indebted to the Party and the people. Only by resolutely opposing individualism can we uphold collectivism and promote socialist literature.

THE STRUGGLE BETWEEN TWO LINES

Comrade Chou pointed out that the current struggle in the areas of art and literature is a struggle between two lines. At issue is the matter of whether literature should serve the cause of socialism or the individual author; should literary affairs be administered by the leadership of the Party, or should literature be free of such influence? Anti-Party writers have not voiced their opposition to the matter of literature serving the cause of socialism. Actually, however, it is exactly this to which they object. They scorn literature that addresses itself to the workers, peasants, and soldiers. For some time now, Rightists, anti-Party individuals, and revisionists at home and abroad have protested vehemently against socialist literature. It is their primary contention that such literature does not tell the truth. They assert that there can be no creative freedom under the socialist system. Their objection to socialist literature is tantamount to a rejection of Marxist-Leninist theory and the entire socialist system.

Comrade Chou vigorously repudiated this argument. He pointed out that from the time that Stalin was criticized at the Twentieth Congress of the Communist Party of the Soviet Union, there has been a worldwide tendency to deny the achievements of Soviet literature of the past twenty years. Socialist literature is still young, he said. Our dogmatic attitudes exist because we have not made a thorough study of literature; we have misunderstood socialist realism as dogmatism. The ongoing discussion, however, has not focused itself on this problem. The problem we are discussing is that certain people deride Soviet literature under the pretext of opposing dogmatism and socialist realism. Soviet literature initiated a new era, and our new literature from Lu Hsün's time onward has also made great achievements.

Why, then, are there so few great works of socialist literature?

Comrade Chou stated that the literature of socialism is in an early stage of its development. Soviet literature dates from the publication of Gorky's *Mother* some fifty years ago, and our own literature dates from the May Fourth movement of thirty-eight years ago. In comparison with feudal literature, which has a background of more than two thousand years, and capitalist literature, with its background of four to five hundred years, socialist literature is still quite young. Furthermore, it has an entirely different nature from other sorts of literature. In regard to form, theme, content, and characterization, our socialist literature differs from that of the past. Seldom in the past did literature present the life and struggle of the working people as its main concern. Those who produce the material wealth, those who wear straw sandals or walk barefoot, these people are of little importance in the writing of the past. Now we not only write about such people, we write for them as our readers.

This situation is unprecedented in the history of literature. All great writers in the past aspired to the ideal of serving mankind. None of them, however, openly allied themselves with the working class, or declared an affiliation with its politics. Only our literature, the literature of the proletariat, has declared itself closely related to the proletarian emancipation of mankind. The people of the past experienced class exploitation. Today, it is our purpose to portray new characters, free of the influence of exploitation, and new relationships between men. The literature of socialist realism is the literature of a new era, a literature initiated by ourselves. We wish to carry on the traditions of the past, but must clearly distinguish between our own modes of thought and the hackneyed ideas of the old society. We must give expression to the new era and create characters of an entirely new nature. This is what is demanded of us by our class and by the times in which we live. If we drift away from the struggle of the common people, from our national tradition and from socialist construction, it will be impossible for us to create a new socialist culture.

In regard to the issue of writing the truth, Comrade Chou stated that a literature which is not true to reality is unacceptable to the people. But what is truth? How shall we write the truth? Some people believe that one should write the truth without regard to purpose. But in this apparent absence of purpose there is a purpose: an attempt to divorce literature from politics. After turning traitor to the Communist cause, Howard Fast[3] asserted: "One cannot write according to what is supposed to be right." The playwright Wu Tsu-kuang[4] observed, "One seldom finds anything genuine in today's literature. Even such a writer as Ts'ao Yü[5] must face the problem of deciding between the way in which he wants to write and the way in which he is supposed to write."

Should a writer be responsible to the people? If so, Comrade Chou stated, the writer should consider the problem of which way he should write. That Ts'ao Yü took this problem into consideration reveals his responsible attitude toward society and the people. A writer is faced with two options: He can strive to give expression to the feelings of the people and to fashion his own sentiments and ideas in accordance with theirs, or he can do the opposite. If the writer takes the bourgeois or petit-bourgeois stand, but writes in the prescribed manner, his work will inevitably become dull and will read like formula writing. If he simply writes what is on his mind, the work will certainly be bourgeois or petit-bourgeois in nature. This would indicate that the feelings of the people have yet to be-

[3] Howard Fast is an American novelist who enjoyed great popularity in the Communist bloc. After the Hungarian incident in 1956, he left the American Communist Party and renounced Marxism.

[4] A veteran playwright who had become famous before the Communist takeover, Wu Tsu-kuang was still popular during the early days after liberation; he was criticized during the anti-Rightist campaign of 1956 and has now been rehabilitated.

[5] Ts'ao Yü was one of the foremost playwrights of contemporary China. He wrote the well-known plays *Jih-ch'u* (The Sunrise), *Lei-yü* (The Thunderstorm), and *Pei-ching jen* (Peking Man). He joined the Communist Party after the Communist takeover.

come his own feelings, and that he is incapable of saying what the people want to hear. In order to solve this problem, he must integrate himself with the masses. This is a difficult process of personal remolding, and an assimilation of the desires of the people. What the people desire will become an impetus to creative writing.

Wu Tsu-kuang also said that a writer must use figurative language in his work, that he does not seem to need logical thinking as the basis of his writing. Gorky's *Mother* was the first piece of socialist-realist literature. Lenin and Plekhanov[6] differed in their opinion of this novel. Plekhanov insisted that Gorky should not write as a Marxist propagandist, but as an artist; he should use figurative language, not the language of logic. Lenin, however, warmly approved of this work. The judgment of history is strict and unprejudiced; who was right? Lenin was right, of course, for literature must reflect the progress of its era.

One of the questions regarding "writing the truth," remarked Comrade Chou, is whether or not one should be allowed to write of the dark side of life. The writer has the right to do so, of course. Our literature should not present one aspect of life alone. Not only should it praise that which is positive, but it should also expose the negative. The crux of all this, however, lies in the attitude we adopt in exposing the dark side of life. If we examine a phenomenon in such a way as to detach it from struggle and class viewpoint, we will hardly be able to distinguish between the positive and the negative. Wang Shih-wei and Hsiao Chün, pioneers in writing about the dark side of life, held that even the sun has its dark spots, and purposely looked for those dark spots. Ting Ling also put this theory into practice, and it is now being adopted by Liu Pin-yen.

We have never stated that the negative aspect of things is not to be presented. It should not be done in an exaggerated manner, however, and there should be no confusion of the positive with the negative. Nor should one delight in the negative aspect of things; rather, one should celebrate its defeat. In portraying the dark side of life, we should give the people confidence. Death can be depicted in our works only if it encourages rather than disappoints us, for then it

[6] Georgi Valentinovich Plekhanov, 1857–1918, a Russian philosopher and leader of the Mensheviks.

represents a sacrifice for some noble ideal. We will certainly criticize decadent literature whenever it appears, for such literature is incompatible with the sentiments of our class. We do not want to be burdened with gloom, and we require that literature be an inspiration to the people. Could there be any nobler objective than this? Is one unfaithful to reality if he maintains such an objective? Moveover, is one faithful to reality if he writes about the gloomy sentiments of the petit-bourgeoisie for fame and money?

In regard to the issue of artistic freedom, Comrade Chou explained that the policy of "letting a hundred flowers bloom and a hundred schools of thought contend" is intended to make science and literature flourish, and to make writers and scientists feel free and open. In our society, literature of any sort can be published except that which is anti-Communist, antipeople, and antisocialist. Could there be any greater creative freedom than this? There are some, however, who feel restrained by mental pressures resulting from direct or indirect criticism. In some instances, such criticism is rude and unjustified, and should be opposed. This applies to both oral and written criticism. Since every manner of literature will meet with the approval or the disapproval of society, a writer must be courageous in the face of criticism. Chairman Mao once observed that a genuine materialist is afraid of nothing. We must therefore oppose rude criticism, while encouraging writers to be daring and courageous.

Comrade Chou stated that certain writers feel a lack of creative freedom when requested to write with a certain end in mind. But it is inconceivable for a writer to write without a purpose. Perhaps some people feel a greater measure of freedom when writing from personal objectives, and feel restrained when they are serving the cause of socialism. Lenin stated that socialist literature is a truly free literature since it is not designed to satisfy monetary goals or personal objectives. Another of the alleged restrictions has to do with the selection of theme and technique. A writer has absolute freedom in selecting his theme. After he has given expression to his theme, however, the people have the right to criticize his work and assess its truthfulness. It is wrong to assert that a writer is restricted in his choice of theme if he is encouraged to write about the workers, peasants, and soldiers. On the contrary, the life of our millions of workers, peasants, and soldiers provides an immense variety of themes. It serves to expand the writer's creative possibilities.

It is wrong to think that our five hundred million people are simply a swarm of rogues, and that only intellectuals are worthy subjects of writing. In order to serve the workers, peasants, and soldiers, a writer must have genuine artistic sensibilities and a desire to create. From where are these to be derived—from the workers, peasants, and soldiers, or from the petit-bourgeoisie? We maintain that writers must follow the road of the workers, peasants, and soldiers. To present the true features of these people, to employ their own language and give expression to our five hundred million people—this is the greatest freedom a writer can possibly have. The portrayal of oneself, or of a handful of people associated with oneself, involves no great artistic freedom. Only by integrating oneself with one's era and one's own people can one enjoy genuine freedom; any other freedom is a sham.

HOW TO INTEGRATE WRITERS AND ARTISTS
WITH WORKERS AND PEASANTS

Finally, Comrade Chou dwelt on the tasks of the future. He stated emphatically that during the period of "big blooming and big contending" many people expressed their ideas, most of which were valuable. Debates should continue in order further to explore ways in which literature and art can go the way of socialism. He explained that "letting a hundred flowers bloom and a hundred schools of thought contend" is a long-term policy and must be continually implemented. We must guard against the possibility of literary groups promoting personal preferences, and substituting their simplistic approach to literature for literary policy.

Chou stated that after the current rectification campaign we must resolve the issue of integrating writers and artists with the workers, peasants, and soldiers. "A hundred flowers blooming" can become a garden where every sort of flower, as well as poisonous weeds, can flourish with the right climate, temperature, and soil. The soil is especially important because the seeds are sown there, and it is there that the roots strike deep. Writers and artists must make their roots strike deep among the masses. Comrade Chou noted that there are significant flaws in our slogans of "experiencing life" and "intervening in life."[7] A few older writers, he said, are rich in social experience but are divorced from the workers, peasants, and soldiers. It would therefore benefit them to experience life among the masses for a while. Writers of the younger generation are obligated to work among the masses for a long time, and to participate in practical labor at the grassroots level. Only in this way can they actually merge themselves with the masses, acquire a rich artistic sensibility, and produce good works of literature. Chairman Mao and the Central Committee of the Party taught us this. It should be the essential principle of our literary work that writers be expected to associate with the worker and peasant masses in work and struggle.

Comrade Chou criticized the idea of "intervening in life." It implies, he stated, that writers do not live among the masses but remain above them. Whenever they see something that displeases them, they step in to intervene. Such behavior would certainly cause a disturbance among the masses. If the idea implies actively influencing the affairs of life through literature, why is it that only the exposure of the dark side of life is regarded as "intervening"? Why is not praise of the positive also "intervening"? This idea implies that writers have yet to discover the proper relationship between themselves and the people, and the realities of life.

In conclusion, Comrade Chou declared the meeting to be a great success. We have experienced severe struggles and have learned hard lessons. We now face even greater tasks ahead. With an awareness of history, as well as of what may be in store for us in the future, we must resolutely rally around the Party, integrate ourselves with the working people, and follow the road of socialism. We must construct our socialist country with our own hands, and create a new national culture of socialism.

[7] "Intervening in life" was one of the terms coined by critics during the debates on socialist realism in the period of the hundred flowers. To intervene in life means to study, think over, and analyze life and to take action. If a writer lives and works in this way, he will have individual views about life and will not portray characters from an abstract ideological standpoint.

NOTES ON MAJOR WRITERS

CH'IEN KU-JUNG   Little is known about Ch'ien Ku-jung's life. While writing "Lun wen-hsüeh shih jen-hsüeh" (Literature Is the Study of Man), he was an instructor in the Department of Chinese at East China Normal University in Shanghai. He was very popular with his students. At the meetings convened by the Shanghai branch of the Chinese Writers' Union in 1960, Ch'ien made ten speeches in succession to advocate his concept of "humanism of the working people." He was attacked by Yao Wen-yüan and others for encouraging revisionist ideas.

CH'IN CHAO-YANG   Ch'in Chao-yang, pen name Ho Chih, was born in 1920, and was one of several young Communist writers Chou Yang cultivated at Yenan in the forties. His short stories and novels use village life as the main theme to illustrate the Communist Party's policies and political line. After Feng Hsüeh-feng was removed from the editorship of *Wen-i pao* (Literary Gazette), Ch'in was appointed to the editorial committee along with K'ang Cho and Hou Chin-ching. At the time of the Hu Feng incident, Ch'in published articles in all the major journals to criticize Hu's literary theories.

   In the spring of 1956 he was appointed to *Jen-min wen-hsüeh* (People's Literature) as associate editor. In the same year he published an article entitled "Hsien-shih chu-i ti k'uan-kuang tao-lu" (The Broad Road of Realism—A Reassessment of Realism) and other related articles, which expounded the concept of "she-hui chu-i shih-tai ti hsien-shih chu-i" (realism in the socialist era) as a way of opposing the restrictions dogmatism had placed on literature. Taking advantage of his editorial position, he revised and published Huang Ch'iu-yün's "Pu-yao tsai jen-min ti chi-k'u mien-ch'ien pi-shang yen-ching" (Do Not Close Your Eyes to the Suffering of the People), Liu Pin-yen's "Pen-pao nei-pu hsiao-hsi" (The Inside News of the Newspaper), and Wang Meng's "Tsu-chih-pu hsin-lai ti nien-ch'ing jen" (A Young Man Arrives at the Organization Department). The publication of these three pieces aroused intense debate. After Liu Shao-t'ang, Ch'in was also criticized as a Rightist. The criticism lasted from the end of 1957 through July 1958. Ch'in made self-criticism, and the editorial board of *Jen-min wen-hsüeh* was reorganized. He was then sent to do labor in a factory in Kwangsi from 1959 to 1961. Presumably his name was officially removed from the list of Rightists in 1961 and he was again allowed to continue writing. In May 1962 he published a short story entitled "A Found Letter" in *Kwangsi wen-i* (Kwangsi Literature). He was writing a novel about the Anti-Japanese War, *Liang tai jen (Two Generations),* which was partly serialized in *Kwangsi wen-i* from 1963 to 1964; he is continuing to write this novel.

His major works include *Hsing-fu* (Happiness), a collection of short stories; *Tsai t'ien-yeh shang ch'ien-chin* (Move Forward in the Fields), a novel; and the essays "Hsien-shih chu-i ti k'uan-kuang tao-lu" (The Broad Road of Realism—A Reassessment of Realism), "Lun 'chien-jui' chih feng" (On the Spirit of "Sharpness"), "Ts'ung t'e-hsieh ti chen-shih hsing t'an-ch'i" (Beginning with the Necessity of Truthfulness in Feature Stories), and "Ch'en-mo" (Silence).

CHOU YANG   Chou Yang, born in Hunan in 1908, was a literary theorist in charge of literary activities and propaganda work for the Chinese Communist Party. After graduation from Ta-hsia University in Shanghai in 1926, he went to Japan to study literature and Marxism. He was jailed for participating in a leftist demonstration while in Japan, and returned to China in 1929 to join the Communist Party. From 1930 on, he served as the CCP secretary to the League of Left-wing Writers. In 1936 he dissolved the league without the consent of Lu Hsün and established in its place the Writers' Association. In consequence, he was involved in an intense debate with Lu Hsün and Hu Feng over the issue of "national defense literature." After the beginning of the Anti-Japanese War, he went to Yenan, where he was appointed in succession minister of education under the Shensi, Kansu, and Ninghsia Border Region Government, vice-principal of Lu Hsün Arts Academy, and president of Yenan University. After the People's Republic of China was founded, his most important work, besides his various bureaucratic positions, was to serve as Deputy Director of the Communist Central Committee's Propaganda Department. He was also in charge of the humanities studies at the university level. Chou Yang represented the Communist Party in organizing numerous literary rectification campaigns to criticize such literary figures as Wang Shih-wei, Hsiao Chün, Ting Ling, Feng Hsüeh-feng, Hu Feng, and Ai Ch'ing. However, from 1959 on, he propounded the literary theory of creation which classifies literary works under three categories: the "beneficial" (works in praise of workers, peasants, and soldiers), the "innocuous" (works that lack positive import in politics but can make life delightful and relaxed), and the "harmful" (works that have a negative political influence). All this was at odds with Mao Tse-tung's guidelines for literature. He was criticized during the Cultural Revolution as a "three antis" element—namely, a person who was opposed to the Party, to socialism, and to Mao Tse-tung's thought. The Red Guards criticized him along with Lu Ting-i, Director of the Party's Propaganda Department.

As one of the "four fellows" singled out by Lu Hsün as his irreconcilable enemies during the "battle of slogans" in the thirties, Chou, together with Hsia Yen, Yang Han-sheng, and T'ien Han, was brutally attacked and persecuted during the Cultural Revolution as representative figures of a sinister line in literature and art. However, at a conference convoked by the Ministry of Culture held in March 1979, the good names of Chou and others were restored and such labels as "ministry serving the bourgeoisie," "ministry of emperors, kings, generals, ministers, talented young scholars, pretty ladies, and the dead people of foreign countries," which Mao had tagged onto the Ministry of Culture, were officially removed. Now Chou Yang has been appointed adviser to the Chinese Academy of Social Sciences and also serves as Chairman of the All-China Federation of Literary and Art Circles. He is a member of the Standing Committee of the Chinese People's Political Consultative Conference. At the Fourth National Congress of Literary and Art Workers, Chou made a keynote speech and openly apologized to Ting Ling, Ai Ch'ing, Hsia Chün, and others, writers whom he had wrongly persecuted in the past.

His works include *Ma-k'e-ssu chu-i yü wen-hsüeh* (Marxism and Literature) and *Chung-kuo ti hsin wen-i* (China's New Literature). He also translated *Anna Karenina* by Tolstoy and *The Aesthetic Relationship between Art and Reality*, by N. G. Chernyshevsky.

FENG HSÜEH-FENG Feng Hsüeh-feng, a native of Chekiang, was born around 1906 and started his writing career as a poet. He joined other young poets—P'an Mo-hua, Ying Hsiu-jen, and Wang Ching-chih—to publish the poetry collection *Hu-p'an* (The Lakeside) in 1922 and another poetry collection, *Ch'un-t'ien chih ko* (The Song of Spring) in 1923. Later he exclusively wrote literary critiques and articles about literary theory, for which he became famous. Most of his articles were collected in *Kuo-lai ti shih-tai* (The Times We Have Been Through) and *Hsiang-feng yü shih-feng* (Spirit of Country and City). In 1927 he joined the Communist Party and in 1930 he joined the League of Left-wing Writers. Feng was a devoted disciple of Lu Hsün, with whom he had close contact from 1928 on. In 1938 he went to Kiangsi to the Juichin Soviet, in 1934 he participated in the Long March, and in 1936 he returned to Shanghai from Yenan. He had considerable influence within the League of Left-wing Writers and persuaded Hu Feng to join the Party. He, Lu Hsün, and Hu Feng were united in opposition against Chou Yang in the "battle of slogans" over national defense literature.

When the war against the Japanese broke out in 1937, because his opinions clashed with those of the Party leaders, he voluntarily withdrew from the Party and returned to the countryside to live as a recluse. In 1939 he reestablished relations with the Party, but after working in the Communist Southeastern Bureau for a few months, he again departed. In 1941 he was captured by the Kuomintang and placed in Shang-jao Concentration Camp in Kiangsi. During his internment he wrote the poetry collection *Lin-shan chih ko* (The Song of Lin-shan). He was released after two years and went to Chungking. There Hu Feng and the Communist Party were in conflict over literary policy, and Feng spoke up in Hu Feng's defense. After the war, Feng lived in Shanghai and wrote fables and essays, collected in *Yu-chin wu-t'ui* (Go Forth without Retreat) and *Yü-yen chi* (A Collection of Fables).

After the People's Republic was established, he served as vice-chairman of the Chinese Writers' Union and director of Jen-min wen-hsüeh ch'u-pan-she (People's Literature Press). In 1952 Ting Ling recommended that Feng succeed her as editor of *Wen-i pao* (Literary Gazette). In 1954 he was criticized for shelving articles by Li Hsi-fan and others because they were critical of Yü P'ing-po's *Hung-lou-meng yen-chiu* (Studies on *Dream of the Red Chamber*), and he lost the editorship of *Wen-i pao*. He was active for a time during the Hundred Flowers movement. During the anti-Rightist campaign he was criticized as an important member of the Ting Ling–Ch'en Ch'i-hsia anti-Party clique and censured as a Rightist. He died in 1976. His good name was officially restored at the Fourth National Congress of Literary and Art Workers held in November 1979.

HUANG CH'IU-YÜN   The date and place of birth of the veteran Communist writer Huang Ch'iu-yün are not known, but he was probably a native of Kwantung. According to certain autobiographical sketches appended to his stories and articles, it can be gathered that he was born around 1910 and spent his entire childhood in overseas Chinese communities, probably in the South Pacific. He was in elementary school when the Mukden Incident of September 18, 1931, occurred and the Japanese invaded Manchuria. In the 1930s he lived in Canton, and after 1940 in Hong Kong. He translated Romain Rolland's *Jean Christophe,* and the translation enjoyed a wide circulation.

After the People's Republic was established, he edited *Wen-i hsüeh-hsi* (Literary Studies). When the report of Khrushchev's criticism of Stalin during the Twentieth Party Congress of the Soviet Union in 1956 reached China, he was so stunned he nearly had a nervous collapse. In 1957, during the Hundred Flowers period, he published "Pu-yao tsai jen-min ti chi-k'u mien-ch'ien pi-shang yen-ching" (Do Not Close Your Eyes to the Sufferings of the People), revised before publication by Ch'in Chao-yang; and "Tz'u tsai na-li?" (Where Are the Thorns?). Criticized during the anti-Rightist campaign for so-called "right-deviationist thinking" and his "revisionist views," he did self-criticism and continued to publish, mostly essays and literary critiques. He was assigned to work at *Wen-i pao* (Literary Gazette) in the early sixties and was a major target during the early stage of the Cultural

Revolution. The historical story "T'u-fu fan chi'a" (T'u-fu Returns Home,) which he published in *Pei-ching wen-i* (Peking Literature) in April 1962, was attacked as a "poisonous weed" that slandered socialist society. Denounced as a member of the "sinister gang of literature and art," he was sent to do labor in a May 7 cadre school.

His works include two collections of essays: *T'ai-hua chi* (Lichen Flower), and *Ku-chin chi* (Past and Present).

HUANG YAO-MIEN Huang Yao-mien, the veteran leftist writer, was born in 1903 in Kwangtung Province. In 1925 he graduated from Kwangtung Higher Normal Institute, majoring in English, and taught in a high school near Canton; in 1927 he went to Shanghai to serve as an assistant editor to the Creation Society. He began publishing articles in *Ch'uang-tsao chou-k'an* (Creation Weekly) and other journals and joined the Chinese Communist Party in 1928. In 1929 he did underground work for the Chinese Communist Youth League and also taught at Shanghai Arts University. During this period he translated into Chinese Turgenov's novel *Smoke* and Upton Sinclair's *Worker Jimmy*. In the winter of 1929 he went to Moscow to work for the Communist International. He returned to China in 1933 and served as director of the Propaganda Department of the Communist Youth League Central Bureau. Arrested by the Kuomintang in the fall of 1934, he was sentenced to ten years' imprisonment. He was released in 1937 on the recommendation of the Eighth Route Army and went to Yenan. After the outbreak of the war against Japan, he traveled through Hankow, Kweilin, and Hong Kong, returning to Hong Kong after the war. Due to his writings and participation in Min-chu t'ung-meng (Democratic Alliance) activities, he was frequently under surveillance and threatened by the Kuomintang.

After the People's Republic was established, he returned to China as a literary critic and became an important figure in the Democratic Alliance. During the campaign against Hu Feng, he actively criticized Hu. He debated with Feng Hsüeh-feng on literary theories, and replaced Feng as one of the editors of *Wen-i pao* (Literary Gazette). He held unorthodox views in the 1956 debate on aesthetics, and also spoke out during the Hundred Flowers period. He was criticized as a Rightist in the subsequent anti-Rightist campaign and was dismissed from the editorial board of the *Literary Gazette*. Presumably he was officially removed from the list of Rightists, and he is now a professor in the Chinese Department of Peking Teachers' University. He was recently elected to the National Committee of the All-China Federation of Literary and Art Circles.

His poetry collections include *Hsi-pan-ya i shih hsüan* (Selected Translations of Spanish Poetry) and *Kuei-lin ch'e-t'ui* (Retreat from Kweilin). His collections of short stories include *An-ying* (Dark Shadows) and *Wo ts'ung chien-yü chung ch'u-lai* (I Came out of Prison). Huang also published numerous collections of essays: *Mei-li ti hei-hai* (The Beautifully Black Sea),

Shu-ch'ing hsiao-p'in (Lyrical Pieces), *Lun Shih* (On Poetry), *Min-chu yün-tung chian-hua* (A Discussion of the Democratic Movement), and *P'i-p'an chi* (A Collection of Critical Essays).

LAO SHE Lao She, of Manchurian descent, was born in 1896 and raised in Peking. He studied at Yenching University and taught language and literature at Nankai High School in Tientsin. In 1925 he went to London to teach Chinese at the School of Oriental Studies, London University. During that period he began writing. His first novel, *Lao Chang che-hsüeh hsüan-chi* (The Philosophy of Old Chang), was serialized in *Hsiao-shuo yüeh-pao* (Fiction Monthly) and made Lao She famous. He subsequently published *Chao Tzu-yüeh* and *Erh Ma hsien-sheng* (The Two Mas). In 1931 he returned to China and taught for three years at Cheloo University in Tsinan, Shantung, then for one year at Shantung University in Tsingtao. After that he quit the teaching profession to concentrate on writing. He published *Mao-ch'eng chi* (Cat City), *Niu T'ien-sz'u chuan* (The Biography of Niu T'ien-sz'u), and *Lo-t'o hsiang-tzu* (Rickshaw Boy).

During the war against the Japanese, Lao She was in Chungking, presiding over the general service department of the All-China Federation of Literary and Art Circles. In 1946 the English translation of *Rickshaw Boy* was published in America. He came to America to give lectures and to continue writing, and then returned to China in 1949. He became vice-chairman of the Union of Chinese Writers and held many other literary and political offices. He often went abroad on official visits, and at home greeted many foreign dignitaries. He took part in many cultural exchanges while continuing his writing. After publication of the play *Lung-hsü kou* (Dragon-beard Ditch), he was proclaimed Artist of the People. He continued to write plays, including *Fang Chen-chu, Ch'a-kuan* (Teahouse), and *Hsi-wang Ch'ang-an* (Look Westward toward Ch'ang-an). However, his play *Ch'un-hua ch'iu-shih* (Blossoming in the Spring and Bearing Fruit in the Autumn) was openly criticized by Feng Hsüeh-feng for inferior artistry. Primarily because of the descriptions in *Cat City,* he was accused of being a counterrevolutionary author by the Red Guards in the fall of 1966. Having been brutally beaten at a struggle meeting, he drowned himself the next day. Now, his good name has been restored. His works have again been incorporated into literature textbooks for university students, and in 1978 the People's Literature Press republished many of his major works.

LI HSI-FAN Born in 1927 in Peking, Li Hsi-fan entered East China University in Tsinan, Shantung, in 1949 and underwent a short period of political training. He then studied literature at Shantung University in Tsingtao. Upon graduation in 1953, he transferred to Peking to continue his study of philosophy. In 1954 he was sent to *Jen-min jih-pao* (People's Daily) to work in the literature department. In that year, he collaborated with Lan Ling on an article called "Kuan-yü 'Hung-lou-meng chien-lun' chi ch'i-t'a" (Concerning "A

Concise Treatise on *Dream of the Red Chamber*" and Others), which was published in the Shantung University magazine *Wen, shih, che* (Literature, History, and Philosophy). He later published "P'ing *Hung-lou-meng yen-chiu*" (Critique of *Studies on Dream of the Red Chamber*). The main content of both articles was to refute Yü P'ing-po's contention that the novel was autobiographical. Li espoused the theory that the novel was a historical record reflecting the collapse of feudal society. The article was personally endorsed by Mao Tse-tung, who then launched a nationwide movement to criticize *Studies on Dream of the Red Chamber* and Hu Shih's subjective idealism. The campaign was directed at Yü P'ing-po, Feng Hsüeh-feng, and Hu Feng, among others. Li's article was reputed to be the first shot in the counterattack against the bourgeois-oriented academic research of Hu Shih's school. Li was then promoted to the Chinese People's University in Peking as a researcher and became a member of the Writers' Union.

From then on, Li consistently upheld the Party's literary theories and actively pursued a career in literary criticism. He attacked Wang Meng's story "Tsu-chih-pu hsin-lai ti nien-ch'ing jen" (A Young Man Arrives at the Organization Department) and repudiated humanistic tendencies in literary creation. He also engaged Ho Ch'i-fang in a debate over "Ah Q" and rhyme in modern poetry. Even after the conclusion of the Cultural Revolution, Li still held a critical view of Ho. According to Li, he had been at odds with Chou Yang in 1964, and from that time on had begun to form ties with Chiang Ch'ing. In 1976 he visited Japan as vice-chairman of a Chinese delegation. However, since the latter half of 1978, he has been openly attacked for his close association with the Gang of Four and his riding roughshod over the entire literary world. His name rarely appears on the list of participants in national conferences on literature and art, though he still keeps his job with *People's Daily*. His works include *Hung-lou-meng p'ing-lun chi* (A Collection of Critical Essays on *Dream of the Red Chamber*) and *Hsien-wai chi* (Connotations).

LIU SHAO-T'ANG   Liu Shao-t'ang, a native of Hopei, was born into a small country merchant's household. He began writing in high school and published several short stories, including "Hung hua" (Red Flowers), "Ch'ing-chih lü-yeh" (Lush Branches and Green Leaves), "Ta ch'ing lo-tzu" (Big Black Mule), "Pu-ku niao ko-ch'ang ti chi-chieh" (The Season the Cuckoo Sings). He received a great deal of aid and support from literary organizations of the Communist government. At seventeen he was accepted into the Communist Party. In the afterword to "Ch'ing-chih lü-yeh," he stated: "I have been educated and brought up by the Party. If I have the least bit of accomplishment, it is wrung from the blood and sweat of the Party." Because he became famous at such an early age, he prided himself in the afterword to his 1955 collection, *Shan-cha ts'un ti ko-sheng* (Songs of Hawthorn Village), as "a prodigy at ten, a talented man at twenty." During the Hundred Flowers movement he spoke at meetings and published articles in opposition to the creative method of socialist realism. He felt that it led to dogmatism and formula writing. He advocated "realism in the socialist era" and called for freedom to create and write the truth. For these views he was criticized as a Rightist. His later writings, "Hsi-yüan ts'ao" (The Grass of Hsi-yüan) and "T'ien-yeh lo-hsia" (Evening Glow over the Fields), were censured as distorting reality.

Featured in the September 16, 1957, issue of *Chung-kuo ch'ing-nien* (China Youth) was Mao Tun's article "Liu Shao-t'ang ti ching-li kei wo-men ti chiao-yü i-i" (What We Can Learn from Liu Shao-t'ang's Experiences). Mao Tun wrote: "Precisely because he encountered no setbacks and had never been tested, it is extraordinarily urgent that his ideology be remolded. Precisely because he had never experienced any change in ideology, the capitalistic individualism of his petit-bourgeois upbringing coincidentally combined with the poison of his backward social thinking to erode and contaminate him. His fame from youth resulted in his becoming unreasonable and arrogant." Mao Tun summed up Liu's literary stance as having been influenced by nineteenth-century French literature. At the end of his discourse, he revealed why the Communists considered criticism of Liu important: "The transformation of Liu Shao-t'ang can teach us a lesson. He was brought up in favorable circumstances, was educated, protected, and nurtured by the Party to prepare him for his initial success. Afterward, due to his arrogance and pride and refusal to remold his thought, he opposed the Party and became a Rightist. Liu should be held up as a mirror for all young writers to gaze into, to find out if therein exists any shadow or fragment of a shadow of themselves." Clearly Mao Tun's remarks were intended to be an explanation of the case from an official point of view. In January 1979 Liu was rehabilitated as one who had been mistakenly classified as a Rightist. He was invited to attend the Fourth National Congress of Literary and Art Workers held in November 1979.

LU TING-I Lu Ting-i, a native of Kiangsu, was born in 1904. He was graduated from the University of Communication in Shanghai, and studied abroad in America and at Sun Yat-sen University in Moscow before returning to China to work as a journalist. He joined the Communist Youth League and became a member of the Communist Party in 1925 as well as a member of the Central Committee of the Communist Youth League. In 1928 he was named minister of propaganda for the Youth League. He traveled to the Juichin Soviet in 1930 and joined the Long March in 1934. In 1937 he became chief of the division of propaganda in the political department of the Eighth Route Army. In 1945 he was elected a member of the Central Committee of the Communist Party.

After the establishment of the People's Republic of China, he became vice-chairman of the education and cultural committee under the Administrative Council and in the same year became chief of the Propaganda Department under the CCP Central Committee. From 1956 on he served as an alternate member of the Politburo. In 1959 he became vice-premier of the State Council, and in 1965 substituted for Mao Tun as Minister of Culture. He was attacked during the Cultural Revolution as a counterrevolutionary revisionist and publicly tried by the Red Guards. According to a report in *Cheng-ming* (Contention), a leftist magazine in Hong Kong, he was one of the high-ranking political prisoners jailed in the No. 1 Ch'in-ch'eng Prison near Peking during the Cultural Revolution. He was released later than the others because he refused to sign his name to the conclusion made of his case. He made his first public appearance at a spring festival party held in January 1979 and was covered by the news media, an official announcement of his rehabilitation. Accompanying him was his wife, who had been accused of being a spy plotting against Lin Piao's life. On March 8, 1979, Lu Ting-i published a lengthy article in *Jen-min jih-pao* (People's Daily) in which he said that things in China had run into difficulties since the Great Leap Forward in 1958 and that those who had opposed Peng Teh-huai were wrong.

MAO TUN   Mao Tun, whose original name was Shen Yen-ping, is one of the most important modern Chinese writers. He was born in Chekiang in 1896 and studied at the preparatory school of Peking University. After graduation he went to work at the Translation Institute of the Commercial Press in Shanghai as a proofreader, later rising to the position of editor. He and Cheng Chen-to founded Wen-hsüeh yen-chiu hui (Literature Study Society) and edited *Hsiao-shuo yüeh-pao* (Fiction Monthly), which advocated that art serve life and reflect reality. In 1925 he was secretary of the propaganda department under the Kuomintang Central Committee. After the split between the Communist Party and the Kuomintang, Mao Tun, because of his Communist leanings, found refuge in Shanghai. In 1927 he began to write novels and published *Huan-mieh* (Disillusion), which made him famous. In 1928 he completed *Tung-yao* (Vacillation) and *Chui-ch'iu* (Pursuit), which became the second and third part of the trilogy *Shih* (The Eclipse). Mao Tun then fled to Japan for refuge.

Although he advocated proletarian literature, his own writings tended to be more naturalistic. He felt literature should measure up to literary standards and not concern itself with slogans and clichés. After *Eclipse,* he published a collection of short stories, *Yeh ch'iang-wei* (Wild Roses), and two novels, *Hung* (Rainbow) and *San-jen hsing* (Three Men). In 1931 he joined the League of Left-wing Writers and became its administrative secretary. In 1933 he published his representative work *Tzu-yeh* (Midnight). He then wrote a novel reflecting life in the small villages, *Lin-chia p'u-tzu* (The Lin Family Store), and the trilogy of peasant life, *Ch'un ts'an* (Spring Silkworms), *Ch'iu shou* (Autumn Harvest), and *Ts'an tung* (The Remains of Winter). When war broke out in 1937, Mao Tun fled to Hong Kong, Canton, and Wuhan. In 1938 he was principal of the School of Literature at the Sinkiang Institute. He then taught for half a year at Lu Hsün Arts Academy in Yenan, and later moved to Hong Kong, Kweilin, and Chungking. During this odyssey he published *Fu-shih* (Corruption), *Shuang-yeh hung szu erh-yüeh hua* (Maple Leaves as Red as February Flowers), and *Ch'ing-ming ch'ien-hou* (Before and after the Ch'ing Ming Festival). In 1946 he was invited to visit the Soviet Union and in the following year published *Su-lien chien-wen lu* (My Impressions of the Soviet Union) and *Tsa-t'an Su-lien* (Miscellaneous Thoughts on the Soviet Union).

After the establishment of the People's Republic of China, Mao Tun returned to China from Hong Kong and held the post of Minister of Culture up to 1965 as well as that of vice-chairman of the All-China Federation of Literary and Art Circles, and chairman of the Chinese Writers' Union. During that time he seldom wrote fiction, instead publishing literary critiques. During the Cultural Revolution he encountered no major setbacks. He is vice-chairman of the Chinese People's Political Consultative Conference, and retains the post of chairman of the Chinese Writers' Union, frequently presiding over meetings with foreign dignitaries or men of letters. He is eighty-five now, and reportedly his eyesight is failing.

PA JEN   The veteran leftist writer Wang Jen-shu wrote under the pen name of Pa Jen, using a country village as background for two early novels, *Lieh-shih* (Martyrdom) and *Chien-yü* (Jail). Later he concentrated his efforts on literary theory and criticism. In 1936, after the dissolution of the League of Left-wing Writers, Wang led the movement to sign up writers for the Chinese Writers and Artists Association, which Chou Yang had organized under the slogan of "national defense literature." More than 120 writers joined the association. Not long afterward, Lu Hsün, Hu Feng, and some 65 others signed "Chung-kuo wen-i kung-tso-che hsüan-yen" (A Declaration by Chinese Literature and Art Workers) under the slogan of "Mass literature for the national revolutionary war." The two sides engaged in a heated "battle of slogans."

After the war broke out, Wang remained in Shanghai. In 1936 he became an editor of Shanghai's *Shen pao* (Shanghai Daily) and together with Lu Hsün's widow, Hsü Kuang-p'ing, undertook the editing of Lu Hsün's complete works. He was dismissed from the paper for attacking Wang Ching-wei's surrender to the Japanese. In 1941 he reached Singapore and taught high school in the South Pacific. In 1947 he was captured by the Dutch in Sumatra and expelled from the country. He went to Hong Kong, and in 1949, after the establishment of the People's Republic of China, he went to Peking. He became the first ambassador to Indonesia from the People's Republic. Returning to China after two years, he became associate director of People's Literature Publishing House. Though Feng Hsüeh-fang was director, Wang was in actual control. During the Hundred Flowers movement he published articles on human nature, and from 1956 to 1960 he was criticized for encouraging revisionist ideas. He died in 1972.

His works include the novels *Lieh-shih* (Martyrdom), *Chien-yü* (Jail), *Ah Kuei liu-lang chi* (The Vagabondage of Ah Kuei), *Ch'en-lun* (In Decline), and

Chiu chia (Old House); and collections of literary essays entitled *Wen-hsüeh ch'u-pu* (An Introduction to Literature) and *Wen-hsüeh lun-kao* (A Discussion of Literature).

WANG SHU-MING Veteran Party writer Wang Shu-ming was editor of the *Kuang-ming Daily*'s literary supplement *Wen-hsüeh p'ing-lun* (Literary Commentary) during the early years of the People's Republic of China, and published critiques of Ting Ling, Chao Shu-li, and others. In 1952, during the rectification compaign, Ting Ling, speaking before a large meeting, criticized Wang, saying: "The editor of *Literary Commentary* lacks serious-ness." Wang subsequently made self-criticism and *Literary Commentary* ceased publication. In 1957 Wang published "Lun jen-ch'ing yü jen-hsing" (On Human Feelings and Human Nature) in support of Pa Jen's essay "Lun jen-ch'ing" (On Human Feelings). In 1960 he and Pa Jen were simultane-ously criticized for their concept of a human nature that transcended class, a reflection, their critics contended, of the revisionist trend in the country.

YAO HSÜEH-YIN Yao Hsüeh-yin, a famous Honan novelist born in 1910, joined the Communist Party in 1929 but soon resigned. Later he lived and wrote in Shanghai. When the war against Japan began in 1937, he rejoined the Communist Party. In 1938 he published *Ch'a pan-ch'e mai-chieh* (The Half-Baked) for which he became famous, and which gained him the reputation of a "peasant writer." Because he refused to accept a job assign-ment from the Communist Party, and because he advocated uniting behind the Kuomintang to resist Japan, he was expelled from the Party. During the early stages of the war, he worked in northern Anhwei, the Japanese-oc-cupied area, with an army service group under the Kuomintang Central Military Council. Later he reached Chungking. He successively published *Jung ma lien* (A Love Story in the Army) and *Ch'un nuan hua k'ai ti shih-hou* (When Spring Is Warm and Flowers Bloom), both of which were criticized by Communist writers. In 1953 he was assigned to work in the Wuhan Writers' Union. He published a series of articles in *Pen-liu* (Torrent) and also wrote the novel *Pu hu chi* (Tiger Hunting), which was not published. In 1957, during the Hundred Flowers movement, he published a number of articles in *Ch'ang-chiang wen-i* (Yangtze Literature) and *Wen-i pao* (Literary Gazette) which were critical of Communist leadership in the area of litera-ture and art. During the anti-Rightist campaign he was criticized as a Right-ist. In the early sixties his name was removed from the list of Rightists, and in 1963 he published the first volume of his novel *Ch'uang wang Li Tzu-ch'eng* (The Rebel King Li Tzu-ch'eng), which has made him the most popular nov-elist today.

During the editor's trip to China in 1976, Nieh personally met Yao and learned more about this novel. According to Yao, 300,000 copies of the novel had been printed in Peking alone, but these were immediately sold out. Now twenty-eight provinces in China each plan to print 100,000 copies.

The first and second volumes have already been printed, a total of 1,300,000 words. The third volume will contain more than 800,000 words and is expected to come off the press in the spring of 1979. When the novel is complete, it will consist of five volumes and three million words. The novel has already been adapted into a movie and operas. Yao disclosed that he started writing the novel while he was subject to criticism during the anti-Rightist campaign in 1957 and has not stopped writing since. He takes no vacations, no Sundays off. Mao read the first part of the novel with approval and personally intervened to have Yao protected during the Cultural Revolution. Because of this, Yao was able to keep all his notes, index cards, and manuscripts safe from the Red Guards; he even moved to Peking in 1972 to dedicate himself to the writing. Yao now serves as chairman of the Hupeh Federation of Literature and Art. He plans to write about the Taiping Heavenly Kingdom and the 1911 Revolution after he finishes *Ch'uang wang Li Tzu-ch'eng*.

His other works include *Hung lo-po yü Niu Ch'üan-teh* (The Carrot and Niu Ch'üan-teh), *Ch'ang yeh* (The Long Night), and *Ch'ing-ch'un* (Youth).

YAO WEN-YÜAN Born around 1925 Yao Wen-yüan, whose native place was Chekiang, was son of the 1930s left-wing writer Yao P'eng-tzu. In 1950 Yao began writing and publishing short commentaries and essays. At that time he worked at the New Democratic Youth League, the Shanghai Municipal Committee, propaganda section, and as a correspondent for *Wen-i pao* (Literary Gazette). In 1951 he was appointed an editor of *Meng-ya* (Sprouts), and frequently wrote literary critiques to join in the criticism of Hu Feng, Ting Ling, Feng Hsüeh-feng, Ch'in Chao-yang, Yao Hsüeh-yin, and others. In 1960 he was on the editorial board of *Chieh-fang jih-pao* (Liberation Daily) and began to come in close contact with Chang Ch'un-chiao. In 1965 he wrote an article entitled "P'ing hsin-p'ien li-shih chü *Hai Jui pa-kuan*" (On the New Historical Play *Hai Jui Dismissed from Office*) under the instruction of Chiang Ch'ing and Chang Ch'un-chiao, an article that was published in *Wen-hui pao* and that heralded the beginning of the Cultural Revolution. Afterward he became a member of the Cultural Revolution Group under the CCP Central Committee and was one of the leaders of the radical wing of the Party. He was elected a member of the Central Politburo at the Chinese Communist Party's Ninth Congress in 1969, with responsibilities for theoretical and propaganda work. He retained the post until Mao's death, when he was accused of being a member of the Gang of Four that attempted to usurp Party and state power. He was arrested along with Wang Hung-wen, Chang Ch'un-chiao, and Chiang Ch'ing. An extensive campaign was conducted throughout the whole nation to criticize them.

His essay collections include *Tsai ke-ming ti lieh-huo chung* (Amid the Flame of Revolution), *Hsing-mieh chi* (On Establishment and Destruction), *Lu Hsün—Chung-kuo wen-hua ke-ming chü-jen* (Lu Hsün—A Giant of the Cultural Revolution in China), *Hsin sung chi* (New Pines), *Tsai ch'ien-chin ti tao-lu-shang* (Forward March), and *Wen-i ssu-hsiang lun-cheng chi* (Polemics on Literature).

BIBLIOGRAPHY

Every book, article, poem, or story to which reference is made in the anthology is listed below. Translations of the names of Chinese periodicals and newspapers appear only once, at the first citation of each. Characters appear in either simplified or regular form according to the original source. Because the materials were collected from a wide variety of libraries and research institutions, it is inevitable that some inconsistencies in citations occur.

Bibliographical information on the articles, stories, and poems translated in this anthology, which appears after each work, is not included here.

Ai K'e-en 艾克恩. "Po Ch'iu-yün ti 'liang-hsin' lun" 驳秋耘的"良心"论 (A Rebuttal of Ch'iu-yün's Concept of "Conscience"). *Pei-ching wen-i* (Peking Literature), August 1957.

Chang I-hsing 张翼星. "'Wen-i tsa t'an' tu hou" "文艺杂谈"读后 (Thoughts after Reading "A Random Discussion of Literature"). *Hsüeh-hsi* (Studies), June 1957.

Chang Kuang-nien 张光年. "She-hui chu-i hsien-shih chu-i ts'un-tsai che fa-chan che" 社会主义现实主义存在着，发展着 (Socialist Realism Exists and Develops). *Wen-i pao* (Literary Gazette), December 24, 1956.

——"Ts'ung i-p'ien wen-chang k'an Huang Yao-mien ti yu-p'ai ssu-hsiang" 从一篇文章看黄药眠的右派思想 (The Rightist Thinking of Huang Yao-mien as Seen from One of His Articles). *Wen-i pao*, no. 19, 1957.

Chang Li-yün 张立云. "Liu Shao-t'ang tsai wen-hsüeh shang ti yu-p'ai kuan-tien" 刘绍棠在文学上的右派观点 (Liu Shao-t'ang's Rightist Ideas regarding Literature). *Pei-ching wen-i*, no. 8, 1957.

Chang Yü 张羽, and Li Hui-fan 李辉凡. "'Hsieh chung-chien jen-wu' ti tzu-ch'an chieh-chi wen-hsüeh chu-chang pi-hsü p'i-p'an" "写中间人物"的资产阶级文学主张必须批判. (We Must Criticize the Idea of "Writing about People in the Middle," a Bourgeois Concept of Literature). *Wen-hsüeh p'ing-lun* (Literary Criticism), no. 5, 1964.

Chao Ts'ung 趙聰. *Hsien-tai Chung-kuo tso-chia lieh-chuan* 現代中國作家列傳 (Biographical Sketches of Modern Chinese Writers). Hong Kong: Hsiang-kang Chung-kuo pi-hui, 1975.

Ch'en Ch'i-t'ung 陈其通, Ch'en Ya-ting 陈亚丁, Ma Han-ping 马寒冰, and Lu Le 鲁勒. "Wo-men tui mu-ch'ien wen-i kung-tso ti chi-tien i-chien" 我们对目前文艺工作的几点意见 (Our Views on Current Literary and Art Work). *Jen-min jih-pao* (People's Daily), January 7, 1957.

"Ch'en Ch'i-t'ung teng 'Wo-men tui mu-ch'ien wen-i kung-tso ti chi-tien i-chien' fa-piao i-hou" 陈其通等"我们对目前文艺工作的几点意见"发表以后 (Following the Publication of the Article "Our Views on Current Literary and Art Work" by Ch'en Ch'i-t'ung and Others). *Jen-min jih-pao*, April 4, 1957.

Ch'en I 陈沂. "Wen-i tsa t'an" 文艺杂谈 (A Random Discussion of Literature). *Hsüeh-hsi*, July 1957.

Ch'en Po-ta 陳伯達. "Hsieh tsai Wang Shih-wei 'Wen-i ti min-tsu hsing-shih tuan-lun' chih hou" 寫在王實味"文藝的民族形式短論"之後 (A Comment on Wang Shih-wei's "Brief Discussion of the National Form in Literature"). *Chieh-fang jih-pao* (Liberation Daily), June 15, 1942.

Chi Shu 季叔. "Tui 'Hsi-yüan ts'ao' ti i-chien" 对"西苑草"的意见 (Comments on "The Grass of Hsi-yüan"). *Che-chiang jih-pao* (Chekiang Daily), June 9, 1957.

Chiang K'ung-yang 蒋孔阳. "Kuan-yü she-hui chu-i hsien-shih chu-i" 关于社会主义现实主义 (On Socialist Realism). *Wen-i yüeh-pao* (Literary Monthly), April 1957.

Ch'ien Chün-jui 钱俊瑞. "Chien-ch'ih wen-hsüeh ti tang-hsin yüan-tse, ch'e-ti p'i-p'an hsien-tai hsiu-cheng chu-i" 坚持文学的党性原则, 彻底批判现代修正主义 (Abide by the Party Spirit in Literary Endeavors and Thoroughly Criticize Modern Revisionism). *Wen-i pao*, no. 8, 1960.

Ch'in Chao-yang 秦兆陽. *Hsing-fu* 幸福 (Happiness). Peking: Jen-min wen-hsüeh ch'u-pan-she, 1951.

——*Tsai t'ien-yeh shang ch'ien-chin* 在田野上前進! (Move Forward in the Fields). Peking: Tso-chia ch'u-pan-she, 1956.

——(also Ho Chih 何直). "Ts'ung t'e-hsieh ti chen-shih hsing t'an-ch'i" 从特写的真实性谈起 (Beginning with the Necessity of Truthfulness in Feature Stories). *Jen-min wen-hsüeh* (People's Literature), June 1956.

——(also Ho Chih). "Lun 'Chien-jui' chih feng" 论"尖锐"之风 (On the Spirit of "Sharpness"). *Wen-i hsüeh-hsi* (Literary Studies), no. 8, 1956.

——(also Ho Yu-hua 何又化). "Ch'en-mo" 沉默 (Silence). *Jen-min wen-hsüeh*, no. 1, 1957.

——(also Ho Chih). "Kuan-yü 'hsieh chen-shih'" 关于"写真实" (On "Writing the Truth"). *Jen-min wen-hsüeh*, March 1957.

Chou Po 周勃. "Lun hsien-shih chu-i chi ch'i tsai she-hui chu-i shih-tai ti fa-chan"

论现实主义及其在社会主义时代的发展 (On Realism and Its Development in the Socialist Era). *Ch'ang-chiang wen-i* (Yangtze Literature), December 1956.

Chou Yang 周扬. "Wang Shih-wei ti wen-i-kuan yü wo-men ti wen-i-kuan" 王實味的文藝觀與我們的文藝觀 (Wang Shih-wei's Literary Views and Our Literary Views). *Chieh-fang jih-pao*, July 28, 1942.

——"She-hui chu-i hsien-shih chu-i: Chung-kuo wen-hsüeh ch'ien-chin ti tao-lu" 社会主义现实主义：中国文学前进的道路 (Socialist Realism: The Road of Progress for Chinese Literature). *Hsin-hua yüeh-pao* (New China Monthly), February 1953.

Fang Shu-min 房树民. "Liu Shao-t'ang shih tsen-yang tsou-hsiang fan-tang ti" 刘绍棠是怎样走向反党的 (How Liu Shao-t'ang Set Off on the Anti-Party Road). *Wen-i hsüeh-hsi*, September 1957.

Feng Hsüeh-feng 馮雪峯 (also Hua Shih 畫室). "T'i-wai ti hua" 題外的話 (A Digression). Supplement to *Hsin-hua jih-pao* (New China Daily), January 23, 1946. (*Ts'an-K'ao tzu-liao* [Research Material] vol. 2, pp. 428–30)

——(also Lü K'e-yü 呂克玉). "Tui-yü wen-hsüeh yün-tung chi-ke wen-t'i ti i-chien" 對於文學運動幾個問題的意見 (Comments on Some Problems in the Literary Movement). In *Kuo-lai ti shih-tai* 過來的時代 (The Times We Have Been Through). Shanghai: Hsin-chih shu-tien, 1946, pp. 55–68. (*TKTL*, vol. 1, pp. 567–575).

——"Min-tsu hsing yü min-tsu hsing-shih" 民族性與民族形式 (National Character and National Form). In *Kuo-lai ti shih-tai*. Shanghai: Hsin-chih shu-tien, 1946, pp. 122–26. (*TKTL*, vol. 1, pp. 797–99).

——"Kuan-yü 'I-shu ta-chung-hua'" 關於"藝術大眾化" (On "Popularization of Art"). In *Kuo-lai ti shih-tai*. Shanghai: Hsin-chih shu-tien, 1946, pp. 69–84. (*TKTL*, vol. 1, pp. 790–97).

——*Yü-yen* 寓言 (Fables). Peking: Tso-chia ch'u-pan-she, 1956.

"Feng Hsüeh-feng shih wen-i chieh fan-tang fen-tzu" (Feng Hsüeh-feng Is an Anti-Party Figure in Literary Circles). *Wen-i pao*, no. 21, 1957.

Hsiao Mei 肖玫, and Wang Chi-hsien 王积贤. "Liu Shao-t'ang pi hsia ti ta-hsüeh sheng-huo" 刘绍棠笔下的大学生活 (University life as Described by Liu Shao-t'ang: A Comment on "The Grass of Hsi-yüan"). *Wen-i hsüeh-hsi*, October 1957.

Hsü Chung-yü 徐中玉. "Yu chung hao-hsiang yung-yüan tou shih cheng-ch'üeh ti jen" 有种好象永远都是正确的人 (There Is a Type of Person Who Always Seems To Be in the Right). *Wen-i pao*, no. 8, 1957.

Huang Ch'iu-yün 黃秋耘. "Hsiu-sun le ling-hun ti pei-chü" 锈损了灵魂的悲剧 (The Tragedy of the Rusted Soul). *Wen-i pao*, July 15, 1956.

——"Chung-yao ti shih yu t'ung-hsin" 重要的是有童心 (The Important Thing Is to Retain a Childlike Heart). *Wen-i pao*, August 15, 1956.

——*Ku-chin chi* 古今集 (Critical Essays on Ancient and Modern Literature). Peking: Tso-chia ch'u-pan-she, 1962.

Huang Yao-mien 黃藥眠. *Kuei-lin ti ch'e-t'ui* 桂林底撤退 (Retreat from Kweilin). Shanghai: Ch'ün-li shu-tien, 1947.

——*Shu-ch'ing hsiao-p'in* 抒情小品 (Lyrical Essays). Hong Kong: Wen-sheng ch'u-pan-she, 1948.

——*Lun tsou-szu chu-i ti che-hsüeh* 論走私主義的哲學 (The Philosophy of Covertly Peddling Individualism). Hong Kong: Ch'iu-shih ch'u-pan-she, 1949.

——*P'i-p'an chi* 批判集 (A Collection of Critical Essays). Peking: Tso-chia ch'u-pan-she, 1957.

——"Shih she-hui chu-i shih-tai ti hsien-shih chu-i hai-shih she-hui chu-i hsien-shih chu-i?" 是社会主义时代的现实主义还是社会主义现实主义？(Is It Realism in the Socialist Era or Socialist Realism?). *Pei-ching wen-i*, no. 5, 1957.

I Cheng 易征. "I-p'ien pu lao-shih ti wen-i pao-tao" 一篇不老实的文艺报导 (A False Report on Literature: Criticizing Huang Ch'iu-yün's "The Spring Wind Has Not Yet Greened the Banks of the Pearl River"). *Tso-p'in* (Works), September 1957.

I Ch'ün 以群. "Chia-ju Lu Hsün hsien-sheng hai huo-che" 假如鲁迅先生还活着 (If Mr. Lu Hsün Were Still Alive). *Chieh-fang jih-pao*, October 19, 1957.

——"Lun hsien-shih chu-i chi ch'i-t'a" 论现实主义及其它 (On Realism and Other Issues), in *Lun wu-ch'an chieh-chi ke-ming wen-i* (On the Revolutionary Literature of the Proletariat). Shanghai: Shang-hai wen-i ch'u-pan-she, 1963.

"I ke ch'ing-nien tso-che ti to-lo" 一个青年作者的堕落 (The Degeneration of a Young Writer: A Report on the Meeting to Criticize Liu Shao-t'ang's Ideas and Behavior as a Rightist). *Wen-i pao*, October 20, 1957.

"Kuan-yü 'hsieh chung-chien jen-wu' ti ts'ai-liao" 关于"写中间人物"的材料 (Materials on "Writing about People in the Middle"). *Wen-i pao*, nos. 8–9, 1964.

"Kuan-yü *Wen-i pao* ti chüeh-i" 关于"文艺报"的决议 (A Decision regarding the *Literary Gazette:* Adopted at the Joint Session of the Presidium of the All-China Federation of Literary and Art Circles and the Presidium of the Chinese Writers' Union on December 8, 1954). *Wen-i pao*, nos. 23–24, 1954.

Kuo Mo-jo 郭沫若. *Ch'uang-tsao shih-nien* 創造十年 (Ten Years of the Creation Society). Hong Kong: Hui-wen-ko shu-tien, 1972.

Li Hsi-fan 李希凡. *Hsien-wai chi* 弦外集 (Connotations). Shanghai: Hsin wen-i ch'u-pan-she, 1957.

——"So-wei 'kan-yü sheng-huo', 'hsieh chen-shih' ti shih-chih shih she-mo?" 所谓"干预生活，""写真实"的实质是什么？(What Is at the Bottom of Such Concepts as "Intervening in Life" and "Writing the Truth"?). *Jen-min wen-hsüeh*, November 1957.

——"Po Pa Jen ti 'jen-lei pen-hsing' ti tien-hsing lun" 驳巴人的"人类本性"的典型论 (A Rebuttal of Pa Jen's Concept of Typification of "Human Nature"). *Wen-i pao*, no. 7, 1960.

——and Lan Ling 蓝翎. *Hung-lou-meng p'ing-lun chi* 红楼梦评论集 (A Collection of Critical Essays on *Dream of the Red Chamber*). Peking: Jen-min wen-hsüeh ch'u-pan-she, 1973.

Li Shao-ts'en 黎少岑. "Erh-shih yüan i-ch'ien" 二十元一千 (Twenty Dollars per Thousand Characters: A Rebuttal of Yao Hsüeh-yin's Essay, "In Praise of the Marco Polo Bridge"). *Ch'ang-chiang jih-pao* (Yangtze Daily), September 4, 1957.

Lin Hsi-ling 林希翎, and others. *K'an! Che shih she-mo yen-lun?* 看！这是什么言论？ (Look! What Are They Saying?: A Collection of Speeches and Wall Posters by Lin Hsi-ling and Others). Peking: Pei-ching-shih hsüeh-sheng lien-ho-hui, June 1957.

Lin Mo-han 林默涵. "Wang Shih-wei ti 'Yeh pai-ho hua'" 王实味的"野百合花" (On "The Wild Lily" by Wang Shih-wei). *Wen-i pao*, no. 2, 1958.

Liu Pai-yü 刘白羽. "Lun wen-hsüeh shang ti yu-p'ai han-liu" 论文学上的右派寒流 (On the Rightist Cold Wave in Literature). *Wen-i pao*, August 4, 1957.

Liu Shao-ch'i 刘少奇 "T'an 'pai-hua ch'i-fang, pai-chia cheng-ming'" 谈"百花齐放，百家争鸣" (A Discussion of "Let a Hundred Flowers Bloom and a Hundred Schools of Thought Contend": An Excerpt). *TKTL*, vol. 2, pp. 480–81).

Liu Shao-t'ang 劉紹棠. *Ch'ing-chih lü-yeh* 青枝綠葉 (Lush Branches and Green Leaves), Shanghai: Hsin wen-i ch'u-pan-she, 1953.

——"Ke ai-hao wen-i ti ch'ing-nien t'ung-hsüeh-men" 給愛好文藝的青年同學們 (A Letter to Young Students Who Love Literature). *Wen-i hsüeh-hsi*, February 8, 1955.

——"Hang-k'ung hsin" 航空信 (An Airmail Letter). *Chung-kuo ch'ing-nien pao* (China Youth Daily), May 14, 1955.

——"Yung-kan ti, chen-shih ti fan-ying nung-yeh ho-tso-hua yün-tung chung ti chieh-chi tou-cheng" 勇敢地，真实地反映农业合作化运动中的阶级斗争 (Courageously and Truthfully Reflect the Class Struggle in the Agricultural Collectivization Movement). *Kuang-ming jih-pao* (Kwang Ming Daily), November 11, 1955.

——"Shou-huo" 收穫 (Harvest). *Pei-ching wen-i*, no. 3, 1956.

——"Ch'u ch'un yeh" 初春夜 (An Evening in Early Spring). *Chung-kuo ch'ing-nien pao*, April 4, 1956.

——*Shan-cha ts'un ti ko-sheng* 山楂村的歌聲 (Songs of Hawthorn Village). Shanghai: Hsin wen-i ch'u-pan-she, 1956.

Liu Ts'un-shih 劉存史. *Yao Wen-yüan wen-chi* 姚文元文集 (The Collected Writings of Yao Wen-yüan, 1965–1968). Hong Kong: Li-shih tzu-liao ch'u-pan-she (Historical Materials Press). 1971.

Lo Chu-feng 罗竹风. "'Jen-tao chu-i' k'o-i shuo-ming i-ch'ieh ma?'" "人道主义"可以说明一切吗? (Can "Humanism" Serve to Explain Everything?). *Wen-i yüeh-pao*, September 1957.

Lo Feng 羅烽. "Hai-shih tsa-wen ti shih-tai" 還是雜文的時代 (Still the Time for *tsa-wen*). *Chieh-fang jih-pao*, March 12, 1942.

Lo Sun 罗苏. "Chien-chüeh fan-tui hsiu-cheng chu-i wen-i ssu-hsiang" 坚决反对修正主义文艺思想 (Resolutely Oppose Revisionist Ideas in Literature). *Shang-hai wen-hsüeh* (Shanghai Literature), no. 6, 1960.

Ma Wen-ping 马文兵. "Lun tzu-ch'an chieh-chi jen-tao chu-i" 论资产阶级人道主义 (On Bourgeois Humanism). *Wen-i pao*, nos. 17–18, 1960.

Mao Tse-tung ssu-hsiang wan-sui! 毛泽东思想万岁! (Long Live Mao Tse-tung Thought!). Reprinted by Gendai Hyoronsha, Tokyo, 1974.

Mao Tun 茅盾. "Kuan-ch'e 'pai-hua ch'i-fang, pai-chia cheng-ming', fan-tui chiao-t'iao chu-i ho hsiao-tzu-ch'an chieh-chi ssu-hsiang" 贯彻"百花齐放，百家争鸣"，反对教条主义和小资产阶级思想 (Implement the Policy of "Let a Hundred Flowers Bloom and a Hundred Schools of Thought Contend," and Oppose Dogmatism and Petit-Bourgeoisie Thought). *Jen-min jih-pao*, March 18, 1957.

——"Wo-men yao pa Liu Shao-t'ang tang-tso i-mien ching-tzu" 我们要把刘绍棠当作一面镜子 (We Must Use the Example of Liu Shao-t'ang as a Mirror). *Wen-i pao*, October 20, 1957.

Meng Ch'i 孟起. "Yao Hsüeh-yin ti pien-tzu" 姚雪垠的鞭子 (The Whip of Yao Hsüeh-yin). *Ch'ang-chiang jih-pao*, September 1, 1957.

Ou-yang Wen-pin 欧阳文彬. "Hsien-shih ho jen" 现实和人 (Man and Reality: A Critique of "Literature Is the Study of Man"). *Wen-i yüeh-pao*, April 1958.

Pa Jen 巴人. *Wen-hsüeh ch'u-pu* 文學初步 (An Introduction to Literature). Shanghai: Hsin wen-i ch'u-pan-she, 1951.

——"Lun shih liang-chü" 论诗两句 (On Two Lines from the Poem "General"). *Wen-i pao*, July 30, 1956.

——*Wen-hsüeh lun kao* 文学论稿 (A Discussion of Literature). Shanghai: Hsin wen-i ch'u-pan-she, 1956.

——"Po 'Yu chung hao-hsiang yung-yüan tou shih cheng-ch'üeh ti jen'" 驳"有种好象永远都是正确的人" (A Rebuttal of "There Is a Type of Person Who Always Seems To Be in the Right"). *Wen-i pao*, July 21, 1957.

——"Chiao hsin p'ien" 交心篇 (Give Your Heart to the Party). *Jen-min jih-pao*, May 20, 1958.

——"Shih hsieh-shih chu-i hai-shih fan hsien-shih chu-i?" 是现实主义还是反现

实主义? (Is This Realism or Antirealism?). *Wen-hsüeh p'ing-lun* (Literary Criticism), no. 1, 1959.

T'ao P'ing 陶萍. "Pa ho-tso-hua yün-tung ti kao-ch'ao t'ui-hsiang ch'ien-chin" 把合作化运动的高潮推向前进 (Advance the Agricultural Collectivization Movement: A Review of Ch'in Chao-yang's Novel, *Move Forward in the Fields*). *Wen-i pao*, December 1955.

Ting Miao 丁淼. *Chung-kung wen-i tsung p'i-p'an* 中共文藝總批判 (A Comprehensive Critique of Chinese Communist Literature). Hong Kong: Hsiang-kang Chung-kuo pi-hui, 1970.

TKTL: Pei-ching shih-fan ta-hsüeh Chung-wen hsi hsien-tai wen-hsüeh chiao-hsüeh kai-ke hsiao-tsu 北京师范大学中文系现代文学教学改革小组 (Group on Revision of the Teaching of Modern Literature, Department of Chinese Literature, Peking Normal University). *Chung-kuo hsien-tai wen-hsüeh shih ts'an-k'ao tzu-liao* 中国现代文学史参考资料 (Research Materials on the History of Modern Chinese Literature), 2 vols. Peking: Kao-teng chiao-yü ch'u-pan-she, 1960.

Ts'ung Wei-hsi 从维熙. "Tui 'she-hui chu-i hsien-shih chu-i' ti chi-tien chih-i" 对"社会主义现实主义"的几点质疑 (An Inquiry into Socialist Realism). *Pei-ching wen-i*, no. 4, 1957.

Tu Li-chün 杜黎均. "Hua lo chih to-shao" 花落知多少 (How Many Flowers Have Fallen). *Wen-i hsüeh-hsi*, no. 8, 1956.

Tuan-mu Hung-liang 端木蕻良. "Ts'ung Wei-hsi ti lun-tiao shih miou-wu ti" 从维熙的论调是谬误的 (Ts'ung Wei-hsi's Arguments are Absurd). *Pei-ching wen-i*, August 1957.

"Tui Wang Shu-ming t'ung-chih ti 'Kuan-yü jen-hsing wen-t'i ti pi-chi' ti p'i-p'ing" 对王淑明同志的"关于人性问题的笔记"的批评 (Comrade Wang Shu-ming's "Notes on the Issue of Human Nature": A Critique). *Wen-hsüeh p'ing-lun*, editorial, May 1960.

Wang Chang-ling 王章陵. *Chung-kung ti wen-i cheng-feng* 中共的文藝整風 (Rectification Campaigns in Chinese Communist Literature). Taipei: Kuo-chi kuan-hsi yen-chiu-so, March 1967.

Wang Chih-liang 王智量. "Ch'ien Ku-jung 'Lun wen-hsüeh shih jen-hsüeh' i-wen ti yu-p'ai ssu-hsiang shih-chih" 钱谷融"论文学是人学"一文的右派思想实质 (On the Rightist Thinking Embodied in Ch'ien Ku-jung's "Literature Is the Study of Man"). *Jen-min wen-hsüeh*, September 1957.

Wang Jo-wang 王若望. "P'ing 'She-hui chu-i shih-tai ti hsien-shih chu-i'" 评"社会主义时代的现实主义" (A Comment on "Realism in the Socialist Era"). *Wen-i pao*, June 1957.

Wang K'uei-lung 王夔龙. "Huan-hu 'pai-hua ch'i-fang'" 欢呼"百花齐放" (Hail the Hundred Flowers Movement). *Chung-kuo ch'ing-nien* (China Youth), no. 10, 1957.

Wang Liao-ying 王燎熒. "Jen-hsing lun ti i-ke 'hsin' piao-pen" 人性论的一个 "新"标本 (A "New" Specimen of the Theory of Human Nature). *Wen-hsüeh p'ing-lung*, no. 4, 1960.

Wang Shih-wei 王實味. "Cheng-chih chia yü i-shu chia" 政治家與藝術家 (Statesmen and Artists). *Ku-yü* (Grain Rains), no. 4, 1942.

——"Yeh pai-ho hua" 野百合花 (The Wild Lily). *Chieh-fang jih-pao*, March 13 and 23, 1942.

Wang Yao 王瑤. *Chung-kuo hsin wen-hsüeh shih-kao* 中國新文學史稿 (Draft History of New Literature in China, 1919–1950), 2 vols. Shanghai: Hsin wen-i ch'u-pan-she, 1953.

"Yao Hsüeh-yin fan-tang mien-mu yüan-hsing pi-lu" 姚雪垠反党面目原形毕露 (Yao Hsüeh-yin's Anti-Party Nature Has Been Entirely Exposed). *Hu-pei jih-pao* (Hupeh Daily), August 30, 1957.

"Yao Hsüeh-yin kung-chi Mao chu-hsi wen-i fang-chen" 姚雪垠攻击毛主席文艺方针 (Yao Hsüeh-yin Attacks Chairman Mao's Literary Policy). *Kuang-ming jih-pao*, September 3, 1957.

"Yao Hsüeh-yin ti k'uang-hsiang p'o-mieh" 姚雪垠的狂想破灭 (The Collapse of Yao Hsüeh-yin's Wild Ideas). *Jen-min jih-pao*, September 3, 1957.

Yao Wen-yüan 姚文元. "She-hui chu-i hsien-shih chu-i wen-hsüeh shih wu-ch'an chieh-chi ke-ming shih-tai ti hsin wen-hsüeh: T'ung Ho Chih, Chou Po pien-lun" 社会主义现实主义文学是无产阶级革命时代的新文学：同何直，周勃辩论 (The Literature of Socialist Realism Is the New Literature in the Era of the Proletarian Revolution: A Debate with Ho Chih and Chou Po). *Jen-min wen-hsüeh*, September 1957.

——"Wen-hsüeh shang ti hsiu-cheng chu-i ssu-ch'ao ho ch'uang-tso ch'ing-hsiang" 文学上的修正主义思潮和创作倾向 (Revisionist Thought and Tendencies in Literature). *Jen-min wen-hsüeh*, no. 11, 1957.

——"Ching-yeh tsa-kan" 靜夜杂感 (Random Thoughts on a Quiet Night). *Wen-hui pao*, November 12, 1957.

——"Ch'e-ti p'i-p'an tzu-ch'an chieh-chi jen-tao chu-i" 彻底批判资产阶级人道主义 (Thoroughly Criticize Bourgeois Humanism: A Rebuttal of Ch'ien Ku-jung's Revisionist Ideas). *Shang-hai wen-hsüeh*, May 1960.

——"P'ing Ch'ien Ku-jung hsien-sheng ti 'jen-tao chu-i' lun" 评钱谷融先生的 "人道主义"论 (A Comment on Mr. Ch'ien Ku-jung's Theory of Humanism"). In *Wen-i ssu-hsiang lun-cheng chi* (Polemics on Literature). Shanghai: Tso-chia ch'u-pan-she, 1965.

——"Tsai t'an chiao-t'iao ho yüan-tse" 再谈教条和原则 (A Further Discussion of Dogmas and Principles: A Debate with Liu Shao-t'ang and Others). In *Wen-i ssu-hsiang lun-cheng chi*. Shanghai: Tso-chia ch'u-pan-she, 1965.

——"P'i-p'an Pa Jen ti 'Jen-hsing lun'" 批判巴人的"人性论" (A Critique of Pa

Jen's "Theory of Human Nature"). In *Wen-i ssu-hsiang lun-cheng chi*. Shanghai: Tso-chia ch'u-pan-she, 1965.

"Yu p'ai fen-tzu Yao Hsüeh-yin yin-hsien chiao-cha i-kuan fan-tang" 右派分子姚雪垠阴险狡诈一贯反党 (Yao Hsüeh-yin Is a Crafty and Deceitful Rightist Who Has Always Opposed the Party). *Ch'ang-chiang jih-pao*, August 31, 1957.

"Yu-p'ai fen-tzu Yao Hsüeh-yin ling-hun ch'ou-o" 右派分子姚雪垠灵魂丑恶 (The Rightist Yao Hsüeh-yin Has an Ugly Soul). *Wen-hui pao*, September 2, 1957.

MODERN ASIAN LITERATURE SERIES

NEO-CONFUCIAN STUDIES

TRANSLATIONS FROM THE ORIENTAL CLASSICS

STUDIES IN ORIENTAL CULTURE

COMPANIONS TO ASIAN STUDIES

INTRODUCTION TO ORIENTAL CIVILIZATIONS

Wm. Theodore de Bary, *Editor*